ANTIGENESIS

D.S. WHITAKER

This is a work of fiction. Names, characters, businesses, places, events, locales, and incidents are the products of the author's imagination or used in a fictitious and satirical manner. Any resemblance to actual persons, living or dead, or actual events is purely coincidental. Certain long-standing institutions, agencies, and public offices are mentioned, but the characters involved are wholly imaginary. The opinions expressed are those of the characters and should not be confused with the author's. We should consider nothing in this book medical, health or dietary fact or advice.

Please note, this work was written and published before the Covid-19 pandemic.

ISBN: 978-1-7342595-0-6 (EB)

ISBN: 978-1-7342595-4-4 (TP)

Library of Congress Control Number:2019918948

Back photo by Diana Lang

Cover Design by DS Whitaker

Virus image CDC Public Health Image Library

To Dad, Nancy, and Irene for your insights and support

To Tim for his love and encouragement

	The	Munson	Library	
**********	Your	Special	Code	**********
Please	mark the	space	below to	record
that you	have	read	this	book

CHAPTER 1

DAY 0

The puppies were born on a snowy evening in late January near the Arctic Circle, having no knowledge of their miniscule invaders.

Their mother, the Russian Commandant's beautiful, pure-breed Samoyed, yawned and closed her eyes. After the Army doctor wrapped the newborns in green woolen blankets, he wiped the bloody mucus from his hands with a damp cloth. Absentmindedly, he scratched his nose and adjusted his glasses before reaching into his medical kit for antibacterial gel.

It was the beginning of the end.

Yet, in that moment, in the glow of new life—in the form of three squirmy white pups with shrouded eyes—the doctor couldn't stop smiling.

DAY 30

Pile upon pile of dead bodies. At first, Darya felt fear and sadness. Now, just the ache in her muscles and back pain. Dead men were like fleshy logs. Difficult to move, particularly in the cold and snow.

Darya thought back to the first few days, when healthy soldiers managed the process, assembling wooden caskets for the high-ranking officers. In hindsight, those were the easy days. During the first week, she and the other healthy females merely continued working their regular assignments.

When the number surpassed two hundred, one of the officers considered leaving the corpses in their beds; to bring in a cleanup crew later. But the rotten egg stench, images of their bloated green skin, and fixed condemning stares became unbearable.

Why didn't the Commandant call for help? Suspend the exercise?

During the early days, as she crossed the field each morning on her way to the supply tent, she studied the troops during muster. The soldiers' coughs grew louder and more persistent. Men expelled chunks of blood through their mouths, still trying to maintain their posture. Some crumpled to the ground.

It defied common sense to continue. Yet, every morning, the PA system crackled and blared commands; as tractors and tanks maneuvered and the men played war games across the tundra and through the adjacent pine forest.

As head supply clerk, Darya requisitioned extra body bags and antibiotics when they ran out. After three days with no reply, she put in the order again. Moscow finally responded—both were in short supply. Delivery would take some weeks.

At the end of the second week of the outbreak, the number of ill climbed higher. Nearly everyone in the camp—five thousand—were sick or dying. The chain of command fell apart; all the officers were in the infirmary or already dead.

Then another blizzard. Snow was a normal part of life in the Arctic Circle, but this was heavy, dense snow. The kind you couldn't see through. Not the typical dry flurries that were readily swept away by the wind.

Darya looked at the calendar. Only twenty-five days ago, they found Doctor Volkov dead in the infirmary. One of the nurses told her how she came across his body, his face sideways on the concrete—eyes pocked with broken capillaries—a large glob of dark red blood near his mouth.

She was exhausted. She saw the same weariness in the eyes of the other women. They didn't talk much now. The days blended together.

Over the last week, she and the other women woke at dawn to begin their new daily routine—alternating shifts of nursing the sick and moving corpses. After trial and error, they found it easiest to roll the deceased onto thin mattresses and pull them outside with the dog sled team.

They debated how to sort the dead into piles. *By rank? By Regiment? Alphabetically?* In hindsight, it didn't matter. During the night, wolves ripped the bodies apart, leaving them unrecognizable.

Still no word from Moscow. The officers' tactical satellite phones were useless without the classified passcodes for outbound calls. After three unsuccessful attempts, it locked them out. She kept the phones charged hoping the Kremlin would reach out and call them. She and Kira debated if one of them should get in a vehicle and start driving south to get assistance. *But what if they spread the disease in the process?*

Darya was leading the dogs back to retrieve another batch. The wind picked up, pushing back her hood. She studied the sky. Dense clouds loomed nearby.

All hope is lost.

She located Kira at the mess tent. "Another storm is coming," she warned. "We need to save ourselves."

"What about the soldiers in the infirmary?" Kira asked.

"The ones still alive are coughing blood. They won't survive another day."

"What's the plan? Do we drive out?"

"Too risky in bad weather. We stick together. Move to the largest cabin and wait out the storm. Spread the word. Have everyone convene at Cabin Three in twenty minutes."

Kira said, "I'm on it."

"Scour the camp. Gather all the blankets, clothing, and rations."

"Heating oil and candles, too."

"Yes. I'll join you soon," Darya said.

After Kira left, Darya unhooked the sled dogs. The dogs would have to fend for themselves.

Would they ever be rescued? What would happen to the rescuers? Would they suffer the same fate?

She sent another message the only way she knew how—through the unclassified facsimile system used for requisitioning supplies.

No one else needed to die.

DAY 32

Ally felt the familiar depressions across her mattress. Gretchen had jumped up on her bed and was now stomping across her legs. She finally settling down with an indelicate sideways crash into her ribs. Ally scratched her cat's head absentmindedly while she contemplated starting her day. After a couple of minutes, Ally pulled back the comforter and slid another pillow behind her head. She stared at the blank beige wall in front of her.

My apartment is a sad, sterile box.

She had lived in her apartment for nearly five months now, but it didn't feel like home. No, home was with Jim.

And Jim was gone.

She pushed the thought out of her head and got up to get coffee. It was nearly eight o'clock. *How had she slept so late?* It was a Saturday, but she hadn't slept past six a.m. in decades. In her previous job, she was constantly traveling for work, spending weeks abroad. Waking early due to jet lag or to catch a flight had been her normal routine for as long as she could remember. Her new boring job had regular hours. It felt decadent starting work at nine, like most of the day had been wasted. But still, the extra sleep was growing on her.

As she waited for the coffee maker, she glanced around her spartan living room. Despite the lack of color, she loved the compactness and efficiency of her Bethesda apartment. It had everything she needed as a single person. After months of cleaning out their old four-bedroom house near Atlanta, her new foray into minimalism seemed right.

She poured the steaming liquid into her large Dr. Spock mug and took it back to bed. Gretchen followed. Ally took a long sip and then traded the mug for her laptop. She opened her browser to read the day's headlines first before opening her model to begin editing. Ally re-ran the last simulation from the night before, changed some parameters and ran the simulation a dozen more times.

She moved the sliders a bit and ran the program again…same results. She tried initiating the outbreak in different parts of the world, China—then the US—then South Africa.

Using traditional pandemic models wouldn't give her the granularity and patterns she sought. Academic models for estimating the spread of epidemics assumed people were smarter and better equipped than in the past, and that outbreaks would be contained swiftly.

The Great Influenza circled the globe three times. Pandemics weren't singular events. She would need to overwrite some variables or perhaps start from scratch if she wanted different outcomes.

She conceived the idea for a more robust model during her time with the CDC. Despite transferring to the NIH last year, the project kept gnawing at her. She wanted a tool that would help quantify the effect of early medical intervention.

Governments and other aid organizations were often late to the problem. Even a day or two could make a vast difference. Data—irrefutable data—was her solution. If she could model viral and human factors on a global scale, showing regional differences in healthcare and prevention, she had a chance to shape new policies.

Her former boss at the CDC, Nancy, supported her project to a point. Nancy hadn't been keen on adding a financial calculation into the model. Ally insisted it was necessary to show the benefits of early action—particularly to spur international aid to poorer countries.

Nancy warned that reducing the decision to save lives to a cost-benefit analysis was in poor taste. Would governments consider some human losses preferable to spending tax dollars? Upper management at the CDC wouldn't touch this with a ten-foot pole. So, Ally pursued it on her own.

Her model became a poor excuse for a hobby. She fell down a rabbit hole of "what if's"—attempting to simulate the worst pandemic conceivable. She tried different iterations to generate maximum contagion rates of the worst diseases—allowing the spread to proceed unimpeded by typical interventions. It was morbid, but she wanted to see what would happen.

What use was a model without a good stress test?

Ally had witnessed, up close, human suffering from diseases all over the world. The mental images could never be erased—children with malaria or whole families slowly dying of cholera, languishing in migrant camps. She didn't take outbreaks lightly.

But the model was different. These were just numbers on a screen. A numeric exercise…like a sinister video game.

Her younger sister, Gwen, said she should talk to someone—a professional. "This obsession with death isn't healthy," she said. "You need to grieve."

Her sister had a point.

Maybe I don't want to confront my feelings. Feelings were messy—inconvenient—unproductive.

It had been easier to focus on her project after Jim died last year. Hunting down data and news stories of novel viruses and unusual outbreaks wasn't meant to be morbid. It was all excellent information for the model, she reasoned.

Deep down, Ally knew she was hiding from the question that

haunted her: *Could she have saved Jim?*

Jim couldn't resist the cookies, pies, or chips. He had joked that every food package was a single serving—even the family-sized chip bags. Around holidays, he would load up on certain treats—like jelly beans at Easter and candy corn at Halloween. Like a kid in a literal candy store.

Jim was the love of her life and they'd been incredibly happy. *Would he still be alive if she pressed more?* No, people are stubborn. They almost never listen to health advice.

After Jim passed, she gained weight too. Allowing herself some comfort eating, but really in hindsight, the grief made everything a blur. When her weight reached an alarming number, she tried several diets, but settled on a high fat, low-carbohydrate diet.

As she lost the weight, she dove into the scientific literature on low-carb diets and their ability to reverse Type II diabetes. Overconsumption of carbs and sugar were contributing to diabolical health problems, including obesity, heart disease, and Alzheimer's.

Metabolic disease was bad enough on its own, but also impaired one's innate immune response to infections. If a serious viral pandemic occurred, the prevalence of metabolic dysfunction could compound the death rate. She made a mental note to add this to her model.

Ally worked on her project until Gretchen wedged herself onto the keyboard. Ally checked the time. The morning had gone by and she forgot to feed the cat again. She dislodged herself from the bed when her cell phone rang.

She untangled herself from her comforter. As she strode out of the bedroom, the cat sprinted between her feet. Ally stumbled sideways into the wall, bracing her fall.

"Jesus, Gretchen!"

She located her phone on the kitchen counter and checked the incoming number. She hadn't seen this number in years, amazed she knew exactly who it was. Ally drew in a long breath and hit accept.

"Hello?"

"Hello, Allison?"

"Hi Walt."

"Um, hi. Wasn't sure if this was the right number. Sorry to call you on a Saturday. I know it's been a long time, but I have something interesting I'd like your opinion on."

Ally wondered if Walt knew about Jim's death. She guessed not. It had been nearly eight years since she talked with Walt at their college reunion. She was surprised he still had her number. But then, she still recognized his.

"Walt, good to hear from you. You know I'm always happy to give my opinion. What's this about?"

"I don't want to go into it over the phone. Maya told me you live in Bethesda now. Can we meet for coffee? I can come up your way—I think you used to like that ancient diner."

"You have a good memory. I live only two blocks away. How does eleven sound?"

"Eleven it is. By the way, do you still have your clearance?"

"It's still active. Why do you ask?"

"I'll tell you later. See you then." Walt ended the call without a goodbye.

Ally's mind raced. *What could he want?*

Her recent position at NIH was more as an administrator—or a glorified paper pusher. Not anything exciting like she used to do—chasing outbreaks all over the globe. She wasn't in a position of authority to help someone of Walt's new status.

This couldn't be a social call. Sure, they had dated in college, but that was three decades ago. There were none of the typical pleasantries exchanged on the phone. He didn't even ask how she was. Walt could be that way. Getting to the point.

But why so evasive? Since when did he need her opinion?

Brushing her teeth seemed like a good first step. She looked up at the bathroom mirror and cringed.

This is what a depressed person looks like.

The weight loss left her with sagging skin on her face and neck—and other places. The laugh lines were fine, but the deeper creases on her forehead were unflattering. She hadn't had a proper haircut in a year and her gray roots were showing against her medium-length, straw-colored hair.

Did she have time for a shower? She lifted her arm for a smell test.

Not presentable at all.

She showered quickly and threw on some clean sweatpants. She tied her still damp hair in a low ponytail and put on her tan, slouchy coat.

Gretchen meowed at her feet. *Shit! Feed the cat!*

The cat jogged beside her to the food dish. Ally opened a can and dumped it in.

She grabbed her keys and phone.

"Goodbye!" Ally called, half-way out the door.

Gretchen didn't look up.

She arrived at the diner a minute before eleven. Walt was already there, staring deep into a cup of coffee—sitting in a booth at the far back corner of the room, as if deliberately hiding.

He looked the same—hardly aged from the last time they'd met. His dark crew cut showed a little thinning, and he had some gray around his temples. He was clean-shaven and his olive skin didn't show many wrinkles.

Walt didn't look up until she plopped down on the red, vinyl-covered bench across from him.

"Hey, Walt! What's up?"

He beamed, "Ally, hi! How are you?"

She grinned. "Busy…I killed six million people this morning…how about you?"

He stared at her with his brows narrowed. "Ok, I'll bite." He braced his hands on the edge of the table. "Proceed."

She took off her coat and folded it beside her. "I've been running global pandemic simulations…it's my new hobby."

"Ok! Nice seeing you!" He pretended to scoot across to leave. He smiled and settled back down. In a moment, his smile vanished and he leaned forward. "So really, how have you been? Maya told me about Jim. I'm sorry I didn't call. I was in the middle of changing jobs and moving. No excuse really. I can't imagine what you've been going through."

Ok, here we go. She didn't want to talk about Jim. Not to Walt, not to anybody. But she wanted to be polite.

"Hey, congratulations on your job," she said with a feigned smile. "It's ok you didn't call. I kept the news of his passing close. I didn't want to talk to people at the time."

"It's hard to believe he's gone," she continued. "It was so sudden. He died in his sleep." She fiddled with the menu, "I think I'm doing ok. The first few months were the toughest. Cleaning out his things…"

Like I was erasing his very existence.

Her eyes got misty. She took a deep breath and forced herself to think about anything else. She raised her gaze and tried to affix a smile, "Anyway, after that, I looked for jobs further north. I left Atlanta and transferred here to NIH last August. The new job is keeping me busy. And when I'm not working, I do some jogging or watch stupid YouTube videos with my cat. You know, normal stuff."

Normal. *What is normal, anyway? What's normal about grief? Or about the loss of true love?*

Most of the time she felt like a robot. Her dad and sister Gwen were robots too. They all had the Scandinavian 'gene' that overruled their emotions and locked them away. Particularly in times of tragedy, one cared for the living and kept plowing ahead, never really digesting the impacts to oneself.

She picked up the menu and placed it in front of her like a wall. "So, did you order already?" She looked over her shoulder for a server.

"No, not yet. Just coffee," he said.

"Now that I'm closer to New Jersey, I can see my family more often, especially my new granddaughter."

"Oh, that's right!" Walt beamed, flashing his perfect white teeth. "What's it like to be a grandma?"

"It's fun. I babysat last weekend." Ally smiled, recalling their interaction. "Baby Charlotte loves chasing my cat around. And I had forgotten how gross toddlers are! Feeding her is a hoot. I gave her some small bits of apple. She would take a chunk, put it in her mouth, take it out, try to feed it to Gretchen—who wasn't happy about it—then drop it on the rug and then offer it to me! As a good grandma, I have to eat it! You know, reinforce the concept of sharing. So, it'll be nice to have some breakfast that hasn't been licked by the cat or dropped on the floor repeatedly!"

Walt laughed. "Of course, who knows what's going on back there!" he said, pointing to the griddle behind the long counter.

Ally turned her head. The head cook, an old, grizzled, skinny man with a white stubbly chin and greasy hair, wearing a ridiculously stained apron, wiped down the steel exhaust hood with an equally disgusting rag.

She quickly turned back around as her eyes cramped with laughter. Walt began chuckling. His eyes watered, his face turning pink and the vein in his forehead protruding, unsuccessfully trying to contain himself. Their conversations had always had a special rhythm and appreciation for the absurd. In that moment, laughing together, their old friendship came flooding back to her.

After Walt gathered himself, he let out a long breath and asked, "And your son, Theo? How is he?"

"Good. Working construction. His wife works at a community college. They bought their first house just before Charlotte was born—not far from my dad."

She should have reciprocated, asking him about his life and family, but didn't want to know.

No ring on his hand. *Was he still a bachelor after all these years?*

She avoided that mine field and changed the subject. "But that's not why we're here. You said I could help with something?"

"Yes, and thanks again for meeting me so quickly," he said softly. "I don't know exactly where to begin. But to make a long story short, the White House received a brief and frankly, there are so many questions. I wanted to get an outside, objective opinion."

"You asked about my clearance on the phone. So, this is classified?"

Walt nodded. "Normally I would ask you to come down to a secure facility to look at this, but honestly, it's not really my place to bring you in. Would raise too many questions. Instead, I redacted enough to downgrade the classification. But I can only show this to you. You can't have your own copy. And you can't divulge this to anyone."

The waitress interrupted, "Can I get you something, darling?"

"I think we'll be here awhile," Ally said. "Can you bring me a black coffee and a side of bacon?"

"I'll have the Belgian waffles with whipped cream and a large orange juice, plus more coffee," Walt added.

Ally grimaced. *And he is the White House physician.*

After the server left, Walt said, "Hey, I biked here. A few extra calories won't hurt."

Yes, he did look great. Why did some men age so gracefully? *Not fair.*

He slid an unmarked folder across the table. Inside was a grainy facsimile with lines of redactions in black marker, blocking out the headers and most of the text. Some remaining text was in Russian, with English translation typewritten in the margins, describing weekly mortality numbers.

"Take your time. I'll answer whatever questions I'm able to."

Ally looked over the information for a few minutes. and then heard a beep. She took out her phone.

"Hey," Walt said in an alarmed tone, "You can't use your phone."

"Just a text message from Theo. I'll put it away."

"Sorry," Walt said, stone-faced, "you have to keep your phone in your bag."

"Ok. Got it. So," she scanned the pages in front of her, "let's see ...roughly five thousand people died over four weeks? How big a geographic area are we talking? How many people lived there? It's hard to understand the scale of the outbreak from these numbers."

"What makes you think it was an outbreak?" he asked.

"Educated guess. If it wasn't viral, you'd be talking to someone else."

"That's the problem. There are different theories. Let's just say we're supposed to believe these people died from starvation. As a hypothetical, this population lives in a remote northern zone that had record snowstorms—that is, maybe they were cut off from supply lines and depleted their food stores. Would this be plausible?"

"Hmm. But what about the death rate? If one in five hundred people died, it's entirely different from, say, one in fifty."

"Our estimate is eighty to eighty-five percent. But our assumptions of the starting population may be imprecise."

She dropped the folder on the table. "What! That's crazy! Even category four hurricanes don't kill that percentage of people. Jeez, even the worst pandemics in history resulted in less than twenty percent mortality."

She sat back and rubbed her face with both hands. "Wait. The earliest outbreaks of Ebola in the Congo had mortality rates of ninety percent. Later outbreaks had lower overall death counts—due to quick response times. Could we be talking about a massive Ebola outbreak in a northern climate? No. That doesn't make sense."

She paused and shook her head. "But to backtrack, there are problems with the starvation theory. People can live off their fat stores for much longer periods, a couple months, if they can drink water, which they obviously had access to—with all the snow. Could they have frozen to death? That would be more likely than starvation. A polar vortex? Temperatures of minus forty?"

She recalled historical accounts of tens of thousands of soldiers freezing to death. They were marching long distances in the snow, or surrounded by enemy forces and couldn't escape—and in these cases, the soldiers were already malnourished and ill-equipped after months of fighting. But she wasn't aware of any northern wars.

Walt wasn't interrupting her. In fact, he seemed to enjoy her antics—with a small smile, resting his chin on his palm. He used to tease her in the old days. When she got on these types of bents, he would patiently let her go on, then eventually say, "World peace, check mark," mocking her garrulous method of problem solving.

The waitress returned with their breakfast and poured additional coffee in Walt's mug.

After the waitress left, Walt whispered, "What about a chemical attack? Poison gas?" He stuffed some waffle in his mouth.

"Unlikely," Ally said. "Deaths would be limited to those in the immediate vicinity of the release, with a larger percentage just sickened. Doesn't fit."

She ate a portion of bacon, then pointed it at him, "I think there is a lot you aren't telling me that would help narrow this down. Maybe a contaminated water supply? But more importantly, I'm wondering why all the secrecy. Classified, right? Probably military-related?"

She studied his face and waited for an answer, but Walt didn't flinch. He took a sip of orange juice.

"Aha! Ok, so maybe you can't say. Fine, let me think this through. Hmm. Let's assume this occurred at a military base. Something killed eighty percent or more of them. You're a doctor, you understand the immune response. During the Spanish Flu of 1918, their own strong immune responses destroyed young soldiers' lungs. The healthier people suffered more."

Ally sipped her coffee and stared at the numbers again.

Finally, she said, "My gut tells me this is a new virus—probably a flu based on the climate—but again, just a guess. But what kind of flu…who knows! Hmm, maybe SARS? You would need to get a lot more information. I mean a lot!" Ally froze, realizing her voice carried too far.

Her fingers drummed the table with anxious energy while she thought about the situation. She leaned forward and quietly continued, "You would need to collect blood samples from both sick and healthy people. Locate and interview any survivors. Find out what differences allowed them to recover. We need to get an estimate of the transmission period."

He just stared at her, so she continued, "You need to locate patient zero. Or at least try to narrow down which people got sick first and where they traveled beforehand. Understanding the origin is important if you want to get ahead of this."

Walt put down his coffee and rubbed his temples. He let out a sigh. "I thought as much, but I needed to hear it from someone I trusted." He pushed away his plate and gathered the papers. He kept his head down as he stuffed the folder into his messenger bag and put on his jacket.

"Whoa!" Ally said. She grabbed his arm and quickly let it go. "Wait, how bad is this? Where and when did this happen? Is the CDC aware of this? What about WHO? Am I allowed to brief my boss at NIH?"

"I can't really go into it now." He reached across the table, placed his hand on hers and looked at her sternly. "And you absolutely can't discuss this with anyone."

She held her breath a little, her body stiffened, processing the seriousness of his warning.

Walt said, "But would you be willing to come to some meetings and get read in…if I can swing it?"

"Sure, whatever you need," she said, nodding.

He slid out of the booth, grabbed the check and said, "I got this."

She got up and they exchanged a polite hug goodbye. "Thanks, keep me posted."

She left a tip on the table as Walt's tall, thin frame exited the front door. She stood transfixed, watching him through the front window as he unlocked his bike from a lamp post and rode away.

When he was out of sight, she picked up the rest of her bacon off her plate and wrapped it in a napkin. She placed it in her large coat pocket, before heading to the door.

On the chilly walk home, her mind raced. This new mystery was thrilling, although she felt like an awful person for being excited by human tragedy. Yet, she couldn't wait to get home to try some new simulations that could come close to an eighty percent mortality rate. She was going to have to make some structural changes to the program, to increase the transmission times and the virus' lethality.

Why hadn't this been reported in the news? *Not a good sign.* She would need to do some internet sleuthing. Five thousand people don't die in a complete vacuum.

Chapter 2

Day 33

It was early morning on a Sunday in Beijing. Zhang Ling, Deputy Director of the Ministry of State Security, read the document over again. *The Russians really used a fax? So quaint.*

He called Dr. Wu on an encrypted line.

"Doctor—you received the pages I sent?"

"Yes. Where was the outbreak, exactly?"

"Northern Russia. Near Granitnyy. The Director will want your team to study it."

"As we should," Dr. Wu said. "It could provide the breakthrough we need. But how do we get a sample?"

"Stand by. I'll call you soon."

Zhang broke off the call. He walked down the hall to his supervisor's office—to discuss the situation with Szu Qiang.

Qiang was sitting at his desk, watching something on his computer monitor. Some kind of surveillance video.

Zhang knocked and bowed his head toward Qiang. "Sir, sorry for the intrusion. Your secretary said you were free. I have something you will very much want to look at."

"Are you presuming that you can read my thoughts?" Qiang asked with a sneer. "Very well. What is so important?"

He handed Qiang the document. "Over five thousand Russians have died just north of the Arctic Circle. The cause—we can only guess at. If this is a new virus, or bioweapon, it could be the breakthrough our team needs."

He waited patiently, standing with his hands clasped in front of him, as Qiang studied the document. Zhang knew that interrupting or saying the wrong thing could result in terrible consequences. He'd seen it with his own eyes—men severely beaten or sent to the work camps for an incorrect turn of phrase. Qiang's brother was China's president, Szu Chen. With this connection, Qiang had nearly unlimited power and often used it for sadistic ends.

After two uncomfortable minutes, Qiang looked up. "Do you think other countries intercepted the transmission?"

Zhang said, "We didn't see any indications. The phone traffic at the WHO appears normal."

Qiang frowned. "The Americans. They did this. You see? Some said I was mad. Now my brother and all of China will understand my vision."

"Yes," Zhang nodded. "You were right to not trust the Americans."

Qiang hit his desk with his fist. The corners of his mouth showed a slight, familiar smirk. "The only way to deter their aggression is with our *own* arsenal of bioweapons. The next war will not be nuclear. It will be biological. An unseeable force."

Based on Qiang's reputation for cruelty and ambition, his plan was not about deterrents. No, Qiang was most certainly considering a first strike. He had seen this same smirk before when Qiang ordered prisoner executions.

Zhang nodded.

Qiang continued, "Our country could be the next target. Is Dr. Wu ready to assist?"

"Yes, the doctor will accompany the insertion team. Our window of opportunity is short."

"Send a team as soon as possible. I want to be briefed on all aspects." Qiang waved a hand in dismissal.

He turned to leave when Qiang said, "Wait. I want you to lead the team. There can be no mistakes."

Zhang bowed and left the room.

He walked a few feet down the corridor and stopped. A sharp pain radiated between his brows—the first signs of a migraine. Leading a team into Russian territory was madness. Up to now, the work at the bioweapon lab had seemed purely theoretical. Even if this virus was a fluke—perhaps nature's own creation—it was deadly enough to be the solution Dr. Wu's team had been searching for.

Dr. Wu was the head of China's secret biological warfare laboratory called "The Farm." Qiang created the lab two years ago, hidden in plain sight within the remote southern mountains. They designed the buildings to resemble old, rustic farm buildings on the outside; but inside were state-of-the-art research facilities.

To further their deception, the scientists pretended to be alpaca farmers. The farm was a dark site, and phone or internet communication were highly restricted.

Would Qiang really use bioweapons? This question kept him up some nights.

But Qiang had a point. In the event this outbreak spread from Russia, Wu's team would have a head start developing a vaccine, saving countless Chinese lives.

He focused on the order at hand. They needed to act quickly. *Opportunity knocks on the door only once*. Another snowstorm was coming towards the region that could provide additional cover for their insertion team.

Zhang returned to his own office and called Wu.

"Yes, the operation is authorized," Zhang blurted. "You are coming with us. Meet me at the airstrip tomorrow morning at daybreak."

He hung up and looked at the picture on his credenza. His beautiful wife of forty years, smiling, holding hands with their two young grandchildren.

China worrying about Russia is like a dog worrying about a flea.

But too many fleas will begin spreading to other hosts.

It is best to find out the truth.

DAY 34

Senator Ruth Cochran briskly took off her suit jacket as she walked into her chambers. Beads of sweat formed on the back of her neck and moisture wicked up along her hairline.

"Who has a copy of the invitation and the doctor's brief? And someone turn down the thermostat!" She tossed her jacket on the back of her desk chair.

Her chief of staff, Sally Taylor, rushed in bringing her an iced mocha and placed it on her desk. "I turned the temperature down to sixty-four." Sally said. "NSA Director Ortega will pick you up in an hour so you can talk in the car. The meeting is all set. The Vice President, Secretary Shelton, and your buddy, Major General Roadfuss will be at the meeting. All the information is in your briefcase."

"Ha! My buddy! I'd rather be friends with a shark. At least it would make eye contact. He's a lousy liar."

"Do you want me to accompany you? Take notes?" Sally asked.

"Thank you, but I need you to keep things running here. Jason will be there. I only wish we had more time to plan!" Ruth collapsed in her leather office chair and threw her black-framed glasses on her carved mahogany desk. "Crap!"

"Relax. It will be fine," Sally said in her usual soothing tone. "Ortega will do the heavy lifting. You said it yourself—he just wants to look them in the eye. It will be short." She picked up Ruth's glasses from the edge of the desk, inspected the hinges, and folded them neatly in front of her.

Ruth leaned forward. "Have you confirmed Dr. Reynerson's attendance?"

"Dr. Braff is walking her over to the meeting. But as discussed, he will not be attending, so she is officially your guest...."

"Yes. Right." She put her jacket back on, her sweat turning cold on her skin. "Fine, let me know when Ortega arrives. I'll meet him out front. But please, find a picture of this doctor so I can at least recognize her when I get there—I don't want to go in blind." She picked up her glasses and put them back on.

Ruth was glad Ortega pushed for the meeting. According to her sources, Roadfuss was not reacting appropriately to the Russian Army memo. She needed to know why and what this all meant. Something fishy was going on.

A year ago, the Army submitted a draft budget line item that looked out of place. One of her interns pointed it out to her. The budget for the chemical and biological weapon surveillance program hadn't changed in over a decade. But there was a small plus-up for new satellites to cover Southern China and Northeastern Russia. The details were masked and the funding request would have been lost in the fine print except for the diligence of her staff.

They dug around and discovered General Dirk Roadfuss at Fort Belvoir requested the funding. This meant something. Something important.

When she discreetly asked her old friend, Director Ortega, about this new line item, he explained that China had begun operating a new biological weapons laboratory. Roadfuss' team was monitoring it and even had a spy on the inside to provide us regular intelligence.

But the budget request for monitoring in northern Russia made no sense to him. Ortega made some inquiries to Roadfuss. He got the stonewall treatment. Something was definitely not right.

Ortega agreed with her they needed to keep an eye on the General. That was easy enough. But now the Russian Army memo—describing mass casualties—raised new questions. They both knew the President was a moron.

Could he really have directed Roadfuss to create a new biological weapon and test it on Russians?

If so, President Merriwether was no longer fit for office.

Ruth knew she could trust Ortega—they had a close personal history going back decades.

She wasn't sure who else she could trust in the Merriwether Administration.

* * *

Vice President Thomas Defoe studied the printout of his daily schedule. It was a mild and sunny February day—an early sign of Spring. Some cherry trees were confused by the high temperatures, and a handful blossomed near his home at the Naval Observatory.

It would be a great day to kayak along the Potomac, Tom thought.

He hadn't had a full day off in the last one thousand and forty-five days. Not since the Inauguration. Counting the days made him feel worse, but he did it anyway. Today was no exception. He didn't have a choice to skip meetings, especially on days when the President was indisposed.

As he entered the briefing room at the Old Executive Office Building, he scanned the attendees, both familiar and unfamiliar faces. He'd learned to skip the pleasantries at the start of meetings. His time was too valuable for that nonsense. "Ok, let's get going. Who's up first?"

The head of the Army Intelligence and Security Command, Major General Dirk Roadfuss stood up. Tom knew the General well. A tall man with a squarish face, thick waist and even thicker neck.

Sometimes a thick head.

But he was loyal. His Army uniform was decorated with a large swath of ribbons and medals. Roadfuss, holding a water bottle, lumbered over to a small lectern next to the projection screen.

"As most of you know," Roadfuss said in a deep, gravelly voice, "the NSA intercepted a faxed data report from a remote area near Granitnyy, Russia. NSA Director Ortega turned it over to the Pentagon due to its military nature. We were well aware of Russia's planned military exercise."

An aerial view of the Russian camp appeared on the wall.

Roadfuss continued, "Translated into English, they called it 'Operation Ice Dagger'. The exercises were routine. Some typical posturing. But then this fax, transmitted through an unencrypted supply system database, was sent directly to the Kremlin. This is highly unusual because there were no attempts at cyber security. Perhaps they didn't think we were paying attention. But the report itself is the troubling part."

A close-up aerial view was projected. "Even with all the snow on the ground," Roadfuss continued, "any land disturbance is visible by our satellites. The Russian's began staging equipment, helicopters and ground vehicles, and building temporary structures in early January. Forces arrived shortly after. The exercise, as we understood it, was for symbolic purposes—a show of strength and an excuse to play with some of their new weapons and vehicles. So, when NSA intercepted this report—alleging roughly five thousand soldiers died within a month's time—we needed to assess the ramifications."

He took a sip of water and then said in a solemn tone. "If this is true, a sizable portion of their Army's ground combat troops were affected. This is what brings us here today."

Switching to another slide, a graph appeared showing the exponential death curve. The General appeared to pause to let the others digest the data before proceeding.

He clicked the remote. A new slide highlighted a portion of text from the Russian fax with a translation underneath. It read,

"Roads are blocked. Too many dead to bury. Will let you know when safe."

The General continued after glancing at some papers. "There were two notable snowstorms in the region during the month of January, but by our estimates, the most severe one may have occurred after the troops had already perished—the report isn't clear on this timing. And this explains why a fax was sent without encryption, probably because of sheer panic. Note the report does not ask for aid or rescue for the survivors; we think they intended it as a warning for others to stay away."

Tom had seen all this in his pre-brief notes. "Why do we care about a bunch of dead Russians?"

Senator Cochran leaned forward and whipped off her glasses, "Obviously, this is quite alarming. What are the chances that this was a biological attack? That's why we're here, right General? I've brought in my own expert. Dr. Reynerson?"

"Senator, could you tell us more about your guest?" Roadfuss said.

"Yes, of course. Dr. Reynerson is a specialist in the fields of epidemiology and pandemic response, currently working for the National Institutes of Health, and before that, she worked for the CDC." She turned to the doctor, "I have that right?"

The doctor—a thin, older blonde woman in an ill-fitting navy-blue suit—nodded. "Yes, Senator."

Ruth put her glasses back on. "She has the appropriate clearance and was brought in as a consultant last night with the approval of Director Ortega. I've asked her to give a brief presentation if you don't mind."

Roadfuss took his water and went back to his seat.

Dr. Reynerson stood and walked around the table, handing out papers. "Good morning! I'm Dr. Ally Reynerson. In my federal career, I've worked in the Epidemic Intelligence Service, identifying the causes of infectious diseases when they arise, both domestically and abroad."

Tom suspected that Ruth was up to something, but he played it cool. "Glad you could be with us today."

"Thank you, sir. The virus—if we can all agree this was the source of the problem—was highly unusual. If you don't mind, I'll go over some basics about viruses and how they spread. I think this will help put this news from Russia into context."

She reached her chair again and sat down. "Viruses need a host to live and multiply. In the northern hemisphere, influenza, for example, is transmitted more readily during the winter based on several factors.

The air is colder and drier, which allows viruses to survive outside a host for many more hours than they would in warmer, more humid environments. The reduced amount of sunlight can decrease vitamin D and melatonin in humans, which compromises our immune systems."

She glanced about the table. "Because of the cold, people congregate indoors—where they breathe the same air, sneeze, cough, and transmit droplets directly or indirectly onto surfaces. Places like cruise ships, airplanes, daycare centers, shopping malls…you get the idea…are ideal for transmitting viruses because of the density of human contact. The spread of viral infection can become exponential.

"However, as people become aware of the magnitude of the contagion, there are the typical countermeasures, such as closing schools, teleworking, hand washing, limiting close contact with others, avoiding unnecessary travel, increasing vaccinations…and all these measures help break the cycle of contagion."

Director Ortega asked, "And what about the Russian army?"

"We can assume, as military personnel, most of the population at the camp would have been generally young and healthy. This leads me to believe the illness is similar to the 1918 pandemic. The youngest, healthiest people had such strong immune reactions, they experienced swollen lung tissue, respiratory failure, and nearly immediate death. Some individuals developed a secondary bacterial infection, like pneumonia—compounding the problem. If this occurred in Russia, it could explain the extraordinary death total."

This is tedious, Tom thought.

"I didn't come here for a biology lesson," Tom said. "I just need to know, based on our best intelligence, whether or not we can confirm if this virus is some type of biological weapon. Do we need to be concerned or not?"

The doctor said, "It could be a weapon. A very effective one, at that. Maybe the most effective one in human history. But it's almost impossible to know without a physical sample to analyze. We would need to do some DNA testing perhaps, comparing it to known viruses. As far as being concerned, yes, we should be concerned something of this lethality and transmission rate exists in the world."

General Roadfuss straightened in his seat. "So, you don't know. Hmmf. But should we worry about it continuing to spread?"

Reynerson replied, "The best method to stop an epidemic is to isolate the infected. As a rule of thumb, the transmission period for most viruses is under seven days. With the snowstorm and the warning letter to Moscow, it's likely there would be little to no transmission outside the original group. Based on the timeline, if this was a virus, it's probably contained by now."

Roadfuss glared. "I understand what you're saying, but do you really think it would be responsible of us to assume it's contained?"

"I'm not here to recommend a course of action," Reynerson said. The doctor looked at Senator Cochran and then Roadfuss. "It isn't my place. As a researcher and doctor, I would want to learn more and work with a specialized government team to develop a vaccine for it."

Tom looked at Roadfuss, but the General appeared to be in a staring contest with Ortega. *What is going on with these two?*

The room was silent. The doctor cleared her throat and looked at Roadfuss. "Because you are absolutely right. Viruses which become, quote 'contained', often show up in other parts of the world or return a year later, sometimes mutated—resulting in worse outcomes. We've all seen Ebola outbreaks come and go. Based on the estimated mortality rate, this new virus is just as deadly and far more transmissible."

A low murmur erupted; side conversations grew louder.

Tom checked his watch. He didn't care about dead Russians. *Lord, even if the virus spread and decimated most of Russia, well, that was good for the U.S., right?* But he had to pretend to care. That's what a VP does. The rising clamor pricked at his ears.

"Hello! Can everyone simmer down?!"

When the room quieted, Tom looked at the Secretary of Defense and asked, "Shelton, what is our next step?"

"Sir," Shelton said, "the General's team and the Pentagon will continue our satellite reconnaissance of the area and monitor all voice and data transmissions coming into and out of the region. Nonetheless, we suggest creating a back channel with Moscow to offer our assistance in identifying and finding a vaccine for the virus."

"Good," Defoe said, rising, "I think we're done. Keep me posted."

The rest of the room leapt to their feet. Defoe walked out, followed by his secret service detail.

That was a waste of time, Tom thought as he walked swiftly down the hall. *If the doctor says it's contained, then why would we care about a vaccine?*

There was no way Russia would ask for, or accept, American help. He certainly wouldn't if the situation were reversed.

Defoe hummed as he walked back to the Oval Office.

The Russians must be crapping their pants!

* * *

Ally watched as everyone gathered their belongings and headed out of the room. Walt had instructed her to hang back and meet him in the hallway when everyone else was gone. The meeting itself left her with more questions than answers. Her head was spinning—like she just walked out of a fun house, the kind with mirrored walls. She was looking at her watch, trying to figure out how long it would take her to get back to NIH, when Senator Cochran touched her elbow.

The Senator said, "You did great. Thanks again for your assistance." Cochran looked at her phone and then locked eyes with Ally. "I've got to run. Maybe we'll see each other again?"

Ally looked at her dumbstruck. *I did great? Was anyone even listening?* With all the staring contests going on, she doubted anyone heard her.

She stood, tongue-tied. The Senator briskly turned and walked away.

But still, in the fleeting moment when Cochran spoke to her, Ally was stunned by the Senator's intensity. There was a power in her eyes—like she was acknowledged in a way she hadn't been for a long time. Maybe that's how politicians *wer*e. They had superpower levels of charisma.

A young man, a civilian, collected all her handouts and walked them over to a shredder. Ally waited until most of the attendees left, as Walt had instructed, before leaving the room.

Walt was waiting a few feet down the narrow hall, his back to her, leaning against the wall. She tapped him on his shoulder.

"Jesus, Walt," she said in a low tone. "That was intense. I still don't understand why you weren't at the meeting. And why I had to be the guest of Senator Cochran…whom I've never met before."

"Ally, thanks for being there." He scanned down both ends of the hall.

She followed his gaze, noticing that the hallway was empty.

Walt whispered, "I'm just the White House physician. It wouldn't be appropriate for me to attend. It was unusual for me to see the report from Russia in the first place.

"Yeah, how did you come across it?"

"It's not important," Walt hissed, glancing again up and down the hall.

"Hey, you came to me. I think I should know what's going on."

"Shhh. Let's just say I came across it in the Oval Office, while I was waiting for the President."

"Shit, Walt! You stole a copy?"

He put his finger to his lips. "Sometimes I read things over for the President—at his behest. He made it part of my job to figure out what's important and what isn't. Look, it doesn't matter now. But the real question is, how did the meeting go?"

"Terrible. The Vice President doesn't care. So, is that it? Aren't we going to contact the World Health Organization or the UN? Will General Roadfuss share this with the CDC and NIH?"

"You have to read between the lines. I'm sure most of those things will happen...maybe not through official channels. We don't really know what happened in Russia. If we raise an alarm and it turns out to be something else, our country, and specifically, our President, could look foolish."

"Hey, speaking of, where *is* the President? Shouldn't he have been here? Instead of Defoe?"

"Don't worry. A synopsis of the situation has been in his daily briefing package for the past couple of days. President Merriwether is away on a short golf trip."

* * *

On the way to the parking garage, Roadfuss saw Senator Cochran stride towards him with deliberation. He pretended to ignore her until she called out, "Major General Roadfuss! Do you have a minute?"

Roadfuss knew better than to avoid the Senator. His budgets would never survive the slight. He slowed until she reached him and then they walked together towards his car. "Senator, I think I know what you're going to ask."

"So, did we do this?" she whispered. "Did we create a biological weapon? I need to know if our President is a maniac or just insanely stupid. Or is it possible the Russians may have been developing a weaponized virus? Perhaps one that got away from them?"

"Ma'am, I've been in the military for thirty-five years. I know sometimes the right hand doesn't know what the left is doing. We're a large organization and this fact isn't lost on me. But I've looked high and low, and there's absolutely no indication we did this or had the capacity to do this. My team is focused on surveillance. We don't create biological weapons."

Cochran stared at him, peering at him over her glasses, her pointy jaw aimed upward. "So, I'm told."

They reached his white sedan with government plates and he took the keys from his pocket. "I sense you doubt my veracity." He looked down at her with a smile, hoping to diffuse the situation.

She cocked her head to the side. "I don't trust—I *verify*. You—more than anyone else—understands this."

The smile left his face, and he crossed his arms. "We both know that Russia is good at keeping secrets. It's conceivable they created something that turned against them. But that's highly unlikely." He put his hands on his hips and stepped forward, closing the gap between them. "Look, their military was already weakened from the tariffs and embargoes. I think they got unlucky and didn't bring enough antibiotics to handle a bad flu. Or maybe they underestimated how much heating oil to bring."

Looking around, he added, "If it reassures you, all the vehicles they brought into their camp before the exercise are still there. Satellite photos confirmed it yesterday. There's no indication anyone left the area. The closest town is over twenty-five miles away, across hostile terrain. Nobody, sick or otherwise, is walking out."

Ruth fastened the top two buttons on her long camel-hair coat. "Thanks, General. But please keep me posted on any new developments. I hope you know you can call me anytime." She locked her squinty eyes on his, as if she was trying to peer inside his brain.

He dismissed her with a curt, "Yes ma'am."

She pursed her lips in apparent disapproval and walked away.

He got into his car and started the engine. He turned the car radio on and scanned different stations, settling for some light rock. He watched her walk away and then stop after a hundred feet—greeting a tall man with dark skin, wearing a dark gray trench coat and a black flat cap.

Was she talking to Director Ortega?

He waited until Ruth was out of sight before he drove away.

Ruth was a real pain in his ass. But she was the least of his concerns.

President Petrov can't be happy.

Hopefully, the situation is contained.

* * *

Zhang stared out his office window. Getting a military team into Russia was a suicide mission. Yet, he couldn't push back. Director Szu Qiang was unequivocal—get samples of the Russian virus at any cost. Qiang was not a reasonable man.

Zhang invited Navy Captain Gao Dong to his office—to meet one on one. He needed a plan on the best way to insert operatives through Russian-controlled waters.

When Gao arrived, Zhang skipped the pleasantries and gave Gao an overview of the events leading up to their new mission.

Gao asked, "Respectfully—you want to do what exactly?"

"I need a small team to infiltrate a remote Russian military encampment and get blood and tissue samples of infected soldiers. Both living and dead."

"Sir, as you know," Gao said, "we have a vessel in the area. We've been keeping a watchful eye for some time. We can drop a team in by helicopter to the boat, but the rest…" Gao closed his eyes.

With new land and waters opening up, a modern-day land grab in the Arctic was underway. Even the Americans were changing their tactics to operate in the cold. The Chinese Navy was patrolling the international waters north of Operation Ice Dagger, on an ice breaker disguised as a Green Ocean research boat. They put out a phony press release about their efforts to track a pod of bowhead whales through the Artic.

Even Petrov didn't interfere with the greenies—he said many times they were a fringe group that was sad and inconsequential. "*Let them chase their stupid whales*," he remembered Petrov once said. "*Soon there won't be any left, so what does it matter?*"

Getting the team onto land—undetected—was the difficult part. One wrong move could cause a major international conflict.

Zhang showed Gao a satellite photo showing cloud cover of the area. "If the weather forecast is correct, another snowstorm is coming. It could mask the Russian's satellite reconnaissance, providing a window for our mission." He continued to explain that the region was largely uninhabited except for a few natural gas pumping and compressor stations.

Gao suggested they bring in members of the Snow Leopard Commando Unit. After their zodiacs reached the shore, the six-mile hike would be easy for them. They would travel by night wearing night vision goggles.

Sure, commandos could make the journey—but the doctor?

Zhang said, "The doctor is eighty years old. Is it feasible he could make the journey on foot alongside the Commandos? During a snow storm no less?"

Gao replied, "The Unit can pull him on a sled if needed. They will get the job done."

"You and the team must understand," Zhang warned, "that if we are captured, we will honor our country and use cyanide pills. This is not negotiable."

Dead men cannot be interrogated. Zhang needed to keep it that way.

Gao said, "Yes, they will comply."

Chapter 3

Day 35

Getting onboard the icebreaker boat went according to plan. Yet Zhang's stomach was tied in knots, trying to anticipate all the things that could go wrong. He studied the maps again, committing them to memory.

At midnight, he and the three Commandos cleaned and inspected their weapons. They had acquired Russian military snow camouflage suits. With the extra padding, helmets and masks, they could pass for Russians—at least from a distance.

When the boat was within a mile of the landing zone, Zhang checked on Dr. Wu.

"Are you ready?"

"Yes, but…"

Zhang sighed with frustration as Dr. Wu fiddled with the fasteners on his suit, unable to clip on his flashlight without assistance, and had difficulty putting on his boots.

He helped Wu get outfitted properly. An unnecessary delay. When the doctor was finally ready, two commandos helped ease Wu into the zodiac and placed him in the center of the boat, under blankets to stay warm. The wind and spray of the ocean were freezing. Zhang wished he also had a blanket. But, as their leader, he could not show weakness.

They reached the shoreline and pulled the inflatable boat out of the water, hiding it behind some boulders. Zhang stayed at the back with Wu as the Commandos marched single file close to the tree line.

He was surprised how well the doctor was keeping up for the first fifteen minutes, but then Wu lagged behind and fell. They needed to quicken their pace. Zhang radioed one of the commandos.

"We need the raft."

Zhang and a Commando pulled the doctor the rest of the way.

When they arrived at the Russian camp, the snow subsided. Zhang scanned the landscape. No lights. No sounds.

Finding corpses was easy. There were unusual mounds scattered on the edge of the camp, some with limbs sticking through the snow. The dead were frozen, but accessible.

They formed two teams. One to do recon for survivors and the other to get samples from the dead. Zhang and one commando stayed with Wu to get tissue samples. Two commandos investigated the surrounding structures.

Zhang found a low mound and wiped the snow off a corpse. He handed the doctor a backpack with instruments and sample containers. Dr. Wu knelt in the snow and went to work cutting the lymph nodes from a cadaver. Zhang looked down and was revulsed by the dead eyes of the soldier staring back at him, frozen yet questioning. He looked away.

Flashes of gray and brown appeared near the tree line. Then a growl. A pack of wolves.

He studied the pack, trying to count. *Maybe five?*

The old man screamed. Dr. Wu's eyes were wide like saucers. He fell backward, his arms scrambling to right himself.

Zhang bent down to cover the doctor's mouth with his gloved hand. "Shhh. Quiet!"

A moment later, a distinct noise echoed from across the field. The clunk of a wooden door. At a nearby cabin, a woman with long red hair appeared on the porch wearing a bathrobe and white combat boots. She was looking in their direction.

One of the commandos slid behind her. The solder knocked her in the head with the butt of his rifle and the woman fell to the ground.

We have our survivor, Zhang thought.

Alive for now.

* * *

The wolves looked so big…like he could reach out and touch them.

Dr. Wu held his breath as he watched the commando dispatch the animals with his silenced firearm. He exhaled in relief and thanked the soldier for his quick reaction.

Now that they were safe, he wasn't having luck getting back up, so he rolled to his side, pushing with his arms to get his knees underneath him. His back ached; his hands frozen. As he struggled, Zhang reached down and pulled him upright, holding onto the back of his jacket.

Before he could straighten himself out or utter a proper thank you, Zhang hissed, "You almost compromised the entire operation! Screaming like a toddler. Haven't you ever seen wolves up close before? They were probably just curious."

He knew Zhang was right for being angry. He also knew his apology wouldn't compensate for his mistake. "My apologies," Wu whispered. "I was…it won't happen again." He kept his gaze downward.

One of the commandos from the recon group came over. "Doctor, we subdued a middle-aged female survivor. Do you want her dead or alive?"

"Alive, please," Wu said. "We don't know what we'll get from the cadavers. If she has the virus, perhaps as a carrier, we have a good chance of identifying it and reproducing it at the lab."

In the distance, additional gunshots rang out near the cabin.

Zhang asked the commando if there were other survivors.

The commando spoke into the radio on his shoulder. He paused as if listening to a response and then replied, "There were. You said you only needed one alive, correct?"

Wu blinked. Killing the others was necessary for their escape, but it made his stomach begin to hurt. He hoped the information they gathered would be worth the human cost.

Zhang said, "Yes, correct. We need to wrap it up here. Dr. Wu—we're leaving in five minutes. See those all-terrain vehicles?" He pointed to a pool of white transport trucks. "If we can get one running, we can get Wu and the Russian woman back to the ship quickly."

The wind gusted and snow began to fall again with large wet flakes.

Wu smiled imagining a comfortable, warm ride back to the shore. Being pulled on the raft was embarrassing.

He finished packaging his tissue samples into an insulated bag, stuffing snow around the jars.

After some tinkering by the commandos, the engine of the tracked personnel carrier roared to life a few feet away, belching black smoke at first but then turning a whitish gray, barely discernable in the snowfall. Wu grabbed the railing at the back door to the vehicle but slipped on the icy bottom step. Zhang, standing behind, caught him and assisted him into the carrier.

Wu took a seat on a bench along the wall, grateful to get out of the wind. He placed the backpack with the samples and medical tools on the seat by his side. His hands were so cold. He took off his gloves and rubbed his bony, wrinkled hands together to increase circulation.

He watched in silence as the Commandos covered the unconscious woman in blankets and propped her body in the opposite corner. They had put a half-face cartridge respirator on her.

Wu looked over at Zhang, who took the seat across from him. "Won't the Russians notice us leaving in one of their large vehicles?"

"There are no people for miles," Zhang explained. "The snow will cover our tracks. It's a calculated risk."

Wu nodded.

The vehicle jerked forward. The ride was bumpy, and the engine was quite loud.

Within a few minutes, the engine noise became a droning beat; warm air from the engine flowed through vents into the compartment. Zhang and the rest of the team were closing their eyes and falling asleep.

Dr. Wu resisted sleep—reflecting on the kidnapping and the killings. It was one thing to take tissue samples from dead people, but he knew what would befall their red-haired donor. But he had his directive. Retaining a survivor was necessary if they were to achieve their goals.

Wu closed his eyes, hoping to settle his mind. Instead, he heard a muffled grunting noise. He looked in the direction of the Russian woman. No, she was still covered up, her chin slumped to her chest—eyes closed—unconscious.

He heard a squeak. A tiny puppy popped out from under his seat. A Samoyed—fluffy and pure white—with round body and folded ears. The dog couldn't be more than six weeks old. It was the cutest thing he had ever seen.

He remembered the time his parents got him a dog, named Gengi, for his seventh birthday. He loved his dog and they were inseparable. But after a few weeks, his dog mysteriously disappeared. He searched everywhere for his friend. Day after day, after school, he walked through the streets calling out 'Gengi'. Asking both neighbors and strangers for clues. He cried himself to sleep many nights. Six months later, to his horror, their elderly neighbor confessed to luring the dog—eating it for supper.

He learned as a child that loving something too greatly resulted in great pain. So, he hardened himself…perhaps too well.

He held the puppy and regarded him with a smile. *Maybe he can help us with the Alpacas.* Samoyeds were known as great herding dogs.

I will keep this little guy and call him Sam.

He glanced around the compartment. Everyone was asleep. He kissed Sam's tiny white head and tucked him snugly beneath his down coat.

Wu drifted into a joyful sleep.

DAY 36

Darya woke to a darkened room. It was swaying. Her head ached. A dull pain in her left shoulder. *I'm on a boat?* She sat up. Something sticky at the bend on her arm brushed against the inside of her nightgown sleeve—it felt like gauze affixed with tape. *They took blood?*

A thin beam of light shone under the door, faintly illuminating the door handle.

"Let me out! Hello!" she yelled. She pounded on the steel, over and over, until her hands were numb. She pressed her ear against the door. No response. Nothing. Just the boat creaking with the waves.

She licked the blood from her knuckles. She looked around her cell, seeing a tray in the far corner. It contained a wooden bowl. She inspected it, then dipped a finger to smell the contents. *Cold chicken soup with soft noodles?* Also, a small loaf of bread and a plastic cup with milk. She picked off a small corner of the bread and placed it on her tongue. It tasted fine. She stuffed the bread into her mouth, chewing large chunks at a time.

Her captors were obviously not people aiming to simply rescue her. But they didn't want her dead either. A small pillow and a couple of woolen blankets were arranged neatly against the wall. After she finished her meal, she tucked the scratchy fabric around her legs and torso. The darkness, the rocking of the boat, and her satisfied stomach created a soothing combination.

She closed her eyes and gave her mind over to the ship's motion.

I must conserve my energy.

I may need it later.

* * *

Vice President Thomas Defoe stood at attention while he watched Marine One approach the south lawn. President Daniel Merriwether's helicopter touched down. After the blades stopped turning, a Marine in dress uniform opened the hatch stairs. Dan forgot to salute as he waddled down. His German Shephard, Rex, bounded down the steps behind him.

A nearby secret service agent spoke into his sleeve, "Ace High arriving."

Tom walked toward the President, smoothing back his gray hair from the winter winds. Rex ran ahead and began sniffing his pant leg.

"Welcome back, sir," Tom said, reaching down to rub Rex's ears.

He hated dogs. But you could never be too careful. Reporters had telephoto lenses and were notoriously sneaky. He was mindful to appear relatable while in public view.

Tom extended a hand to Merriwether, "How was Pebble Beach, sir? How was your game?"

Merriwether shook his hand with a strong pumping action. "Wonderful! I played three rounds—one with Sergio and two with Bubba. Great guys. Did I miss anything?"

He wanted to give a snarky answer. He knew the other reason for the President's trip. Merriwether was meeting Kiki, his girlfriend, a former dancer who, decades ago in her prime, appeared in some of Biggie Small's music videos. *Or maybe it was Tupac. Whatever.* Now she was an Instagram celebrity.

Everyone pretended not to know, at least on the surface, out of respect for the office. Merriwether still wore his ring and kept telling the press his marriage was fine. It was a huge farce.

'Did I miss anything?' Merriwether had the nerve to ask. Of course, he missed things. He rarely read his morning briefs and never

on golf trips.

"No, nothing that couldn't wait," Tom replied, tucking his tie back under this black suit jacket. "I attended a few meetings last week. Summaries are on your desk. The First Lady called. Jack took the call."

The President's stunning wife, Esmé, had become estranged from him a few weeks after the election. It was no secret she had only kept up appearances of a happy relationship during the campaign. The First Lady was a French National with dual citizenship. After the inauguration, she retreated to her family apartment in Paris and made plans to stay there indefinitely.

On more than one occasion, the President confided to him that Esmé's absence gave him more time for golf and his weekly poker game, which suited him just fine.

"Thanks for holding down the fort, Tommy. I think I'm supposed to call Vlad today. Will you be on the call?"

"Yes. The call with President Petrov is scheduled an hour from now. You'll have enough time to change and read the pre-brief." What he wanted to say was, "Please, for the love of decency, change out of those ridiculous golf shorts and wear some goddamned pants!" The President wore shorts to the office quite often. On his "casual" days, his personal style resembled a sorry blend of Rodney Dangerfield and Jimmy Buffett.

"Great, see you in a few."

Tom watched Merriwether as he walked through the portico to the Oval Office and made a weak gesture resembling a salute to the Marine holding the door. *At least he saluted this time.* Dan wasn't good at protocol.

Sweet Jesus, he wasn't good at anything.

I hate my life, he thought. *I hate my life.*

* * *

Forty-five minutes later, President Merriwether strolled in wearing a red polo shirt with an embroidered presidential seal and a pair of cut-off jean shorts.

"Sir," Tom said, "Did you read the brief?" *Still with the shorts? It's February!*

"Yeah, something about a disease?"

"Yes, a virus." Tom handed him a folder. "We need to offer our help. But we need to be subtle. I'll give you a couple of minutes to read this over."

Jack Cunningham, the Chief of Staff, came in and set up the video conference phone. "When you're ready, press this button here." He pointed to the large red "on" button in the middle of the speaker and left again.

Merriwether put down the folder after a minute but kept it open to review his script. "Ok, let's do this!"

Once the video connection was established, Merriwether said, "Vlad! Great to speak with you again."

"Comrade President! Mr. Vice President," Vlad said with a smile. "How nice to speak with you as well. What can I do for you?"

"Well, Vlad, buddy, ya know, the disease conference is coming up soon. We plan to send our best researchers…I hear they made terrific progress on Ebola and other stuff. Are you sending a team this year? I was thinking…you know, just spit-balling here with good ol' Tom…it would be great for our science guys to get together. You know, to solve world problems and such."

Another screw-up. Seriously? Science guys? Tom wrung his hands, aching to jump in.

After a brief silence, Petrov said, "I'm sorry Mr. President, what …what are you talking about?"

Tom motioned to Merriwether to ask "May I?"

Merriwether nodded.

Defoe cleared his throat and turned the camera towards himself. "President Petrov, Tom here. I think what the President, or I mean, what we are trying to say is, the International Conference on Disease Prevention will be held in Switzerland next month. As you know, our latest treaty addresses the free and open exchange of cutting-edge medical research. So, in the spirit of our renewed good will, and given the recent epidemics around the globe, we'd like to be partners with you on leading the charge in the area of world health. More specifically, to initiate a roundtable between our respective scientists to discuss the Ebola situation in Africa, as well as the latest advances in Zika and Malaria vaccines. Would you be amenable to this?"

"Why, yes, of course our scientists will be going, as they do every year. I'm sure they will converse freely with all the other scientists, including yours. I find it interesting you would call about such a mundane event. Is there anything else you wanted to discuss today? I have a full schedule and unfortunately, I must be going."

Tom could sense the underlying hostility. It was unmistakable.

Vlad is pissed.

"Well," Merriwether said, "we should make time to talk about the plans for the space station, but that can wait if you are busy."

"Yes, my friends, let's talk again soon. Do svidaniya, gentlemen." The line went dead.

Tom let out a long breath.

"What do you think, Tom?" Merriwether asked.

"I think he clearly didn't want to talk about diseases or any collaboration with us." *Do I really need to spell this out?* "But you know Russians—they're hard to read. At least he knows we want to help. I'm sure if he was concerned about the outbreak at Ice Dagger, he would accept our assistance. But perhaps he has it under control."

"Yes, he probably does. Well, ok then. We'll just sit tight and see if he comes to us," Merriwether said.

The President acted disinterested in their conversation as he walked over to his set of golf clubs propped in the corner and took out his putter. He began putting golf balls across the carpet towards a mat of artificial turf with a shallow cup.

Did Dan understand what just happened? No. Of course not.

"Right, sir. As you wish."

Tom shook his head as he walked out of the oval. *Only 410 more days…and he would be free.*

* * *

Those ridiculous Americans, thought Petrov. *Do they think they are subtle? Merriwether is such a durak.*

It would be a cold day in the underworld before he would accept their assistance.

In his office, General Nikolayev finished setting up the video feed. "As you requested, we're ready to remove all remains of the encampment. It would have been helpful to retrieve some of the vehicles and equipment, though."

"The advance team described a horrific scene," Petrov said. "I cannot sacrifice more troops to whatever illness transpired to decimate the camp."

"As you instructed," Nikolayev said, "we told the families the soldiers died from the weather. That we chose not to retrieve the bodies to save costs. We posthumously gave each the valor award and paid their families the usual one million rubles to abate any inconvenience. Some family members, as you can imagine, were not happy with this answer. But we have made the prerequisite threats to quiet those that would challenge us."

"Good. When does the countdown start?" Petrov asked.

"The adjacent areas have been evacuated and our planes are in place now. You can give the signal when you are ready. This radio is patched into their cockpits. Just press this button to speak."

"Well—let's go already!" Petrov pressed the button. "Airmen, I want to thank you for your loyalty and service to your country. You may drop the weapons now."

After a few seconds of delay, aerial video appeared on the monitor. Within seconds, projectiles fells toward the earth. Enormous fireballs of red and orange flames exploded over the scene of the former base.

It took a few minutes for the black smoke to clear. Dark areas of scorched earth remained.

Petrov said, "General, thank you for your loyal support. You understand this never occurred. We will not discuss it again."

Nikolayev nodded. "Yes, of course, Mr. President."

CHAPTER 4

DAY 37

A pipe fitter was repairing a valve at the natural gas metering station north of Granitnyy. The explosions unsettled him the previous day. The ground disruption shook loose some fittings and several pressure alarms had gone off. The company was lucky the pipelines didn't suffer more damage.

After he finished his work patching leaks and replacing joints, he walked back to his truck. He heard a whimper nearby. It was coming from a pump enclosure. The hatch was unlocked and ajar. He peered inside. A white dog and two puppies were curled inside. The momma dog rose and smelled his hand. She looked at him with wide eyes and licked his fingers.

The dog was beautiful and sweet...the puppies more so. He rubbed the dog's head and furry neck.

"Hey girl! Where did you come from?"

He looked at the dog's collar. Her silver tag listed an Army Commandant as her owner.

Most likely dead now.

His cousin had contacts in Europe that sold exotic dogs. Sometimes there would be a finder's fee, sometimes a considerable sum for certain breeds.

He picked up the puppies and called to the mother dog to join him inside his truck. She jumped into the front seat and he placed the pups beside her. He looked through his lunch box and took the ham out of his sandwich. As he offered it to the momma dog, she nearly bit him, snatching it and chomping it down quickly.

It was a long ride into back to Severomorsk. When he got to town, finding adequate cell phone coverage, he texted his cousin, attaching pictures of the dogs.

"Yes, they are valuable," his cousin texted back. "Can I come pick them up tomorrow?"

"How much?"

"Thirteen thousand RUB for each puppy. The mom is too old."

"Thirty-five thousand RUB for each," the fitter negotiated.

His cousin replied, "Since you are family, here is my best, twenty-five thousand each plus mom for free."

He looked at the momma dog. She was wonderful. He would have loved to keep her. But he spent days living in a trailer in a frozen, barren part of the world.

This dog deserves a better life.

"Sold. See you tomorrow."

* * *

Dr. Wu smiled when the farm came into view.

Tomorrow, he thought. *Yes, the interview with the Russian woman could wait until tomorrow.*

He needed to regain his strength and rest. Besides, he reasoned, it would give her another day of life.

The woman was placed in a holding room inside the barn, guarded by two soldiers.

The farmhouse was divided into two wings: living quarters and laboratory spaces. They wanted to keep the lab spaces sterile and pressure-regulated so no germs could escape.

They constructed a large furnace in the basement, alongside a morgue for performing necropsies. When the time came to test live virus on living creatures, they could dispose of the carcasses with minimal effort in the furnace. For now, they would test on mice and rats, but they planned to test promising agents on small primates. Wu wasn't surprised that the furnace could accommodate grown humans.

He was well aware Szu Qiang expected them to experiment on people…many of them political prisoners, who would otherwise linger for years in labor camps.

Wu unpacked his samples and placed them in a dedicated freezer. His new friend, Sam, watched him through the glass door, tail wagging. Sam followed Wu to the other side of the house to the living quarters.

In the kitchen, Wu placed some leftover chicken on a plate on the floor for Sam. The other researchers came into the kitchen and they all began cooking dinner.

On the voyage back, Zhang admonished him for bringing the puppy back. But allowed him to keep it. He warned Qiang could never know. He would consider the dog a frivolous distraction.

"We must make sure Sam never enters the lab rooms," Wu warned. "And when outsiders visit, he must be restricted to the bedrooms upstairs."

The others understood.

* * *

Dr. Yi Nian regarded Wu's new pet. *Is the old man insane? He would risk all our lives for a dog?*

She had come too far and risked too much. Zhang was looking the other way, but Qiang would assassinate someone for any degree of mis-step. No, this was madness. As a spy, she needed their work to appear normal, without issue.

Raised near Tibet, she witnessed the persecution of her parents. As a child, she resolved to get an education and find a way to leave China. The Americans promised her freedom for the intelligence she provided. Since college, the NSA groomed her and gave her a new identity. After two decades working in benign laboratories—testing the effectiveness of new medicines—the government directed her to work for a new secret laboratory, researching means to combat biological weapons. The NSA must have guided this move somehow. She didn't ask questions. The NSA had their mole.

She remained at the farm during the Russian expedition. Zhang didn't tell her the scope of the Russia trip, just that they would be gone for three days and she would need to be prepared to receive important new samples.

When she first arrived at the farm, she was shocked to see the lengths they went to disguise the laboratory. When Zhang asked her to take care of the alpacas at the farm, she accepted, not wanted to be labeled a troublemaker. Between her government's elaborate cover story and the NSA's guiding force, Nian understood this was no ordinary lab.

Her first three months at the farm were uneventful. The team spent much of the time configuring the laboratory layout, setting up equipment, and putting in requisitions for items they needed. They installed a new electrical transformer to handle their power needs. Solar panels and batteries were installed to handle potential outages. To eliminate the possibility of computer hacking, no internet connectivity was allowed on the property. Only Dr. Wu was authorized to use the one satellite phone, and then only sparingly.

Her sole contact with the outside world was in the form of coded messages she gave to an NSA spy—a man named Ren—who posed as their grocery delivery man. When she first came to the farm, she asked Ren for a set of current American vaccines to protect herself. China had a very robust human vaccination program, but it wasn't uncommon for Chinese vaccine makers to take shortcuts and manufacture substandard or fake vaccines. And while the lab had modern containment measures, and they wore protective equipment, why take chances?

For the first year, they worked on developing treatments for MRSA. Harmless work. But she became alarmed when their group was instructed to develop a more lethal measles virus. She provided monthly reports to Ren; however, she didn't know exactly who received them and what they did with the information.

When Wu returned from Russia with two soldiers and a hostage, she remarked they would need additional food to feed them and wrote out a shopping list.

Handing the list to Dr. Wu, she saw him add vodka to the bottom.

The wheels were set in motion. Ren would arrive in the morning with their supplies. She needed to encode a new message and place it in the wood bin near the farm's driveway, without raising attention. Her other two colleagues were fascinated with Wu's new puppy.

She slipped out the back.

* * *

Jason Burns reviewed the footage—more activity at the Chinese "farm". Two unfamiliar vehicles had arrived at the farm about seven hours ago. Otherwise, things were quiet. He checked his email. Nothing time critical. He left the SCIF to get a candy bar from the vending machine. The walk and the sugar might keep him awake. Working the overnight shift in this new job was not kind to his waistline or his sanity.

How did he give up his NSA gig for this?

His Aunt Ruth and Director Ortega pulled some strings to get him this civilian post at Fort Belvoir, working for Roadfuss. It meant a lot to Ruth. How she had done this without the General's knowledge, he could never figure out. But since they had different last names, no one put it together.

He worked the midnight to 8:30 shift, when it was quieter and he could snoop around with fewer prying eyes. Ruth and Ortega needed to know why Roadfuss' budget for bioweapon surveillance included a new satellite over northeastern Russia. This didn't fit with the typical locations for Russian weapon labs.

Jason considered it was crazy to spy on the Major General. *Is this what 'deep state' meant?*

Ruth and Ortega assured him it would all be ok. But it made little sense and couldn't be legal. Yet, he had such high respect for both of them, he had to trust they knew something he didn't.

For several months, Jason kept his eyes out for anything Russia related. When Jason intercepted the fax about the outbreak, he gave Roadfuss two days to do the right thing. But the General ignored it.

Jason back-channeled it to Ortega and Ruth. When Roadfuss found out Ortega set up a meeting with Vice President Defoe to discuss it, he flew into a rage. He began shouting something about staying in one's lane and demanded to know if anyone leaked it. But then, curiously, Roadfuss got calm. Too calm.

At the OEOB meeting, Jason sat in the back and had to remain stone-faced as he watched Roadfuss pretend to be concerned by the situation. He enjoyed watching his Aunt and Ortega in action.

The candy gave him enough energy to keep his eyes open. When Roadfuss entered the office at seven o'clock, he straightened and stopped doodling.

"Burns! Bring up the satellite images from Yuxi."

"Yes, sir!" Jason said. "The current images will be ready in five minutes. There's a time delay. Printouts of yesterday's images are on your desk. No word from Dr. Yi in about a week. Our man on the ground, Agent Ren, told us he's filling a grocery order and will be at the compound in a little while."

After a few minutes, Roadfuss came over to his desk holding a can of Red Bull. "Are the images ready yet?"

"Yes, sir. I'm posting them to the central server now." Jason opened other files on the server. "Wait. Holy hell! Um. Sir, I also pulled down the most recent images from Granitnyy. You need to see these."

Roadfuss and the other analysts crowded around Jason's monitor.

Petrov is one crazy bastard, thought Jason. *Is it even legal to use napalm anymore?*

"The camp is gone…like it never existed," Jason said. The images included still shots of the fireball and the charred aftermath.

Roadfuss grunted. "Yes, I can see that. Ok, everyone. Back to work. Jason, print out a copy of those five frames. I need to send a copy to the White House."

"Yes, sir."

And for good measure, I'll make a copy for Auntie Ruth.

DAY 38

Jolie drew in the cool morning air from her open window as she rolled over to look at her bedside clock. Ranger lay snoring by her feet. It was six thirty.

Her two-year-old border collie/wolf mix, picked up his ears and positioned himself at against her ribs, placing his chin on her chest. She stroked his caramel coat and white chest fur for a few minutes before checking the weather on her phone. Low forties going to sixty-eight degrees. A typical February day in San Antonio.

She rolled out of bed, showered and got dressed in her usual uniform of long-sleeve polo, overalls, Doc Martens, and Carhartt jacket embroidered with her company logo. She drew a comb through her brown, pixie-length hair.

Ranger, who had left her side during her shower, greeted her in the kitchen, tail wagging, carrying today's copy of the San Antonio Examiner, retrieved from her driveway.

"Good boy!"

She poured some coffee and then put an English muffin in the toaster. Sunlight streamed through her kitchen window. It was the calm before a flurry of activity and she was savoring the quiet as she ate breakfast and read the paper. Ranger lay at her feet under the kitchen table with his favorite stuffed animal toy, a small reindeer, tucked under his chin.

After breakfast, she went into the yard and completed her rounds by eight, feeding the dogs and inspecting their cages. She played with the youngest pups, passing the time until Jennifer and the other college interns arrived.

Jennifer arrived at eight-thirty, wearing jean overalls with a delicate flower print blouse, her long, curly blond hair pulled back into a messy yet stylish bun. Her nails were manicured with cute flower and bird images. "Miss Jolie, I ran the numbers again. Do you want to go over them?"

"Sounds good. Let's sit in my office. Can I get you some coffee?"

"No, I had some already. I redid the Gantt chart last night. It's going to be tight meeting the delivery schedule. But I think we can do it."

They sat at the round wooden table. Framed photographs of the dogs they'd trained filled the office walls. Letters from appreciative military and police units were pinned to the bulletin board. A picture of border control agents posing with their working dogs was centered on the wall behind her desk.

Jolie held the weighty contract documents. After the latest incursion in Afghanistan, the Army put out a contract for two hundred dogs for bomb and drug detection. Simultaneously, ICE wanted another two hundred working dogs for the southern border.

"I still can't believe we won both. When we put in our bids, I hoped we might get one. Four hundred dogs trained and delivered to the government in six months? Importing them alone will take two to three months."

Her dogs came from central and eastern Europe. The best dogs were Labrador Retrievers, Shepherds, Dobermans, Collies and Schnauzers. After quarantine, they were evaluated for personality, physical ability and retaught commands in English. The government provided most of the dog's specialized training at their own sites, but her facility provided basic screening and training preparation.

Jenny nodded. "I know. But I think if we stagger the import dates and reach out to more breeders, we can conduct the training schedules in intervals. Here, look at the chart."

Jolie studied the schedule. "What about space? I have only a hundred kennels. Ha! Only a hundred. I have the largest private dog training academy in all of Texas, and I still can't handle this."

"Look, we can double or triple up the dogs in the larger kennels.

It wouldn't be hard to build new ones from chain link fencing. But again, if we stagger the deliveries, we might only need two hundred kennels. We could also subcontract. I know you hate the idea, but it would take a lot of the stress off."

Jenny was right. Subcontracting to other academies was the sane approach. But this was her opportunity to expand her business and dominate her competition.

Ranger came in with his small reindeer in his mouth. He dropped the toy on Jennifer's lap.

"Hey boy! Do you want Rein-Rein?" Jenny stroked his ears and then, without warning, threw the stuffed toy into the air, across the room. Ranger bolted towards it and plucked it out of the air, contorting his body in an acrobatic twist.

Jolie smiled. Before she won these huge contracts, she planned to take Ranger to the World Agility Championship in New York City. He had worked so hard last year and she knew he could take the gold. The championship was a month away. Even with Jennifer's planning and attention to detail, the timing couldn't be worse. Yet, the competition was her chance to demonstrate her dog training expertise on the world stage. Ranger was ready. She made a promise to herself that they would go this year. She had to trust her staff to run things when she was away. With Jenny in charge, it just might work out.

Ranger returned with the toy and now placed it on Jolie's lap. Rein-Rein was missing an antler, and the stuffing was coming out of its rear end. Its red nose and white spots had turned brown. She had patched and washed it so often, but it was clearly time for a new one.

"Sorry, Ranger, I have work to do." She pointed towards the door.

Ranger took the reindeer from her lap and walked outside. It broke her heart a little.

Jolie turned to Jennifer. "Your schedule…what about my trip to New York? Can I swing it? Without subcontracting?"

"Yes, you just have to delegate. I can stay over while you're gone, if it makes you feel better."

Jolie looked at the numbers in the attached spreadsheet. "What percent of flawed?"

If some dogs were found to have rabies, or some kind of personality or physical defects, she might have to put them down, or if possible, send them into the civilian adoption system. She accounted for only a handful to be unfit, since most of her breeders in

Europe were excellent. They had long-standing reputations for quality, along with strict health guidelines.

"About ten percent. So, we actually need to import more dogs. But I accounted for that number in the schedule."

"Right. Can you still do this with your other college classes? We are going to need more interns and they all need to be trained."

"I put out a flyer last week on campus. Ten people contacted me already. Look, we can have the newest people do the care and feeding, and the senior interns lead the training sessions. Lots of the work is simple repetition. We'll use a buddy system to train the new folks."

"Ok, but I want to interview all the candidates. They need solid references. I don't need any assholes messing up my dogs."

"I'll narrow down the list to the best. Just relax."

Sitting back, Jolie grinned. "Jenny, I'm so glad you're on the team. You know the offer still stands."

"I'm thinking about it. Graduation is only four months away. I can stay through August, but then I need to go to veterinary school."

"You'll make a great vet." Jolie said.

"Thanks. Now, go see Ranger. I got this."

Jolie went outside and found Ranger standing on the starting platform of his obstacle course. The reindeer toy was lying beside him. She picked it up and smiled. She took her whistle out from under her shirt and blew on it. Ranger sprang into motion, going through the course on his own, with his ears tucked back and his tail down. When he got to the tire jump, she threw the stuffed animal in the air. He passed through the tire and caught it in his mouth before his paws hit the ground.

Jolie commanded, "To the end!"

He ran to the end of the course.

"Good boy!" Back at the starting platform, she rubbed his underbelly and scratched his ears. Ranger dropped the reindeer and looked at her with moist, pale-yellow eyes, his tail wagging.

She didn't need her stopwatch to know he'd run the course in a spectacular time.

New York was going to be a triumph.

Chapter 5

Day 39

Dr. Wu looked out the front window.

Who let Sam out?

Sam bounded along the long dirt road, down the hill toward the front gate. Wu tried to be angry, but it was fun watching Sam run.

Oh, if I could be so carefree. Puppies need to run and play.

He walked outside and called, "Sam! Come here, boy!"

The sound of a high-pitched motor grew louder. Of course, Sam heard Ren's scooter and was inquisitive, wanting to greet the delivery man.

I'd better go get him.

Wu rarely greeted the delivery guy. Twice weekly deliveries were typically dropped in a wooden bin by the gate, and Wu ensured they placed the correct amount of money inside. They developed this system "in case they were busy out back tending to the alpacas," Ren wouldn't have to wait.

Why a man his age was delivering groceries still dismayed him. But the man was obviously a simpleton and quite poor. Wu did not begrudge the man making a living.

When he reached the gate, Sam was already engaged in a game of tug-of-war with his new friend.

"Hello Mister Ren! I see you've met Sam."

"Greetings Mr. Wu. Yes, he is a very cute dog," he replied, throwing the stick again.

"Thank you for bringing the groceries so early."

Ren said, "I placed them in the bin already. I'll take them out for you." He lifted the hatch and placed the box on top. "I'd be happy to carry them to the house for you."

"Oh, no. But thank you for the offer."

Sam returned with the stick in his mouth and dropped it in front of Ren. Ren bent to toss it again, but Sam excitedly chomped down on it. They played a little tug of war and both men laughed at Sam's antics. Finally, Dr. Wu grew weary of Sam's games and became uncomfortable having Sam on display. Wu said, "Here, let me take Sam off your hands."

Wu grabbed Sam around his middle to pick him up, but Sam got snippy—the dog dropped the stick and bit Ren's hand as Ren tried to give him one last goodbye scruff on his head.

"Ow, he has sharp little teeth for one so tiny."

Seeing the blood, Wu offered, "Oh, many apologies. Let me get some antiseptic for your wound."

"I'm fine. Barely a scratch, see?" He showed his fingers, revealing small nicks. "I need to get on my way. My boss will fire me if I don't get back soon."

Wu nodded and handed Ren some small bills. "A little extra for your troubles. Again, my deepest apologies."

Ren got back on his moped and waved goodbye. When the moped was out of sight, Wu picked up the box of groceries. Sam followed him as he walked back up the path. "Bad dog! You are a bad dog!"

We don't need trouble.

Climbing the front porch stairs, he stumbled and nearly dropped the box. He blinked and tried to shake the foggy sensation in his head.

Perhaps the long trip to Russia took its toll. Travel was difficult at his age. He remembered his throat felt parched during the long flight home.

I must be dehydrated.

Yes, that must be it.

Some fluids and I'll be just fine.

* * *

Darya couldn't see with the silky hood over her head, but she could breathe well enough. Someone took her arm and guided her to sit. The zip ties on her wrists chaffed her skin, but she kept tugging, despite the pain. The room smelled dank. She seemed to be sitting on a bale of hay.

She had gotten accustomed to the voices of the guards, even though she couldn't understand them. A few minutes passed. She tried to decipher the different smells in this new place. Many of them were not very pleasant; dung, straw and mold.

Then an unknown voice emerged. He spoke in Chinese with the guards for a minute, then footsteps approaching her.

The new voice took off her hood. He was an older Asian man, bald in the middle with some short, stringy white hair. She flinched when he spoke to her in Russian.

"Hello miss. I am a medical doctor and we need your assistance. We hope you can answer some important questions. Can you do this for us?"

Darya studied the man. He wore a white lab coat. *Kind eyes.* She assessed her surroundings. From the light coming through high windows, she assumed it was mid-day. *I'm in a barn?* It was a modern structure. A guard wearing black sat against the opposite wall, near the door.

This doesn't make any sense.

"What kind of place is this?" Darya said. "Look, I don't know who you are or what you people want. What country am I in?" She continued to scan the barn as her eyes adjusted to the light.

"Vot eto pizdets! What is *that*?" she said, pointing her wrists toward a fluffy creature with a weird face sleeping a few feet to her left.

A baby alpaca?

"Miss, I need you to focus. Ignore the animal. Can you answer some questions?"

"Why should I tell you anything? Take me home—right now!"

"Please, I am but a humble scientist. The death toll at your camp was unimaginable. Our team is hoping you will help us find the cause of the illness. We wish to prevent future outbreaks. We want to save lives."

"So, you kidnap me and bring me who knows where? What day is it? Wait, are you Chinese? Am I in China? Where are the other women? Where's Kira? I don't need to tell you anything."

The old man motioned to a guard. The guard, dressed all in black, came over and cut the zip ties, freeing her hands. With a nod from the old man, the guard receded into a dark corner of the barn.

"Thank you," Darya said, rubbing her wrists.

The old man said, "Let me start again. My name is Dr. Wu. We did not harm the other survivors. We have treated you well. But perhaps we have been over zealous in our approach. You see, we fear you were exposed to a man-made virus. A virus created by the U.S. to overthrow governments such as yours—and ours. There is also a small possibility your own government created a bioweapon that got loose. If you can help us, we promise not to harm you. We simply need information."

It hadn't occurred to her the outbreak could have been the result of a biological attack. "My family probably thinks I am dead. I need to call them."

"Yes, of course. But please, time is of the essence. We do not have access to a phone here on our property. We will take you into town after we debrief you. However, if you wish to remain in China, we can arrange this as well. If your own government created a bioweapon and tested it on its own people, you may not feel so eager to return. It is possible you are safer if your government believes you died at the camp."

I don't feel safer.

Dr. Wu showed her a photograph. "Your government has burned all remains of the camp. They murdered your friends."

Darya stared at the photo. Where buildings and tents once stood, there was nothing but charred earth and burnt out, twisted metal of military vehicles. The picture appeared authentic.

Perhaps I'm safer here?

"First, what is this place?"

"You are at a medical facility," Wu explained. "This is the most advanced anti-viral research facility in Asia. With your help, we can neutralize the threat by creating a vaccine. The vaccine will then be mass-produced and distributed worldwide as a pre-emptive measure. As you probably surmised, we have already taken some blood and tissue samples from you when you were asleep."

"Asleep! You mean drugged, asshole." A guard rose from a darkened corner of the barn and began walking towards her. Her heart pounded. "Look, I have nothing to hide. I'm tired. I want to go home in one piece. Let's get this over with."

The guard returned to his seat. The doctor placed a recording device on the table.

"My head is killing me. May I have some aspirin and a glass of water?"

The doctor left, and after two minutes, returned with a glass of water, aspirin and a bottle of vodka. "Let us start at the beginning. Were people sick before they arrived to the camp? Who was the first person reported ill?"

Darya ignored the water glass and took the vodka. She unscrewed the cap, smelled it, paused and took a swig. She took a deep breath. "I don't know exactly who got sick first. I work in Supply. I make sure all the equipment gets to where it needs to go and track all the equipment and spare parts. I didn't see too many people at first. Because I just sat in my office all day, maintaining inventory and filling requisitions."

"The first week, they reported five people sick and died. One was Doctor Volkov, the Chief Medical Officer…I remember clearly because they found him dead on the floor of the infirmary. Losing him had a big effect on our ability to handle the rest of the sick. His wife also died—she was a nurse—a nice lady. The other three were young, in their twenties." She took another longer swig from the bottle.

"The barracks and infirmary were disinfected immediately. But then others started coming in with coughs, aches and difficulty breathing. Even some sled dogs had the sniffles—but the dogs recovered. The people weren't so lucky."

"After the first hundred died, the Commandant still insisted on holding the exercises. It was insane. People were coughing blood. Finally, we began a quarantine. But people went from their first cough to dying within two to three days. The quarantine didn't work. We had thousands to bury at the end of week three, including the Commandant, all the officers and the remaining two doctors. We took precautions like washing hands and wearing masks. I guess it wasn't enough.

Wu said, "But you survived?"

"I don't know why, but I never got sick," explained Darya. "I had a runny nose for a day, but that's all. A few other women survived…mostly my age."

A rush of warmth from the alcohol made her dizzy. She wrung her hands together and looked at the bottle. Half was gone. She wiped her eyes.

"Just twenty-one of us remained. We grabbed all the food and blankets we could carry and retreated to a large cabin on the edge of camp. There was nothing left for us to do."

"No men survived? Did you or the other survivors take any medications?" Wu asked.

"No and no."

"Very well." Wu signaled to the guard.

The guard zip-tied her hands again.

"Wait! What about my phone call?"

They slipped the black hood back on her head. She felt steel pressed to her temple.

With a loud blast, she was gone.

Days 40 to 43

Nian woke to the sound of moaning.

Dr. Wu?

It was 5 o'clock in the morning. She put on her robe and walked down the hall to his bedroom. The door was ajar. She peeked through the opening.

"Doctor Yi," he called with a croak. "I don't feel well. I may have caught a cold in my travels. Come closer."

Nian entered slowly but kept ten feet from his bed. Sam was sleeping snuggled next to him. "What's wrong?"

"My muscles ache—difficult to move. [cough] Throat is sore."

His face was shiny with perspiration, his pupils dilated. She left his room, put on a face mask and gloves, and brought him another blanket and a glass of water.

She headed downstairs to search for his notebook. The Russian woman, Darya, had been interviewed, shot and disposed of in the furnace yesterday.

Perhaps Wu's notes would provide some insights?

She read the interview. *Hardly distinguishable from a regular flu at first.* They would need to take a blood sample.

Nian pulled the other two researchers aside and raised her concerns. They assumed Dr. Wu was just tired from the expedition. Or perhaps he just had a cold.

She wasn't convinced.

Another doctor took blood samples from Dr. Wu and gave him

anti-viral medications.

She retrieved the quarantine manual from Wu's office and began re-reading it, sitting in a leather chair in the den. Sam nudged her leg. She picked him up, and he slept on her lap as she read.

If Wu has the virus, we're already doomed.

By late afternoon, the test results came back. A strong viral DNA match to that from the Russian cadaver samples. They implemented full quarantine measures.

The following day, Wu had trouble breathing. They concluded that Wu was a liability now. Nian volunteered to end his suffering, injecting him with a potassium solution.

After they disposed of his body, the team suited in Level A gear—with supplied air—disinfected the entire residence and the laboratory. It took all day to complete a full wipe down given the limited dexterity provided by the suits.

Two days later, all the other researchers and the two guards were bedridden. She took blood samples from each and found the same viral DNA. Somehow, she was fine.

All is lost, Nian thought.

She called Ren on Dr. Wu's now unattended satellite phone and asked him for an extraction plan.

"They're all sick?" Ren asked.

"Yes," Nian said. "I don't have any symptoms though. Just like the hostage Darya. I've checked my blood. It will take a few more hours to get the DNA analysis, but my lymphocyte count is normal."

"If you think it's safe, I trust your judgement. Come meet me as soon as you have the results. In the meantime, I'll arrange transport."

She wasn't a killer. The Americans warned her from the start that she may need to take extreme measures during her undercover assignment. She couldn't make her escape until all the others were dead. She went to the lab and filled some syringes.

I'm putting them out of their misery, she convinced herself. She waited until they were all asleep. After killing the first guard, the remaining executions became easier.

While she was having lunch, her own viral DNA test results came through.

All clear.

The SAT phone on Wu's desk rang. She froze. Answering it would raise suspicions, and she had no time. She dropped it in a desk drawer instead. The wooden drawer vibrated with each ring. It was difficult to take her eyes away—as if the phone was an active witness to her crimes.

Snap out of it, she scolded herself. *Time is my adversary, not the stupid phone.*

She quickly packed a change of clothes. Before she left, she needed to assess what items to bring with her. Something to show her worth to the Americans. Perhaps she could bargain for a new life in the States.

She grabbed Dr. Wu's notes, some electronic files and an airtight container with blood samples from both Darya and her fallen colleagues.

As she headed out the front door, her mind filled with worry about how to reach town undetected. She was focused on the journey ahead when she heard Sam's little feet scampering behind her. She turned. Sam had a stick in his mouth.

"Sam, you can't come with me. Stupid dog."

Sam stopped in front of her, dropped the stick and began racing around in tight circles, trying to catch his own tail. In one of his quick rotations, he tripped and tumbled.

"I don't have time for this!" she scolded.

He got up and looked up at her with his moist black eyes and panted with excitement.

Such a sweet puppy. Last week, while feeding the alpacas, she saw a Mountain hawk-eagle swoop down and catch a hare. The same fate could easily befall Sam. "I guess I can't leave you here."

She placed him in her canvas satchel and grabbed her backpack. She wore a paper mask out of an abundance of caution. Nian followed the one-lane dirt road down the mountain. The trip took nearly an hour. When vehicles approached, she shifted her hat below her eyes.

When she finally got to town, she met Agent Ren at the grocery store, where he gave her a new identity and passport.

"I see you brought my friend Sam," Ren said. He tickled Sam under his chin.

"I couldn't leave him. Too young to fend for himself. Can you find him a new home?"

"Yes, of course." He picked up Sam. "But we need to get you out of here. There's a special route. I've marked it for you." He pulled a map out of his back pocket. "It's a long drive but your best option.

Head southeast to Vietnam and continue until you reach Hanoi. A U.S. Army transport at the Hanoi airport will take you to the States. Roadfuss said go to the Avis rental desk. Ask for Albert. He will escort you."

He walked her over to the garage behind the store. "Here, take my moped. I packed food and water for you. There's money folded inside your new passport. Extra gas in the jerry can."

She studied the map. "How far?"

"Four hundred miles." He looked her squarely in the eyes. "If you don't make it to the airport within four days, they'll assume you were captured or fell ill and died. There will be no rescue attempts."

"What about you, Ren? Aren't you coming with?"

"I'm leaving. But for a new assignment." He paused and gave a tight smile. "I hope you find happiness in America."

Nian put the map in her coat pocket. She walked toward the moped and inspected it. It had rust spots in places and a cracked leather seat. But it was her lifeline.

"Thank you, Ren." She gave him a quick hug and kissed Sam on his head.

Ren said, "I wish I could do more."

"No. You are giving me freedom." Her eyes felt watery. "It's all I've ever wanted."

Chapter 6

Day 50

Jolie arrived at the cargo terminal lobby at nine o'clock. She brought extra copies of the animals' Certificate of Veterinary Inspection from their country of origin. Dealing with Customs could be a hassle. It helped marginally that she was on a first name basis with two customs officials. It didn't make the process much faster, but at least friendlier.

She checked in with the reception desk. A woman snapped her gum at her and said in a monotone voice, "We'll let you know when your shipment is cleared."

Jolie brought a book to read, her way to pass the time when things got backed up or the plane was delayed. She waited in the lobby for over half an hour when a familiar customs screener waved from behind a glass door.

He came out to greet her.

"Hey, Miss Jolie, nice to see you again," Darryl said. "Your dogs arrived fine. But we can't release them just yet. Our medical inspector hasn't shown up. We had a little situation yesterday. Two dogs imported by a pet store came in from eastern Russia and one was DOA…dead on arrival. Think they came from one of those black-market puppy mills. So, we need our guy to give your fellas a quick checkup. Don't expect a problem, though. Your sources are top notch and such. But, like I said, he hasn't come in yet…but he should be here soon. Sorry for the wait."

"Yeah, no problem Darryl, I know you guys have a process.

Should I come back later?"

"I really think it shouldn't be more than an hour. I'd hate for you to make two trips. But I guess it's up to you. You could give your cell number to Sheila at the reception desk. She could call ya."

"I guess I'll stick it out a bit longer. Keep me posted, will ya?"

"I'll try, but we're getting to the busy part of the day. If ya don't see me, Sheila will keep you posted."

"Sure thing, Darryl. Have a nice day!"

Darryl headed back toward the hangar bay. Jolie looked over to Sheila behind the glassed-in counter. She did not make eye contact.

So far, none of the dogs she had imported were found ill upon arrival. Today's shipments of dogs were coming from Estonia, Latvia, and Belarus. They comprised Dobermans, Labs, Huskies, Samoyed-Wolf Mix, and German Shepherds.

Jolie waited in the small lobby, seated on a hard, molded plastic chair. Elevator music filled the space that did not enhance her mood. The walls hadn't been painted in decades and the plastic cove baseboards had mold.

A little bleach would do wonders, she thought.

She read several chapters of her romance novel. She shifted in her chair, realizing her butt cheeks were half numb. She looked toward Sheila from time to time. Sheila still refused eye contact.

She began making a mental list of all the things she could do to prepare for her trip. It was close to noon now. She got up and walked up to the office window to ask for the status again.

Sheila slid open the divider, pursed her lips and said, "Can I help you?" as if she were seeing Jolie for the first time.

Unbelievable.

The receptionist made a call and after a few "uh huh's" hung up and said "Vet's here but it'll be another twenty minutes".

Jolie tried reading again, but then put down the book and sighed. The delay was wrecking her schedule.

She picked up her phone and called Jenny. She got voice mail and left a message.

"Hey, I'm stuck at customs. Could you do me a big favor? Give Ranger a bath this afternoon? Nothing fancy. Just a single lathering and rinse. I'll brush him out tonight. Oh, and let him chew on his hedgehog squeaky toy—he doesn't squirm as much during his bath when he plays with it. Thanks again. I'll call you when I leave here.

Make sure Joey has the microchips and the kennels ready for the new dogs. And tell him to meet me when I get back. If he keeps me waiting like last time, I have a mind to fire his ass."

Jolie flipped through her paperwork again.

Yep, everything's in order.

She picked up her novel and regarded the steamy cover. A man's torso with ripped abs, unbuttoned white shirt blowing in the wind. A dark-haired lass with her fingers pressed against his chest.

I need better books to read.

At home, she had a drinking game where she took a swig of scotch or beer every time someone's clothes were ripped off. Waiting at the airport, she didn't have alcohol to enhance her reading experience.

Maybe I'll bring a mystery next time.

At least the ending would be less predictable.

Day 60

Ally looked at her desk calendar and frowned. Nearly a month and Walt was still ghosting her. He could be such a self-important jerk.

Tall, handsome, with a gleaming smile, and crazy intelligent. What wasn't to like? In college, she was mesmerized by his good looks but more enthralled by his wicked sense of humor. In the two years they dated, she thought she knew the real man behind his perfect persona. Sensitive, self-aware, and vulnerable. But right after graduation, she saw a change. He turned coldly ambitious, making choices to promote his career and status.

It became apparent his life did not include her.

She was bitter about their breakup, but it was short-lived. She met Jim soon after. Jim was goofy in all the best ways and the nicest person she'd ever met. He always put the needs of others first.

By contrast, she came to understand that Walt was a complete a-hole.

And now, she was back in the same position. Waiting for him to acknowledge her.

At lunch, she put away her NIH work and did internet searches for any news about the Russian virus.

Damn. When the government buries something, it's as if it never happened!

A trope from a bad movie. No matter where she looked, there were no news stories or internet postings about the Russian deaths.

Over the last few evenings, she channeled her frustration into her model, trying to mimic the results of the outbreak. Making some wild extrapolations and assumptions about the transmission rate, incubation period, and mortality rate, the most severe model resulted in a worldwide pandemic that would eradicate ninety percent of earth's population in less than six months.

That would be ridiculous.

Quarantines and travel bans usually slowed or halted pandemics. Plus, the ability to develop vaccines quickly against all types of new antigens had advanced considerably in the last decade.

It was Tuesday. After work, she changed into her running clothes and took the Metro to Farragut Square to meet up with her weekly running group. The group allowed her to socialize, but reduced the possibility for real conversation, which suited her fine.

She arrived a few minutes early. Most of the other runners were Millennials. They were always late. After a few minutes of stretching, a short, young man with dark, short hair and light caramel skin—another runner—came walking toward her. He had a wiry build and wore a rainbow sweatshirt, long baggy shorts, and tall neon yellow socks with pictures of pandas on the sides. She couldn't recall seeing him before.

"Hey, are you with the running group?" he asked, walking toward the park's central statue.

"Yes, Hi! I'm Ally. Nice socks. Are you new to the group?" she asked as she stretched her calves.

Great, she thought, *another twenty-something year-old. Why can't anyone her own age join the group?*

"Hi Ally, I'm Jason. Nice to meet you. But you look familiar." He paused, "Hey, aren't you the virus doctor? I mean, were you at a meeting with Defoe last month?"

Oh man, this doesn't feel right.

"What?"

"Doctor Reynerson, I'm sorry. Let me start over. I work for Major General Roadfuss. Don't be alarmed. You might not remember me, but I was at the meeting—in the back taking notes. Anyway, I wanted to follow up and see if you would be interested in consulting on the situation further."

"What the hell? Consult on what? What?" Ally's mind was racing. "Oh, screw this."

She turned to leave.

"Wait! Don't go. I understand this is coming out of the left field. And I'm not supposed to be talking to you officially, but I need your help. That's why I'm here."

"Unbelievable," Ally muttered.

Shit. First Walt drags me into secret meetings. Now this clown shows up.

What is going on?

She turned around. "Jason, or whoever you are, I don't need this kind of drama. If the General wants my input, he can pick up the phone, like a normal person, and call my boss at NIH. Her name is Mina Herbert—H E R B…"

"Let me explain. The General is my boss, but he isn't the reason I'm here," Jason said. "Do you remember Senator Cochran?"

How could I forget?

"Sure, I was her guest at the meeting. Why?"

"She's my aunt. She'd like to meet with you again, privately, off the record."

Ally sighed. She looked across the street toward the Metro entrance. Three regular group members walked towards them.

She wanted to scream. *More secret bullshit meetings.* But decided if Walt wouldn't call her back, maybe the Senator had news about the Russian virus.

Ally sighed. "When?"

"Saturday."

"Fine. But this better not be about some political nonsense. I'm a doctor. I only care about protecting public health."

The other runners were getting closer. Continuing in a whisper, Ally said, "I don't like secrets. So, tell her not to bullshit me."

Jason looked around and took her cue. He simply nodded.

Ally watched as Jason adjusted his socks and then walked over to meet the other members. She looked at the back of his head.

Was he the guy shredding my handouts at the meeting?

She wasn't always great at remembering faces. She was more concerned about her presentation at the time.

I really need to pay better attention at meetings in the future.

Chapter 7

Day 61

Sam was a fun companion, but Ren needed to focus on his new task. In fact, he hardly had time to deal with his own care and feeding. Two weeks ago, he left Sam with a family across the street before he headed off in his decrepit excuse for a car.

Since then, the NSA prepared him for his new assignment north of Beijing. He would work at a tailor's shop that routinely made suits for the captain of the regional detention center. With luck, he could sew some tracking devices into the man's trousers or jackets to provide details of his movements. The information would help the NSA develop a plan to rescue a high value political prisoner.

When he arrived in Beijing, he met another local operative—a man who preferred no name—who provided the key to Ren's new apartment along with some cash.

It was an early Thursday morning. The operative introduced him to the owner of the tailor shop, and he was hired without questions. Ren suspected the owner was paid several gold Krugerrands for his cooperation.

Ren said to the shop owner. "Thank you for allowing me to work for you. I will strive to bring honor and prosperity to your establishment."

"Thank you, Ren." the tailor said. "I am happy to have you here. Your friend said you are a fine tailor. Time will see if this is so. Did you bring your own kit or do you require any tools? I can lend you some if needed."

"I would appreciate borrowing tools if you don't mind. All my belongings were lost in a house fire. That is why I moved here…for a fresh start."

The shop owner showed Ren around the back of the shop. Then they moved to the retail space in the front where the owner discussed price structure and record keeping, but also made small talk about the weather and his dislike of narrow-cut slacks.

The bell on the front door rang as three large men dressed in coveralls walked in. It was too early for customers—the shop wasn't officially open.

Ren inspected the men's footwear—combat boots.

Hardly customers needing fine suits.

The largest of the men didn't speak but pointed to the door. As the owner walked towards the men, he bowed, said "Good morning", then walked past them outside, and continued down the sidewalk until he was out of view. The owner showed no signs of coming back.

The three men stared at him in silence.

"Good morning, gentlemen," Ren offered with a forced smile.

The men did not reply.

Ren remembered seeing a teapot in the back room. "I'm sure the owner will be back soon. Can I offer some tea while you wait? I'll go make some in the back." Ren turned to leave. The men walked around and surrounded him in a menacing fashion.

Ren cursed under his breath, "tā mā de."

When the closest man reached to grab him, he tried to run. A thick arm swept around his shoulder. His back hit the floor. He tried to get up. A boot slammed his head.

He recalled going in and out of consciousness: the ground scraping his spine as they dragged him outside; then finding himself crammed in a car trunk.

Ren opened his eyes to a dark, cold room with concrete block walls and a steel door. He assumed a few hours had passed while he'd been unconscious. A small window—barely wide enough to pass a shoebox through—let in enough light for Ren to see the outline of a toilet and a woven mat on the floor.

Ren had been detained by governments before. Several times, in fact. He examined the lump in his wrist where it had been broken all those decades before. It still ached from time to time. He remembered the distinct snap of his bones when his captors smashed it with a hammer. It was a miracle his wrist mended at all.

He was thankful he passed out immediately upon capture. Now that he was awake, things would get rough. In his mind, he began going over his SERE training and details of his cover story.

After a couple more hours, a guard ripped him from the cell and placed him in a small interrogation room. They handcuffed him to a chair.

A man came in. He had seen this particular face before in a dossier. It was one of the highest ranking and most reclusive intelligence leaders, Deputy Director of State Security Zhang.

"Mr. American spy, you are finally awake."

Ren said, "Director Zhang. I consider it a privilege to be interviewed by someone of your status."

"Ha! Interviewed. You make me laugh." Zhang narrowed his eyes. "I have been after you for some time. We were fortunate a smart citizen turned you in. From your file, I see you were born in the Pinggu District. I, too, was raised there. It is a small world. But you have obviously chosen a more treacherous path. You've betrayed your country for the last time, you see."

Zhang walked around the perimeter of the small room. "We learned of your association with Dr. Yi. If you tell us where she is, you may avoid a great deal of pain. Understand," he paused, "you will comply with our demands. Maybe you will be stupid and lose quite a few fingers or other appendages first. Maybe you will talk freely, so we may spare your life. It all depends on you."

"Deputy Director, I am aware of your reputation. I know your boss, Szu Qiang, expects much from you. But you are a pragmatist. You cannot get information out of a corpse. Out of respect, I will share what I know. But I cannot share what I don't know."

Zhang snorted. "Probably all lies, but, yes, please proceed."

"With regard to Dr. Yi, whatever I can tell you now will not make any difference. Nian is safely in America by now. Her flight departed days ago. I did not ask where the Army was taking her. But I doubt they would have told me…knowing I could be interrogated like this. In fact, she may not be in America at all. She could be at any American base, foreign or domestic. I only know a US Army aircraft planned to pick her up in Hanoi. But I'm assuming you already know this. In fact, you probably have more information about Ms. Yi than I do at this point. I have my own missions. My handlers wanted me to focus on my next assignment. Which, of course, is over now." Ren smiled at the General. "I must admit I looked forward to learning to sew."

"I appreciate your candor. However, you understand I cannot take you at your word. For you are a trained spy...and a trained liar. Respectfully, my team will work you over for a time to refresh your memory of any details you may have forgotten. It is also curious that you do appear to be affected by the dog virus. Our medical staff will run some tests as a precaution."

"Dog virus? What dog virus?"

"Aha! Perhaps you did not see what was unleashed. Or perhaps you are playing dumb."

"Sir, are you talking about the Russian virus? I know it killed the other doctors. Miss Yi did not fall ill. But what does this matter now?"

"You really don't know what happened, do you?"

"No. I don't imagine you will tell me, will you?"

"Perhaps you are right. Perhaps it doesn't matter now." Zhang looked down and sighed.

Ren said, "Sir, please forgive my candor. I know what it is like to work for difficult men. If you ever wish to strive for a different life, I would gladly assist. I have lived many places and know many people. If you were kind enough to let me go, as a man of my word, I would repay that kindness without reservation."

Zhang turned to leave. He placed his hand on the door latch and smiled. "You are a funny one. It was nice meeting you, Mr. Spy. In another life, we might have been friends. For what is it worth, I think you are telling the truth. To reciprocate, I will tell you truthfully—I detest cutting pieces off of other human beings, even when they deserve it. It is always better to keep a person intact so they can be productive in the labor camps. Don't you agree?"

Ren assumed this was a rhetorical question, but nodded in response.

Zhang said, "I will come back and see you in a week's time, if you are still with us. Which I hope you are."

"Thank you, Director" Ren said. "I also hope I am alive, and not missing pieces, when we meet again."

* * *

Minister Szu Qiang looked at his watch. He gnashed his teeth, wondering how to contain his fury. His trust in Zhang had been misplaced. The virus was becoming their downfall, all due to Zhang's incompetence.

Zhang tepidly knocked on the door and peered his head inside. "Minister, you wanted to see me? I have good news."

"What good news could you have?" Qiang hissed. "People are dying and we can no longer control the news. Your bio team is dead, and we don't know how to contain the virus. What is good about this?"

"Sir, we have recovered the spy named Ren. He was the agent who helped Dr. Yi escape into the arms of the Americans."

"Wonderful. Make a video of his torture and death and email it to my brother and President Merriwether. You are excused." Qiang considered having Zhang arrested and sent for execution. But this would have to wait, to his chagrin.

"Sir, please. There is more. The spy Ren was exposed to the virus in Yuxi. We believe he was caring for the same dog that was the source of the virus which killed our team. But he did not become ill. He could hold the key to stopping the virus. We should not kill him before we can do some medical tests."

Qiang's eyes narrowed. "He's a survivor? Why didn't you say so immediately? Pathetic. I will need to see Mr. Ren. Ask my physician to come see me at once."

"Yes, Minister," Zhang replied with a bow, before he quickly exited.

Those Americans will pay for this, Qiang thought.

They think they can defeat our country with a virus?

They will never know what hit them.

* * *

Ally checked her email. Still no news alerts about the Russian outbreak. *How was this possible?*

She sighed. *Probably censorship.* Russia tightly controlled its media coverage.

As a condition of attending the meeting at OEOB, she wasn't allowed to discuss the events in Russia. Her meeting with Senator Cochran was days away and Walt was still being an elusive jerk. But she couldn't stand it anymore.

Maya! I'll call Maya.

Maya was Ally's college roommate, and they began their careers together at the CDC. They traveled the globe as a team for years. Now, Maya was an administrator with Doctors Without Borders. She heard about outbreaks from word of mouth—from doctors situated on the front lines. She was the best source of information regarding small epidemics in remote areas that never made it to the news wires.

Ally asked Maya about anything going on in Eastern Europe or Russia.

"Sorry, Ally," Maya said. "I haven't heard about anything unusual occurring in that region. Is that why Walt wanted your phone number? He called me a couple weeks ago."

"Um. We just had coffee together. I don't think he likes working for Merriwether very much."

"Yeah, I could see they would be polar opposites. God, Walt looked really good at the last reunion. So, what did you *talk about*?" Maya said the last part slyly.

"Not much. Um, just catching up."

"Uh, huh. Riiiiight."

Shit. She always could tell when I was lying.

Maya laughed. "Don't worry, chica. He asked about my clearance too. Mine lapsed years ago. You don't have to tell me what this is about. But he's still a fox, right?"

"He's looking very…fit."

Maya laughed. "I think he's still single."

Ally sighed. "I'm not interested."

"I don't know. Never say never!" Maya made kissy noises.

"Shut up! It's not like that and you know it," Ally said with emphasis.

"*Oh, Walt! Take me now!*" Maya mocked.

"Ok, give it a rest. Look, sorry I asked. Just wanted to know about any outbreaks in eastern Russia."

Maya sighed. "It's all diseases with you lately…Alright, fine. I did hear about another outbreak. Have you heard about the dog flu in Asia? Dogs in southern China have been dying quickly…soon after they begin sneezing and coughing."

"Dog flu is getting to be pretty common these days," Ally said. "But it usually isn't a big deal."

"This is different—according to local doctors—there is a similar rise in human illness and deaths in the same area. A doctor friend of mine in Hong Kong heard that farmers in the mountains of southern China are shooting their dogs to avoid getting sick."

Ally said, "You know, there hasn't been a documented case of influenza transmission between dogs and people before. Do you think it's real?"

"I don't know. But since you are the great virus hunter, I thought you might want to look into it."

"Thanks, yeah, I'll check it out," Ally said. "Hey, let me know if you hear of any other unusual viruses or outbreaks." Ally paused and then chuckled, "Or if you hear of dogs and cats living together…mass hysteria!"

"No problem. Tell Walt I said hi. You know, better yet, tell him to ring *me* up for coffee. Maybe some hot macchiato."

"Riiight." Ally laughed.

"If you don't want him, I'll take your old castoffs!"

"Bitch!"

"Love you too, chica," Maya said.

"Yeah. Love you back. Bye!"

Wow! A dog transmitted influenza would be a game changer. But it's probably a hoax.

If it were remotely possible for dogs to transmit influenza viruses to humans, the world would have seen it already.

Ally went back to her desk and found Gretchen, who was rolling around against her laptop.

"Kitty! Why does everyone want me to find a boyfriend?" she said, petting the fuzzy exposed belly. "You are the only furry companion anyone could ever want!"

She picked up Gretchen and rubbed her face into the cat's dense coat. She opened her laptop and played one of her cat's favorite videos of Fum and Gebra—a cat and barn owl playing together. Gretchen was transfixed in her adorable, excitable way.

Maybe I'm becoming one of those crazy cat ladies.

She smiled. *There are worse things, I suppose.*

Chapter 8

Day 62

Deputy Director Zhang was at a crossroads.

Minister Szu and his brother, the President, were maniacs! First Qiang wants the army to kill all the dogs in the country and burn their bodies. Then he orders all the television and internet companies to shut down.

But now, Szu Chen is toying with the idea of sending a nuclear warhead to the United States. He doesn't seem to care about the illness and the effect on the people. Only caring for revenge.

The death toll was accelerating. The President ordered mass graves for the fallen, without any of the traditional ceremonies. Coroners weren't allowed to create death certificates. People were getting very angry—Qiang and Chen were called the "brothers of chaos".

If the illness doesn't kill us all, the Americans will annihilate us with their own nuclear weapons once they discover the submarine.

Zhang and his assistant guided Mr. Ren into the President's ceremonial room at Zhongnanhai central headquarters to meet the brothers.

Ren was blindfolded, gagged, and his wrists chained. He had bruises on his face and his clothes were dirty.

"Excellency, as you requested, I've brought the spy to see you," Zhang said.

"Yes, very good," Qiang said. "Thank you, Deputy Zhang."

"You and your assistant can leave now," the President said

dismissively.

"Sirs, respectfully, are you sure you want us to leave?" Zhang asked.

"Hmm, you have a point," Qiang said. "We will be done with the prisoner soon. Stay by the door."

"Yes, of course." The men took places by the door, about fifty feet away.

Szu's family physician crossed the room and sat Ren down in a chair next to the President. He gave Ren a shot of something…likely a sedative, because Ren slumped down and appeared to be asleep. The doctor then inserted an I-V in Ren's arm; blood wicked into a long, thin tube.

The doctor then inserted a needle into President Szu Chen's arm and connected the tube from Ren. He was performing a direct transfusion.

"What are you doing?" cried Zhang from across the room.

Qiang replied, "You said the traitor had immunity. Now we will have the same immunity. Do you have a problem with this?"

He's only trying to save himself. Zhang's chest tightened. "Oh, now I understand. I'm sorry for questioning you."

After five minutes, the President's transfusion was complete and Chen left the room. The tube was then affixed to Qiang's arm with a new needle. Finally, ten minutes after the transfusion began, the doctor removed the needles from both men.

Szu Qiang waved his hand and the doctor backed away, as if choreographed. Zhang thought the process was complete and assumed he would take Ren back to his holding cell. But Qiang stood up, taking a knife out of his jacket pocket.

Qiang sliced open Ren's neck and blood came streaming out, hitting the ornate tiled floor. Qiang picked up a large silver goblet and caught the red, rushing liquid in his cup.

Zhang froze in horror.

Qiang put the goblet to his mouth and drank the blood in a short gulp, as some trickled down the sides of his mouth.

Am I actually seeing this?

Zhang glanced at his assistant, whose eyes were closed and his head rolled to the side. Zhang grabbed his arm to keep him from falling.

Qiang smeared the blood from his lips and announced, "Men,

would you please dispose of Mr. Ren? As you can clearly see, we no longer need his services."

DAY 64

Late Saturday morning, Ally pondered what to wear to the secret meeting with the Senator. Ultimately, she decided on an all-black outfit with her slouchy coat and running shoes. She took the Red line south to Gallery Place to meet Jason at noon, about a half hour after the museum opened. Why he wanted to meet at the Kogod Courtyard was beyond her comprehension. The courtyard at the National Portrait Gallery was an immense three-story, glass ceiling atrium with horizontal water features, potted trees and stone benches. It was a serene, contemplative space enveloped by the four wings of the museum. Sure, it was a lovely, quiet space, but hardly private.

She walked past the visitor desk. There were already hundreds of visitors packing the hallways.

Jason sat on a bench reading in the corner, wearing a perfectly typical outfit of jeans and a navy hoodie. She coolly wandered around the atrium's perimeter before she sat down on the bench with her back to him.

"What do we do now?" she whispered, careful not to turn around.

"Relax, no one knows who we are. Act like a normal visitor. We'll walk up to the third floor to meet my Aunt by Michelle's portrait. Follow my lead."

As they walked inside and up the semi-circular staircase, Jason explained, "Ruth and I try to meet at typical tourist locations—a different one each time. Sometimes we meet up at a metro platform for quick exchanges. If we dress like tourists, no one bothers us. It's amazing—when she doesn't wear a suit or put on makeup, the public doesn't recognize her!"

I bet that's true, Ally thought. Senator Ruth Cochran was always put together. Her hair notoriously coifed into a perfect chignon, wearing her signature rose colored lipstick, her usual attire consisted of Chanel-style suits, short pearl necklaces, and pointed-toe kitten heels. Ally had always admired the Senator—not just for her style but more so for her confidence and grace under pressure.

Ruth had been a family physician before running for public office.

She was one of those charmed people that made it look easy to win elections. She began her political career as a small-town mayor, but quickly rose to the state house and then to the role of senator.

President Merriwether derogatorily called Ruth "Betty Crocker" because of her love of baking. Every Thanksgiving, she would deliver turkeys and her home-baked pies to homeless shelters in D.C. How the President could make fun of such an altruistic act was stunning.

In an interview with the *New Yorker*, Cochran explained how she learned baking from her grandmother. She enjoyed making pastries from scratch with her own hands. Working in the kitchen allowed her to clear her mind; she admitted she had some of her best ideas while baking.

Sure enough, Ally didn't identify the almond-skinned woman in the seafoam green velour track suit, faded gray Washington National's cap, and red plastic-framed cat-eye glasses until she heard her very familiar voice.

"Glad to see you again, Dr. Reynerson," Ruth said. "I hope I haven't put you to too much trouble. Has my nephew explained why I wanted to see you?"

"No, ma'am. I'm still in the dark. It's nice to meet you—again. I'm quite a fan actually. But what can I do for you?"

Ruth took a step closer. "I don't know if you picked up on this at the meeting last month, but the Army is taking the lead on tracking the outbreak in Russia. They haven't been sharing this information with the CDC or the World Health Organization. Officially, they are telling me that—until they can rule this out as a potential biological weapon—they refuse to inform anyone outside a very tight circle. I've asked my nephew to keep an eye on things in the Major General's office and alert me to anything troublesome."

The senator continued, "Through Jason, I've learned that a hostile foreign government has obtained samples of the Russian virus. Our agent in that country, reporting to the General, obtained both a blood sample from a deceased victim and a transcript of an interview with a non-sickened survivor. I asked Jason to obtain a copy of the transcript. Would you look it over and give me your opinion?"

"Isn't there a more official channel for this?" Ally asked. "I feel like I'm risking my clearance and my job by talking with the two of you. Director Ortega already cleared me to attend the first meeting. Why not just have more official meetings, like the first one, to discuss the new information?"

"If the General were more forthcoming, I surely wouldn't put you in this position. I don't know what his real motivation is for all the secrecy. My worst fear is he thinks our government should weaponize this virus for our own purposes. I might be paranoid, but paranoia has allowed me to survive as majority leader for the last decade."

Ruth casually walked toward another exhibit, as the two followed. "I don't know who to trust in Merriwether's administration. Because Walt brought you into the first meeting, he obviously trusts you. Walt does not abide fools or con artists. So, I know you will give it to me straight."

Ruth took off her velour jacket and draped it over her arm. Underneath she wore a long-sleeve white t-shirt with a picture of Mr. Rogers and the words 'Won't you be my neighbor?' Ally smiled and almost laughed but maintained her composure.

"Unfortunately," Ruth continued, "sometimes there are people in the government and the military that solely care about their own careers and not the welfare of the nation or the welfare of people in other countries." Ruth took a handkerchief out of her pocket and patted the back of her neck with it. "I'd like your independent assessment of the interview notes—I want to know if it's worth fighting the Pentagon for greater disclosure."

"I still don't like the sound of this, but I'll take a look. I don't want to take sides between you and the military." Ally crossed her arms. "I want you to know—I will walk away if I'm asked to do anything illegal or treasonous. And I won't lie for you or Jason. If anyone asks me, I'm telling them the truth about how you involved me in this. At any point, of my choosing, you need leave me alone."

The senator nodded, "Of course. I understand completely. The last thing I want is to cause you problems."

Too late for that, Ally thought.

Ruth put her jacket back on and walked toward the stairs.

She watched Ruth descend. Once she was out of sight, Ally asked Jason, "Ok, what's next?"

"A week from now, Saturday, same time at the National Zoo." Jason said smiling. "Inside the panda building."

* * *

Later that day, Ally scanned the internet again for any news of the dog virus in southern China. Maya's network usually had reliable intel. It was worth looking into.

International news outlets reported movements of troops in China's southern quadrant. Nothing directly discussing a new dog virus or flu epidemic.

After an hour of searching, she found a YouTube video from a farmer in the region. The video had tags with the words *illness*, *dogs*, and *outbreak* in Chinese. To the camera, he described in broken English how his entire village was overcome with sickness; half had already died. He showed their location on a map—just outside the town of Yuxi.

At first, he explained, a couple dozen dogs had died within a day. When their owners got sick, their neighbors became alarmed, and began killing dogs—both pets and strays.

This must be what Maya was referring to.

The man in the video coughed frequently while he spoke. He panned the camera to a bedroom where his wife, daughter and baby son were sleeping on a single mattress, their bodies as still as death. He said they all had high fevers.

He held up the blood-soaked rags from their vomit. He pleaded with his viewers for help. He said the government soldiers would shoot him if they knew about this video. Soldiers were going door to door, wearing respirators, confiscating personal electronics, such as cameras, laptops, and phones. The military ripped out the wiring from small household satellite dishes.

Ally's mind raced. If the Chinese government is suppressing information about a deadly virus, this would be extremely dangerous. The best way to stop an epidemic is to communicate with the public and institute quarantine measures. A lethal virus can't be ignored away.

An hour later, the video vanished from the internet, as if it never existed. Of course, Ally had recorded a copy on her computer and also saved it to her phone for good measure. She was getting sick of this shit.

She emailed a file of the video to Maya and then to her old boss at the CDC, Director Renée Carson.

People needed to know.

Day 71

Jason got off the Metro at Cleveland Park and was looking forward to seeing Ally again. He liked her, despite—or perhaps because of—her healthy paranoia and obsession about the virus. She was the perfect asset. Smart, trustworthy, caring, and had all the right contacts.

Not many other agencies or officials knew about the events at the farm or Nian's role. Now that Nian was in the States, along with her virus samples, Ruth wanted to bring the CDC into the fold.

Roadfuss showed no intentions of involving the CDC. He couldn't be trusted.

Jason walked briskly toward the front gate of the zoo, carrying a tall Starbucks cup. He was dressed more conservatively than his first meeting with Ally. He changed his appearance, just to throw off anyone that might recognize him. Today he wore a gray flannel blazer, a buffalo plaid scarf, dark-wash denim jeans and brown suede slip-on loafers.

I look just like a J. Crew catalog, he thought. He daydreamed about meeting a cute preppy, falling in love, buying a brownstone together and owning two Dachshunds.

At the panda house, Ally sat on a bench along the far back wall, wearing black running tights and a snug-fitting, black running jacket. She wore a blue baseball cap.

Holy hell, this chick is always early. He slid up beside her and opened his messenger bag.

"Hey Ally, what's new with you?"

"Hey, just watching some pandas. You know, the usual. So, whatcha got?"

"Well," Jason said, "I got you a really awesome panda calendar from the gift shop. It's totes adorable. But you should probably open it at home." He handed her the plastic bag holding the calendar. He sipped his coffee.

"Aw, you didn't have to do that—I didn't get you anything," Ally quipped back. "By the way, you look really nice today."

"Thanks. Hey, do you have any cute guy friends? I'm sooo ready to settle down. Dating is crazy these days, ya know?"

Ally laughed. "Sorry, I don't know any cute guys. But I'll keep a look out for you!"

"Appreciate it! Hey, let me know how you like the calendar." In a lower tone, Jason said, "I'm going to be at the Hirshhorn tomorrow when it opens at ten. Want to join me?"

"Do I have a choice? See you there."

"Well," Jason said in a louder tone, standing up, "I'm going to check out the red pandas next door. Join me?"

"Nah, I've seen them before and I'm kind of tired. I'm heading home. Have fun!"

"You too."

Jason watched Ally leave. He headed out of the panda house, into the sunshine.

Poor Ally is going to flip out.

He turned on his cell phone and opened an app. The image resolution was pretty good, even for a rush job. He needed to keep an eye on her tonight for sure.

* * *

Ally slid the deadbolt across the door. She threw her jacket on the back of her sofa, ignoring Gretchen's vocalizations for food. She closed the curtains, grabbed a diet soda from the fridge and took a seat at her kitchen table, the calendar in hand. Tucked inside between June and July, was a manila folder with the words "TOP SECRET" in big, bold print.

She read the transcript of an interview with someone named Darya. She was transfixed with Darya's account of how she, and other women, dealt with the dead and the dying at the Russian military camp.

Whoa, she thought. *The only survivors were women? Weird.*

She continued reading. All the survivors were women in their fifties and sixties. *This made no sense.*

Usually older people had worse immune systems. Women had some slight differences in immune response when compared to men. *But would this be enough to create such a huge disparity?* Twenty-one women within such a narrow age range surviving had to be statistically significant.

Darya told the interviewer that the survivors had similar responses. They reported a little chest or sinus congestion, some aches, but only for a day and they were fine afterward. So, the virus probably got to them, but their immune system targeted the threat immediately, and fought it off before it could invade the majority of their cells and replicate aggressively.

They must have acquired immunity! So interesting!

Reading further into the report, Darya described the typical progression of the flu among the *non-survivors*. The first symptoms were aches, congestion, sore throats, low grade fevers—typical cold or flu symptoms. Within a day or two, however, they became extremely weak and were bedridden. Near the end, some developed high fevers and were coughing up blood. Lastly, they became nonresponsive and passed away within a few hours.

Darya explained how the early victims received infirmary care with I-V's, antibiotics and pain medication. When they didn't respond and the doctors became infected, the medical tent became quarantined.

Some officers took the few respirators from the stock system. They instructed people to stay in their tents or cabins. But they continued to contract the virus and die. When the Commandant and his officers died, the camp fell into disarray.

Darya and the other survivors tried to remove the dead and care for the sick. With thousands to attend to, they worked twenty-hour days. When another snowstorm arrived, they admitted defeat and left the dead where the lay.

Ally's heart went out to Darya. *These women were absolute heroes.* Ally couldn't imagine how they managed to get by for weeks without outside assistance.

She skipped forward to the next section and her heart stopped. A glossy photo of an aerial view showing a large fireball. The caption read, "Napalm by Russian Air Force, February 26."

That was three days after she attended the meeting at the OEOB! Napalm to contain a virus? It was like a B-movie script.

Ally quickly flipped to the next section, this one filled with another interview. This time with a woman named Yi Nian. Nian was an undercover agent working at a secret Chinese biowarfare lab. The NSA recruited her and she reported to Major General Roadfuss at Fort Belvoir.

"What!?" shouted Ally, frightening Gretchen out of a peaceful nap. "Oh God."

The Chinese were the ones interviewing Darya! How did I miss that?

Wait. The Chinese have a secret biological weapon lab?

The outbreak in China...*was this related?*

This was way above her pay-grade.

Ally turned to Gretchen, "Our friend Jason has a lot of explaining to do!"

As she digested this chain of events, surprise and shock gave way to anger.

Oh, screw this.

She emailed Director Carson.

Within ten minutes, the Ally's phone rang.

"Hi Renée. You got my email. Are you free to talk?"

"Allison, thank you for sending me the video the other day. What's this about a Chinese National in Army custody?"

"It's a long story. But I have reason to believe the Chinese virus originated in Russia. Given the death toll in southern China, I think you need to know. A survivor from China, a spy under the cognizance of Fort Belvoir, is here in the DC area."

"Thank you for bringing this to my attention. Who else knows?"

Ally's heart was racing. *Was she disclosing too much? Did she care?*

"Senator Cochran. Again, it's a long story."

"A story I would love to hear in person. How soon can you come to Atlanta?"

Ally finished her call with Renée and called Maya.

She walked to her dresser and shoved a change of clothes and a spare toothbrush into her backpack. It was almost midnight. She didn't know if she could pull this off.

Still, deep in her heart, she knew it was the right thing to do.

It was the only thing to do.

Chapter 9

Day 72

Ally sat on a leather bench in the middle of a darkened room on the second floor of the Hirshhorn modern art museum. A weird conceptual art film played over and over in a loop. Ally could not conceive what the artist was trying to convey.

This film is ridiculous! Why is that woman putting a frog on her head? The word "love" kept flashing on the screen.

But she had to stay focused. She wouldn't allow herself to become distracted from her mission.

Jason came in, wearing his jeans and hoodie combination again.

"We need to talk…now!" Ally said.

"Good morning to you too!" he said in a jovial sing-song way. "Man, don't get your undies in a bind. Talk to me."

"Don't 'good morning' me." Ally poked her finger in his chest. "I need answers." She grabbed his hoodie with her fist and glowered at him. She took a deep breath and released him, tilting her head to the ceiling. "No. Wait. We don't have time to talk. I want you to take me to meet Dr. Yi *right now*."

"Shush!" Jason said in a whisper. "Come outside."

She followed him outside to the sculpture garden and she watched him as he pretended to admire a bronze figure of a contorted man.

"You can't meet her," Jason said in a more serious tone, without taking his eyes off the sculpture. "She's under quarantine in a safe house outside Alexandria, with an armed guard. Nobody goes in or out. Except me and the General."

"I'm done playing." She shoved him in the shoulder. "Look at me. You get me in to talk to her right now, or I'll drop a copy of your folder to the Washington Post."

Jason laughed. "Yeah, right."

Ally crossed her arms. "Try me."

She took out her phone and showed him a picture of a package with a label written in bold letters that read: "Washington Post, C/O Investigations Editor."

Jason's mouth fell open. "You wouldn't!" He paused, his eyes narrowed. "The General would have you arrested. Divulging top secret information is treason."

"Fine, I'll take my chances." She turned and walked away.

She counted in her head and strode purposefully across the grass of the National Mall. When she counted to fifty-nine, she resisted the urge to look. Heavy footsteps, running, were getting closer.

She smiled inwardly. *Got him.*

She pretended to ignore his heavy breathing until a hand touched her shoulder.

"Ally. Think about this for a minute. You can't take this to the press. You'll get arrested. I'll get arrested too. Ruth can't help me…can't help us." Jason paused to catch his breath. "She'll probably go down for this too. Her political career will be over. Are you *nuts*?"

She crossed her arms. "I'm a woman who doesn't give a damn. So yes, maybe I'm a little crazy. But this is *important*."

"It's *important* not to go to jail," he sputtered.

"Ha! You think I'm scared of prison? Outbreaks happen is some very rough places. Me and my friend Maya were held prisoner for three days by Somali pirates. So, think again."

"Wow." He placed his hand over his mouth. "Really?"

She nodded.

"How did you escape?"

"We were resourceful." She shook her head. "But don't change the subject. Focus!" She clapped at his face. "You need to get me to Nian. If you hadn't guessed, I have a copy of the report in a secure location—for insurance. People *will find it* if I die or go missing." She stared at him with her coldest eyes.

He shook his head. "Fine. You win. You can visit Nian. I'll figure out something."

"I want to see her right now. So, you better figure it out fast. Do you have a car nearby?" she asked. "Or are we taking a damned taxi?"

* * *

After weeks of planning and three days of driving, Jolie finally arrived in New York. They stayed overnight in New Orleans and then Asheville, North Carolina, but still, her legs and back ached from the journey. She and Ranger would have an entire day in New York to explore and sight-see before the competition at the Javits Center.

She had never been to New York. On their first morning, she took Ranger to Central Park. It was mid-March and people were weaving in and out of the crowds on rollerblades, old school skates, skateboards, and bicycles.

There were musicians and dance troupes playing for coins, people playing Frisbee and hacky sack, and sidewalk artists doing their thing. Jolie had never seen such a spectacle. Sure, they had the River Walk in San Antonio, but nothing close to the raw energy and diversity of Central Park. Oh, and so many dogs! She was dazzled by all the different breeds.

Jolie and Ranger walked over to the Balto Statue. She took a picture of Ranger with Balto.

I'm going to frame this one.

After crossing the park, Jolie let Ranger loose to romp around Strawberry Fields with the other dogs. A few minutes later, Ranger began panting, sitting down to rest under a tree. She was tired too. Three days on the road could do that.

Looking on with the other dog owners, Jolie explained how Ranger was going to be the next champion at the agility competition.

They all wished her well.

* * *

Ally watched Jason as he gripped the steering wheel tightly, obviously not talking to her, as he drove them towards the safe house.

She wondered if he was ever going to talk to her again.

After a few minutes, he asked, "What am I going to tell the guard?"

"I'm a doctor. If she's in quarantine, don't you have doctors going in and out all the time to check on her?"

"Yes, but the guard knows her regular doctors. Brian will be suspicious because you aren't on the list."

"Just one guard?"

"Yep. Roadfuss keeps things close."

"Tell Brian I'm her lady doctor. You know, for lady stuff. I bet he won't even ask," Ally said.

"Fine, but if he doesn't let you in, you can't say I didn't try."

"Dr. Yi speaks English, correct?"

"Yes. Excellent, in fact."

"Great! Hey, let's bring the guard some coffee and donuts. Soften him up. What do you think?"

"Sure," Jason said. "Although I could go for something stronger than coffee right now."

"I'll buy you a drink afterward if everything goes smoothly. Promise."

Jason turned into a donut shop. Ally trotted in and came out with a dozen donuts and three coffees. She said, "I got you a latte. Black coffee for your friend with some extra creamers and sugar packets."

She hoped her present would lighten Jason's mood, but he just grunted and took the cup.

A few minutes later, Jason turned into a subdivision of tract homes. He pulled into the driveway of a modest single-story house.

"I'm going to call you Doctor Ann Black. You're a gynecologist from Walter Reed Hospital. Don't say too much. Let me do the talking."

They approached the door and Jason knocked four times. After a minute, the guard opened the door. "Hello Mr. Burns. Who's your friend?"

"Hey Brian, I brought you a coffee and some doughnuts. Thought you might need a break. This is Doctor Black. She's here to do an examination. You remember, the gynecologist Doctor Duran asked me to send over."

Brian peered over Jason's shoulders and looked at her. Brian looked like a typical mall cop, minus the uniform. He wore gray sweats with a tactical holster for his gun and taser. On his feet, Converse low top sneakers.

Guilt washed over her. *This poor slob is just doing a job…a tedious babysitting job.*

Brian shrugged and let them in. "Oh, well, no problem. Hey man, thanks for the coffee. The General is moving her to some other black site. Probably best to get all her medical visits done now. I'll be in the kitchen if you need me." He headed down the hall with the box of doughnuts and his coffee. "Lock the door behind you."

Jason and Ally entered and Jason turned the latch behind them.

After Brian was out of earshot, Ally whispered, "What does he mean? Where is she being transferred?"

Jason whispered back, "First I've heard of it. Roadfuss has been acting stranger than usual the past couple of days."

Ally scanned the room. The front room décor was a throwback to the seventies, with brown and gold carpet, vinyl-covered sofa, and a hanging glass pendant lamp in the corner. An awful wood-look Formica coffee table was littered with pizza boxes and soda cans.

"Wow, this doesn't look like a containment zone to me. What kind of quarantine is this?"

"You'll see." Jason opened a door leading a utility room. The walls were covered in aluminum panels. A steel surgical sink was mounted on the wall. The door to the garage was largely made of glass, with a combination lock. Next to the door, a small plexi-glass chute for passing items while maintaining containment.

Doctor Yi Nian was sitting on a twin-size bed, watching a rerun of the American sitcom *Friends*.

Ally walked up to the window. "Hi Nian, my name is Ally. Jason brought me to see you because—like you—I also research diseases."

The short, thin Chinese woman turned off the television. But before she could respond, a loud clamor of breaking dishes resonated through the house.

Jason ran towards the kitchen.

Now alone with Dr. Yi, Ally said, "Nian, how would you like to get out of here?"

"Miss Ally, I've been in here for twenty-five days. They will not tell me when it is safe to come out. But I assure you, I never got sick."

"I know. I read your file. I'm taking you out of here today. I don't trust the General. Neither should you. Pack your things."

Jason rushed back. "The guard is dead! Ally, what in holy hell did you do?"

"He isn't dead. I slipped a couple roofies in his coffee. He'll be fine in an hour or two. Ok, maybe he'll have a slight headache. Did he hit his head?"

"You what?!"

"You heard me. We're getting out of here—now. All three of us.

Are you going to help or not?"

"What are you doing? Have you completely lost your mind? Where do you want to take her? What if she infects other people? Are you trying to kill us all?"

"I told you. I'm not dicking around anymore."

"Ally, wait! What if she's a carrier? Did you think about that?"

"I reviewed her lab results, remember? She isn't presenting with any symptoms." Ally placed her hands on her hips.

Jason just stared at her.

"Look," Ally said, "Dr. Yi might be the only living human with the key to stopping a global pandemic. I'm talking about a pandemic that could decimate over ninety percent of the world's population. You have the opportunity to be one of the good guys in this story. If you want to walk away, do it now. Otherwise, help me pack her things in the car and let's get the hell out of here."

* * *

Jason turned on the engine. "Which way?"

Ally said, "Take a right and head east."

Jason grunted.

"First, give me your phone," Ally said.

He gave it over.

She took out the sim cards from both their phones and threw them out her window.

"You think they can't track us now? Amateur." Jason said.

"We're going to the Amtrak station in Alexandria. We'll ditch your car there."

"Fine." Jason said.

They sat in silence as Jason drove.

Nian sat in the back seat and finally broke the tension asking, "Where are we going?"

Ally replied, "The CDC. Atlanta."

Nian nodded and settled in.

Ally had a plan. The night before, Maya bought them tickets to take the Palmetto Train south to Columbia, South Carolina. The train would take over ten hours—far slower than driving. But with all the highway cameras, toll plazas, and patrol vehicles, it was safer to avoid major roads. Once they arrived in Columbia, Director Carson offered to meet them and drive them to the CDC Chamblee Campus in Atlanta.

After they boarded and the conductor checked their tickets, Jason finally whispered, "Did Aunt Ruth put you up to this?"

"No, of course not. I'm sure she'll be mortified when she finds out."

"Hey, why do I feel like I'm your hostage?"

Ally sighed. Now that they were safe, the tension in her muscles subsided.

"You didn't have to come along. You could have punched me in the face and turned me in to the General. But you didn't. So deep down, you know we're doing the right thing. Stop worrying."

"Stop worrying? You know, I understand you are old and don't care about your career. But I'm young. I have a frickin' life ahead of me. At least I did. How did I let you talk me into this?" He crossed his arms and stared at the ceiling.

"Hmm, did you really have a life? At the rate things were going, you were going to die in the apocalypse anyway. With my help and Nian's, you and millions of other people might actually survive the coming plague!"

"Plague? Really? You and your stupid computer simulations. Yeah, there's a deadly virus, and it got bad in a couple places half way across the globe. But you don't really know what is going to happen. A computer can't tell you that. All I know is, you and I committed twelve kinds of felonies and the government is going to put us away for decades—if they don't shoot first and ask questions later."

"Look, we'll be on the train for a few hours. Why don't you get some sleep? Nian and I have a lot to discuss."

With a pinched mouth, Jason said, "Fine. Whatever." He took his ticket and moved across the aisle to an empty row. He pulled his coat over him like a blanket, nestled his head against the window and closed his eyes.

"Whatever," Ally mouthed back, shrugging at him sarcastically.

Why does he bring out the brat in me?

She looked across to Nian, who was staring at her with wide eyes, as if asking, *'What's going on here?'*

"Sorry, Nian," Ally whispered. "How are you doing? Are you hungry? Thirsty? Can I get you something?"

"No, Miss Ally. I just want to understand what is happening. What is the plan?"

"Yes, well, I read your file and I think you can help us work on a cure."

"I would be happy to help. But how?"

"Reading interviews and looking at test results are one thing. It's another to actually experience how a disease is transmitted…first-hand, like you have. I'm hoping you can tell me your story of what happened at the farm, in your own words."

"Yes, but let me say, I am not proud of my actions. Or my role at the farm."

"I know you did the best you could. I'm not here to judge. I just need the facts."

Nian nodded and recounted her time at the lab. When she got to the part about killing the guards, Ally could see how upset this made her.

"Nian, let's stop there. You've been though things I can't even imagine. Why don't we both try to get some sleep? We can talk again in the morning."

"Yes, Miss Ally. Thank you again for rescuing me."

"No, Nian. Thank *you*. Now, let's get some shut eye. Tomorrow will be a big day."

* * *

The train wheels squealed and the car rocked side to side as it went around a bend. It was still dark outside, just after nine at night. Ally got up to head to the café car before service closed.

Jason opened his eyes. "What did I miss?"

"Not much. I had a long talk with Nian, but I still have lots of questions. We should arrive at our destination in four hours. I'm gonna get some food. Can I bring you anything? A beer?"

"Hey, quick question," Jason yawned. "Since we won't be returning any time soon, who's taking care of your cat?"

How does he know I have a cat?

"I never told you I had a cat."

"Are you sure? I think you mentioned it the first time we met at Farragut Park."

"I don't think so…" Ally reflected on their conversations. "Wait! Oh God. I'm such an idiot. You've been spying on me! Did you bug my apartment? My phone? Did you have me followed?"

Jason grinned. After a long silence, "Of course. Really…did you think I'd hand over state secrets to you and not know what you were up to or who you were talking to?"

Ally sputtered, "Wow! I shouldn't be amazed. But damn. You really are into this spy shit."

"Says the kidnapper," Jason retorted wryly. "Remember when we met Ruth at the museum? I had my guy bug your home and your computer. All I can say is, your browsing history is supremely morbid. And you watch way—I mean way—too many cat videos."

Ally just stared at him with her mouth open.

"But honestly, I was impressed you found that Chinese video last week. Even my group at Belvoir didn't know it existed. But it was kind of a rotten you sent it to Maya and Director Carson without telling me first. I thought we were friends."

She rubbed her eyes. *Fucking spies.*

She motioned him to follow her. They walked towards the café car, but once they reached the first space between adjoining cars, she hit him in the shoulder.

"Ouch."

"You deserved that. And more."

Jason laughed. "Honestly, I was impressed you found that video."

"For what it's worth," Ally said, "I had no idea the stuff in China was connected to Nian until I read the report yesterday. But I'm glad I sent it to Director Carson. This cloak and dagger stuff is ridiculous. The CDC needs to get involved—like yesterday."

Ally lifted her head in thought. "Wait, so you knew I planned to kidnap Nian?"

"Not exactly. Not at first. But when you asked your neighbor to watch Gretchen and said Maya would pick her up the next day, I figured something big was up. Oh, and I thought Gretchen was your human daughter," Jason laughed. "Until I put it together with the cat and chinchilla videos. Then I heard your call to Maya where you asked her to buy you three train tickets to South Carolina. When you called Renée, I mean Director Carson, it wasn't hard to figure out what you might be up to."

"So, all your righteous indignation and pouting a couple hours ago was a complete act? Why would you do that?"

"Sorry, I was having too much fun." He giggled. "I still can't believe you roofied the guard. That is next level girl! Ha! I was going to put him in a choke hold, but you beat me to the punch…literally!"

He laughed, holding his stomach. "Then I couldn't help myself. It was hilarious." He was choking for air now. "You're a frickin' badass!"

"Damn! I thought I was careful…going through Maya. Shush! Stop laughing. People might hear us. But wait—what about your job? If you knew I was going to extract Nian, why did you go along? What are you playing at?"

Jason took a deep breath. "Ha! Madam, first we need a couple of those crappy beers from the café car!" He pushed the button on the connecting door and it slid open. He extended a hand to Ally. "Shall we?"

Ally sighed and took his hand. "Ok, but now you're buying."

* * *

They drank a couple beers in the café car. The car was empty except for an elderly couple who had fallen asleep in the booth across the aisle.

"So, you were a Marine?" Ally asked.

"Yeah. Right out of high school. My mom and sister died when I was fifteen—in a car accident. My dad was Marine, but he passed when I was much younger.

"That's awful."

"Yeah. Ruth was my guardian. I lived with her until I was eighteen. I was a sullen teenager to begin with, but after my mom died, I was even more lost."

"I didn't know."

"I'm good now. Ruth kicked my ass back then. She isn't the motherliest person, but she gave me the discipline I needed. A year before graduation, I told her I wanted to become a Marine like dad—see the world. I was worried she'd be angry. But instead, she threw down the gauntlet. Signed me up for SCUBA classes at the Y, brought home books on military history and strategy."

Jason laughed, "Get this—I had to give her book reports each week. At breakfast she tested me on Morse code. She even did pushups with me in the evenings. Of course, I had to do twice as many—but she's a beast!"

Ally laughed, "Why am I not surprised by this?"

"I can still hear her. She said, '*If you want to do something, do it right. Always be more prepared than the next guy.*' She was a tough drill instructor!"

"Ok, so then what?"

"I joined the Marines. Made the cut, naturally. Did a couple tours in the Middle East. Got shot a couple times, but nothing serious. Ruth freaked out—strongly advocated I change professions. I couldn't argue with her. She was friends with Director Ortega and got me the job with NSA. I worked there for a couple of years, until they asked me to work for Roadfuss and work undercover. You know the rest."

"Incredible. So, you were spying on Roadfuss for the last twelve months?"

He chuckled. "Yep. Remember that first meeting? With Defoe? Well, Roadfuss pretended it was his meeting, but really, he tried to bury the Russian outbreak. He's a shady dude. Ortega was the one that pushed for the meeting with the Vice President."

"And Nian?" Ally asked.

"Roadfuss didn't tell Ortega he brought her back to the states, or that the outbreak in China was connected to Russia. Look, I don't know what he planned to do with Nian. But it couldn't have been good."

"Would you have rescued her? With or without me?"

"Absolutely. But it helped having you on our side. We didn't know if it was safe to move her. So, thank you."

"Huh. You're welcome, I think."

"Hey, something you said a while ago. I have to ask…how did you and your friend get away from Somali pirates?

"Ooh. You really want to know? It's not pretty."

"Well, now I *have* to know."

"Fine, but I warned you." Ally finished her beer and leaned back. "We were working on a meningitis outbreak in Somalia. A dangerous place, but we go where we're needed. We slept in tents at the U.N. camp. One night, after midnight, we woke up to find two men holding guns to our heads. Said they would kill us if we made any noise. We did what we were told. I guess the pirates thought we would fetch a good ransom because we were doctors from America. Like all Americans are rich or something. They drove us to the shore, then ferried us to a large fishing boat anchored off the coast."

"Whoa. You must have been terrified!"

"I guess so. Being with Maya helped. But I have to say, they were surprisingly polite most of the time."

"So? Then what?' He leaned forward, resting his chin on his hands.

"Right. They placed us below deck in a locked room. Brought us water and little bits of food occasionally. Otherwise, they left us alone. But I was severely pissed when they took my wedding ring. Never got it back—those fuckers!" She hit the table.

"Ok, but how did you escape?"

Ally chuckled. "Well, this gets kind of gross."

Jason crossed his arms. "Spill."

"Fine. On the morning of the third day of our captivity, Maya got her period—which got me thinking of a terrible plan. Um. I'll spare you the details. Let's just say we strategically used the blood to convince the pirates we were infected with Ebola."

"No!"

Ally laughed. "They freaked out. Tossed us overboard. Luckily, the seas were calm and we swam the two miles to shore. Once we crawled onto dry land, we laid there, laughing so hard we couldn't see straight. The local fishermen probably thought we were insane."

"Wow. That's amazing! Yeah, I'd say you were resourceful. Ick. I'm kind of sorry I asked."

"Me too."

"Ally, I need to ask you something else." His eyes turned serious. "How much do you trust Director Carson?"

"I trust her implicitly. Worked for her for nearly my entire career."

"But, in the words of my Aunt Ruth, is she a good guy?"

"I'm betting my life on it!" Ally laughed.

He clinked his beer bottle against hers.

"Good enough for me."

Chapter 10

Day 73

Their train arrived at the Columbia Amtrak Station around two in the morning. Before the train doors opened, Ally strained to view the platform.

A woman with short, perfectly trimmed silver hair, wearing a gray suit, was texting on her phone. It was Renée.

So far, so good.

As Ally disembarked, she quickly scanned the rest of the platform. *No police in sight.*

"Well, if it isn't my favorite virus investigator," Director Carson said, arms outstretched.

Hugging Renée, Ally replied, "I'm so happy to see you! Sorry for causing you all this trouble!"

"Allison, I'm glad you reached out to me. As for trouble, well, let's just say everything will be taken care of. Or rather, Senator Cochran will take care of things. I'll tell you the whole story once we're in the car."

Turning to Jason, Renée said, "Well, you must be the famous Mr. Burns. It's great to meet the legend. I just got off the phone with your Aunt."

Jason smiled. "My reputation is probably exaggerated. Nice to meet you too."

Renée said to Nian, "And you must be Dr. Yi. I'm glad to have you on our team. I'm sure your experience in China must have been difficult to say the least. Please let me know if I can do anything to make your stay more comfortable."

"Thank you, Director Carson," Nian said. "I am very thankful to be here."

"Well, you all must be tired from your travels. The drive to Atlanta will take about four hours, and after that you should use the rest of the day to get settled. I took the liberty of arranging hotel rooms. But tomorrow morning, we'll start bright and early. We'll set up your new lab and brainstorm a plan."

Renée turned to Jason, "Mr. Burns, will you be staying on with us long term?"

"Ma'am, please call me Jason. Yes, I plan to stay awhile. I can't help with the lab work, obviously, but I'd like to keep an eye on things—from a security perspective. Will that be a problem?"

"No, not at all. From what I've learned from your aunt and Director Ortega, a little extra security couldn't hurt. You are welcome to stay as long as you wish."

"Thanks, Ma'am. I'll try not to get in your way," Jason said.

Renée asked Ally, "Just the two backpacks? Do you have any other luggage?"

"No other luggage. We were in kind of a hurry."

Jason said, "Ally, I hope you don't mind, but I arranged to have some clothes and personal effects picked up from our apartments and shipped here. Since Nian didn't have many things, I ordered items for her online. I think she's a size two? Anyway, our packages arrive at Chamblee tomorrow."

Ally stared at Jason. "Wait, how did you…? I took your phone. I threw away the sim card!"

"Really? You're so funny," Jason said. He pulled a phone out of his hoodie pocket. "I always have a spare with me."

Ally sighed. "Yeah, I'm an amateur. Thanks, I guess. You're always going to be two steps ahead of me, aren't you? Were you a fixer in another life?"

Laughing, Jason said, "Another life? No, just this one, *Allison*. I have a reputation, if you hadn't heard!"

Ally punched Jason in his shoulder as they followed Renée to her car.

"Ow!" Jason said in a mocking way. He stopped and Ally stared at him. She expected him to punch her back or say something really sarcastic, but instead he laughed, put an arm around her shoulder and said, "I'm sorry. Really. And you're welcome."

* * *

What does Cochran want now? Roadfuss wondered. It was Monday morning. The meeting invite was strongly worded.

He had never been summoned to the Dirksen Senate Office Building before. To make matters worse, he had no time to prepare. This was a big deal. He was asked to—no, ordered to—accompany the Defense Secretary, Arnie Shelton, to this meeting.

On the way over, Shelton asked him what the meeting was about. Roadfuss didn't have an answer. This would not bode well for his next promotion.

They arrived at nine and were quickly seated in the Senator's chamber. Cochran made them wait for an uncomfortable ten minutes before she swept in.

"Gentlemen, sit down. I'm sorry I'm running late. There was a very early floor vote…kind of unusual, but you know we have a budget to pass." She closed the door behind her.

"Yes, Senator, we understand," Shelton replied, evenly.

"Well, I'll get right into it then. I want to show you something." She turned the screen around on her desk to face the men. She hit some keys, and a video began to play.

Fuck. *How did she get the Chinese dog virus video?*

Instead of watching the video, Roadfuss studied Secretary Shelton, who appeared engrossed.

I'm a dead man.

At the end of the video, Cochran asked, "Do you want to see it again?"

Secretary Shelton looked up. "No, Senator. But why are you showing us this? What's this about?"

Cochran set her stare on Roadfuss, "Why don't you ask General Roadfuss?"

Roadfuss looked back at Shelton. Shelton had a confused look.

He needed a good story. "Um, I'm not sure I follow, Senator."

"Do I really need to spell this out? Are you honestly going to play dumb, General?" Ruth said, draping a finger over her chin and crossing her other arm in front of her. "Well, then."

She strode over to a credenza and opened a safe behind a mahogany door. She took out a folder marked Top Secret.

Damn. Is that what I think it is?

"General, are you sure you have no idea what I'm going to say?" Cochran asked. She then walked to her desk and buzzed her secretary to bring in her guest.

A tall, distinguished man wearing in a gray flannel suit walked in. With his dark skin, green-grey eyes, and salt and pepper hair, he was immediately recognizable.

"Good morning, Director Ortega," Ruth said. "Thank you again for meeting us so early on a Monday. Gentlemen, you know the NSA director?"

Shelton reared his head back and stood a little straighter. He extended his arm to shake hands with Ortega. "Yes, nice to see you again, Director."

"You see, gentlemen," Ruth continued, "I've brought Director Ortega in because this concerns him as well. We are both wondering why General Roadfuss has been keeping certain important national security information from the rest of us."

Ruth paused and then put her hands on her hips. "For example, just the mere existence of a Chinese biological warfare lab would be sufficient to brief the Senate's National Security Committee, don't you think? And when there was a deadly virus being spread in the vicinity of that lab, well, that could be another bit of news you might want to share."

Ruth's eyes bored into him. "But then, I had to learn from Ortega that General Roadfuss has a Chinese National—from that same laboratory—secretly hidden in a safe house just four miles away…well, it was more than I could stand."

Roadfuss tried to bring words to his lips, but only stammered.

She raised a finger at him. "Don't! Don't say a word. I'm not remotely finished."

Turning to the Secretary, she said sweetly, "Secretary Shelton. Did the General happen tell you that, yesterday afternoon, your Chinese asset, Ms. Yi Nian, was removed from your safe house and transferred to the custody of the CDC?" She paused and turned her face to each of the men in order.

His face felt hot. *This can't be happening.*

Director Ortega stepped forward and said, "Gentlemen, I know that monitoring the Chinese lab was under your purview. But, regrettably, when it became apparent you weren't going to share any information, I had someone inserted into your team to keep an eye on things. Your man, Mr. Burns, is a former employee of mine. Quite a remarkable young man. He's been reporting back to both me and the Senator from time to time."

Roadfuss felt the heat of Ortega's anger.

Ortega continued, "Frankly, Senator Cochran wanted to open a Senate investigation weeks ago, but I persuaded her to wait. We gave you every chance. Honestly, I must say, not telling us about the Chinese outbreak and holding Dr. Yi hostage was the last straw."

Roadfuss cleared his throat and looked at Shelton, "I can explain, sir..."

Ortega turned to Secretary Shelton, "Senator Cochran and I called the CDC a short time ago. Director Renée Carson will be setting up a new task force to address this new virus. We need to know how to fight this if it reaches our shores. Dr. Yi will be helping their team. I'm working on her citizenship paperwork as we speak. Oh, and Dr. Ally Reynerson from NIH—I think the Major General has met her—will be transferring to the CDC team. I've asked Mr. Burns to tag along. I understand the three of them arrived in Atlanta a short while ago."

Roadfuss continued to hold his head in his hands.

This isn't happening. How am I going to explain this to Shelton on the ride back?

Maybe time to retire after all?

That's it.

I'll put in my paperwork later today...after I wipe the server clean.

Chapter 11

Day 74

Tom received an email shortly after ten. It was from Ortega. *"Meet for lunch? American Grille at noon?"*

Since the primary, Tom detested going to restaurants. But he couldn't let on that it bothered him. He replied, "Sure." Besides, after Roadfuss called him in a panic, he had to get the real story.

His anxiety about the restaurant was assuaged by the rumblings in his stomach. Yesterday was a fasting day. Ever since his bout with colorectal cancer in his mid-thirties, he tried to eat right and exercise. He learned that cancer thrived on glucose. This meant he could starve cancer cells if he changed his diet radically. He'd been on a carnivore diet for the last five years.

His unusual diet made social meals a chore rather than an enjoyable occasion. Invariably people asked him about his food choices. He avoided discussing his history of cancer. It turned pleasant conversations into awkward moments…or worse, people would tell their own sad personal histories.

When he ran for his party's nomination against Merriwether, he avoided the topic of his health as much as possible. No one votes for a candidate, particularly for president, with a history of cancer.

He'd given up alcohol years ago. But since the inauguration, he found himself drinking almost daily as a crutch. The thought of alcohol made his mind race. He imagined the sweet taste. *A little bourbon with his lunch wouldn't hurt.* He debated with himself on the ride to the restaurant. Finally, he decided that drinking around Ortega would introduce unnecessary risk.

When he arrived, Ortega was already seated in the private booth of the back of the restaurant. The room was given the all clear by agents White and Flanders, leaving them alone behind a velvet curtain.

Tom told the waiter, "I'll have the ribeye, medium rare, and an unsweetened ice tea."

Director Ortega said, "Sounds great. I'll have the same."

Kiss ass, Tom thought. "Tell me about your meeting with Secretary Shelton and Senator Cochran."

"I think Shelton was quite embarrassed, sir. And I think General Roadfuss is probably getting a real dressing down right about now."

"Well, they both had it coming. Can you imagine if their debacle had gotten out into the press? Do you think the Senator is satisfied? She got her pet project to research the China virus. I think this should shut her up for now. But honestly, poor Shelton. Did she have to be such a cunt?"

Ortega's dark eyes narrowed. His normally calm demeanor shifted. The Director put down his water glass; his hand resting on the table slowly clenched into a fist.

"Sorry, that was uncalled for," Tom said, shaking his head, hoping to appease Ortega. He didn't need to make an enemy out of the man holding the country's biggest secrets. *But since when did Ortega become buddies with Senator Cochran? Curious.*

"I'm having a bad day. Ruth is a fine person." He hoped the apology was quick enough.

Ortega leaned forward. "I think the Senator was very concerned about the outbreak. Rightfully so."

"Yes, of course."

Ortega changed the subject for a short while—to his relief. They talked about some other national security threats in the world.

After their food arrived and the waiter left, Tom needed to get down to brass tacks. "Did you really plant a mole in Roadfuss' office? You know you could have come to me with your suspicions. God, now that Cochran has the Chinese video and the file from Fort Belvoir, how do we know she won't go public?"

"I've known Ruth a long time. She doesn't play politics with national security. She…actually, we both want to make sure whatever happened in Russia and China doesn't reach our shores. This transcends partisan bickering. Regardless, I think things are back on track. The Chinese scientist, Dr. Yi, will be working with the CDC to help develop a vaccine. The General's office will be transferring all samples and records she brought with her."

"I need you to know," Ortega continued, "the Chinese President is making noises saying the Americans are conducting bio-warfare against them. There's chatter about retaliation. So, if we develop a vaccine quickly and share it with them, hopefully we can de-escalate tensions."

"Agreed. I'll call Director Carson personally when I get back to the office. I'll suggest she re-allocate her Zika and Malaria research funding towards this new virus. By the way, what are we calling it?"

"Well, there isn't an official term yet. But some of us at NSA are calling it the Red Death. You know, like the Black Death, but different."

Tom gasped, nearly choking on his steak. "Lord, that's terrible! I'm sure it won't create mass panic when this gets out," he said, dripping with sarcasm.

Tom finished chewing. "Please get a better name in place, you know, like one of those H1N1 numbers that no one understands. Work with Director Carson on it. We need to get some talking points in place for the White House Communications Director and cabinet secretaries. Understood?"

"Will do," Ortega said.

"Oh, and this goes without saying, but under no circumstances can anyone use the term 'Red Death' in front of the President. Not once. Not ever. Sweet Jesus!" He could sense his blood pressure rise.

"Dan is just like a toddler...he'll repeat back whatever you say without even thinking. He has no filters. We all need to be on the same page. Right now, or we are toast. I need you to pass this message to the other cabinet members. In fact, just to be safe, have every virus-related brief pass through me first."

"I understand, sir. I'll contact the other cabinet members. Don't worry about this. We know the drill."

"Thanks Ortega. You know, you're a good egg. Now finish up your steak. You don't want it getting cold."

"Yes sir, this is a wonderful piece of beef. I'm glad you suggested it."

Tom winked at Ortega. “I've gotten pretty good at ordering at restaurants since the election. I always order a steak, regardless what's on the menu.”

“Oh, no, I'm sorry, sir. I didn't mean—.”

“Yeah, I know. I'm just messing with you. I got over it months ago.”

Ortega exhaled. “You had me there, sir.”

Tom smiled, holding up his fork with a chunk of ribeye attached. “Cheers!”

Ortega nodded. “Yes, sir.”

* * *

Ally lightly rapped on the doorframe to Nancy’s office, unsure how she would be received. She expected raised eyebrows or a bad joke. But instead, Nancy strode around her desk, yelled “Ally!” and hugged her.

As Nancy released her, Ally braced herself for questions. Surely there would be questions. Questions about her sudden return. And her new friends Nian and Jason.

Again, she was taken aback when Nancy simply said, “I’ve missed you! So, what do you need to get started?”

“I...missed you too. Um, what did Director Carson tell you exactly?”

“Oh, we’ve all watched the China video. Really fascinating. Tragic, of course. But the possible dog connection is very interesting.”

“You *all* saw it? All, like who?”

“Well, all the supervisors, like me, and some of the heads of the disease research labs.”

“Wow.”

“Carson asked me to supervise the new team, but I’m sure you’ll want a prominent role. Have you given it any thought?”

Ally said, “Well, you know I’m not a great people-person. If it’s all the same to you, I’d like to be the EIS lead. I haven’t done field investigations since I left. I’ve missed being on the front lines.”

“With your background, that makes perfect sense.”

“What kind of resources do we have? Things were kind of tight, space-wise, before I left.”

“We put our heads together to come up with a compromise. We’ll take over the Zika lab. Some folks were a little upset at first, particularly since they didn't have much notice. But when I showed them the viral video, sorry bad pun, they all became really intrigued. In fact, half of them asked to work with you on it."

"Oh? That's great!" Ally said. "How many staff members do we have? I heard we have a healthy budget. How did you swing it?"

Nancy said, "We have about a dozen virus specialists already assigned. Plus, you and Dr. Yi. And you'll have to thank Senator Cochran for the plus-up in the budget. She championed the whole effort."

"Looks like you have everything covered."

"Just about. We need to get you, Jason and Nian situated. I can't wait to meet them. But first, you have appointments to get badges at noon. Then, to the onsite clinic to make sure you all have the most recent suite of vaccines. I know you're probably up to date, but there is no way around it. Rules are rules."

"You know, I've never seen the agency work this fast before. No offense." She couldn't hold back a grin. "Ha. I should just be glad I'm not in jail."

"Jail? For what?" Nancy asked, one eyebrow raised.

"Oh, nothing. I'm just happy to be here."

* * *

The valet pulled up in front of the hotel with Jolie's SUV. She tipped the driver and Ranger bounded into the passenger seat.

The competition had gone really well. He had won third place overall—not shabby for a first timer. He struggled at first to adjust to the new setting and large crowd. In fact, many of the dogs seemed unaccustomed to the artificial turf. But once he focused, he obeyed all her commands as he'd practiced at home.

It was a close one—Ranger was just two seconds slower than the overall winner. She burst out in tears after his amazing last run of the event. She was so proud. Several other owners and breeders came up to her after the award ceremony to ask if Ranger was available for breeding with their females. Alas, Ranger had been neutered many years ago.

She reluctantly pulled into city traffic.

Time to get back to work.

As she left the Holland Tunnel, the energy of the city subsided and the grind of the coming two-day journey began to sink in. Ranger was quietly snoring in the seat next to her. *If only I could teach you could drive*.

After several hours of highway driving, approaching Georgia, her cell phone rang. She barely the ring over the loud country music she played to help her stay awake. It was nearly ten at night. Nobody ever called her this late. It was Jenny.

"Hey Jolie, it's Jennifer. I'm sorry if I'm disturbing you, but I couldn't put off calling you any longer."

"No problem, honey. We're just getting ready to check into a hotel for the evening. Is everything ok?"

"I hate to give you bad news on the road, but two of the puppies you imported from Yugoslavia last week came down with colds or flu or something. They were sneezing earlier this morning and had a little trouble breathing. I brought the vet out, thinking it was something kinda routine. He gave them some antibiotics, and I separated them from the rest of the dogs. They looked better later. You know, less wheezing. But…and I'm not sure how to say this…so I guess I'll just spit it out. Both dogs are dead. I thought they were just sleeping. But they didn't touch their dinner, so I tried shaking them awake and they were both stiff like boards."

Jenny sniffled and blew her nose.

Jenny continued, "But anyway, that's why I'm calling. I don't know what you want me to do next.'

Dogs die all the time, Jolie thought. She'd seen lots of cases of kennel cough that went badly. *Poor Jenny. She hadn't been around much death.*

Young people can be so sensitive.

"Listen Jenny, I'm sure it wasn't any bit your fault. So, don't go worrying. I appreciate you being there while I'm gone. You know I trust you more than anyone, right? You did good by bringing out the vet. Here's what I want you to do. You ready?"

"Yes ma'am. I can take down some notes if you want."

"Good girl. Ok, so the first thing I want you to do is call the vet back out again. He may not want to come out at night, but it can wait until morning. Ask him to do a necropsy and give a cause of death—something in writing—he'll know what to do. Ask him to check the other dogs. Take their temperatures."

"Right. Got it." Jenny replied. "When are you getting home?"

"In about twenty-four hours. Which ones died?"

"Two of the German Shepherds—Morningstar and Constitution. The ones for the Army contract."

"Tsk, they were such wonderful pups," Jolie sighed. "Ok, well, in the meantime, write down what happened, just like you told me, in the medical log book, using your best recollection. If you can think of any other little details, what they ate last, interactions with other animals, include those also."

"Thanks Jolie. I'm sorry if I let you down. I'll get right on it."

"And sweetie, try to get a good night's sleep tonight. I don't need my best trainer upset and exhausted. Shoot, I'm tired enough for both of us!"

"Sure thing, Miss Jolie. Drive real safe. See you tomorrow night."

* * *

President Szu Chen was losing the fight against the virus. All his provincial leaders were reporting mass casualties. Whole industries were coming to a grinding halt. Exports were delayed or ceased altogether. Power plants were understaffed, causing rolling brownouts, particularly in the rural areas.

He ordered military troops to remain at their bases, with no outside visitors.

We must preserve our forces against the enemy.

Chen closed the airports, then the borders. Already there were caravans of families rushing to the borders to escape the virus. They were rightfully shot in the back as they ran from police.

Only the Americans could have devised such a fiendish weapon.

They will not get away with this.

His brother Qiang and his team of assassins had their instructions; to seek out and destroy specific American targets.

But more importantly, President Merriwether needed to be punished. Merriwether was scheduled to attend a rally in Los Angeles in seven days. A submarine was on its way; with the goal of releasing two nuclear-tipped missiles to greet the American President.

Yes, the Americans will pay with Merriwether's blood, he vowed.

When all his plans were fulfilled, a virus would be the least of their worries.

DAY 75

Ally gathered all the scientists on the team into the main auditorium for a briefing and strategy session. Dr. Yi was her co-presenter. Nancy was the meeting facilitator. As for ground rules, no ideas would be dismissed.

"Ms. Yi," Ally said, "you've come into direct contact with the virus. Could you tell your story again to the rest of the team? Please, even small details could be important."

"Well, I was recruited to a secret biowarfare team roughly two years ago. But also, reported my work to your government. I was, how you say, a double-agent. Our lab was in the southern mountains, near Yuxi. Our supervisor, Dr. Wu, went with the Chinese military to obtain a sample of a deadly virus in northern Russia. They returned with samples and a female survivor named Darya."

Ally addressed the audience, "The interview notes from Darya are included in your packet. Sorry, continue."

Nian nodded. "The day after they came back, Dr. Wu began to feel poorly. He died about twenty-four hours later. Then some other researchers and the guards became sick."

Ally said, "What about you? Did you have any symptoms?"

"No. I was never in contact with the Russian woman. But like the other doctors, I was around Dr. Wu and the samples. I checked my blood for pathogens and other signs of infection. I even analyzed for DNA, but never contracted the virus. I collected as many samples and test results as I could carry before I departed.

"Sam and I walked into town. I drove to Hanoi, where an American Army plane flew me to Virginia. I was kept isolated for over three weeks."

Ally interrupted, "Sam. Who's Sam? Was he also a researcher?"

"Oh, no." Nian blushed. "I'm afraid the report doesn't mention him. No, Sam is a dog. Actually, a puppy. Dr. Wu found him in Russia and brought him back as a pet. It was supposed to be a secret. Director Szu Qiang would have been angry if they found out we had a dog. Sam was a Samoyed, a few weeks old. Cute."

"Wait…all this time…you had a dog from Russia at your facility and never mentioned this before?"

"He was just a puppy. Why would this be important?"

Ally sighed. "I didn't show you the China video. Why didn't I show you the video?" she said, her hands in the air.

Ally placed a thumb drive into the laptop, dimmed the overhead lights and projected the video on the auditorium screen. Ally examined Nian's response as it played. Nian gasped and covered her mouth with her hand. She muttered something in Chinese...*an expletive?*

After the video finished, Ally turned up the lights and leafed through her thick folder of notes as the other scientists began murmuring.

A half-minute later, Ally held up a page. "Aha! Everyone—go to page two of the interview with Darya. She mentions sled dogs. She said some of them got sick but recovered. Do you know what this means?"

Nian asked, "No, what does this mean?"

"What if the dogs are carriers? We know Darya wasn't sick when they picked her up. Perhaps she had innate immunity. We all assumed the team got sick based on their exposure to Darya. But what if she wasn't the cause of the infection in China? What if Sam was a carrier of the virus? Dogs often carry viruses that they themselves aren't affected by."

Nancy walked over to look at the interview notes. "A theory worth looking into. Nian, what happened to Sam after you left?"

"I left him with my friend Ren—in town. But Ren said he was leaving also. I assumed he gave Sam to the family he was staying with."

Ally stared at the ceiling, "So now we could have all kinds of dogs throughout Eastern Russia and Southern Asia infected with a virus that can be transmitted to humans. No wonder the video talks about killing dogs. There could be a strong association after all."

Nancy picked up the wall phone and put in a four-digit code. "Can you send someone from APHIS here immediately? We need them on our team."

* * *

Jolie arrived home a few minutes before midnight. Jenny was asleep on the worn leather couch. She was facing towards the back, a striped wool blanket draped over her legs. There were crumpled up tissues scattered around her, as if she was sick or perhaps crying. Jolie reached over to tap her gently on the shoulder.

"Oh, Miss Jolie," Jenny yawned. She rolled over, slowly opening her eyes. "I'm so happy you're home. [cough] What time is it?"

"Late. Why don't you go home and we'll talk in the morning?"

"No, No. You don't understand. I have *so much* to tell you." Jenny sat up and began folding the blanket on her lap. "The vet was here this morning. Half the dogs had high temperatures. I had to isolate them. And Joey, the intern—he went home sick. He was having trouble breathing." Jenny stood up and began pacing, "Do you think it's related? Oh, and the vet will have the results of the necropsies by Wednesday. But he wanted you to call him right away…first thing." She handed Jolie the vet's business card.

"Sure, wow. But what about you? How have you been holding up? Are you ok?" Jolie asked.

"Yeah. I'm super tired. Been coughing since lunch time. But it probably is just Spring allergies. [cough] I didn't want to leave until you got home." Jenny gathered the used tissues and placed them in a trash can.

"Hey, don't worry about anything. Stop tidying up. I'll take care of that in the morning. I'm going to make a snack before I call the vet. Did you have dinner? Can I get you anything? Or do you want to go straight home? I'll drive you if you can wait about twenty minutes. I want to do a quick check on the dogs."

"I think I'm going drive myself home and sleep—if you don't mind. I wrote down all the notes in the medical book like you told me. I'll be back tomorrow morning, [cough] if that works for you," Jennifer said.

"You take care of yourself. I want you to take the day off tomorrow, hear? You've been working yourself to the bone while I've been away. Go feel better. I'll call if anything important comes up."

After Jenny left, Jolie ate a quick bite over the kitchen sink. Then she grabbed the medical journal and began making rounds with Ranger. She walked outside with her flashlight and did a quick scan of the cages. The cage which previously held the two dead dogs was empty.

Was that blood on the chain link? In the darkness, she couldn't be sure.

She inspected the other cages. Before there were two to three dogs in some of the larger cages—now they were now all separated.

She leafed through the medical notes by flashlight. The dogs with temperatures had received antibiotics. The dogs were sleeping and she watched each one to check for the rise and fall of their chests—to verify they were breathing.

Back at the house, she called her vet, Dr. Berg. He explained that he had concerns over the rapid spread of the dog virus across her ranch. He requested she send the vaccination records over to him in the morning. Dr. Berg wanted to see if there were any lapses or additional vaccinations needed for the remaining dogs. She said she would scan them and send them over in the morning.

What a shitbag show, she thought. *Thank goodness for Jenny.* But this mess would set her back considerably with her contracts.

Damn!

Jolie yawned and whistled for Ranger. A few seconds later, he came bounding into her bathroom and sat by her feet as she brushed her teeth.

She got into her pajamas and then cuddled with Ranger in bed.

"Good night, boy," she whispered as she closed her eyes. In the stillness, the aches in her joints and muscles, from the hours of driving, kept her awake.

Tomorrow would be no reprieve.

Another long, crappy day.

CHAPTER 12

DAY 76

Jolie started her day at dawn and went straight away, gathering all the dogs' health records. As she suspected, all had all their vaccinations in order, as well as the documentation from the import process. She scanned them and emailed them to Dr. Berg. She then began her normal rounds.

So far, all the dogs appeared ok. The five with the temperatures were a little listless, but ate their breakfast and wagged their tails when they saw her.

At nine, her phone rang. It was Dr. Berg.

"Hey, Dr. Berg."

"Jolie, I'm hope I didn't wake you. I couldn't sleep last night, so I finished up the necropsies. You won't believe what I found."

"So, what killed the pups?"

"I'm not exactly sure. Both dogs had unusual sores in their lungs. Like chicken pox or measles, but internal. I've never seen anything like this. Were they exposed to any dust, or toxic smoke, or other irritants? Maybe asbestos or silica?"

"No, not that I'm aware of. I mean, we get dust storms sometimes…we're in Texas after all. But there aren't any sources of hazardous dust on the property."

"Ok, I figured as much but had to ask. I'll do some cultures on their lung tissue to see if the source is viral. It may take another five days to get the assays completed. How are the other dogs looking this morning? Did you take their temperatures yet?

"Not yet. They look ok…a little tired but not sick. They had healthy appetites this morning. I'll take their temperatures in a little while and email you the results. I compiled all their immunization paperwork for you. I checked it again this morning, and it's all in order. Hey, do you think you should call APHIS about the two dogs? Or should we wait for a better diagnosis?"

"I called their hotline yesterday. I got back an automated message saying they'll contact me within forty-eight hours. I'll let you know what they say and if they decide to send out an inspector."

"Thanks, Dr. Berg. I appreciate you coming out while I was gone. Let me know how much I owe you."

"No problem. You can pay me at the end of the month. I'll try to keep the lab expenses reasonable. I'll call you when I know more."

"Appreciate it. Bye, Doc."

Jolie continued making her rounds.

Odd. Quiet.

The interns should be here by now.

Where was everyone?

* * *

Jolie began receiving texts from her interns around ten. The four scheduled to arrive that day wrote they weren't feeling well and would be in tomorrow. She assumed they went to the college bonfire last night—after the big basketball game. They were probably hung over. Every year she saw the same pattern.

Still, she needed them. She decided to wait a couple hours and then read them the riot act. She had a list a mile long of other students who wanted to work at the ranch. Everyone knew Jolie wrote the best reference letters in the business. All her kids ended up in really great jobs in the fields of veterinary science and animal behavior research.

After lunch, Jolie took all the dogs' temperatures again. One of puppies wasn't looking so good. She had named this puppy Garner because he had beautiful brown eyes and bushy eyebrows that reminded her of one of her favorite actors, James Garner.

She bundled him up in a blanket and brought him into the house. Jolie normally had a strict rule about bringing other dogs into the house. But she needed to keep an eye on him. She mashed up some chicken livers into a paste and fed Garner by hand. He sniffed the dish and rested his jaw on his front paws—refusing to eat. She wrapped him back up again and put out a dish of water.

Jolie called the vet. "Hey, Dr. Berg. I know you won't have results for me for a couple days, but one of the other puppies is looking quite poorly. Can I bring him into you this afternoon? He's refusing to eat. Maybe you can put him on a I-V?"

Dr. Berg coughed into the phone, "Hey, [cough] Jolie, I think I'll have to refer you to another vet. I'm coming down with something myself. Flu seems to be going around. Anyway, my friend Dr. Marla Berry is taking over my cases and will finish the viral cultures. I got a call back from APHIS. They left a message saying they won't have someone to come out for another five days. In the meantime, why don't you bring your puppy to Marla's office? Tell her I referred you."

"Hey, no problem, Dr. Berg. You take care of yourself now!"

Man, when it rains, it pours.

Maybe the interns really are sick?

She couldn't think about that now. Her first concern was getting the puppy to the vet.

She scooped up Garner and placed him in a travel cage. She threw in one of Ranger's other stuffed animals, a gray squirrel, for good measure.

"Hey buddy, we're going to see Dr. Marla! You hang in there. Ok, sweetie?"

As she walked out the front door, she called out, "Ranger! You have the con! See you later!"

* * *

Fifteen hundred miles off the coast of California, two Navy P-8 aircraft circled at low altitude. The Navy had been tracking the progress of the Chinese submarine since it crossed into international waters. U.S. Navy squadrons from the Marianas and Hawaii had been following its movements as it crossed the Pacific.

Then a curious thing happened. The submarine appeared to lose power. It drifted along as if no one was steering it but didn't surface. The submarine had been running deep—a half-mile below the surface—well past divers' abilities to investigate.

After consulting with the Pentagon, the Pacific Command received direction to drop an autonomous underwater vehicle near the submarine to explore further.

Pictures from the AUV showed no signs of cavitation or damage to the hull. When the submarine did not respond to the presence of the vehicle, the Navy hailed it on all frequencies. With no response, the Navy tried knocking. They gently rammed the AUV into the hull, so it could be heard but not cause structural damage.

Again, no response.

The Navy consulted the Pentagon. They decided to raise the submarine and tow it back to the closest Naval base—San Diego.

They waited until midnight to tow the sub the final five nautical miles to their port, under tight security. Once the submarine was secured, sailors used a torch to open the hatch.

Petty Officer Derrick Powell peered into the opening. The odor was overpowering.

It was the putrid smell of death.

Derrick called down. "Hello?"

No answer.

He descended the metal rungs cautiously into the dark enclosed space. His eyes watered from the stench. It smelled like the time they found the rotten turkey in the abandoned refrigerator of the old mess hall.

He knew the truth, but had to verify.

Holding his breath, he scanned compartments with his flashlight.

All the Chinese crew members were dead.

Day 77

Bob Parks, APHIS epidemiologist and inspector with the Veterinary Services National Incident Management Division, began his morning by pouring a hot cup of coffee and chatting with his coworkers. They were discussing a story out of Minnesota, where a crate of dogs arriving from Yugoslavia was DOA. The unit there didn't have a diagnosis yet. While interesting, Minnesota was a world away from their office in Austin, Texas.

Bob got down to business and reviewed the previous night's entries from the Emergency Management Response System. There were the usual cases of rabies being reported. But one entry caught his eye. Two six-month-old German Shepherds in a ranch in San Antonio had some type of flu. The attending veterinarian, Dr. Jacob Berg, didn't have a definitive diagnosis on what kind of virus the dogs had. But both dogs were recently imported into the country from

Europe, had died fairly quickly and most noteworthy, they had strange looking sores inside their lungs.

Not like any dog illness I've ever heard of.

The forwarding email from the scheduler set his visit five days from today. That might be way too long a time to wait. He made some calls and got approval to accelerate the case. They bumped it up on the priority list.

He arrived at Dr. Berg's clinic by eleven o'clock, despite the usual heavy I-35 traffic.

Dr. Berg's small office building appeared deserted. No lights on. No vehicles in the parking lot. A note on the door directed patients to a veterinarian named Dr. Marla Berry.

That's weird.

He called Berg's office number. No answer. He didn't have a personal cell number for the doctor.

He then looked up Dr. Berry's practice. Her office was about a mile away. He called Berry's office number.

A receptionist answered on the fifteenth ring. "Hello, Dr. Berry's office. Can you hold?"

"No, ma'am, please don't put me on hold. I'm looking for Dr. Berg."

Instrumental music.

"Mary Mother of God," he muttered. He kicked a rock across the parking lot. He held the phone, tapping his fingers on his elbow. After a minute, he sat in his car to wait.

After five minutes of elevator music, he hung up, slammed his car door and asked his phone to navigate to Dr. Berry's office.

He pulled off the two-lane highway and slammed on the brakes. It was now eleven-thirty on a Wednesday and her parking lot was completely full. Some cars were double-parked. A few at strange angles or on the grass.

What in heaven was going on?

His anger vanished as curiosity and anxiety bubbled up.

He backed out and parked at the closest lot; a fast-food restaurant across the highway. He crossed the road, clipboard under his arm, and cautiously approached the building.

He opened the wood front door. There were dozens of dogs and their owners in the small waiting room. He wedged his way through the crowd to the front desk. The receptionist was on the phone, oblivious to his presence. Bob stared at her, hoping she would look up.

"No ma'am, Dr. Marla doesn't have any openings today," the receptionist said forcefully into the receiver. "I know, but she is full up. You'll have to take Muffins to another vet. Yes, I know he's a regular patient…no, don't bring him here. There is no chance she can see him today. There is an excellent vet a town over…Dr. Harris. Yes, I'll try to send over Muffins' records, but I can't promise anything. Please don't use that tone with me. I'm sorry, but it can't be helped. Well, if you can't be civil, I'm going to have to end this call…." The receptionist hit the next flashing button.

He couldn't take it anymore. He walked around the desk and took the phone out of her hands. "Ma'am…"

She stood up and slapped him across the face. "I told all of you! You wait your turn. I have half a mind to call the police on you."

Rubbing his face, "Ma'am, no disrespect. I'm Inspector Parks. From APHIS. I need to know what's going on right now!"

She stared at him. He held up his badge.

All color left her face. "Oh! I'm so sorry, officer. Let me call Marla. Better yet, head down this hall. It's the fourth door on your right. She'll be happy to see you."

He walked down the narrow, dimly lit, wood-paneled hallway. The office building, based on the architecture, was clearly once a residential home built in the late 1950s. The doors were wood veneer and the location of the exam rooms indicated they were small bedrooms, now converted. The dark décor and narrow, claustrophobic hallway reminded him of walking through a haunted house at a second-rate amusement park. He could hear the whimpers of dogs through closed doors. The air smelled pungently like Lysol.

When he arrived at the fourth door, it was open half-way. This room was a proper office with a large wooden desk. A petite woman with thick, curly brunette hair, wearing a white lab jacket, was writing furiously on what appeared to be a medical folder. There were stacks of them on her desk in a disheveled mass.

"Dr. Marla Berry? Bob Parks. I'm an inspector from APHIS." He handed her his card. "I received a message from Dr. Berg. But his office was closed and I don't know how to reach him. He left a note referring patients to you. So here I am. Are you normally this busy?"

She looked exhausted. She put down his card and walked over to the attached bathroom where she turned on the faucet at the steel sink. "Hold on a sec, let me clean up a little." She began scrubbing heaps of foamy soap on her hands and then her arms up to her elbows.

"You'll have to pardon me for not shaking your hand." After she dried her hands, she continued, "No, I'm not normally this busy. I'm really glad you're here. If you weren't here now, I'd be calling your office to get some advice." Marla went over to the window and stared outside at her parking lot. "Dogs all over town are sick. A couple dogs died in my office this morning. And the phones won't stop ringing ...I'm...I'm about to have a nervous breakdown to be honest with you."

"Ma'am, I'm from the government, and I'm here to help." He smiled and waited for her to laugh. But the look she gave...not amused. "Sorry, bad joke. But I think you'll have to start at the beginning. Are any of these cases connected to the report from Dr. Berg? Where is Dr. Berg?"

"No one's heard from him in twenty-four hours. I've called and texted his cell phone and tried his house a number a few times. In fact, since I'm up to my eyeballs in sick animals, perhaps you can drive over and check on him? Here, I'll write down the address."

"Might as well. I'm not going back to Austin until I get some answers."

* * *

Three hours later, Inspector Parks was back at Marla Berry's office.

"I'm sorry, Dr. Berry. We have to shut down your practice. I need a list of all the dogs and the owners you've come into contact with over the last forty-eight hours. I also need your help to call all the owners and insist they isolate their dogs from people and other pets for the next ten days. They need to report any additional deaths directly to this number." He handed her a flyer. "I'll be back tomorrow with a larger team."

Parks looked up at the ceiling and took a deep breath. "I think you should sit down for this next part."

Sitting, she said, "You're scaring me. What could be worse than shutting down my practice and town full of sick dogs?"

"I came directly from Dr. Berg's house. I was there a long time. The police were interviewing me and his neighbors for the last two hours. They didn't know if he had kin in the area."

Marla stared at him; her head tilted.

"Dr. Berg is dead."

Marla clasped her hand to her mouth. "What? When? How?"

Parks grimaced. "His neighbors said he'd been in perfect health until now. Perhaps I'm being paranoid or I've watched the movie 'Outbreak' too many times, but if this dog virus is connected to his death, we have a real problem on our hands. Out of an abundance of caution, you and your staff should call your family doctors and quarantine yourselves as well."

Chapter 13

Day 78

Explaining the situation to her clients yesterday did not go well. Marla didn't have enough antibiotics in stock for every dog, but she split up what she had as equitably as possible.

Still, the pet owners yelled at her. Only when two cop cars arrived, the angry holdouts took their dogs and left, carrying their crumpled quarantine instructions.

She decided to conduct her own quarantine at her office.

Why put her family at risk?

She affixed paper signs to the front door, 'Closed for Quarantine' with the APHIS hotline.

Last night she called pet owners who may have been exposed. They were not pleasant calls. She had to hang up on some of them. Not very professional; but, in the interest of time, necessary.

Now, in the clear light of a crisp March morning, her head ached. Maybe from stress. Maybe from sleeping on the uncomfortable bench in the reception area.

She padded barefoot into one of her examination rooms and got her stethoscope. Checking her own lungs, she detected no wheezing or congestion.

At least for now.

Nobody knew what the precise incubation period was. She took her temperature—normal. She emailed Parks with her stats.

Her phone rang. Her husband greeted her with a video call. Their daughter, ten, bounced up and down in the background and said "I love you, Mommy!" but then promptly began begging dad for a cupcake for breakfast.

Marla assured her husband she was ok. "Just a few more days," she said with a half-smile.

But how many things would go wrong while she was away? Did he know what to pack in their daughter's lunch box and to give her milk money?

She wanted to rattle off a million instructions, but then her husband called, "The bus is here," and the call was over.

She took out a clean sheet of paper and began brainstorming all the daily details she managed. A few minutes later, there was a knock at the door.

Please, not another upset dog owner.

She pulled back a sliver of the heavy curtain from the picture window. *No, it was much worse.* A news van pulled up in front.

Not heeding the quarantine warning, a reporter and a camera operator walked up to the door.

What did they want?

What was she allowed to tell people?

She called Inspector Parks again and got voice mail.

Shit.

The knocking got louder. She paced the waiting room. *Should I talk to them?*

After prolonged knocking, it was clear they weren't going away. She scribbled her phone number on a piece of paper in bold print and held it up to the window. There was no way she was going to open the door.

She watched as the reporter, a young man with thick brown hair and a crooked nose, pulled out his phone.

In rapid-fire speech, the reporter said, "Dr. Berry, my name is Harry Zinke. I'm a reporter from Channel Four news. We're doing a piece on the quarantine. Would you be willing to do an on-camera interview? I'm under a deadline."

"Fine. It would probably be helpful to the public—to inform them about the virus. But I'm not going outside."

"Um, we can do it through the phone and we can take video of you through the window."

"Look, it may turn out to be nothing but a normal flu, but if it isn't, more people should know about it. Let me get myself together and brush my hair. I'll be back in two minutes."

She put on a clean lab coat and some socks and pulled her unwashed hair into a bun. She didn't have any makeup or toiletries at the office. She found some dog toothpaste and cleaned her teeth. It tasted like chicken, but better than nothing. When she returned to the window, the camera operator had already set up his equipment and was doing tests with the reporter's cell phone to optimize the audio quality.

Harry gargled with some water from a bottle and spat it on the ground. He said to the camera man, "You know, I can't recall a time I interviewed someone like this. But this is ratings gold."

She stared at the reporter through the window. *He doesn't realize I can hear every word...*

Harry waved at her and called.

"Ma'am, you ready?"

"Sure, go ahead."

Turning to the camera, the reporter began, "This is Harry Zinke for Channel Four News. I'm outside the San Antonio office of veterinarian Dr. Marla Berry. Dr. Berry is under self-imposed quarantine due to a potential dog virus, which is believed to have jumped to humans. Dr. Berry, can you tell us the events leading up to this?"

"Thanks Harry, I..."

"Dr. Berry, could you look at the camera instead of me? Just turn your body a little to your left...good, that's it. Start from the beginning and we'll splice it later."

Taking a deep breath and looking directly at the camera through the window pane, she continued, "Thanks Harry, well, it all started yesterday morning. I was asked by another local veterinarian, Dr. Berg, to take on his caseload. I was glad to help."

"Why was that?"

"Dr. Berg suddenly became very ill. I thought he had a normal flu. I mean, it *is* March. Getting the flu this time of year is pretty routine. Anyway, I later discovered, rather, APHIS discovered...."

"Can you tell us who or what APHIS stands for?"

"APHIS is the Animal and Plant Health Information Service. They're a division of the Department of Agriculture." She took a deep breath, "APHIS discovered Dr. Berg had died in his home yesterday. It appears Dr. Berg performed necropsies of two dogs that had died from a mysterious new virus. That seemed very suspicious. But at the same time, my office received dozens of calls from pet owners. Yesterday I had a record number of dog appointments. About twenty times more than a typical day. A few dogs died."

"Hold on, so you are telling us you may have the same deadly virus that killed Dr. Berg and all these other dogs?"

"I feel fine. I don't have any symptoms. After APHIS advised us—me and my staff, and the dog owners I saw yesterday—to quarantine ourselves, it was the right thing to do. As they say, out of an abundance of caution."

"Dr. Berry, can you describe the symptoms you're seeing in the dogs?"

"I don't know if all the sick dogs have the same illness. I don't even know if what they have is actually transmissible to humans. You have to understand, we're still in the early stages of the investigation. But the sick dogs, they had moderate to high temperatures, some were dehydrated. In the advanced cases, the dogs had trouble breathing. The earliest signs are congestion, runny noses and fatigue."

"Dr. Berry, exactly how many infected dogs did you, and your staff, treat yesterday before the government shut down your office?"

"I don't have an exact count, but on the order of about seventy."

Turning to the camera, Harry said, "You heard it here first, San Antonio. There are several dozen dogs infected with a deadly virus in our very city…one that can kill humans."

"Wait, I said I'm not sure if it's transmiss…"

"This is Harry Zinke. Channel Four Evening News. Back to you at the news desk." He paused a four count and said, "OK, we're out."

"Hold on, you totally mis-characterized what I said!"

Harry ended the call. He and the cameraman gathered the equipment and packed it into the van.

I wanted to warn people, not completely terrify them!

She called Inspector Parks again.

It went directly to voice mail.

What should she say?

Sorry?

The damage was done.

She didn't leave a message.

* * *

On a one-way flight from Hong Kong, the assassin Ju-long sat comfortably in First Class, sipping his champagne and eating a chocolate-covered strawberry. He studied the picture of Dr. Yi to commit it to memory. Tracking her would be difficult. At first, he assumed his mission was to bring her back alive—that somehow, she might know the cure for the virus. But Minister Szu Qiang was adamant—he wanted her dead.

The spy, Ren, told them Nian was on her way to Washington DC. Ju-long doubted she was still there.

He had two missions. One to kill Nian, the other to disable America's infectious disease labs. He was given a list of potential locations. At the top of his list was Plum Island.

Yes, they do some freaky things there. Even weaponized ticks?

It was the most likely place for the Americans to have developed the dog virus.

Even if Nian wasn't there, Qiang was adamant that Plum Island must be destroyed.

Ju-long understood why he was chosen for this mission. He had a special set of skills.

And he thoroughly enjoyed watching things go 'boom'.

* * *

Petty Officer Marty loaded his duffel bag in his jeep. The guys were already in Vegas, partying without him, while he helped the morgue move and bag the bodies from the Chinese submarine.

He checked his phone. The boys sent him pictures of the penthouse suite and a coffee table filled with empty bottles. They sent selfies with hot chicks. Usually he would fly out, but it was cheaper to drive the five-hours. Plus, he could bring additional food to save money.

After their short break in Vegas, they would be deployed for months at sea. As bachelors, they saved for weeks for this one big blowout excursion. He wasn't much of a gambler, but he enjoyed walking the strip at night, sipping on a tall plastic cup of hooch. The last time they were in Vegas, he met a really nice girl. He still had her number. *Will she remember me?*

After driving two hours, his phone rang. It was Jones.

"Hey buddy!" Marty said. "What's the good word! Hey, leave some of that Jack for me! I'll be there soon!"

"Dude," Jones said, "you may want to turn around."

"What? Did you find some honeys?" Marty grinned. "Trying to keep them for yourself? Afraid of a little competition?"

"No, man. I'm serious. Derrick got real sick. We're at the hospital now."

"Man, that guy could never hold his liquor!"

"Yeah, he was puking all over, but this time it was all bloody. Totally gross. We tried to clean it up before the maid showed up."

Marty laughed. "Like that time, you moved the couch over the spot Melendez crapped himself? Damn, tell me you got Derrick on video this time, bro!"

"Hey, it's not funny, man. I mean, at first, we were all cracking up. But then he passed out. Unresponsive. Cameron began CPR. I called 911."

"Oh, damn! Is he ok? What's happening now?" Marty asked.

"We're trying to reach Derrick's mom in Utah. The hospital asked us to locate his next of kin."

"Whoa."

"The doctor said his pulse is dangerously low. They put him on a ventilator."

"From alcohol poisoning?"

Jones said, "The doctor doesn't know the cause. They put him on steroids. Doing a bunch of tests. Anyway, we're just waiting at the hospital until his mom arrives."

"Does the CO know?"

"Not yet. We figured they would pump his stomach and would go home. If he gets better fast, we don't want to rat him out. Plus, the CO would berate us for weeks; and it would go on Derrick's permanent record."

A highway exit sign came into view. Marty pulled off the interstate and parked at a convenience store.

"Look man," Marty said, "I'll be there in two hours. I want to help. Maybe let the other guys get some rest. We can take turns at the hospital."

"Ok, bro. I just wanted to give you the option to head back. No reason to ruin everyone's vacation. Text me when you get in."

"Roger that."

Marty did a U-turn to get back on the highway. A shiver went up his spine. He turned up the heat. The back of his throat felt dry. He coughed.

I better not be getting a cold.

Visions of the dead Chinese sailors crossed his mind. The doctors made everyone wear gloves and surgical masks before handling the bodies.

It was Derrick who opened the hatch.

Was Derrick infected like the Chinese?

The base infirmary made sure everyone got their flu shots after the sub arrived.

Marty scrolled through his phone contacts and called the CO's office. On the third ring, he reconsidered and ended the call.

Nah, Derrick just drank too much again. He was never a strong drinker.

A road sign indicated 120 miles to Las Vegas. He made a bargain with himself. If Derrick wasn't breathing on his own when he got there, he'd call the CO.

And if the guys give me crap about it...

They can all fuck off.

Chapter 14

Day 79

Ally couldn't sleep. It was four in the morning. She started her day, checking her Google news alerts on her laptop at the hotel. Her alerts included terms like 'dog virus', 'dog illness', and 'canine flu'. Most mornings, the results turned up stories of heroic family pets that stayed by the bedside of a sick child, or warnings of isolated cases of rabies. So far, more of the same.

The tenth story made her heart pound. In Texas, an APHIS alert went out describing a very contagious dog virus. It went on to say investigators were seeing a strong correlation with human illness and even the death of a veterinarian.

Could it be?

Ally jumped out of bed and phoned Nancy. It was now four thirty. She got voice mail and left a message.

"Nancy. You need to check the APHIS database. Get the phone number of the San Antonio branch. I think…I'm not a hundred percent sure, but the virus has arrived in Texas. Shit. I'm heading to the office. Call me!"

Ally didn't bother to shower. *My coworkers will just have to deal with it.*

At the office, she applied to get her own APHIS database login account. The automatic reply email said it would take two to three working days for her account to be activated. Ally found a phone number for APHIS. Both the Washington DC and San Antonio offices played automated messages announcing their business hours.

It was five o'clock now.

Screw it. She called Renée's cell phone.

On the third ring, Renée answered, "Hello?" A loud yawn followed.

"Oh, shoot, I'm sorry. I woke you, didn't I? But I didn't know who else could help me. I wouldn't have called unless it was urgent. And it really is. I mean, ok, sorry, I'll just spit it out."

"Good morning to you, too. Yes, Allison, what is it?"

"The dog flu is in Texas. I mean the Chinese flu. Whatever. Ah. You know what I mean. At least, I'm pretty sure it is. There was a news story overnight. I was trying to get more information about it, but I don't have an APHIS account and I tried calling their main numbers but no one's answering."

Ally looked at her watch again. "Oh shit, yeah, it's only four am in San Antonio…they're on Central Time, right? I always get mixed up about time-zones. Do you have any contacts there I can call?"

After a long pause, Renée said, "I'm glad you called. Really. I'll go through my contacts. But let me make the calls. I'll have their people get in touch with both you and Nancy directly. In the meantime, send me whatever news you have on this. I'd like to read it for myself."

"Thanks, Renée. Again, I'm sorry I woke you. I'm hitting send on the story right now to your email."

"Be prepared to come brief me at nine with a plan. I'll clear my calendar to fit you in."

"Absolutely. Thanks!"

* * *

Ju-Long kept the motor at low speed as he approached the island. Despite the cloudy night sky, the lighthouse illuminated his path. He hadn't anticipated the bright beacon.

Brighter than I expected.

He pulled the small aluminum fishing boat up onto the rocky shore line. With deliberation, he hiked toward the three tall above-ground fuel tanks. There was a security road and a chain link fence in his path. A white government utility truck was parked nearby. But he didn't see any people.

He took off the poncho, revealing his gray coveralls with a red embroidered name tag, "John". He grabbed his backpack and other weapons, and set the boat adrift. Leaving the boat on the shore was too risky. He would need to find another way off the island after his mission.

Ju-Long climbed the fence which surprisingly did not have any barbed wire. He placed the bomb at the base of the center fuel tank and set the timer for one-hour.

Ju-long walked through the dark swampy woods towards the main dock area. He placed his collapsible semi-automatic rifle in a plastic, wheeled trash can he found behind the main office building.

With his coveralls and the trash can, he looked like an inconsequential janitor. He hunched his shoulders and slowed to a more leisurely pace. He placed more explosives near a few of the administrative buildings.

About two hundred feet away from the dock stood a large abandoned building. Vines and saplings were taking over the half-collapsed structure and parts of the lower roof were gone.

The Americans made this far too easy.

He entered the building and ascended the moldy stairs to the shaky second floor roof. The roof of the decrepit building provided an excellent vantage point. There was a straight line-of-sight to the docks where employees arrived and departed the island. The sun was coming up. He looked through the scope of his rifle.

The explosives would detonate in half an hour. During the panic to evacuate, he could pick off employees with ease.

Like fish in a barrel, he grinned.

* * *

After her meeting with Director Carson, Ally went back to the hotel, showered quickly and took the first flight from Atlanta to San Antonio that afternoon. It was a relatively short flight, a little over two hours nonstop. She was supposed to stop at the APHIS office first to meet their director. But she lied about her arrival time. She wanted to visit Ms. Walker first—her ranch might be ground zero for the current outbreak.

Arriving at the ranch, there were dozens of buildings and sheds, all in the same barn wood siding, scattered across the flat, sparsely-vegetated ranch. It looked rustic and homey, like out of a western movie. On top of the barn, the largest building, there was a beautiful green patinaed copper weathervane of a greyhound—in a running pose.

She left her lab coat and mask in the back seat. Grabbing her medical bag, she knocked on the craftsman style door of the residence.

A petite brunette, with pink skin, light freckles on her cheeks, a short haircut and green eyes, looking to be in her mid-forties to early fifties, answered the door, wearing a gray t-shirt and faded brown canvas pants.

"Hello, my name is Dr. Reynerson. I'm with the CDC. Are you Ms. Jolyssa Walker?" Ally asked.

"Yes, but just call me Jolie. Everyone does. I'm assuming you're here because of Dr. Berg?" Jolie said.

"Yes. I'm wondering if I could ask a few questions. We have a team working to develop a vaccine for a certain virus. There's good reason to believe Dr. Berg contracted this new virus."

A blur of fur brushed up against the back of her legs. She took a step sideways. A large collie with beautiful auburn and white fur licked her hand. The dog had a red, white and blue bandana around his neck.

"Come in. Don't mind Ranger. He gets excited to see people, but he is harmless. Just wants to sniff y'all, ya see."

"Hey, Ranger," she said, dropping to rub his chest fur. "Beautiful dog!"

"Yep, he's a keeper. Can I get you a cup of coffee, doc?"

"Yes, thanks, black is fine. And please call me Ally. Do you mind if I wash my hands first?"

"Sure thing. You can wash up here at the kitchen sink. So, tell me about this virus you're studying," Jolie said.

"Well, it's kind of a long story. But there's an outbreak in China that's linked to dogs. The Chinese government has been trying to hide it from the rest of the world. A nationwide news blackout. Anyway, the CDC managed to get some blood samples from sick individuals and we're trying to learn more about it. When I saw the APHIS report this morning, I came right away."

Ally rinsed and dried her hands. She sat down at a small wooden table across from Jolie.

"Yeah, poor Dr. Berg," Jolie said. "He was a great vet. He worked with my dogs for over twenty years. I don't know if I believe what the news is saying—about him dying from contact with my dead dogs. Doesn't seem possible. If there was a deadly dog virus, I would the first one dead, right? I mean, I was with those dogs every day for the last two months. Even Ranger here." She patted Ranger's neck as he sat at attention by her side, tongue out and panting. "He hasn't been sick. A couple other dogs got colds last week, yeah, but they rebounded fine."

"I hear what you're saying. I've been studying pathogens for the last three decades. Viruses are interesting. Some people can become very sick, or even die, while other people don't. There can be a lot of factors."

"Well, you tell me what I can do. I'm under a deadline to meet my government contracts. But if the Feds think my dogs are sick, I could lose hundreds of thousands of dollars. I need to find out—just like you—what's going on."

Ally paused then shook her head. "What…what government contracts?"

"My business. This is the largest training facility in the south for military and police dogs. They rated us number one in Canine Training magazine last year! For the past three months I've been importing dogs from all over Europe to meet the quota. They stay with me for about sixty to ninety days while I make sure they pass health requirements. My interns and I train the dogs in most of the basics. My second delivery to the Army is due next month. So, I'm happy to help or do whatever to speed this up."

"Second? Wait, so you've been importing dogs from Europe and you've already delivered some to the U.S. military?"

"Yep. And Border Control. Lucrative contracts, too. They will keep my ranch going for the next couple years."

Ally took out her phone and opened her medical kit. "Jolie, I think we have a major problem. First, I'd like to take your temperature—just to be sure. If it's normal, as I suspect it will be, I need you to come with me to the APHIS office right now. I also need you to bring all the files on the dogs you've delivered to the Army so far."

* * *

Ally took a cab to her hotel in San Antonio. The meeting with Mr. Parks went as well as could be expected. They sent out notices to all their offices nationwide and sent a directive to Homeland Security to block all new dog imports into the country. They set up a phone bank to call every veterinarian, kennel and pet adoption agency within a hundred-mile radius. They ordered all dogs quarantined.

Next, the contacted local mayors to have the public dog runs closed and locked for the next two weeks. Jolie talked to the Army's Contracting Officer to alert them about the dogs she delivered previously.

Ally asked Inspector Parks if they had the capability of sending Wireless Emergency Alerts. APHIS told her they didn't consider mobile alerts necessary at this time. Alerts were for natural disasters like hurricanes, tornados and flooding—not for illnesses—they explained. Ally hated their short-sightedness.

After she checked in, she called Jason. He would understand. She needed to know she wasn't insane.

"Hey, Jason, how are things at CDC? Are you getting bored babysitting a bunch of nerdy scientists?"

"Hey, Ally. Things are fine here. They said you went to San Antonio. Did you really call Dr. Carson at four o'clock? I thought you liked working here!"

"Funny. Look, things are really bad here. Or, at least they will be soon. I have an awful feeling about all of this. APHIS is doing a good job sending out warnings and notices, but not going as far as I'd like. I'm waiting around to get some cell cultures from the dead dogs. They say it might take them another day or so. So, I'm stuck here for now. Oh, get this. The owner of the first dead dogs just came back from a road trip to New York City. She was at a dog show of all places!"

"What? Do you think she spread the virus in New York?"

"Could be. Interestingly, she hasn't been sick at all. Does that remind you of anyone?" Ally said.

"Let me guess, she's between fifty and sixty years old. Like Darya and Nian."

"Bingo! So weird, right? And the veterinarian who died was also in his fifties but a man. Maybe the virus is more gender specific than age specific. Come to think of it, I'll need the coroner to send us samples from Doctor Berg. They are doing some of the routine tests, but CDC can do more comprehensive tests."

"Hey, if it isn't Miss Marple, virus detective! Be safe and let me know if I can do anything."

"Will do. I'll be leaving tomorrow. If you see Nancy, tell her I'll be driving back instead of flying. There is no way I'm bringing samples of deadly pathogens on a commercial airplane. I'll send her an email tonight with my notes."

"Actually, Nancy said something about the Director getting a military helicopter to bring you and the samples back. Carson announced she is getting incredible support from the White House and the military on this. But wait, aren't you scared of getting the virus yourself? If there are potentially dozens of dogs and humans exposed, you could get it also."

"You have a point. If I see anyone coughing up blood, I'll head in the other direction! But seriously, I think I'll be ok. I know what to look for and I have a respirator with me. From what Ms. Walker told me, I suspect the virus is airborne. But from Nian's accounts, people get sick almost immediately."

"Well, you better not come home and infect the rest of us. Typhoid Ally! I'm going to tell Nancy to quarantine you when you get back."

"If I come down with any symptoms, you'll be the first to know. I promise."

"You know I'm just kidding. Come back soon. I found a great gelato place down the street. It will change your life."

Ally laughed. She always had a weakness for good gelato. "Ok, looking forward to it."

"Great!"

Ally hung up and initiated a video call to Theo. It was baby Charlotte's first birthday tomorrow. She hated missing it. Working for the EIS, she missed lots of family birthdays and holidays while Theo was young. She could never make up for that time.

"I'm sorry I can't be there," she told Theo.

"It's ok, mom. Just come back home when you can," Theo said.

Little Charlotte grabbed at the phone, her nose and one blurry eye filling the screen. *Oh, she is getting so big now*, she thought. "Hey Lottie! What are you doing? Did you have a nice day?"

Charlotte began chewing on the edge of the phone and made silly noises. Ally made silly faces back at her.

Theo came back on and said, "It's almost her bedtime." He put Charlotte back up to the camera and said, "Boo boo, blow kisses to grandma! Say bye-bye!"

Charlotte blew kisses and Ally reciprocated.

After the call, she hung her head. She wanted to ask Theo if Charlotte was up to date on her vaccinations. But she was afraid of the answer. They had argued about it months ago. The irony of the situation wasn't funny. No amount of reason or science would convince them. Yet still, if they saw the situation in San Antonio, they might think differently.

Her sister Gwen calmed her down several times during the past few months, saying, "They will have to vaccinate her before she begins daycare or school. I've seen lots of parents like this. Just give them time."

Ally tried to be patient. She just wasn't sure what time would bring.

Should I kidnap my own granddaughter and vaccinate her?

She wouldn't really do that, but it was tempting. She knew where to get the vaccines. Perhaps she was overreacting again.

Crazy Grandma Ally.

She placed a call to Gwen and got voicemail.

After the beep, she said, "Hey, sis! I'm on the ledge again. Tell me again why I shouldn't kidnap Charlotte! Call me!"

* * *

Jason watched Nian like a hawk. Several questions kept him up at night. What if Nian had been working with Darya in Russia? Did she know about the origin of the virus? Did Darya say anything to Nian in China about where the virus came from?

He wasn't sure where to look at CDC. It wasn't as if he would stumble upon a folder that said "Secret Russian Doomsday Virus."

He didn't know if he could trust Renée. Ally trusted her, but Jason understood that people weren't always what they seemed. People in power usually got there from political maneuvering and sometimes subterfuge, rather than experience and technical knowledge. He couldn't trust anyone in management—they were all suspects in his book.

Nian was a quiet person. She exchanged pleasantries with her colleagues but never talked about herself. They had arrived at the CDC four days ago. He snooped through her limited belongings at her hotel room. She was reading a worn copy of an old Harry Potter novel she acquired at the local used book store. There were forms for applying for U.S. citizenship on her desk half filled out. She had a smart phone but there weren't any contacts stored in it except for Ally, Nancy and himself.

She also had a personal tablet but there were only games like FreeCell and solitaire on it, and she had written poems in Chinese.

Thank goodness for Google Translate. The poems were about sunrises, the mountains near her childhood home, and her regret that she never had a family of her own—very sweet and sentimental topics.

Her computer browsing history was also very benign. There were internet sites for English slang words, restaurant reviews in Atlanta, a Tibetan news site, weather forecasts, and various forums discussing local biking and hiking trails in the area. Rummaging through her waste baskets, he found tea bags and energy bar wrappers.

She took long walks in the early morning hours. He followed her a few times, but she always took the same path, making a circle around the CDC on nearby residential streets. She never stopped to talk to anyone and wasn't distracted by anything around her.

Following Nian didn't reveal any clues. His attempts to get information from the other CDC staff were equally fruitless.

Someone had to know something!

He decided to confront Nian and some other staff. In his NSA training, he knew that if you rattle someone hard enough, or fool them with a bluff, they could get sloppy.

He made individual appointments to interview everyone at her lab. When it was Nian's turn, he simply asked, "Nian, how long did you know Darya?"

"Jason, you know this. I met her only briefly after Dr. Wu brought her to the farm."

"You can drop the act. We found the phone records. I totally understand. General Roadfuss left you in a precarious position. I can help you but you have to help me. There are people I still trust in the government. They can give you a new identity and a safe place to relocate."

"What are you talking about?" Nian said. "All I've done is help, at great risk to my own safety. I was scared all the time. Then your General holds me hostage. Now I am free. Soon I'll be a citizen. I am very grateful to you and Ally. Why are you talking to me like this?"

"Nian," Jason stood up and glared at her. "I am your friend. So is Ally. A powerful man was behind the attack in Russia. I'm scared, too. Tell me where to look. That's all. No one will ever know you said anything. I'll make sure of it."

"Jason, I don't know what you mean. If I knew where the virus originated and where to find a cure, I would tell the team. If Darya knew these things, I think she would have told Dr. Wu. I have read the interview notes and there is no indication she understood what she was dealing with."

"I don't believe you. I think you are trying to save your own skin. You've been through a lot. I have sympathy. I really do. Just know, if I find out you had the ability to help us, and you chose not to, I will make it my personal mission to end you myself."

* * *

Ruth received regular updates from Director Carson, but she needed to know what was happening behind the scenes. She called Jason.

"Hi Jason, how are things at CDC?" Ruth asked.

"Hold on, let me walk outside." After a few seconds, Jason said, "Ok, we are good now."

"So, who are the good guys and who are the bad guys?"

"It's still early, but I think Carson is a good guy. She's genuinely helpful. A life-long, public servant that cares about people. Not in Merriwether's pocket. Actually, so far, they are all good guys. I'm not seeing anyone trying to interfere. But I need to get closer to several researchers to see if they know about the origin of the Russian outbreak."

"As we discussed, Ortega is monitoring all the phone lines. He got the FISA warrant yesterday. If anyone there calls Roadfuss or Defoe, they will flag it. If Nian makes any international calls, we'll know about it. Ortega and I both appreciate you being our eyes and ears down there."

"I want to nail the assholes as much as you both do."

"How is Ally? I heard she went to San Antonio. Is there really an outbreak there?"

"Yeah. But Ally is helping them with the response. Oh. That reminds me. You might find this interesting. Older women seem to be immune to the virus."

"Really? In all my years of medicine, I never heard of such a thing."

"Well, all I can tell you is, so far, all the survivors are women over fifty."

"Hmm. Can you imagine what would happen if women ran the world? That would be something. A dream come true! Maybe I can win the next election if there were higher numbers of older women voters!"

Jason laughed, "Auntie, you are going to win anyway. Merriwether is a joke. He won't even know what hit him. I can't wait to see the first debate. You'll annihilate him!"

"Thanks, kiddo. I've been stockpiling material for months. I'm trying to resist going after his character. That would be too easy. I want people to vote *for something*, not just against that twat."

"Ha, knowing you, you probably have your whole administration planned—with dozens of executive orders ready to sign!"

"I have a few ideas…some would say they are somewhat radical. But I need to be centrist for now."

"Well, if this virus gets any worse, we will all be begging for universal health care."

"One of my top priorities. Anything else to report?"

"No, otherwise it's quiet here. Hey, if you make some chocolate chip cookies, could you send me a care package?"

"Of course. I miss you! Call me tomorrow, ok?"

"Yep. Miss you, too."

"Got to run, take care now!" Ruth hung up and went over to her desk.

The latest polling numbers looked very good. But she didn't want to be complacent. Her social media team was ramping up, and she needed to brush up on all the latest platforms—particularly streaming video. She needed to become more comfortable in front of cameras.

Her team was setting up portable lights in the other room for some test runs. *Everyone needs to be a movie star these days,* she sighed. *I'm too old for this nonsense.*

"Ma'am, are you ready for makeup?" Sally asked.

"Sure, bring her in." It was one thing to dress smartly but another to wear lots of goop on your face. But it made her look younger, perhaps more relatable to millennials, her advisors said. She hated playing this game.

I'm old. Let me be old.

A world run by women…the notion stuck in her head. *Ha! The first thing I would do is outlaw eyeliner and false eyelashes!* The thought made her smile.

If women were in charge, life would be so much more practical.

* * *

In Brazil, President Merriwether prepared for the G20 meeting to begin. He put on his favorite blue suit and red tie, and searched the web on his phone to check the leaderboard of the Masters Tournament. He missed the first day of the Masters, but hoped to go to Augusta to watch Day Four in person.

Secretary of State Johnson knocked on his hotel door. "Ready, sir?"

"Do I really have to sit down with Russia and China today?"

"Yes," Johnson said. "Did you read the briefing package last night? There is the matter of the Chinese submarine and how to send back the dead crew for appropriate burial. We also need their cooperation on the Climate Change treaty. Are you sure you don't want me in the room?"

"Yeah, yeah. I got this. Don't worry. I'm a fantastic negotiator," Merriwether said.

"Even to take notes?" Johnson asked.

"We don't need notes. Gets too formal that way. Hampers my style."

Johnson walked him downstairs to the ballroom. "I'll see you afterwards."

Merriwether, Szu Chen and Petrov met inside the ornate room, with chevron patterned wood floors, tall ceilings with crystal chandeliers, and oversized, gold-framed oil paintings.

"President Szu, President Petrov, how nice to meet with you again," Merriwether exclaimed, breaking into a broad smile and outstretched arms. The men shook hands briefly.

Szu remained stone-faced.

"How nice to see you again, Mr. President," Petrov said, smiling with his mouth, but with dead eyes.

The men took seats around a marble table in the center of the room.

Merriwether turned to Szu Chen. "Well, since we are alone, I'm inclined to tell you, President Szu, we recovered something that belongs to you."

"What could you possibly have that would interest me?" Szu asked, the corners of his mouth turned down.

"A sub. Found it drifting in the Pacific. The crew appeared Chinese. Dead inside, like sardines. I heard the smell was worse than a refrigerator full of rotten meat…"

"Oh, it could not possibly be one of our submarines," Szu Chen said, his voice rising in pitch. "Are you insinuating I would not know if my government lost a submarine? First you send a plague to my country with your bioweapons, and then you sit there insulting me. You have interfered with the wrong country. I should blow your United States into tiny pieces. Unless you have an antidote for the poison you sent to us. Vlad, can you believe this buffoon? Does he think we are stupid?"

"I'm sure our American President did not mean any harm," Petrov said. "Perhaps his military did not develop the virus. We cannot be sure of that. Sometimes these things are simply, how you say, unfortunate mutations of nature. President Merriwether, don't you agree?"

"Uh, yes," Merriwether said. "A virus could come from anywhere. You know, I'm not a scientist, but I hear of bugs mutating all the time. Remember the swine flu? Animals are real disgusting. And then some sick dude has sex with a monkey and we have Ebola on our hands. Maybe the same thing happened in China? Ya know, I had a buddy in college. He was a crazy son of a bitch! One time, he got so drunk after the big football game, he took a dare to go make whoopee with the other team's mascot. I think it was a goat? A miniature donkey? Anyway, it was hilarious…you should have been there."

"What!" Szu got up from his chair and narrowed his eyes towards Merriwether. "How dare you imply Chinese people are monkey fuckers or pig fuckers. Or whatever you are saying. I will not tolerate being talked to this way! You are a stupid, stupid man. You have no honor." Szu's face reddened with anger. "I hope this plague finds you and you die with great pain and suffering."

Szu turned to Petrov. "We are finished here. Good day, President Petrov."

Once Szu exited, Petrov said, "My American friend. Now you have done it. I tried to talk sense to him…smooth over his anger. I should have known I cannot save you from your own ignorance and incompetence."

He watched Petrov get up from the table, but then circle around. Dan's muscled tensed as he remained seated, with Petrov's icy presence over his shoulder.

Vlad whispered in his ear, "I know what you did. You had better find a cure for your mistake or I will send my own nuclear weapons. And trust me—mine will not fail. You have two weeks."

Chapter 15

Day 80

Ally woke up early at the hotel in San Antonio and reached for her laptop. A slew of emails loaded on her screen—some from individuals and others were automated news alerts.

An email from a Petty Officer Raymond from the Naval Medical Research Unit told her he would pick her up at the APHIS office at five that afternoon. He would transport her to Kelly Airfield on the Joint Base. From there, she would travel by helicopter back to the CDC.

Several news articles caught her interest. The first was about a deceased dog, but not just any dog—a famous one. The show dog, Mitzy Lucy Carmichael, had recently won Best in Show at the Westminster Kennel Club. The Pomeranian died suddenly while on a press tour event in New Jersey.

Whoa. Wasn't Ranger just at Westminster? Wasn't the agility competition a subset of the larger dog show?

She wondered if she was concocting viral death connections where there were none. S*till, better safe than sorry.* She emailed Jolie to ask. She also texted Jason and asked him to make some calls to the Kennel Club and Mitzy's owner. He needed something useful to do.

The next news alert was a story about a flu outbreak at a Naval base in San Diego. Thirty percent of the sailors were sick. Missions were being postponed as a result. *This could be completely unrelated*, she thought. But thirty percent was high. She forwarded this to another member of Nancy's team.

The next alert was a blurb about a measles outbreak in New Jersey. But it was centered on a tight-knit religious community. *Probably a bunch of anti-vax'ers who are learning the hard way.* She skipped through the remaining headlines.

The last story was about a hunter near Severomorsk, Russia who died after he had finished taxidermy on a gray wolf. The hunter was found to have unusual lesions in his lungs. A local doctor feared he had contracted an ancient version of frozen Anthrax that sprang to life from global warming.

She remembered a similar story. A boy died from Anthrax last year from contact with defrosted Anthrax. But the key word which triggered the alert was the town of Severomorsk. *That is very close to where the Russian Army died!*

This was all too much. Her head throbbed.

Wolves and dogs carrying a deadly disease. People dying suddenly all over the place. Potentially ancient diseases coming back to kill humanity. Where does one even begin? A person could go crazy thinking about all this stuff.

Ally headed to the bathroom and began brushing her teeth. She looked at her face in the mirror. She put her toothbrush down and moved the hair away from her face. The bags under her eyes looked darker than usual. If Jim were here, he would tell her to get more sleep and stop worrying. Though, in the past, she never followed his advice.

Maya! I need Maya.

She looked at her watch. She learned her lesson about checking time zones. It was seven in the morning on the East Coast. She placed the call.

"Chica! How are things in Atlanta?"

"Hey, Maya, I'm in San Antonio right now. How's Gretchen?"

"Gretchen is loud! I think she misses you. She yowled several times last night. I thought maybe she was sick. But then I would check on her and she just looked at me with a confused expression. Weird cat. So—when can I unload her? Are you coming back soon?"

"Um, that's why I'm calling. The Chinese dog virus is here in Texas! Maybe even New York and California. I really need your help."

Maya exhaled with a grunt. "Ok. What kind of help?"

"Come to Atlanta. Join our team. Please? You have tons of contacts in Eastern Europe. The infected dogs are coming from that area. I think this thing is going to explode. I feel it with every fiber."

"Chica, you know I love you, but some of your hunches…"

"You know I was right about the Congo…and New Delhi. Honestly, I think this is going to be worse. Just look at China! This virus has a basic reproduction number higher than measles. Maybe triple! Some of the millennials at the CDC don't get it. But you've been there. And look, Renée said we have a good budget. We can hire people."

Maya groaned. "I've been hearing stories, too. If half are true, you might be right. But come on. You expect me to pack up and just leave on your wild theory?"

"Don't you want to stop the senseless deaths of millions?"

"See, I knew it. You've lost your mind."

"Ha. I wish. I can send you my statistics—"

"No. Don't."

Then a long pause.

"Well?" Ally asked.

"Fuck. You aren't going to stop asking, right?"

"Am I that much of a pest?"

Maya laughed. "I think they teamed us together back in the day because no one else could deal with your three a.m. calls and hundred-hour work-weeks. Ha! Remember the time you forgot to have dinner in Cairo?"

"How was I supposed to know? I was hungry!"

"It was midnight and you walked up to a stranger on a dark street corner, asking to buy his sandwich. You almost got us killed!"

"Hey, I didn't know he was an opium dealer. And the sandwich *was* delicious! Fine, point taken, I'm an enormous pain in the ass."

"Exactly."

"But, honestly, this disease is unlike anything I've seen before. Someone with your background can really make a difference. And I need you to keep me sane. Please! Pack up Gretchen and drive down. I'll ask Renée if she can arrange a sign-on bonus. A sizable one."

"Ok, ok. Let me talk to my boss. I could use the bonus for a decent vacation. Non-profit work is rewarding, but damn, I need to get away."

"You won't regret it!"

"Famous last words. You know, a sizable government contribution to our organization would be nice too. If this gets as bad as you think, Doctors Without Borders could really make a difference."

"I'll ask Senator Cochran," Ally said. "I'm sure she could make that happen. She was a doctor, you know."

Maya sighed. "You win. But there will be rules—like sleep and regular meals. Look—I don't care if fucking flesh-eating zombies are breaking down our doors—we are having breakfast, lunch, and dinner. Got it?"

"It's a deal. I promise!" Ally looked at her watch. "I've got to go. Call me after you talk with your boss. Love you!"

"Crazy chica! Love you back."

* * *

Merriwether was relaxing under a sun shade with a mint julep watching Tiger advance the ball down the fairway.

It doesn't get much better than this.

The crowd swelled when Tiger approached and the mass followed him and cheered him on from the sidelines. The noise was deafening one minute and then quiet as a church as he prepared his next swing.

During the roar of the crowd, an attractive woman with short silver hair, wearing a white suit jacket approached. The agent cleared her.

"Miss," Merriwether said, "could you round up another one of these drinks, and maybe some pretzels for me and my boys?"

"Respectfully sir," the woman in white said, standing over him, "my name is Renée Carson. I'm the director of the CDC. Your Chief of Staff, Mr. Cunningham, told me to meet you at one o'clock."

"Oh. Oh! I'm terribly sorry, Miss Carson. The servers are all wearing white jackets. My mistake." He smiled his biggest smile, hoping to win her over.

"Doctor Carson."

"My yes, sorry," he frowned. "Doctor Carson. I'm very glad you could come out to meet me. I hope I didn't take you away from anything important."

"Mr. President," she said, crossing her arms. "I'm sure whatever you wish to talk about is also important. Is there somewhere more private we can talk?"

Scanning down the fairway, Merriwether said, "Sure. I guess Tiger is done with this hole. He's quite a golfer, wouldn't you say

Miss Carson? Um, let's head to the clubhouse. They set aside a meeting room for us."

Merriwether led the way into the clubhouse, flanked by agents Becker and Tanner. They had an advance team clear a path into the building, although Merriwether stopped along the way to sign t-shirts and programs from his fans.

Merriwether motioned for Renée to sit across from him at an oak table. Secret service took stations by the exits.

"Renée, can I call you Renée? I was never one for formalities. Anyway, I've been hearing about a virus in China and now this outbreak in Texas. Can you tell me where we stand?"

"Sir, we're building up our team to study the problem. This new virus is unlike any we've encountered before. Lethal and highly contagious. Because it acts so quickly, by the time someone knows they are infected, antiviral drugs are insufficient."

"I just came back from the G20 meeting," Merriwether said. "The Chinese President asked for our assistance and I'm inclined to help. I don't want to alarm you, but there could be some international problems if we don't find a cure or antidote for this disease soon. How long will it take your guys to make a potion or shot to stop the virus?"

"Do you mean a vaccine? Well, again, the virus is new to us. But if we use the history of other unique viruses as a gauge, then I would say it will take at least six months to develop and test a trial vaccine."

"Oh. Geez Louise. Really? Six months? You can't have it ready in, say, two weeks? A lot of people could die if it takes that long."

"Sir, six months is the quickest we've ever developed a brand-new vaccine for the annual influenza virus. But I also said trial vaccine. Only about twenty percent of developed new vaccines are proven effective. Even if we get lucky and our first attempt is effective and safe, production on a large scale takes considerable time. It takes weeks to culture large amounts of inactive virus. Each batch of antigen takes at least two weeks to cultivate, then another two weeks for quality control."

"Well, that's unacceptable," Merriwether said, his arms crossed.

She kept her voice level. "Ok, let me give you some context. Did you know it took ten years to develop, test, and obtain FDA approval for the new shingles vaccine? Even the seasonal flu vaccine—the one we all get every year—begins production six months ahead to meet demand. There are strict protocols and safeguards we need to follow.

If developing vaccines was easy, we would have cured HIV, Malaria and Ebola thirty years ago!"

"Well, let's say you develop a shot that works," Merriwether said, "work with me here. Can we send the recipe over to the Chinese and other countries and let them figure out how to produce it?"

"It isn't exactly a recipe. But we can give them a protocol to follow. They would face some of the same issues in terms of testing and production though."

"Great. Well, I want you to finish the vaccine in two weeks and send out the protocol. You know, to the W-H-whatever you call it."

"W H O? The World Health Organization? Of course, we would share it with them. But it will be impossible to develop a viable vaccine in two weeks. You have to understand, if we get the vaccine wrong, it would be reckless to give people a false sense of security." Renée's voice rose in pitch. "They would continue to spread the virus, or become infected, through contact with others, all the while thinking they were invincible!"

"Well, I'm not going to give you more time. I want you to find a cure within the next two weeks or I'll have to get a new Director. You can hire whoever you want and I'm going to double your funding." He waved his hand at her. "And forget the FDA approval nonsense."

He got up from the table and headed to the door.

"Sir?" Renée said. "I don't think you understand."

He called back over his shoulder to Renée, "I'm heading back to the viewing stand. Call me after you have a fix."

* * *

Jason was having a late dinner at the CDC cafeteria. He had all the major food groups: pizza, French fries, chocolate milk and a cookie. Half way through his fries, his phone rang. Ortega.

"What's up, boss?"

"Did you see it?" Ortega said.

"What? What's going on?"

"Plum Island."

"The animal research lab?"

"Yes. Someone blew up several of APHIS' office buildings on the island. A sniper was reported on a rooftop."

"When?"

"Yesterday morning. The FBI has been handling it. Thought it was domestic terrorism. The facility manager had a theory about a disgruntled employee. The entire facility is closing in two years. Some might lose their jobs. The union has been stirring up the workforce."

"But what? You don't believe it?"

"No." Ortega said. "There's been lots of chatter from China. We won't have results from the explosives lab for a few days, but this wasn't an amateur. The assailant disappeared into thin air. A pro."

"Anything I can do to help?" Jason asked.

"Keep an eye out. If they targeted APHIS, they could come for CDC next."

"Roger. But I have to say, things are quiet here. I'm bored to tears. At least the cafeteria has good pizza." Jason bit off another piece of his slice.

Ortega said, "Jason…can you stop chewing? I'm going to call the Atlanta Police and FBI just in case. Can you coordinate with them? I need you to be my point person."

"Sure, boss."

Then silence. Ortega had hung up. Joking around with Ortega never went well.

He looked at his phone, tracking Ally through an app. Her helicopter was expected to touch down in a few minutes. He bussed his tray and headed outside. It was dark, even with the sidewalk lights. He flipped up the collar on his jacket and hurried along the path to stay warm.

It occurred to him that Ally reminded him of his older sister, June. He had never really appreciated his sister when she was alive. They poked fun at each other, sometimes in very not nice ways. *Maybe this is why he felt an attachment to Ally?*

She had only been gone a couple of days. *Why did it seem like weeks?*

As he got to the landing zone in the empty parking lot, he scanned the dark sky for blinking lights. A shadow of a figure on a nearby roof caught his eye. Maybe a maintenance worker, given the time of the evening. Then a dim light appeared; the flicker of a lighter and then a lit cigarette.

Ah, just a smoker.

The CDC had strict rules against smoking on the property. It went against their image as an agency trying to promote health. Despite the campus' tobacco-free policy, it wasn't unusual for people to sneak the occasional cigarette on roof tops or near service entrances by the dumpsters.

He heard a familiar reverberation in the air, a Seahawk, coming from the west. He walked back to the sidewalk, outside the hazard zone. He sang a little tune to the percussion of the blades as the helicopter approached.

If she isn't contagious or being a keto killjoy, he chuckled to himself, we can go straight to the gelato shop!

A blinding light streaked by. He dropped to the ground. A loud boom resonated through his body. He tucked his head under his arms. He hadn't heard this particular noise since Afghanistan. A second boom followed a second later.

He lifted his head. A large chunk of the nearest laboratory building was simply gone. Flames and black smoke emanated from the remnant structure. He rolled to his side and watched the aircraft gain altitude and fly in the opposite direction. The rocket-propelled grenades had likely missed the helicopter by only a few feet.

He shed his jacket and sprinted toward the building where he had seen the dark figure. He drew his weapon from his waistband and entered the building. The metal door opened into a corner stairwell with unpainted concrete block walls.

The man, dressed in black body armor, stood in front of him. The terrorist raised his gun. Without hesitation, Jason shot the man in the chest but heard another shot. He collapsed to the ground. Blood was leaking from his abdomen. His cheek raw against the rough concrete floor. He couldn't move. He closed his eyes, relaxed all the muscles, and slowed his breathing. He needed to play dead.

The man kicked him lightly in the ribs. He let his body move with the blow.

A moment later, the outside door closed with a metallic clang. He placed his hand over the entry wound to apply pressure. He tried to sit up.

Then everything went black.

Chapter 16

Day 81

Pain radiated along her spine. Ally rubbed her lower back. She shifted in the chair several times, trying to sleep, until she finally admitted defeat and got up. She checked her watch—3:30 a.m.

She longed for cold water on her face.

She walked quietly past Jason's hospital bed toward the restroom. Her toe hit the rolling tray table, causing a loud clatter.

Jason said in a soft voice, "It's ok. I'm up. Where am I?"

She whispered, "You're at University Hospital. They brought you in about six hours ago. You came out of surgery a little while ago."

"How…did the other guy do?" he asked, with his eyes half-closed.

"They got him. But don't worry about that," she said, sitting beside him. She held his hand. "Can I get you anything? Some water? Another blanket?"

"I'm fine. Ok, maybe a little water. My throat hurts. But first, who was it? How did they catch him?"

"Look, you got shot. You could have died. Everything is fine now. Well, the laboratory isn't fine, but no one else was hurt. Your only job is to get rest and not worry about the terrorist."

"Ally, I know you want to be a mother hen," he said, fiddling with the button on the large remote and adjusting his bed into a more upright position. "Ow." He lowered the bed back down a few degrees. "I've been shot before. I promise to rest—just tell me what happened."

Ally sighed. "Ok, I think I should tell you; Ruth is in the waiting room. She left to make some calls, but she was here when they brought you out of surgery. She's been talking with the authorities. I'll get her."

Ally left and found Ruth near the nurse's station.

"He's awake."

"Thank Almighty Lord," Ruth said, clasping her hands together. The floor nurse and Ruth followed her into Jason's room.

The nurse looked at his monitors, swapped out his I-V bag and took his temperature while the women waited. She also took Ally's temperature. It was normal. The nurse brought over a cup of water and a straw and placed it on the table.

After the nurse left, Ruth bent over to hug Jason.

"Jason, I came right away. I'm so sorry this happened to you," Ruth said.

"You're really here? Who's running Washington?" He tried to laugh, but said, "Ow, holy hell!" He reached over and sipped some water.

"Ruth," Ally said, "Jason was asking me about the terrorist. Do you want to fill him in?"

Ruth ran her hand over his hair in a tender fashion. Ally had never seen this side of the senator before.

Ruth whispered, "Are you sure you are up to this? We can come back later."

"Please," Jason said. "I don't think I can sleep unless I know everything will be alright. Ally said they caught the guy?"

"Yes. I was on the phone with Director Ortega and local police. Based on the timeline as we know it, the Navy pilot saw the man on the roof. When the pilot saw he had a rocket launcher, he aborted the landing and flew away. He radioed Air Traffic Control and they notified the police. But he kept his eyes on the situation and he said he saw you run toward the building. Only the terrorist come out. The helicopter went into stealth mode and followed the man's movements until local police arrived. There was a shootout near a local motel. A cop was hurt, but they took out the terrorist. It all happened quickly—from what I'm told."

Jason asked, "Was it the same person? From Plum Island?"

Ruth continued in a more hushed tone, "We think so. When they ran his fingerprints, there was a match from the Interpol database.

Ortega confirmed the terrorist was a Chinese operative named Ju-long. He was part of President Szu's personal network of spies and assassins. You are very—I mean very—lucky to be alive, my boy."

* * *

After leaving Jason's hospital room, Ally took a taxi back to the CDC.

He'll be in good hands with Ruth. There were police guarding both his room and the entire floor, both to protect Jason and the Senator.

When she got back to the CDC campus, there were National Guard units at the entrance checking badges. The place looked like a war zone. There were FBI vans littered everywhere, and nearly all the roads and parking lots were cordoned off. With all the extra security, it took her twenty minutes to reach her office. It was a mess, but largely intact. An FBI officer stood by and told her to collect her things. They couldn't stay long. The building wasn't considered safe.

She quickly looked around.

Nothing much to salvage.

Thankfully she had her laptop with her during her trip to San Antonio. She tried her desk phone. Miraculously, the voicemail system was working. She transferred her work number to go directly to her cell phone and left the building.

Once back at her hotel room, she called into the voicemail system.

Message 1: Nancy told her to take the day off after her ordeal and to tell Jason she's thinking of him.

Message 2: Jolie replied she and Ranger had been at Westminster and met Mitzy's owner. "*Was that a problem?*"

She hesitated opening her email.

Email 1: Another team member said the situation at the Navy base in San Diego is actually worse than what they reported yesterday. The local hospital is reporting increasing numbers of emergency room visits with flu-like symptoms.

Email 2: Director Carson distributed an all-hands message saying they would move their research lab temporarily into a series of rented trailers on the campus. They were considering moving the team to Johns Hopkins in Baltimore. She was working on the negotiations. Security and speed to implement the move seemed to be the driving considerations.

Email 3: A coworker stated the samples Ally brought back from Texas had made the trip safely, despite the tumultuous journey. She explained how the Texas samples from both humans and dogs had the same viral signatures as those from China.

The bad news exhausted her. She didn't even want to open this morning's Google news alerts page. Ally opened her mini-fridge and ate cold peanut butter directly from the jar; then found some dark chocolate and ate that too.

Her phone dinged. A text from Maya.

Was it only yesterday she asked Maya to come to Atlanta?

It felt like weeks ago. Maya texted she saw the news about the bombing and asked her to write back so she would know she was alive. She texted back,

"I'm ok. I'm sending today's news alerts. Could you go through and follow up on anything relevant? I need a nap. Will call you after."

* * *

Maya touched her gold cross necklace and prayed.

Please be alive.

The footage on the television was unbelievable. She had worked in that building. Now it had a gaping hole with black smoke. She texted Ally.

She was glued to the television instead of packing. Gretchen wedged next to her on the sofa. Maya regarded the rotund feline. "Your mom better be ok."

After the news about the CDC attack, the station switched to major breaking stories out of Texas.

In San Antonio, the National Guard had been deployed to patrol the city—seeking out and killing stray dogs. Apparently, several dog owners were upset by the outbreak and instead of quarantining their dogs, removed their collars and let them loose.

Other dog owners killed their dogs themselves and set their bodies on fire in their back yards. The news footage showed an aerial view of various fires in one neighborhood. These actions prompted more people to do the same.

Then a story about a gang carrying pistols and rifles, driving pickup trucks, shooting dogs like vigilantes—even those being walked by their owners. This led to fistfights and other deadly altercations all over the city.

Incredible.

Her phone beeped. She sighed with relief reading Ally's text. She whispered, "Thank you, Lord."

Maya wanted to tell Ally about the news out of Texas, but waited. She was under so much strain right now.

Maya's phone rang. *Walt.*

Heat rose to her cheeks. *This is all his fault.*

"Walt, what do you want?"

"Have you heard from Ally? I just saw the news about the CDC. Is she ok?"

"Yes, she just texted me. She's fine. No thanks to you. You know, I don't know if I can forgive you for dragging her into this mess. If she was in that building, she would be dead right now! Hmmf. You call yourself her friend. You know, she tried calling you for a month after that meeting with Defoe. Now you pretend to care."

His voice softened. "Maya, I thought she could help…things are complicated for me."

"No. I don't want to hear your lame excuses. You are some piece of work. Don't call me again. And if you know what is good for you, don't call her either. I mean it."

"You're right. I've behaved badly. I don't deserve her as a friend. I can't go into it, but there have been some things I've been dealing with, too. Would you tell her I'm sorry?"

"Yeah, you are sorry. Don't try that cloak and dagger shit with me. Go fuck off."

Maya pounded the red icon on her phone and let out a guttural scream. "Motherfucker!"

Gretchen jumped away in alarm and ran down the hall.

"Oh, I'm sorry, Gretchen. Come back! I won't yell anymore. We'll see your mom soon. I promise."

* * *

Deputy Director Zhang paced the floor, waiting to see Qiang.

Perhaps he will slice my neck open also, Zhang thought.

Finally, the door opened and he entered Qiang's office. "Zhang, what is the situation?"

"Sir, I regret to tell you one of your four assassins, Ju-long, was killed in Atlanta."

"Hmmf. Did he accomplish his mission before he died?"

"He hit two hard targets, one in New York and the other in Atlanta. However, the spy, Dr. Yi, is still at large."

"She knows too much and has betrayed us too deeply to remain unpunished. Do you have another agent available to complete the task?"

He stared at the floor. "Sir, I have been looking. Many of our operatives stationed abroad have gone missing. We suspect that they learned of our troubles here and defected. Although some may have also succumbed to the virus. It is difficult to know precisely the cause for their lack of response. We have conventional soldiers available to select from. Would you like me to send you some top candidates to interview?"

Qiang sighed. "I am becoming an old man. Sometimes I think I should retire and spend a nice, quiet life by the ocean." He leaned back and asked, "Do you think I am an old man that should retire?"

This was a trick question. He had seen Qiang ask such questions to more naïve people. It never ended well.

"Sir, you and I are about the same age. I, too, feel like an old man sometimes. But you are strong and decisive. Retirement would be an insult to your intellect and drive."

"Aha! Good answer!" Qiang laughed. "This is why you are my favorite deputy. Well, find me a new assassin or two. Or maybe four or five. I would like to see Dr. Yi hanging from her fingernails and flogged; but I need to aim higher. Merriwether needs to die." He slapped his hand against his thigh. "No. Wait. I want your men to bring him here to me. I want to watch him beg for mercy. Over and over. Perhaps then I will sleep at night. Can you make this so?"

"Sir, I will take this as my primary directive above all else," Zhang replied. He walked over to the window. There were massive fires burning in the village down below. People were burning corpses in the city squares with the help of the military, but also burning wood in their fireplaces to stay warm. The power outages, plus a cold spell, were wreaking havoc on basic shelter.

"Good," Qiang said, without turning around. "That is all. The next time I see you, I expect that Merriwether will be with you—shackled and beaten—ready for my interrogation."

Zhang silently exited the room.

Once outside, he let out a slow breath and steadied himself against the wall.

I still have my head on my shoulders.

But how am I going to kidnap a U.S. president?

Perhaps time I should defect as well.

* * *

Renée had seen a lot of strange things in her thirty years at the CDC. But she'd never experienced an actual terror attack. Under any other circumstances, she would be rattled. But instead, she only cared about the effect it had on their work.

Although the blast only affected one corner on the first and second floors, the engineers told her the entire building was structurally unsafe. All the labs and offices in the five-story structure were off-limits. Millions of dollars of equipment would need to be moved or replaced.

As she discussed the situation with the facilities engineer, her cell phone rang.

"Director Carson? Can you hold for Vice President Defoe?" a woman's voice said.

"Yes." Renée was put on hold to a marching band's rendition of the Star-Spangled Banner. She excused herself from the engineer and found a quiet bench in the courtyard. After a minute, a man's voice replaced the music.

"Director Carson, Tom Defoe. How are you holding up?"

"Mr. Vice President, I'm fine. Our staff is shaken. But the building is the primary concern."

"Please call me Tom. I'm glad to hear there weren't any casualties. Now, what can I do to help?"

"We need spaces to continue our work. We can transfer most work to our regional network of laboratories. But I'm reluctant to relocate our local team coordinating strategies for the Yuxi virus."

"I understand. I'll personally call the General Services Administration and have them locate some temporary space. Just send me some specs—square footage, utilities, search radius. Whatever you think will help them. I'll have them put out an emergency repair contract."

Renée closed her eyes. GSA was not known for their lightning speed. The FBI building in DC was disintegrating. Quite literally, concrete was breaking loose, and they put up nets outside the building to prevent passersby from getting clobbered. After several years, GSA still didn't have a plan to move them.

"Thanks, Tom. I'll send you our requirements by this time tomorrow. I appreciate your help."

Defoe said goodbye and the call was over. Renée appreciated his offer, but would not get her hopes up.

At least no one was in the building, and the computer backups in the cloud were safe.

They had lost all the physical samples from China, with only electronic images and DNA data to work with.

Renée called the WHO Director. They needed to work together in a more deliberate manner, sharing research results among several nations, to reduce duplication and expedite a vaccine and effective medications.

During a pandemic, the true enemy was time.

DAY 82

Mayor Alex Beshara was enjoying a bagel for breakfast at his desk when his phone rang. He put it on speaker.

"Mayor Beshara! This is Bob Parks from APHIS. With me is Doctor Ally Reynerson from CDC. Thanks for taking the time to talk with us."

"Sure, what can I do for you?" He glanced at his calendar. *More meetings with Sanitation later.* All he needed was another strike and garbage piled ten-feet high.

"We have strong evidence to believe that there was a deadly disease transmitted at the Westminster dog show a few days ago. The dog that died, Mitzy, was exposed to a dog named Ranger. Ranger might have been a carrier."

"Ok. But what can I do? The show, like you said, was days ago." Alex chewed another bite of his bagel. His coffee cup was empty.

"Mister Mayor, this is Dr. Ally Reynerson. Have you seen the news of the outbreak in San Antonio? Ranger and dogs from the same dog training facility were confirmed sources. New York could be the next hot spot."

Bob spoke up, "There are several measures we feel are prudent at this time. We've been notifying veterinarians and hospitals about the disease and its symptoms. But we will need your help to institute further measures."

"What measures?" Beshara asked. *Was there a fresh pot ready in the break room?*

Bob said, "Dogs are very social creatures. There are probably half a million dogs in the city. But until we understand how the virus is transmitted and how to stop it, all the dog parks need to be closed. And leash laws need to be strictly enforced."

"We have about 140 dog runs in the city. You want me to close all of them?" *Are these people high?*

"Sir, New York could become another Texas," Reynerson said.

"I've watched the news and seen the images. But we are not San Antonio. People don't run around with guns, and we don't let our dogs run loose all over the place."

"Well, we can't make you do this," Parks said. "But please think about it. The NIH will come out with a public service announcement; warning dog owners not to allow them to congregate with other dogs. We'll email you some guidelines."

"I understand. I'll be in touch." Alex hung up.

Yes, more coffee was needed. Right away.

The deputy mayor, Jamie Ryan, walked in.

"Jamie, did you hear that? Can you believe this? Tell me something. Any unusually high levels of ER activity?"

Jamie put his hand to his chin. "Not to my knowledge. I can ask Health and Human Services if you'd like."

"Sure. Ha! These people. Nervous Nellies. This is fuckin' New York City. A germ's paradise! Look at the goddamned subway. We don't touch public surfaces—unless when absolutely necessary—and we wash our hands all the fuckin' time."

"True," Jamie nodded.

"And we have the toughest leash laws and enforcement in the country. Hell, we run emergency health drills all the time. No city is more prepared than ours."

"Just the same, I'll get a staffer to work up a list of public dog runs," Jamie said.

"Good enough. Let me know what HHS says. We'll stay in front of this thing, just in case."

Chapter 17

Day 83

At the New York Stock Exchange, Mayor Beshara went to ring the opening bell alongside Mr. Billy Roberts, host of the late-night cable show, Last Week Yesterday. Billy was accompanied by his miniature dog, who was tucked like an infant in a quilted harness affixed to his chest.

The Mayor greeted Billy and escorted him to the podium. They waited for the clock to turn to the top of the hour.

Beshara stared at the dog. Its eyes were runny and ears drooped. *Sick dog?*

“Don’t mind Oscar,” Billy said. “He goes with me everywhere. This morning he didn’t feel like eating, so I didn’t want to leave him with the maid. We’re going straight to the vet after this.”

The clock showed a minute until nine. Beshara tried to make small talk, finding it uneasy conversing with a bona fide celebrity.

The traders on the floor erupted with applause.

“Here we go!” Beshara said.

The clock officially struck nine. Billy pressed the bell and rang it for a few seconds amid more applause. Dozens of traders began shouting and hand waving.

As the Mayor escorted Billy to the exit, a high-pitched scream broke through the general clamor.

The room quieted. The crowd turned toward the scream.

A woman was pointing at a man on the floor, who was gagging on his own blood. Instead of helping, the other traders panicked and ran toward the exits. Billy, the late show host, also ran to the exit. Beshara froze, watching the horrific scene from above.

Just the way APHIS described it.

He closed his eyes and fished a pill bottle from his pants pocket. Then put the bottle away. He took his cell phone from his jacket pocket and called 911.

"911—what is your emergency?"

"This is Mayor Beshara. There's a medical emergency at the Stock Exchange. We need a biohazmat paramedic team immediately. Pay attention. Do not—I repeat—do not send Fire, Police or EMT. Just a single ambulance and biohazmat for now.

Jesus, maybe APHIS was right after all.

The trader stopped convulsing, his body downward and still.

Was he dead?

Within five minutes, a series of police, fire, paramedic, and hazmat vehicles pulled up outside the exchange, in a blare of sirens and lights. The other traders were standing around on the sidewalk, and other passersby stopped to watch the commotion. Beshara ran up to the incident commander to explain the situation before they entered the building.

Beshara followed them inside but took the stairs to watch them work from the balcony above. Paramedics, suited with respirators, checked the man's vitals.

The stockbroker was still alive! The team gave him oxygen, but needed to get him to an emergency room. Beshara remained on the balcony, as if in a trance, watching the team continue their work of cleaning and sterilizing the floor.

The exchange will be down for days.

I picked the wrong fucking week to quit smoking!

His phone rang again. It was the chief health inspector.

"Should we call in the CDC?" his chief asked.

"Yes! Goddamnit. Yes!"

The phone rang again. The Wall Street Journal wanted to send in a reporter to interview him. *How did they know so fast?*

"No, I have nothing to say right now. Don't come down here! There will be a press conference in two hours at City Hall."

Beshara called Jamie, his deputy. "I need someone from the CDC here for the press conference. Have emergency services call me right away. I'm heading back to the office shortly." He put his phone back in his suit pocket and closed his eyes.

Fuck. What if I was exposed? How are we going to get names of people possibly infected?

His phone rang again. He didn't recognize the number, but it said District of Columbia underneath.

"Beshara. Who's this?"

"Mr. Mayor. Thanks for taking our call. This is Senator Ruth Cochran. I'm here with your Senator, Marleen Davis, and the head of the CDC, Director Renée Carson. We're all conferenced in. Do you have a minute? We know you're dealing with a grave situation. We wanted to extend our help. What do you need?"

He moved his phone to the other ear. "Thanks for reaching out. I need to review our contingency plans. We've had lots of training in biological attacks before, but nothing like this. We assume it's airborne. Can you confirm?"

"Mr. Mayor, this is Director Carson. We don't have a full dossier on the virus. But this is what we've learned so far. It's highly contagious between people. We have to assume that it remains active for days on surfaces, particularly in the cold. We are doing some trials but had some setbacks after the attack three days ago."

"Ok, we know how to handle MRSA and measles. Should we follow the same protocols?"

Carson replied, "This virus has higher transmission and fatality rates. My recommendation is to close every public venue, including mass transit, for at least ten days. Maybe longer. All your first responders should suit up to Level A. Create isolation wards in the hospitals. If it becomes widespread, you may need to dedicate facilities just for the infected."

He rocked back and forth, noticing that the biohazmat team was leaving the building. "I'm waiting to hear from the Governor. Closing down transit is going to upset lots of people. Our police force is the best in the world. I'm not doubting they can keep the peace. But bringing in the National Guard might reinforce the seriousness to folks. They need to know this isn't a typical flu."

Senator Davis said, "Sir, the scene at the Stock Exchange was live-streamed on the internet. People already know. Most of the news channels are re-running the footage."

Great. All I need is mass hysteria.

An incoming text message got his attention. Jamie Ryan had a special set of "codes" for getting his attention. He rated his messages A through D.

"D" was a minor issue that was information only. An "A" was something urgent—it meant drop everything. The message was coded "AAAAA!"

"Um, Senators, Director—I have another emergency I need to deal with. Can I put you on hold for a minute?"

"Yes. We'll hold," Renée said.

The Mayor texted back, "What?"

Jamie texted:

"Hospital won't take the trader. Won't put
other patients at risk. Called around. No others willing.
Call me!"

Beshara texted back, "Got it. Hold on."

He returned to the phone call. "Ladies, I have a bigger problem. We can't find a hospital willing to take our stockbroker patient. The ambulance was turned away. Fucking…sorry. Have you dealt with this before? What legal standing do we have? Can I force the hospital? Christ!"

Carson said, "This is outrageous! Are there any city or state-owned hospitals you can use? What about military hospitals in the area?"

Senator Davis chimed in, "There are VA hospitals in Manhattan and Brooklyn. I'll make some calls with Director Carson to make those the primary emergency rooms for the Yuxi virus. Tell the ambulance driver to proceed to the closest one."

"Thanks Senator. Director Carson, do you have someone on your staff that can help us with the planning going forward? Our current plans only deal with influenza epidemics. This is a whole new situation."

"Yes, of course," Renée replied. "I'll have Doctor Maya Rivera call right away. She's on loan to us but has vast experience with setting up field hospitals for infectious diseases."

"Thanks, Director Carson. I have to go. Appreciate you reaching out. I'll be in touch."

"We're here to help. Hang in there! Call anytime," Senator Davis said.

Where was the flood of relief he expected? Not there. Not yet.

He called Jamie. "What's the situation?"

"The ambulance driver doesn't know where to go," Jamie explained. "Twenty other patients were turned away from the ER with similar symptoms. They are literally sitting on the sidewalk. One is coughing up blood. The driver flagged down a cop and we forced our way in to see the hospital administrator. The network they belong to includes San Antonio. They couldn't isolate the virus with existing protocols. Their whole system collapsed. The New York administrator refuses to put existing patients at risk. Says they are already immune-compromised."

Beshara sighed. "What about other hospitals?"

"The paramedic drivers are calling the other hospitals; they said the same thing. We need you to make the call. Do we send in police? Make them take these people?"

"Hold off for now. Senator Davis is working out a deal with the VA. Send all the infected to either the Manhattan or Brooklyn VA. I'm heading back to the office now. Have the head of HHS, the police chief, emergency management director and anyone else you can think of meet me there. I need you, too."

"Will do boss—the entire emergency services team. Be safe."

Beshara hung up and felt eyes on his back. He looked around. Three men were standing behind him; he knew them immediately. The Chairman of the Federal Reserve, Mario Reed, and the CEOs of two of the biggest financial services firms in the country—Dillan Bates Investments and Maxwell Oaks.

How long had they been hovering there?

"Gentlemen," Beshara said, "whatever you need, it has to wait. I'm dealing with matters of life and death. The stock market will have to fuckin' wait until we deem it safe."

The shortest of the trio, CEO Dillan, said, "That's why we want to talk with you. We have an idea. We want to help."

The oldest of the group, CEO Maxwell, inserted, "We overheard—about the hospitals. Sir, we need the markets open. We need to instill confidence in our financial system. We're ready to pledge our financial support for this effort." His eyes twinkled with sincerity and the wrinkled skin around his mouth formed deep dimples when he smiled.

"What effort?" Beshara asked. "Whaddaya talking about?" He

checked the time on his phone.

"Creating dedicated medical facilities for the infected," Chairman Reed said in a deep, somber tone.

"Look, I'm on my way back to City Hall. Tell me on the way over. If you don't mind the ten-minute walk."

"Our thoughts exactly," Maxwell said. "But perhaps we could all take my limousine? It's waiting just outside."

Beshara desperately needed good ideas. The optics of riding in a limo during a health emergency would be awful. But then, he had bigger problems than optics.

Listening never hurt.

"Sure, let's go."

* * *

Beshara could sense the flurry of activity as he entered City Hall. He headed to his office first with the CEOs and Fed Chair in tow. On the way, he briskly walked past the conference room. He could see it was packed—agency leads were milling about and some were already arguing.

Jamie Ryan came rushing towards him, waving at him for attention. "Sir, I got a call from Dr. Rivera at the CDC. She said she would like to help. I can patch her into the conference room."

"Yes, great." Beshara entered his office and threw his black wool coat on a side chair. Jamie stared at his entourage of white-haired men with expensive suits. "Deputy Ryan, these fine gentlemen represent the Fed and Wall Street. They also want to help."

"I guess the more the merrier. Nice to meet you." Jamie said.

Beshara asked, "James, could you arrange for our intern to get us some coffee and water for the conference room. Maybe order some sandwiches? We may be here for a while."

"Sure, boss."

CEO Maxwell handed Jamie a card. "Our company has a contract with this catering service. Order whatever you think the staff would like. Tell them to put it on my bill."

"Thanks, Mr. Maxwell!" Jamie stared at the card as he exited the room.

"I know I could use some good coffee." Beshara said. "I'm gonna hit the head. We'll begin the meeting in five minutes. Gentlemen, I'll meet you inside."

Beshara hurried around the corner to the men's room.

The restroom was empty. He took off his suit jacket and rolled up his sleeves. His hand was shaking. From his pocket, he took out a bottle of pills and popped two of them into his mouth. His addiction to painkillers wasn't known to many.

He heard the door open. He quickly swallowed the pills and pretended to be washing his hands. It was CEO Dillan.

"Quite a day, right?" Dillan said rhetorically, as he walked to a urinal.

Beshara said, "Yes, yes. Ok, see you in a couple minutes."

He went back to his office and read through his stack of messages: people were running late to the meeting; the head of Sanitation was out sick; several media outlets wanted interviews; hospital administrators sent threatening emails saying "don't send us the infected or we'll sue the city"; the head of traffic safety reported that panicked drivers leaving downtown caused so many accidents that most bridges and tunnels were blocked. People were jamming the ferries and walking across the Brooklyn Bridge to escape the island.

It was like 9/11 all over again.

He walked into the conference room and everyone stopped talking. They all took their seats quietly and looked at him expectantly.

"Everyone, thank you for getting here so quickly." He looked at the speaker-phone in the center. "Dr. Rivera, are you with us?"

"Yes, Mr. Mayor."

"Great. We all know the situation. We need a plan of where to send the infected for treatment. The VA hospitals can only accommodate so many. We also need to disseminate information to the public *now* on how to protect themselves. We need to tell them specifically what to do and who to call if they or their family members become ill."

Beshara brought the center speaker-phone closer to himself. "Dr. Rivera, does the CDC have any published materials on the symptoms of the disease. How can people tell if they have this new dog virus, instead of the usual seasonal flu?"

"Good question," Maya said. "From what we've learned in San Antonio and from the little information out of China, the virus acts quickly. The symptoms begin to show about twenty-four to thirty-six hours before a person become bedridden or dies. Depends on the initial health of the victim. First signs are a low-grade fever and coughing. The coughing gets progressively worse as the virus invades lung cells and destroys them. If a person coughs up blood and spikes a high fever, more often than not, it could be too late. Anti-viral medications might not help."

"You said low-grade fever. What temperature exactly?"

"We only have anecdotal accounts so far, but we believe temperatures as low as ninety-nine point five."

The head of Health and Human Services chimed in, "That is very low. That's on the upper range of normal!"

"I'm afraid this is why the virus is so lethal. Many people won't know they're infected until it's too late...meaning they're probably transmitting the virus to others for hours or days before they show signs."

A collective groan rang out.

The anesthetic coursed through his veins. Beshara poured himself a glass of water from the center of the table. "The hospitals may not be as paranoid as I thought. Ok, everyone, I had an interesting talk earlier with the three men at the end of the table. They have an idea. I suggest we listen and then we'll discuss. Mr. Maxwell?"

CEO Maxwell stood up. "Thank you, Mr. Mayor. As you know, the financial markets took a beating after 9/11. Just like many large cities, our financial firms developed their own emergency management plans. We have alternative work sites and backup servers to handle almost any situation. After the terrorist attacks, the term 'risk management' took on new meaning. We developed strategies to preserve markets during times of war, natural disasters, and other catastrophes. New York is the center of global commerce. I think we can all agree on this. Our companies and financial futures are inextricably linked to this great city. In that spirit, we want to help."

The Chief of Police said, "Hey guys, I know you want to help, and that is great and all, but what can a bunch of rich guys in suits do to stop a virus? I mean, let's get real."

CEO Dillan held up his hand to Maxwell and said, "I got this."

Dillan stood up and walked over to a map of the city on the back wall. It was a black and white aerial image from the 1950s. "Sir, you have an excellent point. My dad was a beat cop. We don't mean any disrespect. This city has given me so much. I've been fortunate. Mr.

Maxwell and so many others feel the same way. We just want to give back. All of you in this room—and on the phone—are the experts. You know how to handle a crisis. What we are offering is funding and a viable idea."

Beshara said, "I think we should hear them out. Ok, everyone?"

People around the table nodded.

Dillan pointed to the Hudson River. "Do you know what that is?"

Maya asked through the speaker-phone, "What is he pointing to?"

Beshara said, "Ellis Island. A former hospital and infectious disease facility."

Maya asked, "Those were closed almost half a century ago. Aren't those buildings falling apart?"

Dillan responded, "You are correct. The National Park Service estimates it would take $900 million to restore the buildings. We expect over a billion to make them working hospitals again."

Beshara said, "Wall street offered to put up the money. It would help create a quarantine zone."

The city director of Health and Human Services said, "But that could take months or years! We don't have that kind of time!"

"It's still winter." Beshara said. "Most of the trade unions have folks laid off right now. If we cancel all our other city improvement projects, we could have an army of framers, plumbers, electricians and inspectors on the job tomorrow. CEO Maxwell said they could pay triple wages. We would have all the help we needed. With the right number of workers, we would aim to open for patients within three weeks. But as the first step, we take over the museum and other intact structures. The National Guard can set up a field hospital in those buildings now."

Ryan raised his hand, "Sir, this all sounds nice but we don't own Ellis. It's managed by the Park Service and a conservancy group. Would they let us do this?"

"First, we need to decide if this makes sense. We'll go around the table. Does anyone object?"

There were no objections.

"Ok, let's get the Park Service, the ferry operators, public transit, and the Public Health Service in a room. What about Governors' Island? I think those buildings are in better shape. Everyone here has a homework assignment—look for other locations to house temporary hospitals. We'll meet back here in two hours. Go!"

After the department heads left, Jamie asked, "Sir, why would Wall Street put up a billion dollars for this effort? Isn't that extreme? And why are they so interested in a remote location for treating the infected?"

"Ryan, did you know that nearly seven trillion dollars of shareholder wealth was lost in the 2008 crash? All the brokerages are panicked. They think this outbreak could be more devastating than 2008. If the city has a solid plan to isolate the sick, they think they can weather the coming storm. A billion is nothing to these guys."

"Geez. So, not altruism at all."

"Hardly," Beshara said. "It's self-preservation and capitalism at the highest extreme."

"Well, if this works, I'm all for it. What about New Jersey? Don't they own part of Ellis?"

"Yes. I'm calling both Governors next. We can probably do a sharing arrangement. New Jersey has lots of leverage. The only bridge to the island originates in Jersey City. Plus, all the utilities are tied into the Jersey side."

"Damn. Right. But we have leverage too. About half a million New Jersey residents work in the city. Our fortunes are linked."

"Exactly," Beshara said. "Hey, I need you to talk to head of the Governors' Island Corporation. See if we can work a deal there too."

"I'm on it. See you in a couple," Jamie said. In a quieter voice, he added, "By the way, lay off the pain pills. You were looking a little glassy-eyed in there. Maybe I'm the only one who noticed. Remember, we are all here for you."

Heat radiated in his face. "Jamie, look, it's been a bad day. I'll be better tomorrow. I promise."

"Should I hold them for you?" Jamie asked, his palm outstretched.

He handed over the pill bottle and left the room without looking back.

Chapter 18

Day 85

President Merriwether watched his favorite morning news show in the Oval Office. He knew he should read his morning briefs instead. He pretended to read them while paying more attention to the television.

A headline flashed on the screen, "DEATH AND MAYHEM IN TEXAS". Merriwether watched footage of National Guard troops patrolling the streets and shooting animals. People were getting into fistfights on the long lines for flu shots at pharmacies and doctor's offices. Store shelves were bare. Most offices were closed. Individuals were openly carrying guns and other weapons. There were a couple reports of coworkers pummeling the other if they sneezed in their direction.

Then the newscaster described the news blackout in China, but how there were multiple reports of mass casualties from what appeared to be the same virus. Next, he showed the footage of the attack on the CDC. A roundtable of panelists then discussed how bioterrorism was occurring across the planet and how we, as a nation, were ill-equipped to deal with it. One commentator believed strongly that the flu vaccine was to blame. Another so-called expert said people needed to arm themselves and build underground bunkers. A reverend on the panel commented that this virus was foretold in the Bible as a sign of the End of Times.

Merriwether asked Jack to come in.

"This disease looks kind of serious. Isn't there some kind of emergency bunker I need to go to? To stay safe?"

Jack sighed. "Sir, one of the first briefing books we gave you when you took office had a chapter on disaster preparedness. There is a protocol for evacuating you and the Vice President to separate offsite shelters. Do you want me to fetch it for you?"

"Um, how about you just give me the main points," Merriwether muttered.

"Well, first, as you've probably already read in last week's brief, the White House has taken numerous steps to protect you and the staff. We have a nurse from the Surgeon General's office taking temperatures of all staff and visitors before they enter the building. All the admin staff and Dr. Braff are constantly assessing the health of individuals who ask to come in to see you. As Chief of Staff, I can send anyone home that presents symptoms. We have antiseptic gel stations throughout the building. I've instituted a liberal telework program and we are holding most meetings via video conference, out of an abundance of caution. However, that being said, until we believe you or the Vice President are in actual danger, we won't institute Condition Delta. Delta is when we would transport you both to remote sites or what we like to call the alternative White House.

"Can I send my momma and Kiki there now? Just in case?"

"Sir, as President, you can implement whatever measures you wish. However, it may send a poor signal to the public and increase panic even further."

Merriwether sat back in his chair. "Hmm. Ok. Well, I'm gonna move them into the White House for now. The news folks think this is End of Times. I was never a religious man myself. But I have to admit this dog thing has got me a little rattled. Hey, before you leave, ask my secretary to get the CDC lady on the phone for me."

"Yes, sir. Anything else?" Jack asked.

"Yeah. Does the secret bunker have cable? I don't want to miss the next season of Medieval Crowns. I love that blonde chick. You know, the short one with the dragons and the battle axe. Not the tall ugly one."

"I'll look into it, Mr. President."

* * *

"Are you frickin' kidding me?" Beshara's head ached, like it was in a vise. "We have legions of workers ready. Materials are being trucked in."

"No, Mr. Mayor, the Ellis Foundation won't allow the renovation of the hospitals," Jamie said.

"Why the fuck not? The place looks like bull crap."

"Their mission is to preserve the history and architecture of the buildings. They said any renovations have to be historically accurate. They said it's painstaking work that has to be completed with approval of the Historic Preservation Office. We can't just replace floors, doors, and windows with anything we want. It has to look like the original. In fact, they said we had to fix the windows instead of replace them. There are over a seven hundred broken windows. Hurricane Sandy really mangled them."

"Jesus Christ," Beshara shouted, slamming his hand on his desk. "We offer to put a billion dollars into the place and they won't accept it? Are they nuts?"

"I can put their historian on the phone if you want."

"Yes! I want to talk to this asshole," Beshara fumed.

They went into the conference room. "Let's bring in Maxwell and Senator Davis too," said Beshara. "Maybe they can help us wrangle some agreement out of this guy."

Once the call was placed, Beshara took a deep breath.

Stay calm, he told himself. *Be nice.*

Beshara said, "Dr. Zinser, I understand you are the Foundation's historian. We heard you have some concerns about the offer to renovate and reuse the Ellis Island hospital facilities. Also, on the line are Mr. Maxwell, one of our benefactors, and Senator Davis. Perhaps we can put our heads together."

"Well," Zinser said, "as you know, our Foundation has an exclusive lease on the property…."

"Yes, it has been renewed every five years…," Beshara's voice remained even.

"Um, correct," Zinser said. "And as part of our mission, we must preserve the historic and architectural aspects of the buildings. We've worked very hard over the last decade to raise the funds to stabilize the buildings and preserve everything in place."

"Yes, your Foundation is great," Beshara said. "A good friend of mine is on the board."

"Thanks," Zinser said. "But what you are proposing would radically alter the buildings. All the historic aspects would be lost.

Real restorations take years. Every window needs to be replaced with an exact replica; we need detailed drawings that need to be pre-approved by the Historic Preservation Office. We need to do consultation in accordance with Section 106. The approvals would take months."

"Mr. Mayor, this is Senator Davis. Dr. Zinser is correct. Under normal circumstances, restoring buildings like this would take considerable time and consultation."

"Exactly," chimed in Zinser.

"But," Davis said, "I would argue that these aren't normal circumstances, right?"

"Well…," Zinser stammered.

"In fact," continued Davis, "the Historic Preservation regulations have an emergency situations clause. The Governor approved the emergency declaration two days ago. In the words of Section 106, we are responding to an immediate threat to life. My office is helping the Mayor draft the letter to the Advisory Council, describing our undertaking."

"But, but…the regs refer to disasters like building collapses…not renovating buildings to reuse them. You are manipulating the system!" cried Zinser. "You don't have to use Ellis!"

"We have a public health disaster," Davis said. "No one disputes this. Creating quarantine conditions in a large, crowded city like New York is particularly difficult. I spoke with Vice President Defoe this morning. He is backing our proposal. In fact, Defoe is ready to call the Secretary of the Interior to have your lease cancelled if you try to block us. That said, Dr. Zinser, we appreciate your passion and certainly don't want to harm the buildings. With your assistance, we will use materials and techniques to preserve as much of the original elements of the building as practical. Mr. Maxwell, for any renovations that are not historically accurate, made in the name of speed, could we agree that your group will fund additional efforts, later on, to correct those items?"

"Of course, Senator," Maxwell said. "After we get through this initial disaster, we pledge to make the building perfect. We would want a long-term agreement that the facilities could be used again in the future, should similar need arise."

Beshara added evenly, "With all the hospitals that have closed over the last fifty years, New York direly needs medical flex space.

We would want to be a party to the agreement, allowing us to use the facility for other public health and welfare issues."

"Hold on," Zinser said. "You can't just take over the place! We have a lease! What about the Park Service? This is outrageous!"

"Sir," Beshara said, "The Park Service is ready to terminate your lease if you choose not to cooperate. We are talking a billion dollars. It would take the Foundation a hundred years to raise this amount. Without our intervention, the buildings won't survive anyway. Look, here is the bottom line. We can pay for your consulting services. Hell, you can hire an *army* of historians to monitor the construction. Make a list of all your requirements and email them to my Chief of Staff. As soon as possible. Ok?"

Zinser sighed heavily. After a pause, "Um, Ok."

Beshara smiled and hit the phone's disconnect button forcefully. He called back Senator Davis.

"Did you really call the Vice President?" he asked. "Did he really threaten to cancel their lease?"

"No," admitted Davis, "I haven't spoken to him yet. But I needed to shut this guy down. I'll call Defoe right away."

Beshara grinned. "I knew I liked you."

"Thanks. Call me if you need anything else."

Beshara ended the call. A minor victory. But they were still losing the war.

A quarter of the office staff had called out sick.

Day 86

In the days since Ally returned from Texas, she had never been busier. The outbreaks in San Antonio, New York, Las Vegas, and San Diego showed no signs of stopping. The first case in Atlanta surfaced.

She took a taxi to the hospital.

When she got to Jason's room, he was sitting up, stuffing his face with a blueberry muffin, watching the news on the ceiling-mounted TV.

"Ally, you have to try one." He took another muffin out of a box. "You'll die." He muted the television.

"Ruth sent another care package, I see."

"The doctor gives me dirty looks when he sees the packages, but the nurse lets me have them."

"Fine. Just a taste." She bit off a tiny piece. "Yep, pretty good."

"So, what's new in virus land?"

She took a seat in the visitor's chair. "I don't know where to begin."

"Is it true people are leaving dead bodies on the curb now?"

Ally sighed. "It's gross, but San Antonio doesn't have enough ambulances to keep up. Now residents roll the dead in a sheet, attach a birth certificate or driver's license, and put them out for the sanitation truck."

"Like with the garbage?"

"No, they have two crews. One truck for trash, one for bodies. Workers suit up for both. They have to assume any touched by human hands is potentially infectious."

"Damn."

"That's not the worst." She chowed down the rest of her muffin.

"Eating carbs? Now I know it's bad."

"One town, about an hour from Austin, put out guidelines. Told residents to mark their mailboxes with an 'X' if there were any sick people inside—to assist first responders. It was well intentioned, but vigilantes began targeting those houses, throwing Molotov cocktails at them, trying to burn them to the ground."

"Holy hell."

"And colleges. Bastions of contagion. A whole fraternity—gone in one weekend. The parents confronted the dean with shotguns."

"I can't imagine. How are you holding up?"

She reached for another muffin, then put it down. "Jason, please put these away."

He placed the box far out of her reach.

She continued, "I'm ok. But I'm here to see how *you* are doing. When are they discharging you?"

"Soon, I think."

"Good, because this is the worst fucking place for you to be. God, the San Antonio health care system completely collapsed. The hospitals kept cleaning and sterilizing everything, but the virus hit everyone. Even the people in out-patient care. Broken legs turned into death sentences. Look, I know Ruth pulled some strings and got you this private room at the furthest end of the hospital. But the sooner you leave, the better."

"But the virus isn't in Georgia, right?"

"It was on the news." She gestured to the television. "You didn't see it? Last night, a flight attendant died at the Atlanta airport."

"Fuck. Well, I'm going to enjoy Ruth's baking and look on the bright side. Not much else I can do until I get discharged."

"I'm sorry. I shouldn't be dumping all my frustrations on you."

"It's ok. I appreciate you coming down. Do you want to watch some TV? Take your mind off things? My favorite sit-com is coming on soon."

"No, thanks. I'm supposed to meet Maya. There's a meeting tonight to go over some new findings." She gave him a hug and said goodbye.

On the ride back to her hotel, Ally thought about how rich people had remote vacation homes, doomsday bunkers or private islands. They had more than a few days of food stored and could easily hide from the virus. So far, the highest death rates were among the homeless; bringing them into shelters made the situation worse.

She went to her new office. The CDC took over an old IRS office building about a mile down the road. She finished adding the most recent mortality data into her model, then emailed the results to Nancy. Maya came by and they walked to the auditorium for the eight o'clock session.

At the top of the agenda, a presentation from APHIS researchers. Veterinarian Marla Berry joined the APHIS team after she was found to be immune from the virus. They allowed her to give their exciting news.

"We've all been focused on the virus," Marla began. "The virus is the component that infects lung tissue and ultimately causes death in both people and dogs. But we overlooked something. We know Ranger from the San Antonio K-9 Academy was in New York, where he interacted with several dogs, both in Central Park and at the competition. But Ranger wasn't sick. So, if he didn't have an active virus in his lungs, how did he spread the disease?"

Marla turned on the projector and a slide came on the screen, displaying a magnified image from a petri dish. Murmurs erupted throughout the audience.

"Um, that is a bacterium, not a virus," Nancy said.

"Exactly," Marla said. "Dogs and other animals are prone to picking up bacteria from the soil and from other animals. Dogs in particular are very social. They rub against each other and roll around on the ground. I call them dirt magnets. Bacteria on a dog's fur is easily transferred to other dogs…but also to humans. By petting an infected animal, a human could spread the bacteria to themselves…and also deposit it on other people, pets and surfaces."

"But what does this have to do with the virus?" Nancy asked.

"Viruses are tens to hundreds of times smaller than bacteria. We thought outside the box and took samples of the fur of sick dogs. We found the virus inside the bacteria. Like a Russian nesting doll of disease. And it wasn't just any bacteria. It had elements similar to that of pneumonic plague."

"Wait, so let me process this," Ally said. "The bacteria were infected with a virus, that was carried on the fur of dogs, and when the dogs traveled from Russia, to China and Eastern Europe, the bacteria were spread to other dogs and humans."

"We believe so," Marla said. "But after the virus lodges in a human's respiratory system, the virus itself becomes airborne for further human to human transmission."

She clicked to another slide. "From the outcomes in Texas, it was apparent that a few dog breeds are immune to the virus. Dogs with a degree of wolf DNA may be immune. This would explain why Ranger wasn't sick but could transmit the bacteria to other dogs in New York. Healthy dogs acting as carriers would explain the high transmission rates."

Ally looked at her notes. There were approximately ninety million domesticated dogs in the U.S. One dog for every 3.6 people! No wonder the disease spread so quickly. It was curious why cats and other household pets didn't become ill or act as hosts. But then again, she wasn't well-schooled in the physiology and epidemiology of animals.

"But we still don't know how to combat the virus in humans," Ally said.

"No, but we have a plan to stop the spread from dogs." Marla said. "I talked to Ms. Jolie Walker last night. When I told her about our bacteria findings, she suggested treating it like ringworm. She's working with APHIS back in San Antonio today to test the effectiveness of lime-sulfur baths."

"But even if we disinfect all the dogs," Ally said, "we still have an extremely contagious airborne virus to deal with."

Nancy got up, "I'm working with the international team to

decipher if there is a genetic component to the virus. Perhaps if we can understand why mostly women are immune, we can develop a treatment."

"You mean women over fifty," Ally gently corrected. "There are some differences in the immune systems of men and women. There are studies showing higher estrogen contributes to increased immune response. But older women have less estrogen. It's bizarre. What is it about being older?"

"We have to follow all leads," Nancy said. "We've compared the virus to every one known to medicine. There are no exact matches yet. We're also looking at other innate and acquired immunity factors, like diet, overall health, and vaccination history."

Ally said, "What about chicken pox? Older people, myself included, had chicken pox as kids...before they invented the vaccine. Could this new virus be similar enough that our immune system recognizes it? Maybe not an exact match, but enough so that our acquired immune system attacks it before it takes root?"

"Varicella-zoster fits in terms of when the vaccine came out," Nancy said. "Nian, Marla, did you have chicken-pox? As kids?"

They responded in the affirmative.

Maya said, "It's worth looking into but still doesn't explain much. First, chicken pox causes lesions on your skin, not in your lungs. Second, shouldn't the current chicken pox vaccine work for the younger people? Lastly, boys and girls got chicken pox at the same rate. Both should survive equally."

Nian raised her hand. "It's possible this new version of pox targets lung tissue preferentially over external skin. I've read about cases where a virus will target atypical areas. When our group in China was researching measles, we came across cases where lesions formed in people's brains."

Ally stared at Nancy and made a cutting motion with her hand across her neck...as in, "time to wrap this up." Not everyone in the audience knew Nian's history working on bioweapons. For Nian's sake, they needed to change the subject. Nancy nodded back to Ally.

Still, Ally thought, *Nian had a good point.* Viruses mutated all the time.

"These are all excellent questions," Nancy said, "and we could debate this for hours. But we have to get back to work. See you all tomorrow—same time. Dr. Berry, keep me posted on any progress.

Ally, could you stay back for a minute?"

After the room cleared, Nancy said, "The results from your model…are terrifying. I decided not to tell the team. I want to keep their spirits up."

"The rate of transmission keeps going up," Ally said. "Despite all the efforts at the local and state level. Why hasn't Merriwether closed all the airports yet? God, and NASCAR events…don't even get me started on those."

"Renée calls the White House every day. Merriwether won't sign an Executive Order for a national quarantine. He just says, 'Find a cure'."

"Jesus."

"Your friend Dr. Braff has been trying to convince him. He isn't getting anywhere either."

"How many people have to die before Merriwether gets it?" Ally said.

"An excellent question," Nancy said. "Keep sending me the daily updates on the actual and projected mortality. Is it ok for Renée to send your model results to Dr. Braff? Maybe if he puts a copy on the President's desk, he might pay attention."

"Sure thing," Ally said.

Walking back to her office, Ally thought about Walt and what his days must be like.

If Walt can't convince the President, things will go from bad to worse very quickly.

Day 90

Being trustworthy had its disadvantages. *Like working every Saturday.*

Walt dallied outside the residence staircase on the lower floor, waiting for the inevitable call. He had a bottle of aspirin, a green smoothie with a splash of vodka, and a cold compress ready.

He was ready for the aftermath of the President's Friday night poker game. The game broke up around one in the morning, usually after the President became so drunk he couldn't read his cards correctly. Walt didn't even want to consider how much money Merriwether lost at those games.

After the first couple of months, as the new White House doctor,

Walt decided it made more sense to come in every Saturday—instead of making plans that would ultimately be ruined. Sometimes Dan would get up at five. Sometimes at ten. So, Walt just came early and waited.

Dan loved Walt's signature hangover smoothie. And no one was allowed to give the President a pill except for Walt. Allegedly, before their separation, Esmé tried to poison him through his food or medications. But Merriwether trusted Walt.

Walt strained his ears for signs of life upstairs. *Nothing.*

He walked to the Oval Office. The room was dark. The CDC reports were still on the President's desk, untouched. He shook his head in disbelief.

It was a morning just like this, he thought.

The morning when I came across that stupid fax.

In mid-December, as Walt paced around the West Wing before daybreak, he heard a weird combination of screeching, beeping and clicking noises. With lights off, except for the red emergency bulbs above exit doors, he scanned the empty offices until he located the source.

It was a fax machine. A very old one going by the discoloration of the plastic outer shell. It was tucked behind the admin desk outside Jack Cunningham's office, covered over with binders and other office supplies. Walt remembered being surprised it was plugged in and contained paper.

Out of boredom and curiosity, he picked up the incoming pages, already crumpled from smashing against a broken stapler resting on top. The first sheet was a plain cover. No hint of the sender and no recipient or "to" line. The second page was a brief note; small handwritten block letters saying something like, "The blankets were received. Operation Granitnyy is a go."

He had put the papers back on the tray gently and walked down the hall.

A few seconds later, in the dim lighting, he nearly bumped into Vice President Defoe.

"Sorry sir, I didn't see you there," Walt said.

Defoe looked around. "Good morning, Dr. Braff! Are you here for our favorite patient?"

"Yes. No signs of life yet. I hope you didn't have an early meeting planned with him. I'm sure he will reschedule."

"Oh, yes. I guess you're right. I also came to pick up a report in my office. Have a nice morning."

"You too, sir."

A few minutes later, he heard Defoe call out a distant, "Bye, Walt."

Walt walked back to the fax machine. The pages were missing.

It was only when he read the report on Merriwether's desk about the Russian Army deaths, that he made the connection. It was weird that the earlier fax talked about blankets, which is why it stuck in his mind weeks later. Putting the two together, he suspected someone in the government sent the Russian Army infected blankets, obviously taking a page out of Native American history.

He didn't want to believe it.

Calling Ally was his best option.

After their meeting at the diner, he wondered if he should simply confront Defoe. But the next morning, he learned of a meeting at the OEOB. Seeing the invite list, he called Director Ortega and left a message with his office.

The return call he received was from Jason Burns. Burns asked Walt if he could get a copy of the fax machine's log. *Why hadn't he thought of that?* When no one was looking, Walt pressed a series of keys to obtain the dates, times and phone numbers of incoming messages.

Two days later, as people began arriving to the meeting at the OEOB, Walt passed a copy of the log to Jason.

Jason later called Walt, saying he was shocked—but not surprised—that the fax about the blankets originated from his own Fort Belvoir.

CHAPTER 19

DAY 93

Tom got into the black sedan to head to the White House. Merriwether wanted his advice on something. He expected they were going to discuss the possibility of a nationwide quarantine.

Has it really come to this? he wondered.

On the way, he stared out the car window, frowning.

I hate my life. I should have been President.

That stupid viral video changed everything during the primaries. It made him look weak and indecisive. An undisclosed entity developed a video from cellphone footage of him ordering at a fancy restaurant. Tom made the mistake of calling the server back to the table to change his order twice—before he finally decided on the porterhouse. It became an internet meme with his image, wearing a cartoon top hat, waving paper cut-out arms at the server, singing in an electronic voice:

"Oops, I can't decide.
Oopsie doo, oopsie dee, oopsie doo, oopsie dee
Oops, I've changed my mind!
Oopsie doo, oopsie dee, oopsie doo, oopsie dee.
If you vote for me,
Up shit's creek is where we'll be.
Oopsie doo, oopsie dee, oopsie doo, oopsie dee."

It was infantile. What did ordering a meal have to do with one's ability to govern or make informed decisions?

But the unsophisticated morons of the country loved it. Afterward, on the campaign trail, someone at a rally would inevitably begin singing the Oopsie song. The audience would join in, like a sing-a-long. His polling numbers dropped like a stone.

He suspected the Russians created the video and that their bots disseminated it thousands of times over, across multiple social media platforms. The Russians made no attempt to disguise the fact that they wanted Daniel Merriwether in office; but it was hard to prove they interfered. Tom doubted Dan knew about the subterfuge. For that matter, Dan didn't know much of anything that went on.

It especially burned him when, during a televised debate, Merriwether clumsily knocked over his bottled water.

As Dan bent over to pick it up, he lifted his head and winked at the camera, saying "Oopsie!"

The room went wild. Despite the moderator's protests, the audience sang the oopsie song in unison, over and over again, waving their arms in the air. It went on for an uncomfortable three minutes. The pundits and news outlets reported on it incessantly, playing it on repeat for days. Political analysts debated whether Merriwether had dropped the bottle on purpose.

Tom couldn't stand it. His campaign was finished.

A few weeks later, Tom was surprised to get a call from Merriwether's campaign chair. He initially laughed when they asked him to join the ticket. He thought it was a cruel joke. But they were serious.

Tom's former colleagues from the Senate told him to just take it. "We need a serious person as Vice President...someone that knows how to get things done."

It was scary to contemplate some of the other candidates on Merriwether's short list. One was a fringe talk-radio host, one was a gambling buddy that owned a chain of supermarkets, and one was a famous actor that was rumored to have a huge cocaine habit.

"Please, take one for the country," Tom's friends pleaded.

With great skepticism and distaste, Tom accepted the offer.

On the night of the election, Tom hoped Merriwether would lose. It was one thing to lose to him in the primary and then pretend to be honored at the offer of Vice President—but he couldn't imagine the American public actually choosing Merriwether over his more intelligent, well-spoken, and experienced opponent. It made him sick to his stomach.

The Russians got their useful idiot—or maybe just an idiot. Either way, Petrov was probably still rolling on the floor laughing his little black heart out.

* * *

Merriwether paced the Oval Office, wringing his hands behind his back. He looked at his watch again.

Tom will know what to do.

The two weeks were up since he had seen Vlad.

In all his worry, he hadn't noticed until that moment, that the cleaning staff hadn't removed all the beer bottles from the night before. They were scattered around the room like little tattletales, revealing his weakness.

Tom wouldn't approve.

He picked up a waste basket and began placing the empties inside.

"Good morning, Mr. President," Tom said in a booming voice, striding into the room.

He almost jumped out of his skin. "Tom, whew. I didn't hear you coming!"

He put down the trash can. "Hey, Tom, thanks for coming right away." He sat down on the couch and motioned for Tom to join him. "I need your advice. We're in a kind of a pickle here. I hoped we'd be further along finding a cure for the dog virus by now."

"What sort of advice?" Tom asked, remaining standing.

"Well, you remember the G20 meeting? Oh, of course you do. I mean, I didn't take you with me, but you remember. Anyway, I met with ol' Vlad and Szu for a private session."

"Right, I remember you said it went well."

"Um. Well, parts of it did. Other parts not so good. Not so good at all. For some cockamamie reason, Szu and Vlad think we created this disease. Szu was totally unreasonable and stormed out. I mean, that guy never smiles. Never understood people like that. How did he get people to vote for him? Not a likeable feller at all."

From under the President's desk, Rex came walking out sleepily with a long yawn and a stretch. Tom froze, staring at Rex.

"Oh, don't mind Rexie here. He got a checkup yesterday. Didn't you, boy? He's not allowed to play outside anymore."

"Um, ok," Tom said. "I'm sure you reassured them we don't have the capacity or will to create such a virulent and deadly agent, right?"

"I tried. I really tried. But like I said, they're not reasonable people. But that's not the worst of it." He got up and started pacing around the sofas again.

Defoe sighed and aimed his eyes at the ceiling. "Ok, what could be worse?"

"Vlad said if we didn't have a cure within two weeks he would start sending over nukes."

Tom chuckled and kept an eye on Rex as he went over to the bar cart and made himself a drink. "And you took him seriously? He's just playing mind games."

"He was *real* serious. You had to be there. Damn. He gives me the willies."

"Honestly sir, I've known Petrov for two decades. We even played golf together during my congressional visit to Moscow back in '98. He likes to be a tough guy. It's his persona. Russians love his macho image. But he cares more about money than politics or war."

"So, like, maybe we can send him some money and he'll cool off?"

Tom gagged on his drink. He coughed and then downed the rest of the contents. He returned his empty glass to the cart. "Sir, by now President Petrov realizes that we are facing the same health crisis. Did Director Carson reach out to Russia to offer them participation in the task force? Never mind, I'll call her myself. Don't worry about it, sir. He was messing with you…getting in your head. He knows better than to start a nuclear war. There are no financial winners in nuclear war, and he has a vast fortune to protect."

"Woowee! I guess you're right, as usual. Dang…he really had me going." He walked over to Tom and put his hand on his shoulder. "What would I do without you, Tom?"

"I'm just glad to help. Well, if that is all you needed. I'll see you again soon."

Merriwether slapped him on the back and grinned.

Tom smiled back and strode out of the room as quickly as he had entered.

After Tom left, Merriwether yelled out, "Petrov, you dirty dog! Hot dang!"

He called his mom.

"Momma, it's Danny. You don't have to stay in the fall-out shelter after all.... Yes, it's safe to travel to D.C.... Oh, you and Kiki are going to be best friends, you'll see. Yes, I told you she was coming to stay...Well, you know, I'm a grown man and can make my own choices. Just come stay with me, please? It would make me feel a whole lot better. I love you, momma."

Day 96

Her email was nearly full again. Ally stared at the screen. The New Jersey Medical Examiner sent her a new mortality report. So had many other states, but this one made her pause. She hadn't called her family in a few days.

Was no news good news?

The mortality numbers had been coming in haphazardly from state vital statistics offices. With so many dead, coroners and medical examiners were overwhelmed with paperwork. Most death certificates were hand-written hastily, with minimal information. Instead of the usually detailed evaluation of causes of death, they wrote "B99"—meaning "other and unspecified infectious diseases". States simply tallied the B99's and emailed numbers to the CDC when they got around to it. The delays in reporting were staggering.

As a work around, Ally connected with some regional administrators from FEMA, who were getting daily reports by way of National Guard units. They kept imperfect, but timelier, records of the bodies they picked up daily. But there were no zip codes or even city information to pin point where the deaths took place.

The Guard and FEMA also didn't list cause of death. They didn't have time to interview the families. Ally couldn't readily determine which deaths were directly attributable to the 'red death'.

APHIS tried to collect information on canine deaths; but the results were confounded by the indiscriminate murder of dogs, whether or not they were infected.

Murder, she shuddered. Random killings weren't limited to dogs now. In Chicago, the police reported individuals were using the virus as 'cover' to poison their enemies or spouses. With the morgues overwhelmed, it wasn't practical to do autopsies on every victim. Revenge seekers and gangs were having a field day. It was horrifying.

Was this a modern day "purge"?

In any case, the numbers of human deaths were increasing at an unprecedented rate — irrefutably orders of magnitude higher than previous years. Assuming the current rate of transmission and death, her model results were astounding. Over eighty percent of all urban populations would be gone within three months. In more remote areas, a little longer…perhaps four to five months.

This virus was moving fast. Faster than she could have predicted.

Why won't Merriwether order a national quarantine?

It would buy more time.

Ally called Nancy. "Director Carson needs to see this."

Nancy said, "I agree."

"Like right now! This is scary."

"I said *I agree*. Email us both a copy. I'll call you back in five minutes."

Nancy got an appointment with Renée for later that afternoon.

* * *

Jason called Walt as soon as they released him from the hospital and could get a new burner phone. The investigation seemed pointless now that all of humanity was imperiled. Still, if their suspicions were correct, perhaps there was a vaccine or course of treatment to be had after all.

"Walt—are you free to talk?"

"Yeah, but only for a few minutes."

"Did you and Ortega have any luck?"

"Yes, I got the bug in place last week," Walt said. "I met with Defoe to discuss the quarantine. I tried to poke around, but it wasn't safe. No luck putting a bug on him directly. So far, he has had no visitors. But I've been chatting up his secretary to find out what appointments are on his calendar. She said he met with General Roadfuss yesterday at the Pentagon."

Jason sighed. "I tried for months to locate evidence in Roadfuss' office. Either he is very smart or very lazy. He didn't keep any written notes."

"Well, if it's any consolation, Roadfuss handed in his resignation."

"Nope. Don't feel better."

"Ok, well let me know if you think of anything," Walt said. "Ortega and I aren't sure what leads are left to follow."

“Maybe we wait for him to slip up and he says something at the Observatory. See if you can talk to his personal physician. There might be clues there. I’ll let you go. Keep me posted on anything that comes up.”

“Will do. Hey, Jason, take it easy man. Don’t go chasing any more terrorists for a while!”

“Sure, doc. You be careful too.”

* * *

Ally presented her results to Director Carson.

"Allison, you developed this program yourself?" Renée asked.

"Yes, I worked on it in my spare time. I know it’s sort of morbid, but I find it numerically interesting. The spread of a virus isn't linear…more like its own organism that moves and grows and dies in fits and starts. Sometimes it’s like a fractal, where pieces shoot off and create new pathways. Other times it’s like creating a ripple in still waters. A small disturbance creates larger ripples further away but then they gradually dissipate. Then again, when two waves meet, they amplify into a larger wave or cancel each other out. Human interaction and immune responses can cause vastly different outcomes. So, I included a Monte Carlo element to distill a range of values into a probability distribution."

"You have a lot of data in here, so I'm not challenging the baseline information. But how did you factor in the potential effects of the quarantine?"

"Well, that’s an interesting problem in itself. This comes down to how many people will adhere to the quarantine. There isn't much information on that since we don't have severe epidemics frequently."

Renée lifted her eyebrows. “Well?”

“I’ve tried to use cruise ship outbreak data. The transmission rate is usually high in such a closed environment. However, the chief strategy is disinfection. Generally, only the sick stay in their cabins. The healthy still roam freely and use hand sanitizer.

Ally continued, “But I think this particular virus has more in common with natural disasters—where everyone is at risk. Hurricanes, tornados, floods, and such. There is always a small subset of individuals that don't take the warnings seriously. They don't get off the beach in a hurricane. Or they loot during a flood event. Or they take pictures of an oncoming tornado. I call them the ‘Brave Souls’ or BS'ers for short. During any natural disaster, I estimate them to be about one to four percent of the population between the ages of thirteen and thirty-five. It may not be fair to make these kinds of generalizations, but that's what models do.

"A real quarantine would close all the schools, businesses, houses of worship, festivals…it would drastically reduce transmission. Again, no model is perfect. I've added in all the risk factors that mimic real human interaction. I'm not trying to be politically correct here. Humans are imperfect beings and their behavior can be erratic. I've tried to simplify and generalize transmission routes using a set of reasonable assumptions…backed up by data and real-world observations."

"Allison, this is all very well and good, but if you want me to ask the President for a national quarantine, we need this to be rock solid."

"I understand. I would feel the same if I were in your position. Tell me what I need to do."

"If I gather some more experts, can you be ready with a presentation tomorrow morning? I'll create a red team…to pick this apart and challenge every assumption. Are you up for that?"

"Absolutely. No model can ever predict the future with a hundred percent certainty. But my baby is darn good." Ally frowned. "I only wish the results were more hopeful."

"If I'm being honest, I hope, for all our sakes, you missed a decimal point somewhere."

Ally bit her lower lip and nodded. "Me too. Me too."

CHAPTER 20

DAY 100

They all rose as Defoe and Merriwether entered the situation room. Ally took a deep breath. She watched as the men joined CDC Director Carson, Secretary Shelton and Director Ortega at the long, rectangular cherry table. Merriwether sat at the head with Defoe to his right. Renée invited Ally in case there were questions about her model. But her role was that of a silent observer. She sat in the row of chairs lining the wall. Walt sat next to her.

Renée began her presentation. "Mr. President. Mr. Vice President. Thank you for meeting with us. As you know, we are no closer to finding a vaccine or effective treatment for the virus. We have the best scientists in the world working on the problem, and we are fast tracking any potential formulations with rat studies. However, the spread of the disease continues—despite strong quarantine and prevention measures implemented at the city and state levels."

She hit a button on a laptop and the large LED screen turned on. The lights over the table faded to dark, leaving small lights around the perimeter of the room. Renée faced the President and began running the simulation.

A large map of the United States appeared on the screen. A series of orange dots began appearing on the map, growing in size in a time-lapse fashion. As the time stamp in the corner progressed, the dots turned red and then black. The model zoomed in on Washington D.C. and then the simulation stopped. D.C. looked like a large red stop sign with black holes.

Renée said, "You've just watched the outbreak until present day. Mind you, these are provisional mortality numbers. These results are themselves troubling. Based on the data and daily reports being made available to us, we have rather dire predictions. We believe that once you see them, you may understand our strong recommendation for a national quarantine."

Defoe said, "We've looked at your briefing package. You don't have to bother with your fancy dog and pony graphics."

Ally's heart sank. They didn't even want to see the predictions she had spent so much time on.

Merriwether chimed in, "You know, it's bad enough our manufacturers are having trouble getting parts from China, but Christ, now you want to shut down the whole economy? Look, I know you are scientists and all, but I know business. This quarantine of yours would tank our country's GDP and stock market for decades! Sure, some more people will die, but people die every day. Remember that hurricane in the Virgin Islands? It killed a bunch of people and it didn't affect our economy at all."

"Sir, respectfully," Director Carson said, "if you don't begin a national quarantine right now, there won't be any American's left to buy American products. There will literally be no economy at all."

The overhead lights brightened.

Merriwether dismissed her with a wave of his meaty hand, his bright gold watch flashing. "See, there you go again. I'll have you know that I just bought something on Amazon and they still delivered it on-time, in just two days. The economy remains strong. We've had some setbacks in some cities—ok, some big cities—but I think your predictions are a bunch of scare tactics."

The President pushed back in his chair from the table and sat in a more reclined pose. "Even my campaign manager told me to stop holding rallies. I told him, absolutely not. People are still coming out in high numbers to hear my speeches. If this disease were as bad as you say, how come all these people are still showing up?"

Ally blinked and shook her head. *The President was proud that large crowds were congregating to see him? What an asshole!*

She wanted to chime in. She leaned forward and sat on the edge of her chair, ready to erupt. But Walt touched her arm and gave her a look. She knew that look. It meant '*don't*'.

He knew the President best. Perhaps she had to trust him to work behind the scenes. She sat back in her chair and bit her lip.

Defoe interceded, "Sir, I think you're right. Why *shouldn't* you attend your rallies? At times like this, the people need to hear from their leader."

Ally furrowed her brow. *Does he want Merriwether to catch the virus at a rally? So fucking evil!*

Defoe continued, "But perhaps we can compromise. Let's say that we stop all immigration and visitation from foreign countries. That might reduce the spread of the disease, especially from certain countries that have less advanced health care systems. We know the virus originated in China. It might make the public feel safer if we stopped foreigners entering the country, illegally or otherwise."

Merriwether sat up in his chair and smiled. "See, that's why you were a great pick for VP! Tom, would you work on this? Close all the border crossings and deny entry to all non-citizens. Yes, that's a swell idea."

The President got up from his chair. "Well, I've got another engagement, so I'll be on my way." He placed his hand on Defoe's shoulder, "Tom, give me an update tomorrow morning, ok?"

Merriwether didn't wait for an answer. He simply turned and left the room.

* * *

Beshara sat in his office, watching the city on his computer through several web cams. Even at noon on a Saturday, in a city with nearly nine million people, he couldn't get over the sight of empty streets.

New York was under the strictest quarantine measures in its history. Beshara had to change his phone number to stop the angry calls after he shut down the mass transit system. There were a few people that protested vocally, but New Yorkers were tough and understood the stakes. Beshara went on television and called the protesters a bunch of whiners. Popular opinion was on his side.

After 9/11, most city offices had teleworking emergency plans. The very rich retreated to their mansions in the Hamptons or their Caribbean vacation homes. Homeless people and the people living in public housing fell victim to the virus at alarming rates. People began stealing food at gunpoint. The police were stretched thin.

Through the webcams, he watched a few National Guard and

FEMA trucks distributing food near Washington Square Park. In Harlem and SoHo, ambulances and fire trucks were picking up the sick and the dead.

Beshara turned off the webcam screens and looked out the window. Two ambulances drove silently by. Emergency vehicles no longer needed to use their sirens on the deserted streets. But they flashed their lights when they were carrying the dead. Other drivers pulled over and stopped briefly—not out of necessity—but out of respect for the fallen.

He placed a call to Dr. Rivera to check in.

"Hi Alex," Maya said. "How are you holding up?"

"Hey, Maya. Well, I'm still getting hate mail." He laughed. "Would it be wrong to stop mail delivery? No, just kidding. Well, maybe."

"You're doing great. Jamie texted me last night. Your recent PSA about the quarantine was spot on."

"Thanks. I think the locals understand. But the tourists! I shut down all public venues, museums. I told the local tourists to go home. But with the airports closed, international visitors are stuck in hotels. A few of them aren't listening. The police have to keep arresting them. Did you know some guy broke a window at the Guggenheim Museum to get in? Motherfuckers!"

"If it makes you feel any better, there are similar problems in other cities. All the tourism sites are closed across the country."

"At least Ellis is up and running," Beshara said.

"That was fast! How did that go?"

"Jamie managed the day to day. Thank God, because I would have had a stroke dealing with that bullcrap. Can you hold? I'll put him on the line."

After a minute, Jamie joined in. "Maya! Great to talk with you!"

"You too. How are you?"

"I'm ok, but I can only stay a minute. So, here's a recap on Ellis. Getting the heating system working was a huge job. All the old radiators and water piping had to be replaced. Corroded beyond repair. That twat of a historian, Zinser, gave us hell about running new pipes outside of the walls—but we had to do it to save time. Oh, and don't get me started about painting the walls! Heavens to Murgatroyd! You would have thought I asked him if I could murder his grandma! But the windows were the true battle. Hundreds of them—metal frames bent and every pane of glass broken. No way to have custom replicas manufactured quickly. We lost days arguing about it. Finally, we framed stock windows in plywood to fit the openings."

"But you did it. You should feel proud," Maya said.

"You know what," Beshara said, "Jamie deserves a medal."

"Aw, thanks Alex," Jamie said, "Got to go. Maya, nice talking with you! Bye!"

After Deputy Ryan left, Beshara said, "Hey, the Mayor of San Francisco called me. They're considering reopening Alcatraz as a hospital."

"I didn't know that. I'm glad you are all talking to each other. I wanted to ask you about a news story about the 'Gray Berets'?"

Beshara laughed. "Yeah, kind of catchy, huh? Remember how you were telling us that some older women were immune to the disease? Well, we are seeing more and more cases. I put out PSA's asking for their help. Most of them are volunteering at the hospitals. But we have so many critical municipal jobs to fill. So, we gave them crash courses for all types of jobs. They're driving garbage trucks, helping EMTs, delivering food and body bags, and we have a couple that learned how to run our sewage treatment plants."

Maya said, "That's incredible. In Chicago and Detroit, they are using the term 'Omegas' after the Charlton Heston movie. But using the lower-case symbol."

"I like it." Beshara said. "But the real reason I wanted to talk to you—do you have any idea on how much longer we need to keep the quarantine up?"

"The CDC has been checking in with FEMA to get daily stats. The death rate has slowed only slightly. We're trying to convince the President to institute a national quarantine. I'd say it's best to stay the course until we see the number of new cases drop to near zero."

"Got it. But I have to say, it's hard to distribute and deliver food, door-to-door, to millions of residents."

"You saw what happened in San Antonio! Not only were people fighting at the supermarkets, the stores were hotbeds of transmission. Someone would sneeze on a crate of apples and then we had hundred new cases!"

"No, I get it. We've allowed certain restaurant owners and supermarkets to deliver food once they pass health code training. And we have a 'ten-foot rule'. Anyone authorized to move around the city has to keep ten feet from any other person and wear masks and gloves. We've asked everyone to get inventive with using the food in their pantries. The rich folks have lots of stored food. But some people living paycheck to paycheck began starving. To make things fair, we're delivering food on certain days, using modified alternate side parking rules. Gray Berets are running food donation drives—primarily canned food where they can disinfect the exterior with bleach. We're still working out the kinks."

"It's the same problem everywhere," Maya said. "Even Atlanta. They just started a new system."

"What's that?"

"Regional food distributors now make sizable curbside deliveries once a week to each apartment building or complex. The residents nominate a food coordinator that places the order for the entire building and collects the funds."

"I'm open to all ideas. Right now, I'm wondering how to keep the masses happy in confinement."

"I wish I knew how to help. It's the same in Atlanta. Some bad people are not taking it well."

Beshara's cell phone rang. "Maya, I'm sorry—I have another call. I'll talk to you again in a couple days, ok?"

"Sure. Call anytime. Take care of yourself!"

Beshara hung up his desk phone and answered his cell. The police commissioner asked to see him right away.

A few minutes later, Commissioner Johnson came into the office. "Mr. Mayor, we need to discuss the food situation."

"Yes, Johnson, what's on your mind?"

"Sir, two tractor trailers full of non-perishable food were hijacked this morning, right outside the Holland Tunnel. Our police force is down more than seventy percent. We can't be everywhere. Just to enforce the curfew takes half our people."

"What do you have in mind?"

"We need more eyes on the street and escorts for food trucks," Johnson said. "The National Guard was helping enforce the quarantine, but I'd like to put them exclusively on food security. Now that we've stopped parking enforcement, all the meter folks are patrolling. But we need to go further. I'd like to pull all the available city workers to conduct patrols. The schools have been closed for over a week now. The school maintenance workers, janitorial and other support staff could easily be given police uniforms and badges. I wouldn't give everyone a gun, but they could radio in problems. Having uniformed presence could curtain criminal activity."

"The school unions might balk," Beshara said.

"Respectfully, fuck the unions," Johnson said with a hand gesture.

"Agreed. Let's call the union leaders and see what they have to say."

* * *

President Merriwether looked out the window of Air Force One as it descended near Des Moines, Iowa. All those corn fields. *As far as the eye could see.* He enjoyed the deep-fried butter at the State Fair, but could never understand how people lived in the middle of nowhere.

He had two rallies planned back to back. His advisors told him to stay home, but he couldn't deny his fans. His campaign manager said it was going to be standing room only in the Wells Fargo Arena. He always gave the same speech, but people loved it regardless.

Senator Cochran was running for president within the opposition party and she was his biggest obstacle for re-election. In his speeches, he would call her "Little Betty Crocker" and the crowd howled. He then added, "If ya can't take the heat, stay in the kitchen!" or "If the country needs a recipe for macaroons, we'll call ya!"

The crowds ate it up.

He didn't invite Tom to his rallies. The Vice President had all the charm of a cod fish. He considered replacing him on the ticket, but everyone said it would be politically incorrect.

No one really cared about the Vice Presidency anyway. Tom was good at handling all the boring meetings and never complained. So maybe he was ideal after all.

Merriwether finished eating his lunch of fried chicken in the SUV on his way to the first event. He beamed with pride at the long lines of people outside the arena.

He followed his handler and security detail through the rear door and waited backstage for his introduction. The crowd had been there for quite a long time already. A congressman was on stage getting the audience stoked for the main event. "What do we want?" he cried.

"Less government!" shouted the audience.

"Who are we voting for?"

"Merriwether!"

"Who loves our country?" the congressman roared.

"Merriwether!"

"Ladies and Gentlemen, here he is. Your Commander-in-Chief! A true American and our next two-term President, Dan—the Man—Merriwether!"

The crowd exploded with applause and whistling. People stomped their feet to the song blaring on the speakers. The arena quaked with energy.

Dan strode onto the stage, waving and blowing kisses to the audience. His body swayed with the music; his chest buoyant with pride.

These are my people!

I am their king and they love me.

He tried to speak, but the din of chanting drowned him out. "Settle down, folks," he said a couple of times, but to no avail. He smiled and waved back to the crowd.

After a full minute of continued applause, Merriwether jogged down the stage steps toward the nylon barricade tape. Agents Becker and Tanner, standing at the bottom of the stage, tried to stop him, but he ducked under the tape and began shaking hands down the front row. The cameras recorded his movements in close-up and transmitted them to an overhead Jumbotron.

He greeted a couple holding a toddler. "What a cute child!" he told the parents. He picked up the small girl and kissed her on the cheek. She instinctively grabbed locks of his hair with her chubby fists, disheveling his comb-over. The audience groaned with an "aaawww" at her funny antics.

He laughed and turned to give the child back to her mom. Before he could do so, the girl sneezed, accompanied by a splatter of wet mucus on his cheek.

The audience gasped and grew still.

Merriwether looked up at his image on the Jumbotron. The green and red nasal excretion on his face was magnified in extreme close-up. He froze.

Agent Becker reacted swiftly and dove through the crowd, pushing back bystanders to snatch the baby away. Her cries pierced the near-silent arena. They ushered her parents out behind the child.

The audience remained motionless until they removed the girl from view. Then all hell broke loose as people fled toward the exits. Under the ensuing mayhem, a half-dozen security agents whisked Merriwether out of the side door of the arena.

Back at the SUV, Merriwether wiped his face with antibacterial cloths. His traveling physician called Dr. Braff.

Christ. Maybe that director lady was right after all.

Sweat ran down his cheek into his collar.

"Sir," his traveling physician said, "We're taking you to the nearest hospital. We should be there in ten minutes."

"No! Take me the hell home. I am not going to a goddamned hospital!" He clawed at his tie to loosen it. "That is an order! Cancel all my events for the rest of the week while you're at it."

He slumped against the leather seat. He picked up a small bottle of water next to him, looked at for a moment, and threw it on the floor.

"Goddamn, Goddamn!"

"I'm fucking fucked."

Chapter 21

Day 103

Ally met Jason at the cafeteria for lunch. She put down her tray and gave him a hug. "Oh God, wait until I tell you about the meeting with Merriwether. That guy is unbelievable. How are you feeling? Does it hurt? What did the doctor say?"

"I'm much better," Jason said. "The stitches were taken out a couple weeks ago and I have my energy back."

"That's fantastic."

"Well, I won't be going to kickboxing class any time soon," he smiled.

Ally laughed.

"Hey. I need to tell you something." Jason looked somber.

This is serious, she thought. It always amazed her how he could go from a lighthearted, somewhat juvenile-minded millennial to a serious, stone-faced government operative so fast. She was never sure which version to expect.

"You may not be happy with me after I tell you this," Jason said.

"Fine. Whatever." She took the bun off her hamburger and cut the meat into small bites.

Ally listened to Jason's story.

Walt found what?

"What?" She picked up the butter knife and stabbed the table. "You could have told me this weeks ago! Like all those times I visited you in the hospital."

"Well, I'm telling you now."

"Blankets. Someone in our government sent the Russians infected blankets. All this time, you knew this was a biological attack! Here I've been wondering what kind of mutation created this mess, and now you are telling me it could have been man-made? You know what? Maybe you deserved to get shot. I want to kill you myself right now." She stabbed the table again.

Jason reached out and took the knife out of her grip. "Ally, I wanted to keep you out of that mess. It's bad enough that Walt is mixed up in it. Some secrets are too dangerous. I wanted to keep you alive."

She tapped her fingers on the table. "So, what changed?"

"I'm at a dead end. I thought I could snoop around here and spy on Nian. Maybe find any connections between the CDC and this virus. Someone had to develop it, and someone had to give it to General Roadfuss to send to Russia. I thought maybe Nian was working with or at least was cognizant of Darya's role in the outbreak. Darya worked in Supply. Maybe she knew about the blankets and facilitated their arrival. But Nian has been a double agent for years under a brutal regime. Even if she knew something, she's a tough cookie. I don't think she'll crack."

"Ok, let's look at what we already know," Ally said. "Walt found a fax that linked the White House to the outbreak in Russia. We have lots of reasons to believe the Vice President was behind this, right? Defoe could certainly despise the Russians. Considering what happened during the primaries and all those social media campaigns against him. Defoe might feel justified in seeking revenge. It's the best motive so far."

"Yes, so? We've tried bugging his residence and talking with his staff. We aren't getting anywhere."

"I'm surprised Ruth hasn't thrown Defoe in prison. Why not interrogate him?"

Jason sighed. "Oh, it's crossed her mind. Many times. But you see what's going on. The world is dying! She doesn't want to waste her time on him. Plus, she doesn't have concrete proof. Ortega wants to keep the investigation quiet until we have hard evidence. We want to find the people that actually created the virus and flip them."

"Jesus. Ok. Personally, I find it doubtful Nian developed the virus in China and sent it to Russia."

"Why? She had the opportunity *and* she reported to Roadfuss.

Why isn't she a good suspect?"

"Put yourself in her shoes. If you created a deadly pathogen at the direction of the U.S. government and then your own team spreads it in China, where would you go? Do you trust the United States to keep you alive? Or do you consider yourself a loose end that they want to get rid of? The fact that she got on a military cargo plane and came here tells me she didn't know the extent of our government's involvement."

"Ok, but how about this? What if she made the virus and an antidote that miraculously spares older women, and then contaminated the farm herself as her means to escape? What if their deaths had nothing to do with Sam the dog?"

"Oooh. That's an interesting idea." She paused and looked at the ceiling.

Could meek little Nian have created this doomsday bug? It didn't feel right.

"Hmm, I still don't buy it though," Ally said. "She would have to be a stone-faced killer. But I don't think a stone-faced killer would risk coming to America. I think she would evade all law enforcement and disappear. That's what I would do. But Defoe has a greater motive and opportunity. If you don't confront him directly, you need to find the middlemen."

"What do you mean?" Jason asked.

"So, let's assume Nian didn't play a role in creating the virus. People had to be paid to create the virus and deliver the blankets to the Russians. You know what they say, *follow the money*."

"We tried that. During the last election, all his funding came from Super PACs. Dark money. Plus, he's a straight arrow. No scandals, no bribes. A boring guy. Walt's been poking around Defoe too. Nothing."

"What about much further back? There could be a thread he can't cover up. What do we really know about the Vice President? How did he begin his political career? Who are his known associates?"

"Shit. I thought I'd have more luck sleuthing here, where all the virus scientists congregate. I'll work with Ortega to do a deeper dive on Defoe's financials and early contacts. But still be careful around Nian. To me, she's a question mark. We really don't know much about her…and what she's capable of."

"Sure. I'll be careful. Hey, you know, I have an idea. I'll let you know if anything comes of it. When you look at the money trail, look for medical research connections. We need to find the lab that created this monster and—more importantly—the monsters responsible."

DAY 104

The CDC virus vault...why hadn't she thought to check?

It was located in the basement of the now condemned building. Some types of viruses were copied and stored in other labs around the country, but those were usually ones actively studied. They had samples going back to World War I and II—although the CDC only began actively managing them in the early 1950s. The Army created a biowarfare lab at Fort Detrick during WWII. That lab had contained much more deadly items. However, that lab was disbanded in 1969 by President Nixon, who also ordered the destruction of all its bioweapon agents.

Ally went to see the vault manager to examine the log book and get a key. The last audit occurred last June; the report didn't mention anything missing or misplaced.

She ducked under the caution tape outside the building and snuck into the stairwell. The power was off and it was eerie going into the basement with just a flashlight. There were puddles on the floor, remnants from the torrent of water used to put out the fire. It bothered her that no one cleared out the vault letting samples deteriorate. But then again, they had bigger problems, like a global pandemic to solve.

The freezers were now warm. Decades worth of virus samples were now trashed. She went through the racks methodically. She had a paper inventory map, showing the physical locations of samples by type. She opened each drawer to compare to the inventory list. Nothing looked out of place.

If someone really wanted to steal a tube of virus, all they had to do is replace it with another similar looking vial with a new seal. It would require laboratory analysis of each vial to determine its actual contents. She sighed. That process would take weeks.

This is futile.

Maybe the visitor log would hold more clues?

She went back to the vault manager and asked for a photocopy. She took the pages back to her hotel to review.

It was going to be a long night.

* * *

Walt looked at his phone. He walked toward the outer doors and exited before he answered it.

"Jason, I'm at the White House. I can't talk long. What's up?"

"Ally asked me to call you. What's the status of the national quarantine order?"

"I've been trying. But he isn't getting it. The rally spooked him, but he doesn't watch the real news and he's shut himself inside."

Jason said, "You told Ally that you sometimes *read his briefs*. What if…hmm…what if there was an Executive Order, typed up, ready to go, and it *happened* to get on his desk, maybe shuffled among some other papers, do you think it would *get signed*?"

"As a hypothetical, it *might* be possible." Walt looked up and saw a Marine walking towards him. "Hey," Walt said in a louder voice, "how about those Atlanta Braves…they have quite a lineup this year!"

Jason laughed. "Sorry, I haven't had time to keep up with baseball. I'm guessing you really can't talk."

"Yeah, their new outfielder is amazing. When the outbreak is over, we should go to a game sometime."

"Ok, well, keep an eye out. Maya is working up some language and will email you."

"Sure thing. Talk with you soon!"

Walt hung up and tried to act casual.

The Marine that walked by didn't give him a second look.

* * *

Walt spent the evening on the phone with Maya after she sent her first draft of the Executive Order. He had some thoughts about the wording and they collaborated for a few hours to make it perfect. When they agreed it was ready, Walt printed a hard copy and brought it over to Cunningham's office.

I think he'll back me up, Walt thought. He rapped his knuckles on the doorframe of Jack's office.

"Jack, I need to show you something." Walt handed him the draft.

Jack took the pages and began reading. His lips moved as he read.

"Damn, Walt. Where did you get this?"

"Does it matter?"

"You know how the President feels," Jack said, peering over his reading glasses at him.

"Most of the cities and states are already under quarantine orders. This would reinforce the quarantine at the federal level, closing loopholes. Come on. This is serious. Um. What if he signs it…by accident?"

"Shhh. Look, I get it." Jack got up and closed the door to his office. In a whisper he said, "I appreciate you getting those MMR vaccines for my kids. I owe you a solid." Jack placed the papers on his desk. He wrung his hands together.

Walt smiled. "Yes, you do."

"Fine," Jack said. "I'll bring it to his secretary and have it put on Presidential stationery. But the rest is on you. I don't want to know about it. We never spoke about it. And we are even. Ok?"

"Got it," Walt said. "I'll throw myself on the sword if needed. You'll be clean. I promise."

Jack turned and opened his office door.

As Walt reached the doorway, he said, "I need it by Friday afternoon."

"Yeah, yeah." Jack shooed him out and closed the door.

Day 105

Jack Cunningham walked into the Oval Office and turned off the television. Merriwether was wearing his Grateful Dead t-shirt and sweatpants. "Sir, you really need to address the nation."

Dan wiggled the club without looking up. "Yeah? And say what?" He putted a golf ball across the oval office rug.

"People need reassurance, Mr. President. The disease is now in every state of the union including Hawaii. People are scared. So many of their loved ones have died. Businesses are closed because they don't have enough healthy workers. Vigilantes and gangs are continuing to kill stray dogs and now homeless people. Stores are being looted. National Guard personnel are pulling shifts around the clock to keep the peace."

Merriwether putted another ball and walked over to retrieve it.

"Sir, look at me! We need you to reassure the public, keep people calm."

Merriwether looked at him. "How in Christ am I supposed to do that? I don't feel calm myself. I'm going crazy cooped up in this stupid place. I can't even visit my winter home in Texas because a bunch of lunatics set it on fire."

Dan threw his putter on the floor. "All the golf tournaments across the country have been cancelled. There's nothing new on Netflix. Momma and Kiki are fighting like…like cats being baptized! On top of all that, my phone won't stop ringing. I didn't sign up for this!"

Jack's eyes narrowed. "Actually, sir, you did. Elections have consequences, as they say. But you must understand that the public needs to hear from you. Senator Cochran has been giving live YouTube vlogs every day for the last month. People are tuning into her by the thousands because they want to know our government is doing something…anything. Heads of other countries are calling her—instead of you—to get information. You are essentially handing her the presidency by staying silent."

Dan bent down to pick up the club. "So, what do I say?"

"We'll have the speechwriters put something together for you. We'll workshop it tomorrow morning and put you on air in the evening. Do I have a go-ahead to set it up with the networks?"

"Yeah. But keep the speech short. And don't use a lot of flowery poofy words. I don't want it to be like blah, blah, blah. People like me because I'm not a politician. Remember that."

"Yes sir. I'll have a draft to you in a few hours."

"Hey, send a copy to Tom. I want him to look at it beforehand." Merriwether yawned and stretched his back.

Jack wanted to smack Merriwether in the face and yell, "Wake up, nitwit!" But he took a deep calming breath and said, "Very well. In the meantime, maybe you should take a nap so you look rested for tomorrow." He began walking toward the door.

"Good idea. Just wake me by dinner. I hear it's mac and cheese night."

Jack grimaced and steadied himself next to the sofa for a moment before continuing out the door. "Very good. Have a good rest, Mr. President."

* * *

Tom spent some time with the speechwriter at the White House. The draft was short. *Probably all Merriwether could handle*. Still, it could use some punching up.

Over the last few months, he, the speechwriter, and Cunningham informally created their own version of the Merriam-Webster dictionary, that they called the Merriwether Dictionary. It consisted of shorter, less complicated words the President liked to use. Mark Twain said, "Don't use a five-dollar word when a fifty-cent word will do." In Merriwether's case, they looked for ten and two-cent words.

Trying to make a speech presidential—and address complex subjects—using these low-level words was the real challenge. All nuance was gone.

But the world was falling apart. Did speeches even matter anymore?

He needed to concentrate. He headed to the White House library. Merriwether rarely used it, storing a pallet-sized crate of his unsold memoir inside. It was a quiet place to think. As he approached, he smelled smoke. His body tensed. *A fire?*

He opened the door. Kiki was sitting in a high-back wing chair next to the fireplace, reading a thick hardcover book. Next to her, on a side table with a silver tray, a teapot and fine china cup and saucer. She was wearing a spandex top with sweatpants; her hair in long thick braids and her face was free of makeup.

"Sorry. Didn't mean to disturb you."

"Hey Tommy. Come on in."

"I smelled the fire and got alarmed."

"Oh, after what happened last week? That asswipe."

"Yes, I'll admit I'm a little jumpy. They electrified the fence, but the number of protestors in the park has doubled. Did you see the size of their bonfire?"

"I'm not scared. I had a mind to throw back my own present." Kiki smiled.

Last week a protestor scaled the fence and security gave chase. The deranged hippie made it up to the building and smeared excrement on an East Wing window before his capture.

Kiki lifted her butt and made a hand motion mimicking scooping a turd and tossing it like a grenade. "Feewww. Blam! Sheeet. Ha! They don't know who they dealin' wit!" She gave him a bright smile.

Tom laughed. *All we need is a war of flying excrement. That would certainly embody Merriwether's entire presidency.*

He changed the subject. "What are you reading?"

She showed him the cover. "Team of Rivals."

"That's a hefty book. I'll confess, I only made it half-way before giving up."

Kiki smiled, "I love Lincoln. I'm a total fan-girl."

He wasn't too surprised. During their other conversations, she appeared cognizant of world politics and spoke with very informed opinions. "Kiki, can I ask you something, candidly?"

"Keep it a hundred, I always say." She sipped from her tea cup.

He took a deep breath. "Why Dan?"

She put down her cup. "Why not Dan? You think I'm not good enough for him?" Her eyes narrowed.

"No. Quite the opposite. You are a beautiful woman. Smart. Appear to be well off financially. Fearless. In contrast, he's a slob. A moron."

"Oh. You think I'm beautiful?" She twirled a long braid, thrust her chest forward and smiled in a teasing way.

His cheeks felt hot. "I'm not saying you're my type, but…you know what I mean." He broke her gaze, staring at the fireplace.

"I'm just playin' wit you. You nice and all, but not my type either. Look it, Danny makes me laugh. Sweet as sugar. After he helped my cousin with a pardon. we hung out a few times. Clicked, ya know? We have a lot of fun. Takes me dancing. Treats me special."

Yet, she could do so much better. He didn't know how to counter. "Ok, I just…I'll let you get back to your book."

"Nice seeing you Tommy. You have a blessed day." She blew him a kiss as he exited.

He headed home to the Observatory. Tom got into the black SUV, thankful that it had ballistic protection. When they reached the gate to turn onto Connecticut Avenue, some teenagers surrounded the car and pounded on it. The crowd chanted, "We are dying! Dan, stop hiding!"

His driver nearly ran over one of the damned kids. Tom didn't know why he even bothered going to and from the White House anymore. He was much safer anywhere else.

Tom arrived at the Observatory. To his amazement, protesters didn't bother him there.

He sat down on the sofa and reached over to turn on the lamp on the side table. Tom missed his mark and knocked over his silver wrestling trophy.

He picked it up. Something odd inside.

A bug!

He knew he couldn't trust Ortega.

He went to his office, smashed the chip with a hammer and threw it in the trash.

Oh Lord, he choked back panic. *Did they know? Were agents White and Flanders in on this? Did Ortega trace the virus to his uncle's pharmaceutical company?*

He thought long and hard about all the calls he made to his uncle, Anders Cullen.

No. They were careful. Still, maybe Roadfuss talked. Despite his retirement, the Major General was a weak link. He should have killed him weeks ago.

Tom turned on the news and tried to clear his mind. The news showed the usual daily coverage of Senator Cochran's video speech, but scrolling along the bottom, a headline read:

"China goes dark—ninety percent of all towns are without power as other Asian countries experience daily brownouts."

The news anchor finished her piece and said, "After these messages, we'll talk to two former national security advisors about the global effects of the Red Death and what the current administration should do next."

Tom turned off the television. That simulation from the CDC stuck in his head. He hadn't intended to kill millions of people. All he wanted was a tiny little virus to take out a portion of the Russian army. After what Russia did to him, they deserved to be punished.

He knew from the start there wouldn't be a vaccine or anti-viral to stem the disease. But after he learned the death toll in Russia, his uncle confessed that they used a form of pneumonic plague as the host bacteria.

Sweet Jesus—plague.

The bacteria acted as the host for the hundred-year-old strain of chicken pox to ensure it got to Russia intact. Uncle Cullen was a madman. At least Cullen had the good sense to leave for his own private island when the first cases hit Texas.

The virus was never supposed to leave the Arctic. General Roadfuss was entrusted to ensure its containment.

Damned Chinese.

The just had to get involved. It might have been manageable

except for them. Now, the world was chaos and death.

As Tom headed upstairs to bed, the lights flickered for a few seconds and then returned to normal. The hum of the outside generator vibrated through the plaster walls.

Here we go.

Nearly time to head to the bunker.

CHAPTER 22

DAY 108

It was the first day back after a long Easter recess. Ruth stayed in D.C. although most of the other senators and congresspeople went back to their home states during the extended break.

Ruth walked into the Hart building, carrying a shopping bag and a briefcase. The hall was empty.

Where were the guards?

The building was as cold inside as outside. She walked up the staircase. Her heels on the marble treads echoed off the walls—none of the usual workday sounds to mask them. She looked down the second-floor hall—also empty.

She looked at her phone. It was still early, but there should be at least a few dozen staffers and representatives milling around, discussing their vacations.

She opened the door to her office. It was unlocked. Sally was there drinking coffee and typing on her computer. A small fire was burning in the fireplace and a space heater was oscillating next to her desk.

"Good morning! Where is everyone? It *is* Monday, right? Don't we have a session today?" She emptied her shopping bag, pulling out a cake covered in plastic wrap.

“Morning Ruth,” Sally said, “I got here an hour ago. I checked out the entire building, even the basement. I think it’s just you and me. Oh, and Miss Marilyn from food services. I found her in the boiler room, fixing the heating system. It was off again. But she called the superintendent, and he walked her through the steps to restart it."

"Did you call any of the other Senators? Do we know where everyone is?"

"I've been going through email. A few senators called out sick and decided to stay back home. A few others are taking care of sick family members. But most folks are M-I-A."

"Well, we knew the outbreak would hit our own at some point. What *was* on the agenda today?"

Sally leafed through her notebook. "A law indemnifying schools and other public and private organizations from lawsuits stemming from providing vaccinations. We also have legislation for increasing the debt ceiling, a resolution to re-name some public libraries, a change to the school lunch program dietary guidelines, suspension of acquisition regulations for purchasing emergency medical and burial supplies, and a motion to re-institute the draft for medical doctors."

"Hellooooo!"

Ruth and Sally peeked outside. Two more female senators, Mertz and Davis, waved at them from the end of the hall. They were wearing their coats and gloves.

"Hey!" Sally said. "So, there are other people here! Thank goodness!"

"Good morning, ladies," Ruth said. "It appears many of our colleagues are ill."

"Yeah, that's what we thought. I got a text from the head of the woman's caucus at the House. She said there are only about a couple dozen over there," Davis said.

"All women?" Sally asked.

"Yep!"

"Well, let's go!" Ruth said.

"What do you mean?" said Mertz.

"I want to see who's still left," Ruth said. "Maybe we can have an impromptu session."

"Session? We don't have anywhere near a quorum," Sally said.

"Ha! Says who?" Ruth said. "Let's go over and we can discuss it over some coffee. I brought in a pound cake. We can share it."

"Nice. I brought in bagels and cream cheese," said Mertz.

"I have a bag of Easter candy. But I think it's too early for jelly beans," Davis said.

Ruth looked at her feet. "I'm going to change into my sneakers. I suggest you all do the same if possible. Give me a minute."

"I'll get my coat and my laptop," Sally said.

Ruth and Sally re-emerged wearing sneakers, each carrying a large briefcase and laptop bag. The group headed down the hall towards the stairs.

"Wait!" Sally said. "What about Miss Marilyn? I'll find her and ask her to come with. If anyone else shows up, she can tell them to meet us over there."

"Hmm," Ruth said. "How about we leave a note on the front door and we bring Marilyn with us? We can't leave her here alone to rattle around these frigid, empty halls."

"Who's got a marker?" Mertz asked.

The women left a note on both entrances to the building.

"Go to the House chambers.
Possible session today. Wear sneakers.
Bring snacks!"

* * *

At Rayburn, the three senators greeted twenty-five congresswomen. Some of them were wearing gray hats. The women sat together, chatting and eating, waiting to see if anyone else would show up. A half-hour later, another ten female senators arrived.

"Ladies, this is a unique situation," Ruth announced.

"Yes, how can we accomplish anything?" Representative Valendez asked. "I've been going through the recall list all morning. Many of our counterparts are self-quarantined or too ill to travel. I think we should all go home until the virus subsides."

"You mean not govern?" Ruth asked. "Don't be silly. We swore an oath to uphold the constitution. As long as there is breath in my lungs, I'm going to show up and do my job."

"Ruth, stop campaigning. At this rate, we'll have to postpone the election in November. We don't have adequate representation to hold any sessions."

"Ladies, put on some comfortable shoes, bring your coats and come with me."

They looked at each other, perplexed. "Where are you going?"

"The Capitol, of course. Just humor me. What else do you have planned today?"

The women followed Ruth to the Capitol. As they passed through the Rotunda, the sunlight beamed across the ornate floors, almost on cue as they walked along. The heat of the rays crossed her face.

Yes, it was time to shake things up.

Ruth escorted the women into the Senate chamber. A camera operator from C-SPAN was sorting out electric cords on the floor.

"Good Morning, Senator Cochran!" the camerawoman said. "I wasn't sure if there would be any sessions today! Where is everyone?"

"Hey Carly, we're getting a late start. Are the cameras on?"

"Kind of. We have the overhead shot as a screen inset while we replay some old interviews. My producer and I were just on the phone wondering if I should just head home. When do you expect to begin this morning?"

"Momentarily. Is the sound off?" Ruth said.

"Yes, ma'am," Carly said. "I see some House members are here. Are you having a joint session or something?"

"Um, no, they are just here for support. I'll signal you when you can begin transmitting. Why don't you get some coffee? We won't be starting for another fifteen minutes."

"Got it. I'll be right back," Carly said.

After Carly left, the other women stared at Ruth.

"What is going on, Ruth? What are we doing here?" Davis asked.

"We're going to have some fun." Ruth smiled. "I'd like you all to play along. Who's with me?"

Senator Mertz said, "Like we have anything better to do? I'm game."

Ruth looked at the others. They shrugged and raised their hands.

"Great, we don't have much time," Ruth said. "I grabbed the old healthcare bill out of my filing cabinet. We are going to have a floor vote!"

"What?" Senator Davis cried. "But it won't mean anything. We don't have enough members present."

Ruth took off her coat. "Everyone! Pay attention. I'll keep the electronic voting open for forty minutes. Who knows how many people will show up? I think a few people over at Hart and Russell said they are voting electronically from their office today." She winked.

Davis said, "Wait…you mean…oh! Ok!"

Some women laughed and talked amongst themselves.

"Damn, now I know why you wore your sneakers!" Sally said.

"Ok, who is a good runner here?" Mertz asked.

Representative Smith cracked her knuckles. "This is so frickin' illegal. Let's do this thing!"

They continued laughing.

"Keys! Who has keys?" Mertz asked.

Miss Marilyn walked up to Ruth and whispered in her ear.

"Great!" Ruth said. "Go show Sally where to get the master key. We'll meet you over there in a few minutes. Try to open as many as you can. Go! Go!"

Sally and Marilyn headed out the door, whispering to each other.

"My distinguished colleagues of the House, let's synchronize our watches," Ruth said. "The quorum call begins in fifteen minutes and the vote begins at ten o'clock sharp. I expect we will see many affirmative votes, yes? We'll all meet back here afterward."

The House representatives departed, whispering plans to each other. Only Ruth, Mertz, Davis, and a few other senators were left.

Ruth went to the podium and typed in the health bill information. She waited until Carly returned. The red light illuminated on Carly's camera, and Ruth opened the session with her gavel.

"Today we will vote on S.R. Bill 2004, titled the Medicare for All Modernization Act, otherwise known as MAMA."

Senator Davis requested a quorum call.

"Yes," Ruth announced, "as you can see, a quorum call is warranted based on the number of empty seats. Many of our colleagues are voting from their offices to preserve the quarantine. An electronic quorum call is in effect for the next twenty minutes."

The vote count began increasing on the monitor. When the number of 'present' reached sixty, Ruth announced the quorum was reached and voting would begin.

The senators signaled their votes within the chamber and promptly left. Ruth watched the monitor. The votes for yes came rolling in slowly and steadily. She could only imagine the mayhem over at the office buildings.

Ruth looked over at Carly.

Carly was grinning.

She knows what we're up to...and she doesn't care!

Ruth took deep breaths, trying to remain straight-faced. The cameras were on. *This needs to look official.*

After forty minutes, all the votes were cast. Carly turned off the camera, walked over to Ruth and held up her hand for a "high five."

Ruth didn't do high fives. She offered a handshake instead. Carly gave her a fist bump as a compromise, then gathered her belongings and departed.

When Carly left, Ruth walked outside to the hallway. Several women come jogging up. They stopped and bent over, catching their breath. Their coats were gone. Their faces were red. Beads of sweat ran down the sides of their faces.

"Are you guys ok?" Ruth asked.

"That was the most fun I've had in a long time!" Valendez cried.

"Yeah, it was epic!" Smith said. "Half-way through, I slipped on the stairs and scraped my arm." She held up her arm and showed where her sleeve had a tear and had spots of blood. "But otherwise, it was fantastic. I wish you could have seen us!"

The other women hobbled over. They were also sweaty and breathing hard. Miss Marilyn was the last to arrive—being helped by Sally.

"Well ladies, as you can see," pointing to the monitor, "The ayes have it!"

"Miss Ruth, I want to thank you," Miss Marilyn said. "This was the best day of work I can remember. I've seen a lot in my time, but nothin' like this."

"Hold on. This doesn't mean a thing," Senator Davis said. "Even if the Senate passes bills—legally or otherwise—we can't enact laws without the House and the President. Goodness, it would take hours to try this in the House. And even if we got away with it, the President wouldn't sign it."

"I believe the Speaker can set whatever time limits they want for a floor vote," Ruth said. "If I recall correctly, I remember a floor vote that remained open for two days. As for the President, just leave that up to me."

"Ruth, this was great," Senator Mertz said. "It made my day…actually my year, but we are seriously out of bounds here. We have a constitution and laws. This was a fun game, but we can't govern this way!"

"Well, tell me this…how can we govern at all if we follow the rules?" Ruth said. "We don't know who is dead and how they will be replaced. We can't physically retrieve our fellow legislators to bring them out of hiding. Did the framers ever envision this situation? Do we abandon all government because we're in crisis? This is precisely the time that the country needs us most. I would argue that we are within the spirit of the constitution to keep congress functioning."

The women began talking amongst themselves. "Damn, I don't know." "It's wrong, but we can do some good." "What do you think?"

"I agree with some of your arguments," Smith said. "I'm all for fun, but we need to be practical. If our current constitution and rules of order can't be adapted to our situation, perhaps we need to consider changing them."

Ruth turned to the senior member of the House and said, "I agree. But I'm not sure we have the time or ability to get ratification from the States. Look, we don't have to decide right now. I think we need to take some time and consider our options."

"Hey, we saw Carly heading out," Senator Davis said. "Did she say anything to you? Is she *cool*?"

"Ladies, I think we are just fine," Ruth said. She held up her briefcase. "So, what do we want to vote on next?"

The women laughed and hooted.

"Hey, I vote we all get shit-faced!" Davis cried. "I have a fifty-year-old bottle of bourbon and some champagne in my office."

"Seconded!"

Thirty-eight!"

Ruth said, "The motion carries. Senator Davis, lead on!"

CHAPTER 23

DAY 109

Ally took a break from reviewing the vault's log book and researching papers on both new and ancient viruses. She called her dad again…still no answer.

Did he forget to charge his phone again? Maybe that's it.

She tried her sister and also got voice mail but left a message. She called her son, Theo. He didn't pick up but texted back,

"We're at the hospital. Charlotte has a high fever.
We'll call when we know more."

Her heart stopped.

Is Charlotte dying?

Her mind raced, doing the math. *Thirteen? Maybe a fourteen-hour drive?* She looked at the clock on her phone.

There were a hundred scientists working on the antigen for the vaccine.

They wouldn't miss her, right?

Yet, what if she or Jason could find the creator of this abomination? It could save the world. And Charlotte, too.

Gretchen came over and yowled.

"Yes, kitty, come cuddle." Ally stroked her fur and thought about Jim. She got off the sofa and went to the dresser and put on his old flannel button-down shirt and her pajama bottoms. The shirt didn't smell like him anymore, but she found the volume of it comforting.

She turned on the television to watch the news. But her mind was elsewhere.

After all this is over, she vowed, *I'll never leave my family again.*

Her mind flashed back to her childhood growing up in Central New Jersey. Some of her earliest memories were spending time with her mom, tending their tiny backyard vegetable garden. She loved playing in the dirt. The fuzzy stems of the squash vines pricked her young skin. The sun bleached her hair nearly white. She remembered her attempts at pulling weeds. Many good plants suffered at her small hands. How was she supposed to know the difference?

Mom put her in charge of picking the cherry tomatoes—but she called them baby tomatoes. She ate more than she gathered.

These memories made her happy and then sad. *Will I ever get to pick baby tomatoes with Charlotte?*

She turned off the television, went to her bedroom, and set her alarm. Gretchen followed her up onto the bed and wedged herself next to her pillow.

She closed her eyes, trying to push images of death out of her mind.

Maybe Charlotte will be just fine.

Maybe dad just needs to charge his phone.

She would call Dad and Theo in the morning.

DAY 110

When Ally arrived at work the next morning, Jason was waiting for her. His feet were propped up on her desk and he wore a huge grin. Her world was crumbling. *What could he possibly be so happy about?*

"Hey Jason. I don't know if we'll find a smoking gun here at CDC. The log books didn't show anything worth looking into. Why are you here so early?"

"You were right," Jason said. "Just like you said. I followed the money. Or rather, I looked into all of Defoe's donors, friends and family. I also checked his legislative history during his time in the Senate. As a senator, he received a disproportionate amount of donations from big pharma. That isn't unusual, right? But, wait for it...," Jason paused and did a pretend drum roll. "Did you know he's related to the CEO and founder of Cullen Pharmaceutical?"

"No! Wow. That could explain a lot."

"Well, I looked into more. Their CEO, Anders Cullen, is believed to have left the country two months ago, not long after the Chinese video came out. No one has seen him or his private jet since. So, my bet is Cullen developed the virus for Defoe and left when things got bad."

"It's definitely worth looking into. But it's such a large company. They have labs across the country. Where do you think we should start?"

"I think we need to drag that sorry prick Cullen back to the States and throw him in a dark cell until he talks!"

"I have no problem with that! But I think we need to find the person who created the virus. Even if Cullen was behind it, CEOs don't normally work in labs. Do you think you could get him to tell us the names of people who created it?"

"I'll do my best."

"But how will you find Cullen?" Ally asked.

"Remember the Panama Papers? Well, they showed Cullen bought a small private island in the Bahamas through a shell company seven years ago. It has its own airstrip. If I were Cullen, that's where I'd go."

"When are you leaving?"

"I have a call into Aunt Ruth and Director Ortega. I'm hoping they can requisition a government plane for me. There are some other kinks to work out. We can't broadcast our plans too widely. There's still a chance the Vice President could catch wind of it and warn Cullen. It will be a two-person job, just me and a pilot."

"Great, I'm coming with you."

"What? No. It's too dangerous. You're a civilian. Cullen won't go with us quietly. He reportedly had bodyguards before this whole situation. I bet he still has armed security."

"Look, I'm a big girl. You aren't the only one who spent time in war zones. I went on all kinds of missions in dangerous places trying to halt outbreaks. We don't have time to waste. If he has information that can save some lives, I need to talk to him immediately. Besides, you're still recovering from your gunshot wound. Let me have your back."

He shook his head. "Ally, I'm fine."

"I'm still going with you. Don't argue with me."

Jason rubbed his temples. "Will you do everything I say?"

"Promise."

Jason sighed. "You understand I can't protect you and find Cullen at the same time. If you go, you're going to have to carry a gun and fire it at very bad guys. And not accidently shoot yourself or me in the process."

"I can handle myself. Jim took me to a gun range before my trip to Kosovo in 1990."

Jason crossed his arms and frowned. "Lady, that was decades ago."

"Ok, point taken."

"This is such a shit idea." He held his face with both hands.

"Did I ever tell you the story of how I saved a U.N. worker who was shot in the leg?"

"No."

"I had to improvise. A real bleeder. Used my bra as a tourniquet." Ally smiled at him.

Jason frowned. "This isn't funny."

"It kind of is."

"You need practice. There's an indoor range a couple miles from here."

"Fine. Let's go."

* * *

After an afternoon of target practice with Jason, Ally arrived back at the hotel and tried calling her dad and son again. *No answer.* She called her sister, Gwen.

"Sis, what's going on? How is everyone? I haven't heard from dad in days. Any update on Lottie?"

"Things are really bad here," Gwen said. "I'm taking care of everyone. I know what you're doing is really important. I didn't want to distract you."

"Nothing is more important than all of you. So please, tell me."

"Everyone here is sick, although I'm still ok. Charlotte has been on a respirator in intensive care for two days. She's a real fighter. The hospital told Theo and Rose to go home. They came down with fevers; might be infected."

"Oh, my God!" Ally eased her body down to the floor, let out a deep breath. "I knew Charlotte was sick, but they didn't say how badly." She tried to focus. "What about dad?"

Gwen paused. "Sorry, haven't heard from him in two days; he's not answering his phone. I've been meaning to head over there but haven't found time."

Ally held her head with her free hand. "Wait, you said everyone is sick. So that means George and all the boys?"

"Yes. I'm also making meals for the church to distribute to the sick and elderly. I haven't slept much."

"You should have called! I would've come home. I can still come home."

"Ally, if you and your team don't find a cure soon, it won't matter if you come home. I know you want to be here. I wish you were here too. Let me take care of things. I'll look in on Dad, Theo, and Charlotte tomorrow. I promise! Oh, I have to go. One of the boys is calling me. I really have to go. I'll call you soon."

The call disconnected.

Tears welled up and she found it difficult to breathe. Ally remembered when Charlotte was born—the wonderful smell of her warm baby skin, her tiny fingers.

She hugged her torso, rocking back and forth, imagining Lottie's small body lying in a hospital bed connected to tubes and machines. And Gwen might lose her husband and kids. It was too much to process.

She crawled into her bed, her body trembling, her throat choking on tears. She clutched her pillow and buried her face, the pillowcase become soaked. The question "why?" reverberated in her mind. Her head throbbed; her chest tight.

Exhaustion and sleep eventually took over.

Sometime later, she woke to a darkened room. She turned on the lights and splashed some cold water on her face. Her eyes were red and swollen. She splashed more water on them, but the puffiness remained.

She stared at her face. Her eyes went from a dark blue to bright cyan when she cried. She always found it fascinating…like a science experiment. Crystal-like orbs, surrounded by red splotchy skin. She had forgotten how freakish crying made her look. *Not since Jim's funeral…*

She checked the time. Late for dinner with Jason at the cafeteria. She texted him to go without her.

Ally blew her nose. Then she became angry.

Why did Senator Cochran bring me into this?

She thought back to her first meeting with Walt. She understood his reasons. After he found out about the blankets, he probably didn't know who he could trust. But Cochran was the leader of the damned Senate! She could have taken the intel Jason acquired and made it public. She could have rescued Nian and contacted the CDC herself. Ruth was a doctor, after all. She probably knew what was going on with the Vice President the whole time!

Ally tried to distract herself by turning on the television and watching a rerun of Mary Tyler Moore. But her dark thoughts kept coming back.

I'm so stupid. So excited about a new virus, I didn't ask basic questions.

I should have walked away the first time I met Jason.

All her fretting was unproductive. *Sleep. I'll go back to sleep.*

She shut off the TV. The hotel room door opened.

Maya.

Ally jogged into her bedroom, closed the door, and turned off the light. She pretended to be asleep. Tomorrow was a big day. Her new handgun was tucked in her backpack. At dawn, she and Jason were flying to the Caribbean to find Cullen.

Cullen better have a treatment or vaccine.

He had to.

Otherwise, her family and the planet were doomed.

CHAPTER 24

DAY 111

At the break of dawn, Ally accompanied Jason to the municipal airport. When the walked into the small hangar, two women were standing next to a Twin Otter. They were comparing side-arms. To Ally's surprise, one of them was Jolie Walker.

Jason approached the younger female. "Ally, this is Kristina." Jason extended his hand to Jolie. "You must be Ms. Walker. Thanks for helping us today."

Ally shook hands with Kristina. She seemed to be close to Jason's age, with a round face, shaved head and a tattoo on the inside of her forearm of a pin-up girl wearing a sailor's hat. "Jason told me great things about you."

"Jason and I go back. Did he tell you about Betsie here?" She patted the plane.

She looked at Jason. "No."

He grinned.

Kristina said, "It was seized from a notorious drug lord. I'm not supposed to tell you his name. But its reinforced with Kevlar and bulletproof glass. Could come in handy."

Ally looked at the faces of the team. They all seemed confident and energized. Their confidence should have calmed her nerves.

Jason showed them an aerial image of Cullen's private island. It was small—but large enough to include a three-thousand-foot dirt runway. It wasn't on any aeronautical charts, but easily visible on satellite images.

They went over the plan. Jason emphasized that Cullen's guards would likely shoot anyone attempting to land on the island. But their secret weapon should give them the advantage.

"Are we ready to go?" Jason asked.

They piled into the plane carrying their Kevlar vests.

After two hours in the air, Kristina went on comms to tell them she would circle around and approach from the south. As the passed over the island, Ally peered down at a large, Tuscan-style house with gaudy Italian marble statues lining the back patio. The place looked uninhabited.

Ally didn't know whether to be angry or relieved. Her heart was beating out of her chest thinking about the possibility of confronting armed security. She took her handgun out of her backpack.

The plane descended quickly—too quickly. Ally looked out the window; holding her breath as the plane lined up with the airstrip.

I hope Kristina knows what she's doing. She gripped the armrest, her fingers turning white.

Finally, the plane hit the dirt and bounced violently down the field.

Through the small round window, Ally saw two men running toward them from about four hundred feet away. The men had crew cuts, wore shorts and Hawaiian shirts, but were holding AK-47's.

Oh God, Ally thought. *We're all gonna die.*

She took out her vest and put it on. She fastened her handgun at her waist.

Her instructions were to stay back and let Jason, Kristina, and Jolie make the first moves. They had a plan—more of a scheme really. It was a little bizarre, but they were the experts.

Before the propellers stopped turning, Jason jumped out of the aircraft and opened the rear side hatch. Kristina and Jolie followed Jason outside and laid down cover fire. He pulled down a narrow aluminum ramp and unlocked the cargo area.

Jolie blew a whistle in a long, loud burst. "Go Go Go!"

Ally watched as six enormous Rottweilers, wearing armor, emerged from the cargo bay. The dogs ran toward the armed men. Jason fired toward the guards, aiming high to avoid the dogs.

Damn, Jolie's dogs are fast!

The men stopped in their tracks once they saw the dogs. They looked at each other. One of them turned and ran toward the house.

The other one shot at the dogs and missed a couple times before he ran in the opposite direction toward a grove of wild vegetation.

Ally followed Jolie, who was following Jason, who was following the dogs, who were chasing the guards. Kristina stayed with the plane so they would be ready to take off at a moment's notice.

It worked! I told Jason his idea was stupid. *I should trust him more.*

Actually, it was Jolie's idea. Jolie's Rottweilers were intended to go to a Federal drug interdiction team at the border. Those contracts were cancelled weeks ago.

Ally tried to keep up. It felt awkward to hold a gun while running. Much heavier than the baton she used in high school track.

When he finally slowed near the residence, three of the dogs were viciously mauling one guard next to the in-ground swimming pool. Flesh ripped from the man's arms and legs. A huge chunk was removed from the guard's throat. He died quickly.

Jolie snapped her fingers at the dogs and the three left their target and sat obediently in a row next to the diving board.

The other guard and three dogs were nowhere in sight.

Jolie whispered, "I'm going to stay outside and keep watch with the dogs."

The house had a series of French doors facing the pool. Jason picked up the guard's discarded weapon and motioned to Ally to walk behind him. He peered inside and quietly entered a grand, high-ceiling living room. A television was on but silent, tuned to CNN International with no news anchor…just scrolling text and images describing the death tolls in various countries.

Ally shivered. The air was cool inside, but it was the décor that made her skin crawl. A bearskin rug scowled at her with large teeth. In the corner, a taxidermied lioness with her two cubs stared at her with glass eyes. Down the hall, toward the foyer, a stuffed polar bear stood on its hind legs.

She remembered reading that psychopaths usually collected animal predators like lions. *Was Cullen a psychopath?*

A half-full glass of wine sat on the side table beside a green leather chair. Jason placed his hand on the seat. He whispered, "warm."

He couldn't be far.

"Stay here," Jason whispered.

Ally nodded and looked for a place to hide. She ducked behind the lioness. As she waited, she strained to hear Jason's footsteps on the stairs. After a few seconds, much louder noises—a door smashing—the grunts of a skirmish—a body hitting the floor—and then a man's voice sobbing.

Cullen!

Cullen pleaded with Jason to let him go. She heard scuffling on the stairs. From the thudding noises, she imagined Jason dragging him.

"Look," Cullen cried. "I have everything you'd ever want." [thump] "Stop! This place is solar powered. I have food for fifty years…and a wine cellar." [thump] "Wait! Books! I have books!" [thump thump] "Ow! Do you like movies? I have hundreds of them! Ow!" [thump crash] "It's all yours. Don't kill me!"

Jason said, "Shut up. Shut up or I'll shoot you and ask questions later."

When they entered the room, Ally came out from the corner. "Anders Cullen? We have some questions for you."

"Tell your goon to lower his weapon," Cullen said, trying to straighten his shirt. He was missing one shoe and there was blood on his lip. "What did you do to my guards?"

Jason pointed toward the patio.

Cullen screamed—seeing chunks of limbs with shredded, bloody Hawaiian fabric scattered next to the pool. Cullen placed his hand over his eyes. "Who *are you*? What do you want?"

She grabbed Cullen's arm and walked him to the chair. "Sit! Our names are not important. I'm a doctor. I'm trying to stop the virus. We aren't here to kill you. Just get information—information that could help save millions of people. If you cooperate, I promise my goon—I mean Jason—won't kill you."

Cullen picked up the wine glass and drank the rest. He looked at the gun in Jason's hand. "I suppose I don't have any choice now, do I?"

Ally took the wine glass from Cullen's hand and transferred it back to the side table. "First, I need the names of the people that created the virus and where we can find them. Then, please tell us you were smart enough to have a vaccine already developed…there are labs all over the world ready to begin production."

"Oh, you silly woman." Cullen wiped the sweat from his forehead on his sleeve and then touched his swollen lip and sucked the blood from his fingers. "Do you really think I would be on this stupid island if there was a vaccine? No, this is Armageddon, sweetheart. Does it matter who created it?"

"Yes, if we could talk with them…" Ally said.

"Hey, shit for brains," Jason said. "Answer the questions now or I can take off body parts…or better yet, I can just call the dogs in here." He put a whistle to his lips.

Cullen raised his hands defensively. Sweat glistened on his forehead. "Oh, no need for that. I guess nothing really matters anymore. You just won't like what I have to say." Cullen paused and sighed loudly. "Well, I'm sorry to say that the researcher who developed this nightmare is gone. It's a sad tale..."

"What do you mean? Keep going," Ally demanded.

"Fine. Well. I had a brilliant scientist on my staff, Dave. He was a master at infectious diseases. Began his career with the CDC before coming to the private sector. He came up with several of our patentable drugs. But I suppose this is beside the point."

Cullen rubbed his temples. "I didn't know at the time. He was emotionally unstable. Sure, there were inklings of him having trouble at home. Office banter. Something about his wife being an alcoholic. But Dave was an excellent employee. He never talked about his personal life with me. He showed up to work early and stayed late. An ideal subordinate in every way. I trusted him completely. Only after the fact, sadly, did I learn the real story."

"Yes, keep going," Ally said, tapping the gun at her waist.

"A year prior, Dave came home from work and found his twelve-month-old son drowned in a bathtub—while his wife was passed out drunk. A horrible tragedy. Unimaginable really." Cullen paused and looked around. "Would you get me some more wine from the kitchen?" Cullen held up the empty glass.

"No." Jason swatted the glass onto the floor. It shattered, pieces flying across the terra cotta floor. "Don't change the subject. Go on."

"Well, in my defense, when I approached Dave to create this virus, I didn't know his mental state. He was severely depressed. I found out afterward…too late. Yes, maybe I should have known. But what I'm trying to say is—unfortunately—he may have been a little overzealous or angry and created something far more lethal and persistent than we intended."

"So, you didn't plan a mass-extinction level virus? Is that what you're saying?" Ally asked.

"No, not at all. Just wanted to take out a few Russians. You know, send a message."

"Fuck," Ally muttered.

Cullen paused and rubbed his eyes. "But there's more. A couple of days after Dave delivered the virus to me, he committed suicide."

"Shit!" Ally said.

"Holy hell!" Jason said. "You let an unhinged, grieving father create a deadly bioweapon! Are you fucking insane?"

Jason turned to Ally. "Ally, let me kill this prick right now!"

"Jason, don't. Did this Dave person leave any notes about how he created it or how to stop it?"

"Sorry to say, he didn't. He left a different kind of note though." Cullen pulled out a folded piece of paper from his shirt pocket. "I carry this around with me…I'm not sure why."

Ally took the paper and unfolded it. It was a suicide note. It read,

"My Charlie is gone. I don't want to live in this world anymore. I need to be with him. I'm sorry, Dave."

Tears formed as she contemplated the level of pain that Dave must have been in. She recalled the similar idea she had after Jim passed. She did not subscribe to the notion of an afterlife. Yet, there were days she wanted to join Jim…to end it all, and make the pain stop. She was having these same thoughts right now.

Was baby Lottie already dead?

She passed the note to Jason. As Jason examined the paper, she unhooked the gun from her belt. She imagined holding the cold metal to her temple.

It would be over so quickly.

But self-pity turned into a blind rage.

She whispered to Cullen, "You killed…the world."

Her fingers trembled. She raised the gun to Cullen's forehead and pulled the trigger.

Jason flinched at the blast and dropped the note. "Holy hell…"

Cullen's body went limp in the chair, surrounded by the splatter of blood and brains.

"What did you do?" Jason cried. He braced Cullen's body as it lurched forward, but then let it slide to the floor. He wiped his hands on his pants.

She slipped her gun into its holster and closed her eyes. She wiped away her tears with the back of her hand. "Let's go home."

She walked toward the patio door and kept walking past Jolie and the dogs toward their plane—she didn't look back.

As they got to the airfield, screams and growls pierced the air. The dogs had gotten their other mark.

"Ally," Jason called out as she reached the plane. He took her by the shoulders and looked her squarely in the eyes. "Do you want to talk about this?"

She handed her gun to him and said flatly, "No. I'm good. Let's get the fuck out of here."

In the distance, Ally heard three staccato blasts of Jolie's whistle.

"I'll be inside," Ally said, climbing into the back seat.

Shortly after, Jolie and the six dogs emerged from the tree line, walking toward the runway. Ally watched as the dogs went back up the ramp into the cargo bay and Jolie closed the hatch.

Ally could discern the three whispering outside the aircraft.

"She did *what*?" Kristina said.

"Is she ok?" Jolie asked.

Then some other indistinguishable murmurs.

Jason said, "Let's give her some space."

The three boarded and didn't say a word.

Normally, she would have felt awkward or apologized. But she didn't care. Not about them, not about herself, not about anything.

She glanced at her watch. The flight back would take a couple hours.

How many people would die in those two hours?

Would her family be alive when she got home?

During the flight, Ally envisioned their plane crashing into the ocean, splintering into tiny pieces…instant death. Like all those episodes of *Air Disasters* Jim loved to watch.

It was all she hoped for.

* * *

Jason gave Ally some space. He sat next to Kristina in the copilot's chair. Kristina started to ask questions but Jason just said, "Later."

He waited for Ally to open up. After take-off, he offered her some bottled water. She shook her head and turned away, staring out the window. For two hours, she didn't say a single word. When they touched down at Peachtree-DeKalb Airport and got off the airplane, Ally acted as if nothing happened. He watched her walk through the empty terminal.

"Wait! You still won't talk to me?" Jason said, trying to keep up with her. "Look, I understand. If *you* didn't do it, *I* may have. He was a piece of excrement…human garbage. But at some point, you will have to deal with this. I know. I've been there."

"No, I don't think you know what I'm going through. I don't give a shit about Cullen. A bullet was too kind for that asshole."

"So, what is it?"

She stopped walking. "Did you know that my entire family is dying? Including my granddaughter? I thought I knew what pain was when Jim died. I was wrong. I was so wrong."

"What? When?"

Ally gave him a cold stare. "Just go home." She turned and walked through the airport terminal.

Jason stopped. *How did I not know about her family?*

Oh. Right. He never asked her.

All this time he never once asked her how she was doing. What he could do to help her.

He watched her leave through the automatic doors. Through the glass, he saw her put on a face mask and gloves, and then hail a ride. An Omega-Car pulled up with the 'ω' logo on van's side window, driven by a woman with white frizzy hair.

Jason turned around and retraced his route back through the terminal and found Kristina. Nearby, Jolie was giving the Rottweilers fresh water.

"After we bring Jolie back to Texas, I'm returning to DC. It's time I went home."

As they took off, he texted Maya.

I'm going back home.
Please take care of our girl.

* * *

It was late afternoon when Ally walked into the Director's office.

Renée's secretary looked at her, head tilted.

"I don't have an appointment," Ally explained, rubbing her eyes.

The receptionist waved her on toward Renée's office.

Putting down her glasses, Renée said, "How was your expedition with Jason?"

Ally planted herself in the visitor's chair in front of Renée's desk. "The scientist that created the virus—he killed himself. He didn't leave any notes. It was stupid to have hoped."

"Allison, it is never *stupid* to have hope. Are you ok? You look tired."

Ally picked at her fingers. "That must be it. I'm tired. Did the team discover anything while I was away?"

"Actually, yes," Renée said. "Based on another review of the interviews and some additional questioning of the survivors, we now have reasonable certainty that they all had the new shingles vaccine."

Ally closed her eyes. "So that explains maybe why their immune systems attacked and defeated the chicken pox-like virus." She leaned forward in the chair. "But what about the bacterial component? Pneumonic plague is extremely deadly."

"The shingles vaccine not only includes the chicken pox antigen; it also includes an adjuvant. It produces more antibodies plus a twenty-four-fold increase in CD4 T-cells. These helper cells increase the body's response to infections.

"Ok, so let me see if I have this straight. The shingles vaccine is usually administered to people over fifty. But why are women surviving more than the men? Shouldn't men over fifty have the same protection?"

"I was puzzled by this too—at first. Let me ask you something. What is the worst case of shingles you've ever heard of?"

Ally leaned back in the chair and stared at the ceiling tiles. "Oh, there are quite a few to choose from. My mother-in-law got shingles around her eyes! Even when the rash subsided, she still couldn't make her own tears. Had to use eye drops for the rest of her life. And a friend of mine had shingles pain for over six years. She tried every type of painkiller with little relief. She finally discovered acupuncture—she went three times a week. Oh, and my sister had shingles last year. Right under her arm. She couldn't wear a bra for two months."

"Now, let me ask you another question. Of all the men you know over fifty—that don't have chronic illness—how many regularly get checkups of their own volition?"

Ally thought for a moment. Then she shook her head and then stared at Renée. "Wait, you mean…"

"Exactly. Men are not as diligent about pre-emptive care. But, in fairness, women contract shingles at a higher incidence than men. They are also more likely to share their painful stories with other women. You came up with three without having to think about it. So, it isn't surprising that when the new vaccine came out, more women than men signed up to get it. The number of people who have received it thus far is fairly low—about seven million—less than two percent of the U.S. population."

"Does the vaccine work on younger people?" Ally asked.

"We hope so. We're working on some other ways to boost people's immune systems. Senator Cochran introduced a bill to nationalize the company that holds the vaccine patent. It's expected to pass overwhelmingly."

"Maybe there is hope after all," Ally said.

"Allison," Renée said, leaning forward. "I don't want to give you false hope."

"Why? We might have a way to protect people! The quarantine is in place. The protocol to disinfect the dogs is working. This all sounds promising."

Renée picked up a stack of papers and flipped through them. She placed a page on top and handed it to Ally.

Ally scanned the paper. *No. Is this real?* She got to her feet. "Wait, I thought New York was doing better than this. The death count is that high? And…hold on…the number at the bottom…is that the national total? No, this must be a mistake."

"I wish it was. Between the confirmed count and those currently sick, we will have lost at about 250 million people by the time this is over—in the U.S. alone."

Ally handed the sheet back. "What about other countries? How are they faring?" She scanned Renée's desk for similar reports.

"With the blackouts and reduced internet access, the reports are spotty. But they tell a similar story. We played with your model. Using these reports, about eighty to ninety percent of the earth's population could be gone by the end of the calendar year."

"What are we going to do?" She slumped back into the chair.

Renée re-sorted the piles of paper on her desk and picked up her phone. "I don't know about you, but I'm going to get back to work."

"You know," Ally said, resting her neck on the back of the chair, "Cullen's private island has enough food and supplies for fifty years."

Renée put down the phone. "Really? Are you thinking of going back there? I wouldn't blame you if you did."

Ally shook her head. *Maybe nothing matters anymore.* "It's tempting on one level. Maybe after this is all over, we can go there to forget about death for a while."

"Sounds good. I think we could all use a break," Renée said. "Now, I've got some calls to make and e-mails to send. Maya was just looking for you. Get some dinner and report back tomorrow." She pointed to the door.

Ally nodded and rolled up slowly from the chair.

She wandered out of Renée's office, through the halls of the lab building, and ambled catatonically towards the cafeteria. She contemplated food, but wasn't hungry.

Food used to make her happy. Lots of things *used to* make her happy. Now she couldn't think of anything worth smiling about.

She changed direction to walk back to the hotel. The sun was going down and the streets and sidewalks were empty. Faint sirens in the distance blended with a chorus of crickets. An Omega-Ride vehicle slowed down, but she waived them off.

A few minutes later, a family of skunks bobbed and undulated in a tight pack down the center of the street, unfazed by her presence. *A surfeit?* She recalled in grade school that a group of skunks was called a surfeit; making up the mnemonic that skunks "sure can fight." The encounter should have made her smile.

Instead, only emptiness.

She wondered if she would ever be happy again.

Chapter 25

Day 112

On a sunny early Sunday morning, Merriwether stared at the leather-bound folder on his desk. He wracked his brain and couldn't remember signing the Executive Order for the national quarantine two days ago. But Walt assured him that he signed it Friday night, right after the poker game. He must have blacked out afterward. Now, it was too late to walk it back. Cunningham had already posted it on the White House website and given it to the media.

Dan decided to let momma and Kiki sleep a little more. He put on the television. A lone newscaster, a handsome woman wearing a black suit and an obvious face-lift, described the mayhem caused by the National Quarantine order. People panicked and raided supermarkets to prepare for being shut in for a solid month. There was a great shuffle as families moved in together to share resources.

After a commercial break, they ran a story about how hundreds of Americans were flooding the southern border to Mexico. People understood that viruses don't like the heat.

Merriwether didn't like the idea of his citizens fleeing. The border crossings were officially closed, but so understaffed that enforcement was limited. After consulting with Homeland Security, border agents decided their only job was to stop infected people from entering the country. They looked the other way for those wanting to leave.

Several CNN pundits praised him for the Executive Order—saying he showed great leadership. One called him a hero.

At least they got that right.

But overall, things were bad. CNN cut to live footage outside the White House, where dead homeless people and protesters were being picked up by FEMA trucks.

Jack Cunningham insisted that he and the Vice President needed to get out of D.C. for their own safety. The District was nearly shuttered. Mass transit was halted. Federal offices were essentially closed, except for the few remaining healthy individuals. The Speaker of the House died last week, and his home state refused to hold another election or send a replacement for the congressman. Six of the nine Supreme Court justices were deceased—leaving only the three liberal female justices.

DC was becoming a ghost-town.

Jack explained that the Presidential "bunker" was located in western Maryland, about an hour outside DC. Usually the President and Vice President would go to separate facilities, but there weren't enough secret service agents available to staff two locations. Based on the threat of contagion, physically separating the President from the rest of congress and his cabinet—the few that were left—was the most prudent strategy.

Merriwether watched the television and grimaced as the camera focused on a dead protester's bloody face.

Jack knocked on the door frame and walked in.

"Sir, I'm glad you're up early."

"Yeah, I'm ready to get out of here. There are dead people littered all over the place." He put on his suit jacket and pointed to his golf bag. "I'm ready."

"Sir," Jack said, his hands clasped. "I don't know how to say this, but I have some bad news."

"Spit it out. We need to get on the road soon. Did the chef make me a goody bag for the ride?"

"Sir, look at me," Jack said in a somber tone.

"What?"

"Your mother passed away last night. Her maid found her. I called in Dr. Braff. He said she passed peacefully."

"What? Momma's gone! Oh, Christ. Momma. Momma." He sat down on the sofa, staring into the distance, hugging a pillow, rocking back and forth.

Streams of salty water rolled down his nose. Jack offered his handkerchief.

"Oh, Lord!" Dan blew his nose. He handed the soggy fabric square back to Jack. "Go! Get out of here!"

Jack threw the handkerchief in the waste basket and turned to leave.

"No. Wait! I need to see Momma. I don't believe it. You're lying."

"Sir, it's highly unadvisable. It isn't safe."

"No. Momma was fine yesterday. She was watching her stories and looked right as rain. Walt took her temperature every morning. She wasn't sick. She wasn't coughing or anything. I mean, hell, she's ninety years old. Maybe she had a heart attack. I need to see Momma now!"

"Sir, respectfully, Walt had her removed from the residence. We're arranging her burial near the National Cathedral. There won't be a public viewing. In fact, Walt wants to give you a quick examination. He can come in whenever you are ready."

"How dare you! You two keep treating me like a goddamned child. You had no right to take momma from me!" He went to his desk and swept all the papers on the floor. He tried to throw his desk phone, but it got hung up on its cord. He pulled on the cord, but it resisted. He tugged again. *Goddamned thing.* He pinched the plastic tabs on the jack, freeing the phone. He threw it at Jack, but it missed his head by a couple feet.

"Sir, are you ok?" Jack asked, walking toward the phone and picking it up.

"No, I'm not ok! That's it. Neither of you get to come with me to the bunker. I don't want to see your faces ever again." He stomped his foot and motioned to the door. "Get out or I'll have the Marines throw you out. Now."

Jack returned the broken phone to the President's desk. With a calm stare, he said, "Fine. I quit." He exited the room without looking back.

Now alone, Dan sat on the tufted, gold fabric sofa, and counted backwards from one hundred. When he got to twenty, his breathing slowed. He wiped his face with his sleeve and straightened up. He didn't need Jack. Or momma. He just needed Kiki.

He pulled out his cell phone.

"Kiki, sweetie. Are you ready yet? We're heading out soon. Did you hear about Momma? They won't let me see her. I can't breathe.

It hurts in my heart. I need you, honey. I need you with me. I can't do this without you. Please hurry up. I don't want to be here anymore."

* * *

Seated in the back of the SUV, heading to western Maryland, Defoe kept playing it over in his mind.

How am I going to spend the next four weeks living with the President? I'd rather have my skin boiled off than spend all my waking hours with this fool.

He didn't mind Kiki though. He could stomach hanging out with her.

Board games.

The President wanted to play board games at the bunker. "We'll play all my favorite childhood games!" Merriwether told him the night before. "Sorry, Monopoly, and even Twister!"

Envisioning Dan's blubbery bottom contorting on the floor made him shudder. *Dan's sweaty hands reaching for plastic circles, his smelly socks.*

His head throbbed with pain. He considered other options—like walking into the woods, living like a mountain man in a remote cabin—giving up all his ambitions. He could forget he ever met Merriwether.

No. I've worked too hard. The presidency was within reach. With the world ending, what did he have left to lose?

His car arrived a few minutes early. He drank some whisky from a flask in his jacket pocket. He gulped down the rest as the President's vehicle arrived.

The Secret Service exited first. Then Merriwether and Kiki, with Rex following after.

He brought the damn dog?

Tom exited the car and strode over to Merriwether with his fists clenched and his face red. "Damnation! Why the hell is Rex here?"

"Rex is family. You know momma just died. Rex is my baby. He goes with us."

Defoe stared at Rex. Rex let out a low growl and bared his teeth at him.

"Look, Tom," Dan said, "Don't go riling up Rexie boy. He's a real sweetheart but he doesn't like it when you raise your voice."

"Sir," Defoe said trying to be calm, "once we are underground, we don't come up for at least a month or until the pandemic is fully resolved. You won't be able to take Rex for walks outside. Isn't keeping him with us impractical?"

"Tom, I thought of everything. We have bunches of wee-wee pads for Rexie. He'll be just dandy."

Dan clapped and turned to agent Tanner. "Ok, let's do this thing!" Tanner, Becker and Flanders escorted the President, Kiki and Rex to the elevator.

Tom closed his eyes and imagined the stench of the dog's feces wafting through the enclosed spaces of the bunker.

Perhaps they were entering the seventh circle of Dante's hell. The dogs have come to rip apart the dissolute and the reckless.

Tom hung his head. *I guess I have no choice now*, he thought. "Fine, you go ahead. I'll take the next elevator." He placed his hand in his coat pocket, feeling for his pocketknife.

"If you say so, Tom," Merriwether said. "Don't be too long now. It's almost lunch time."

The elevator door closed and Dan, Kiki, Rex and three agents were on their way down. This left just himself and agent White.

He looked at his watch.

After the elevator descended, Tom bent down as if to tie his shoes.

Tom turned to agent White and made some small talk. "Kind of a nice day, don't you think? The weather's getting warmer. Too bad we can't hit the links for a while longer. Hey, do you know if our luggage arrived yet?"

In an awkward attempt at acting, Tom stood up and turned his head suddenly. He pointed wildly off in the distance behind White. "Whoa! What's that? Over there?"

As White turned to look, Defoe grabbed his shoulder and plunged the knife into his neck, at his jugular. Blood gushed from the gaping wound and agent White dropped to the ground, gagging.

After a few seconds, White stopped moving. Tom pulled the body toward the bushes and rolled him under the foliage. He unstrapped White's vest and holster and put them on under his suit jacket. Next, he removed his sidearm and checked the chamber.

He holstered the gun and straightened his jacket.

Stage One accomplished. He took another swig from his flask.

Time to rock and roll.

* * *

The Chinese assassin Pei peered through his binoculars. He was assigned to stake out the bunker in Maryland. His counterparts were scattered around the country at the other "remote White House" sites to keep watch as well. They had to cover all the bases. He was fortunate to cover one of the more likely sites, closest to Washington D.C.

When the first black SUV came into view, his heart began thumping. He'd waited nearly a week—camping in the wooded hillside—hoping he would be so lucky. He was tired of cooking over a fire and eating canned rations. Once he returned to China, he would be an accomplished hero. Perhaps he would be rewarded with money and prestige. More important, perhaps Szu Qiang would consider releasing his sister from the work camps.

He became more excited at the second SUV. He scanned his reference cards—a playing deck he was provided with pictures of the President, Vice President and members of the cabinet. The President and Vice President were confirmed. The woman was not in the deck. He did a quick count—only four guards. Easy to manage.

He made several calls on his satellite phone to notify the other operatives that the President was indeed in Maryland. He wasn't sure whether to wait for their arrival or take matters into his own hands.

Pei examined the contents of his duffel bag: a .50 caliber rifle, three Glocks, a few hunting knives and half a dozen hand grenades. He had taken out far more men with far fewer weapons in the past.

He planned to wait until nightfall to make his move. He couldn't hear what the people were saying but watched what appeared to be an argument.

Pei paid particular attention to the German shepherd. *The dog was old but you could never underestimate them.* They had great hearing and could be nasty. He wished he had a steak—to pacify or distract the dog when the time came. The closest grocery store was a couple of miles away. He did not relish the idea of hiking to the store.

The President, the woman and his detail went down the elevator first. Pei yawned. He had not slept well outside in the cold these last few days.

But then, something spectacular. He rubbed his eyes and looked through his binoculars.

Yes, the Vice President was dragging a body.

He took out his telephoto camera and began taking pictures. At this distance and with the intervening vegetation, it would be difficult to make out the faces, even using a zoom lens. Still, perhaps if he got photographic evidence, he might convince himself this was truly happening.

The Vice President was alone now. He could take him with a single shot and no one would be the wiser. But then the Vice President stripped the bullet-proof vest off the dead agent and put it on himself.

This guy's crazy!

The Vice President entered the elevator and the door closed.

He had never been in this situation before. He took his handguns, a knife and two hand grenades and crept out from his hiding area on the hillside. Dressed in green camouflage, he stayed within the tree line as he circled the facility. When it was apparent there were no other security guards, he approached the elevator from behind and waited. He sat still, trying to listen, but no noises emanated from the structure.

The dog was still a wild card to him. *Could I make a steak from the dead agent? Would a dog eat a human steak?* That would certainly save time.

He decided to wait.

The Vice President was on a mission. It would be impolite to disturb him.

* * *

Tom swiped Agent White's keycard on the wall-mounted pad outside the elevator. Taking a series of deep breaths, he entered the elevator and hit the down button. There weren't any floor numbers. From the time and rate of descent, he estimated the bunker was about sixty feet below ground.

He tried to quiet his mind and put on a casual or even jovial demeanor.

The elevator door opened and two agents were waiting.

"Sir," Agent Flanders said, "where's Agent White? He should have come down with you."

"Oh, yeah. He went off to take a leak and smoke a cigarette before coming down. He said he'd be down in fifteen minutes."

"Thank you, sir. The President and Miss Kiki are in the game room. Can we get you anything? Or would you like to see your room first?"

"Yes, show me my room. I'd like to get settled," Defoe said with a smile.

The two agents, Flanders and Becker, motioned for Defoe to follow them.

"As you can see on this wall map, we are here in Corridor B," Flanders explained. "The main living areas are in the center of a cross formation, with four corridors extending to the north, south, east and west wings. This bunker was designed to house seventy-five people. The north wing, wing A, is where the President is staying. You'll be in Wing B. My team will be in Wing C. More than enough space so we won't be on top of one another. Follow me."

They walked down a long concrete corridor with overhead fluorescent lighting. At the very end of the hall, Flanders opened a door and walked in ahead of Defoe, while Becker entered behind him.

"Every bedroom has a private bath and a phone line," explained Flanders. "Your luggage is in the corner. We don't have a butler or chef down here, but the fridge is stocked in the central kitchen. We also have a large pantry with non-perishable foods. Becker and I are going to make some sandwiches. Is there anything we can get you?"

"Thanks guys," Defoe said, turning on the television. "Actually, could one of you show me where the safe is and how it works?"

"Absolutely, sir," Flanders said.

Agent Becker left the room.

"You'll see, here, this safe works like any you'd find in a hotel, but a bit larger," Flanders said, as he walked toward the closet.

Defoe followed behind and quietly took a pillow off the bed.

He peered over Flanders' shoulder as if studying the man's instructions.

The agent entered a number combination. "You set the combination..."

While Flanders was fixated on the safe, Defoe wrapped the pillow around the handgun. He shot him in the head, although the pillow did not mute the noise as much as he had hoped. Defoe pushed the body into the closet and closed the doors.

In less than six seconds, Agent Becker ran back into the room with his gun drawn. Defoe reclined on his bed with the television on.

"Sir, what happened? I heard a gunshot."

"Oh, sorry. I was flipping channels and the movie *Die Hard* came on. I guess the volume was a little too loud."

Becker squinted his eyes, scanning the room. After a moment, he said, "Well, sorry to disturb you, sir. Is Agent Flanders still here?"

"He's in the bathroom trying to fix the faucet. He said you might know where the tool kit is?"

"Sure, let me see what he needs."

Agent Becker walked into the bathroom and looked around. Agent Flanders wasn't there. Before he turned around, Defoe was on him. He shot Becker in the head and a spray of blood coated the walls.

Defoe kicked the body to the side and checked his image in the mirror. A little blood on his jacket and collar. He'd have to change. He closed the door and prepared for Stage Three.

* * *

Ruth read through her notes to prepare for her daily video blog. There were so few congressional delegates left now. The ones that hadn't died left DC to be with their loved ones back home. She couldn't blame them. She was happy that Jason was around. He was a good sounding board now that she was essentially running the government.

Do I tell the public about Cullen and the Vice President?

Most government agencies were barely functional. The Justice Department was a shell of its former self.

What would happen if I had Tom arrested? Would that only create a side-show? There were so many more pressing issues now.

She called Director Carson.

"Director, any good news?"

"Senator, yes and no."

"Is the shingles vaccine working?"

"It's too early to say. On balance, people with lower innate immunity, like smokers, people with heart disease, diabetes, poor diets…they aren't surviving at the same rate. No. That is being too generous. To be blunt, they don't seem to be helped at all."

"But there is some good news?"

"Yes, the transmission by dogs appears to be halted."

"That's encouraging."

"Senator, we have more problems. With loss of manpower and closed factories, cities are reporting severe food shortages and water systems are being shut down."

"I've heard. I have several committees working on these issues with State and local authorities. Call me again tomorrow. And keep sending me items to add to my daily videos."

"Yes, Senator."

Ruth said goodbye.

She needed to practice her speech. When she felt she was ready, Sally turned on the camera.

"My fellow Americans. As you may already know, President Merriwether and Vice President Defoe have been placed in quarantine outside of the city for their safety. They are still governing the country and will be communicating directly with Congress and our emergency responders. However, due to their limited capacity in quarantine, the President delegated many of the day-to-day operational decisions to me. I take this responsibility seriously and will work tirelessly to protect you and your families."

"I will speak with you every day for as long as I can. Power outages and food shortages are occurring more frequently. I'm forming several committees here in Congress to address the basic survival issues we are all facing. We are working with State and local governments to ensure food, clean water and other necessities are delivered and accessible to all. The quarantine has been, and will continue to be, difficult. We have never faced an epidemic of this magnitude in the history of the world. All our actions have a direct impact on the outcome. We can stem the transmission of this terrible virus and get our lives back to normal, all the sooner, if we all adhere to the guidelines."

"I have one favor to ask. Please take care of one another. You are all in my thoughts and prayers. Good evening and God bless the United States of America, and each and every one of us."

* * *

Defoe entered the game room. There was a bar along the wall. He examined the bottles and poured himself a shot of whisky.

"Tom!" Merriwether said. "Glad you could join us! We were getting ready to play another game of pool. Kiki kicked my butt in the last one, didn't you pumpkin? Want to play the winner of this round?"

Defoe scanned the room. Agent Tanner was sitting in a club chair in the corner reading a graphic novel. Rex was sleeping under the pool table.

Tom walked over to Tanner and waited until the agent looked up from his book.

"Can I help you, sir?" Tanner asked.

"Oh, I'm sorry…did I disturb you from your comic book? Aren't you supposed to be standing guard or something? You don't look like you're on duty. Is this what they taught you at the academy?"

Tanner put down the book and stood up. "Sir, with all due respect, we are in an impenetrable fortress down here. There are three other agents plus myself to keep you safe. If I see a terrorist come down the elevator, I'll take care of it."

Merriwether said, "Now Tom, I told my boys that they need to feel at home here. I know they made quite a sacrifice to be here with us for such a long time. We all have to treat each other like friends."

"*Friends*?" Tom exclaimed in a high-pitched voice. "*Friends*? I wouldn't call you my friend if you were the last living person on earth."

Merriwether stared at Tom with his mouth open. Kiki put down her cue stick.

Tanner held up his hands and took a step back. "Sirs, I can see you have things to discuss. I'll be in the kitchen." He turned and walked towards Corridor C.

After a short pause, Tom followed Tanner and shot him between his shoulder blades.

Merriwether and Kiki screamed. Rex woke up and began barking. Merriwether backed himself into the corner and held Kiki in front of him as a human shield. Kiki yelled curse words and flailed her arms and legs.

Tom kicked Tanner's body on the ground and then reached down to take his pulse. Tanner was gone. "Shut up, both of you," Tom said, turning to point the gun at them.

Rex bared his teeth at Tom with a deep growl.

"First things first." Tom pointed the gun at Rex and with a loud bang, Rex went limp.

Merriwether screamed, "Stop! Tom! Tom! Why Tom? Have you completely lost your mind?"

"Ms. Kiki," Tom said calmly. "Do you love this man? Would you die for him?"

Kiki's eyes went wide as she pulled against Dan's grip. "Well, he wouldn't die for me, hiding behind me like a lil' bitch!"

"Exactly. So, I trust that given a choice, you could leave here and never come back…and never tell anyone what happened here."

Kiki nodded.

"Ok then. I'm going to count to fifty. If you manage to leave by the time I stop counting, you will be free. Otherwise, you can share a grave with him."

Merriwether tried to keep his grasp on Kiki but lost his hold when she stomped on his in-step with her stiletto. She sprinted past Tom toward the elevator and lost a shoe in the process. She didn't stop to retrieve it.

Tom continued counting, "ten…eleven...twelve."

She pushed the up button repeatedly, her legs shaking. After a few seconds the doors opened. She rushed inside.

Dan crawled over to Rex and cradled the dog's lifeless head in his lap. Tears filled his eyes. "Tom, what are you doing? Why do you want to hurt me?" He sobbed. "I've been your biggest fan. I made you Vice President when everyone else in the party wanted me to pick the other guy. We had some good times, didn't we? Remember the inauguration? That was a party! You enjoyed it, right? We've had good times, me and you. Christ! Please tell me what you want!"

"This is all your fault," Tom said stone-faced, still pointing the gun on him.

Dan looked up and stopped crying. "What? What is my fault? You shot Tanner!"

"Everything. The virus, the death of humanity. It all rests on your shoulders."

"You are talking plain nonsense now. We've all been under a bunch of stress lately. Is that it? I have some Quaaludes in my bag. Have you ever tried 'ludes? I also have weed. Everyone loves weed! You'll feel a lot better. Right? Hey, let's go smoke a joint and talk about this."

Tom kept the gun aimed at the President.

"Christ! Say something, Tom!" Merriwether looked down at Rex and began crying again.

"You made me do it."

"Do what?" Dan sobbed.

"I deserved to be President. *Me!* Not you. I went to Harvard for Christ sakes. I was a Senator for sixteen years!" He walked closer to Dan, waving the gun from side to side. "You owned a tabloid. You were a draft dodger. You cheated on your wife. You rejected God. You know nothing about how government works." Tom pushed the gun against Merriwether's skull. "Everything is a damned party to you."

Merriwether stopped sobbing. "Look, I know…I know I'm not perfect."

"Not perfect? Are you fucking *kidding me*? You made terrible decisions that hurt the country. You refused to govern. You humiliated me during the election. You continued to humiliate me as Vice President. At every turn you rubbed it in. I did all the heavy lifting. I kept the administration functioning. Things would have gone to *shit* without me! I was your damned handmaid. Every success I had, every good decision I made, you took all the credit. All the while you were on your vacations, playing golf, partying with a bunch of bimbos."

Tom cocked the gun at Merriwether's head.

Merriwether clasped his hands together as in prayer. "Please Tom, don't do this. I forgive you for Rex. I won't tell anyone you killed our guys. You can be President now. I'll resign. Get me some paper. I'll put it in writing. Stop! Jesus, Tom! Just tell me what to say!"

"Oh no! I can't *decide*," Tom said in a mocking tone.

He pulled the trigger.

"Oopsie doo!"

He placed the gun on the pool table and looked down, glowering over Merriwether's crumpled body. He frowned at the blood and guts on the side of his shoe. He wiped it off on the side of Dan's corpse.

"I hope you rot in hell."

* * *

After a few minutes of contemplating ways to distract the dog, Pei heard the whir of the elevator moving. He ducked behind one of the SUVs and tried to conceal himself but still kept an eye on the door.

A young woman of caramel skin-tone came running out clumsily in bare feet, holding a single gold stiletto. She raced towards the closest SUV and tried the doors frantically—they were locked.

She would try his vehicle next. As she approached, he scooted around to the back, keeping to the opposite side of the car as she raced around trying all the doors. These were all locked as well. It was funny to him. She was in such a panic that he could have been standing next to the car and she wouldn't have noticed him.

He scratched his head. *Where did he know her from?*

She hit the driver's window over and over with the pointed heel of her shoe. These were hardened windows. Her attempts to break them were futile.

The woman gave up on the vehicles and began jogging down the access road, holding her boobs with one arm to keep them from bouncing out of her skimpy dress. *A good runner despite her poor clothing choices.* Pei wished he had his good camera for this. He took out his cell phone and tried to capture some video.

After the woman was out of sight and earshot, Pei sat down on the hood of the car.

Americans. All fucking insane.

He retrieved the agent's bloody clothing, minus the armor that the Vice President had commandeered, and tried it on for size. Not a bad fit. Too bad the collar was full of dried blood. But he looked official enough. He found a set of car keys in the agent's jacket.

Pei opened the second SUV and sat inside. He turned on the heat. He soaked up the warmth and held his hands to the vents. He turned on his iPod and listened to his catalog of American rap and hip-hop music. His English wasn't perfect but he could follow the songs. Except for a few of the newer slang words. He loved learning new slang.

After the temperature inside the car reached a comfortable level, he turned off the engine and took a nap. The other operatives would be arriving in a few hours. He might as well get some sleep while he waited.

Pei was awakened a few minutes later by a noise. He slid down the seat but peeked through the window. The Vice President was now dressed in sweats, dragging another corpse across the dirt toward the tree line. He stared, trying to discern the identity of the latest victim.

Another Secret Service agent.

This guy is doing everything for me!

Pei knew he should wait it out. Strategically, that would be the smart thing to do. *If the Vice President is piling up bodies down there, maybe I should let him continue?* But his curiosity was too great.

The Vice President finished dragging the body to a clump of shrubs and began walking back towards the elevator. Pei opened his car door and trained his gun on Defoe.

"Freeze!"

Defoe halted in his tracks and put his hands in the air.

"Turn around, slowly!" cried Pei.

Defoe turned. "It's me. Vice President Defoe! Don't shoot. What is your name, son?"

He thinks I'm an agent. I could have fun with this.

Pei replied, "Sir? Are you ok? What happened to that agent?"

"Oh, he had the virus and died suddenly. I offered to take bring him topside."

"That's terrible! How can I help? How is the President? What about the President's girlfriend and the other agents? Are they ok?"

"Oh yes, the President is fine. Kiki is making dinner and the other agents are helping the President set up his new office. Do you want see? Follow me."

Now it clicked. *Kiki from Instagram.* He loved her. *Poor thing. Probably still running.*

Pei followed the Vice President as he opened the elevator with the key card. They entered the elevator, standing shoulder to shoulder. He kept a sharp eye on him; Defoe began fishing around in his pants pocket.

Pei was ready when Defoe made his move. He readily twisted the knife out from Defoe's grip.

Defoe stiffened, with dropped jaw and wide eyes.

"Mr. Vice President. Can I call you Tom? I'm not secret service. My mission is to kill Merriwether. I should probably kill you also…but you are a curious fellow. I'm interested in your story.

Pei pocketed Tom's knife. He took out some plastic zip ties. "I won't harm you if you behave. Do you understand? Please turn and give me your wrists."

Tom nodded and turned around.

Pei zip-tied Tom's hands and checked they were secure. He turned Tom around as the elevator chimed and the doors opened.

Tom stared at him and said, "First, tell me who you are."

"I think you know." Pei shoved him out of the elevator. Pei held him at gunpoint as he peered into the room.

It was a bloodbath. Literally—blood pooled around the room in little vignettes of horror. The dog and Merriwether were slumped on the concrete floor next to the pool table. There were smears from other victims in the opposite corners.

"Wow," was all he could utter. He sat Tom in a chair and said, "Stay there and be quiet."

Pei crept silently over to the President and took his pulse. *Nothing.*

"You did all this?" Pei whispered.

"Yes. Yes, I did. Are you going to turn me in?"

"Shhh. Be quiet. Is there anyone else down here? *Alive*?"

"No. Just me."

"Dang, bro! You one freaky muthafucka," Pei said with a bad rapper impersonation.

"Ha! Like I give a damn. I hated him. I would do it again. What are you going to do about it?" Tom slouched in the chair, wiggling to get his hands free from the zip ties.

"Whoa, dude. Chill. Look, all I want is Merriwether's head. Actually, my boss wants it. Then, honestly, I don't care what the fuck you do."

"Really? No way! You should have just told me. Sure thing. I was thinking of cutting him up anyway. He weighs a ton. Or do you want to do the honors?"

"Hey, bro, I'll take care of the bodies. I'm known for my knife skills. I'll take Merriwether's head and maybe we'll forget that we ever saw each other. Deal?"

"Deal."

Pei knelt down and held Merriwether's head in his hands. It occurred to him he needed something, a box perhaps, to transport it. "Hey, do you have a box or a suitcase?"

"Ha! Yes!" Tom grinned. "I've got a great idea. But can you cut me loose first?"

Pei cut off the zip ties and Tom went down one of the long halls. When he returned, he held the President's suitcase in one hand and a golf club in the other.

Pei looked over the suitcase. It had the Presidential Seal.

"What's with the golf club?" Pei asked.

Defoe grinned from ear to ear. "Consider it a present to your boss. It was signed by Arnold Palmer. It was Merriwether's prized possession."

Chapter 26

Day 113

Tom wrung out the mop again. Cleaning up the blood was quite tiring. He snapped a picture of Merriwether's dead body before Pei began the dismemberment. He emailed it to Senator Cochran the following day with a story about how the President had committed suicide. Dan was distraught over his mother's death.

Before he took his own life, President Merriwether admitted to sending the virus to Russia and couldn't live with the pain he had caused the nation and the world. Tom described how all four agents—Tanner, Becker, Flanders and White—tried to stop the President, but he shot them all during the standoff. Tom described Dan's last words, saying, "*Tom, promise to lead the country and be a better president than I could ever be.*"

Sure, Kiki was a wild card. A loose end. *But who would believe her version over mine?* She was a smart girl. *She won't cross me.*

A few minutes after he hit send, Cochran initiated a private video conference with him.

"Christ, I'm sorry, Tom. I can't imagine how you are coping with this! How are you? What can I do to help? Let me send in a team in to collect the President and the agents. We need to set up a memorial service, even if it's only televised. *Oh God*, is that blood on your shirt?"

Pretending to cough violently, Tom replied, "Yeah, I coughed up a little blood. You know, I'm not feeling too great. I think I must have picked up the virus somewhere. Merriwether brought his stupid dog with him. Maybe I got the virus from Rex."

"Is Kiki there with you? Is she sick also?"

"The President spared Kiki. She ran off. Where, who knows? She wasn't sick when she left. Anyway, it isn't safe to send more security down here. I've already buried the President and the others up top."

"You already buried…? Oh, I see. Well, if you have the virus, can I send a medical team over to you? They could be fully suited. Make you more comfortable. We are experimenting with immune system boosters for those already infected. It makes a little difference, even if it isn't always a cure."

"I appreciate the offer. I've already taken all the recommended anti-viral medicines. I'm still processing what happened…I think I'd prefer to be alone for a while. Plus, I couldn't live with myself it I caused anyone else to get sick. We need to maintain the quarantine. Just keep me posted on the President's memorial service. I'll pre-record a video eulogy while I'm still strong enough to do so."

"God bless you, Tom. Um, or rather, Mr. President. I'll take care of notifying Congress and the public. I'll be praying for you. You get some rest—try to beat this thing."

"Thanks, Ruth. You were always a class act. I appreciate you managing things."

"Bless your heart. Well, I have a lot to do. Call me tomorrow. Let me know how you're doing."

"Will do, Ruth. Thanks." Tom disconnected the video feed.

Jeez, she is gullible, he thought. At least no one would bother him down here for a few days. He went back to his mop and continued cleaning.

He hummed a little tune.

He was free.

Screw my diet! I'm going to have a big plate of pasta for dinner. Followed by some chocolate cake for dessert!

He went back to the lounge and looked through the video library. He never had much time to watch TV or movies before. *Maybe I'll binge-watch House of Cards. Maybe Dexter too.*

This was going to be a great and long overdue vacation.

* * *

Maya pulled on Ally's comforter. "Get up!"

"Go away," Ally groaned, tugging the blanket back across her chest.

"I'm not feeding your stupid cat anymore. Get the fuck up."

"I'll feed her later. Go without me."

"Hey, you begged me to come here. Don't get me wrong. We're doing important work. But you can't check out on me—on us."

"I don't feel good."

"You don't *feel* good," Maya mocked. "Nobody feels good! Suck it up, buttercup."

"Go away. I have no idea if my family is dead or alive. I haven't heard from them in days. Just let me sleep."

"Hey, I have a family too. Thanks for asking."

Shit. Ally rolled over. "Are they ok?"

"My cousin in Florida died two weeks ago."

"Were you close?"

"Yeah, we grew up together. He was like my brother."

"Oh, Maya, I'm so sorry! You should have said something."

"Everyone has a story, Ally. But we can't dwell on that right now. Not until the virus is stopped."

"I've been a terrible mom…a terrible grandmother…a terrible sister…"

"A terrible friend…."

"Right." Ally rolled over and put the covers over her head.

"Chica, you have a guilty conscience, I get it."

Ally uncovered her head. "Get what?"

"We both ignored our families for years…"

"What?"

"All those years with the CDC. We traveled constantly…chasing every outbreak. You missed half of Theo's birthdays while he was growing up, remember? And all the times you cancelled anniversary trips with Jim. And Christmases. Remember that December in Yugoslavia? We made a sad tree out of some branches and decorated it with gauze."

Ally sat up and looked at Maya.

"No wonder you feel like crap, Ally. You know, I remember in college when you used to cry to me about your breakup with Walt. *He doesn't spend any time with me…he's obsessed with his career.*" Maya mimicked.

"So, you think I'm just like Walt."

Maya sat down on the bed next to Ally.

"No, I *know* you are like Walt. Actually worse. You know, I was mad at him for a long time."

"Walt isn't a bad guy. He got the President to sign the quarantine order."

"I know. My point is, you and I were far more career-focused. I came to my senses a few years back and took an office job. Stopped traveling constantly. It took a long time, but I eventually repaired relationships with my family."

"I might not get the chance to repair things."

"I know. But don't lose hope." Maya held open her arms for a hug.

Ally hugged Maya for an extended time.

"Thanks, chica," Ally said.

Maya broke their hug and said, "Now take a shower and cry on the inside like a winner."

Ally nodded and blew her nose with a tissue. She swung her feet onto the floor, but hesitated. "You know I killed Cullen."

"Yes, Jason told me."

"Is it wrong that I would do it again?"

"After Cullen literally murdered millions? Don't give it a second thought."

"Ok." She headed to the bathroom.

"And feed Gretchen," Maya called out to her. "I swear that cat has lungs on her."

DAY 117

Ally met Maya at the cafeteria for lunch. It was mid-day, but the room was dark. Their building had electricity and a back-up generator, but conservation was the new norm.

"Did you know about this?" Ally asked, placing her tray on the table.

"What?" Maya asked, sipping some coffee.

"Gwen called me yesterday. Walt got a hold of some the new monoclonal antibody serum. Jason drove it up to New Jersey for my family three days ago."

"Yeah, I know the guys were working on it," Maya said. "Walt called in all kinds of favors...we weren't sure he could get enough."

"You should have told me! It's the best news I've had in a long time."

"Well, we still don't know if it will work," Maya said.

"I know. It probably won't, but I'm hoping for a miracle. What about your parents? Did they get the vaccine yet?"

"Yes, they got it before the outbreak, so I think they'll be ok," Maya said.

"The pharmaceutical companies are ramping up production, right? Do we know how long it will take to cover everyone?"

"Renée said between sixty and ninety days. There are still people dying...even ones who received the vaccine. Mostly people in poor health to begin with."

"I think I'm done with my model," Ally said. "I can't take it anymore. I don't want to read any more mortality reports."

"I get it. Right now, we just have to hope for the best."

"How are things going in New York and Chicago? Are you still working with the Mayors?" Ally asked.

"New York is leveling off. Their quarantine was strict. They have one of the better survival rates. Chicago adopted many of the same procedures, but isn't doing well."

Nancy walked up to their table, holding a tray with a bowl of soup and some crackers.

The CDC cafeteria was out of fresh fruit and vegetables, and most other food staples. They had pallets of canned soup from FEMA. Lunch and dinners now consisted of soup heated in the microwave.

"You know, I've been thinking," Nancy said. "Now that summer is around the corner, the outbreak should subside."

"The spread is slowing down," Maya said. "Unfortunately, it might point to the fact that there are far fewer people alive to transmit it."

Nancy said, "The mortality data is still sketchy. The numbers of men dying are astounding, though."

"How is our civilization going to continue? With so fewer men?" Maya asked.

Nancy shrugged, "The issue isn't the lack of men. We still have sperm banks. The issue will be the lack of women of childbearing age. But think about this. We're heading back to the population levels of the late 1800s. The world population was getting a little out of control.

Some people say we needed a course correction."

Ally said, "Yeah, fringe environmental groups are saying terrible things. Did you see the latest Twitter threads? All about how our planet couldn't sustain the rampant population growth. They are happy about the pandemic. Yeah, sure, carbon emissions and greenhouse gases will be reduced. But that doesn't excuse them for being complete assholes."

"The widespread blackouts are scary," Nancy said. "People are losing their minds without power. I heard Senator Cochran ordered all the nuclear power plants mothballed—because of possible cyber-attacks. So, I guess the greenies got their wish on that front, too."

"You think blackouts are bad? Did you hear about the fires out West?" Maya asked. "California and Oregon are letting them burn. Hundreds of thousands of acres! They don't have the personnel. Oh, and cellphones! The Chinese took out many of our satellites in retaliation. Talk about the 1800s! Cochran is trying to consolidate the population towards the cities, to share resources. The homesteaders and the doomsday preppers will probably stay where they are."

Nancy said, "Ally, maybe we should all head off to that Fantasy Island of yours!"

Ally laughed. "Jason told me he wants to be Tattoo to my Mr. Rourke. He is crazy."

"You're talking to him again?" Maya asked.

"Yeah. Did you know he's working with his Aunt on plans for a new system of government? I don't know if that scares me more than the blackouts."

Day 124

Senator Cochran wore her blue suit with a black scarf. She pulled down on her jacket and straightened her flag pin. She stepped up to the podium in the Senate chamber, a bank of American flags behind her. Carly, now wearing a jacket with an omega logo, trained the C-SPAN camera on her and gave the cue to begin.

"My fellow Americans," Ruth began. "This Memorial Day will be like no other. There will be no parades. No picnics. No fireworks. No family outings to the seaside. Because of the quarantine, there will be no ceremonies."

"However, earlier this morning, I went alone to Arlington

National Cemetery. In solitude, I placed a wreath at the Tomb of the Unknown Soldier. There were no crowds. No military. I know many veterans and their families would have wanted to go. I thank everyone for their restraint and for their patriotic adherence to the quarantine.

"We are facing dark times. Many of us have lost loved ones. Some have lost entire families. It's been reported that more citizens have died in the past three months than during all our nation's wars. On this Memorial Day, we must remember all those who have been lost and keep them forever in our hearts and minds."

She paused reverently before going on.

"The disease that has ravaged our country—and the world at large—has been unforgiving. It has touched all of us, regardless of our race, age, gender and economic status.

"But through the darkness, we have all experienced the amazing generosity of the human spirit. Neighbors helping neighbors. Medical and military personnel working double shifts. Food pantries making deliveries to those too sick to leave their homes." She placed her hands together and rested them in front of her on the lectern.

"I want you to know that your government is doing all it can to stem transmission of the virus. I know the quarantine has been hard. And we must be prepared to face this difficulty for the next few days, or perhaps weeks. We are working to stabilize our electric grid and internet, so you can communicate with your loved ones and draw hope from them."

"We are Americans. We will get through this. We will persevere. Our country is great because our ancestors were immigrants with enormous will of spirit. We carry these traits today."

She placed a hand over her heart. "God bless our country, and each and every one of us."

DAY 138

Long wave radio. *It's come to this,* Ruth thought. *We are approaching the Stone Ages.*

At least there were almost no new cases of the virus being reported. The quarantine would have to remain for another few days, just to be safe.

Jason found a way to patch into and reactivate the old Public Emergency Radio station in Chase, Maryland. Using long wave would provide the best chance to transmit to Europe and Asia now that satellite communications were diminished. The station in Chase hadn't been used since 1990. Since Jason returned to DC, he began chatting with all his international contacts in his radio club. His club friends began working with their governments to resurrect the former long wave stations since they used the most basic technology.

He provided Ruth with a rundown of the international news every afternoon. Most interesting, his friend in China told him that President Szu Chen was gone. He and his brother left the country a few weeks ago. There were many rumors. But the one most repeated was they boarded a warship headed to New Zealand. The ship never arrived and was believed to have been lost at sea.

Two fewer mad men in the world.

Ruth was weary. She was tired of giving speeches; speeches trying to put a hopeful spin on all the tragedy. It ate at her soul.

The other female congress members were helpful and competent. She tried to focus on all the positive work they were doing. They organized into new committees to generate solutions for challenges of the day. Farming and food distribution were a huge problem.

Most farming was automated, but farms had been producing junk for years. They didn't need corn or soy, or high fructose corn syrup. They needed organic leafy greens and non-starchy vegetables. The committee on farming proposed smaller, localized cattle and chicken ranches, situated closer to metropolitan areas.

Money was a bigger problem. Money, paper or electronic, really didn't mean anything anymore; and when folks used it, it resulted in hyper-inflated prices. People were bartering now. It got complicated at times. The Finance Committee looked at standardizing the dollar based on the value of four chicken eggs, three ounces of beef, or a quart of whole-fat milk. All financial transactions were measured in some form of food-based equivalent. The committee and Ruth were working with other countries to see if they wanted to adopt a similar system.

Another committee was managing the new census and looked at alternative forms of government. There was an opportunity to eliminate gerrymandering and find a fairer system that resulted in less partisan stalemates. A merit-based system would help weed out the uninformed and unqualified zealots from government appointments. There would be minimum requirements, including work experience, written exams and advanced degrees, for cabinet members, congress and even the President.

A group worked on strategies for developing new healthcare systems. Keeping the remaining population healthy was integral to the fate of the country—and even mankind. Medical care had to be free, not a privilege. They would not take chances with unnecessary or avoidable illnesses again. All the remaining medical practitioners would become high-salaried government employees.

Ruth had read once that the bubonic plague created the Renaissance by leaving wealth and land to a smaller population. It would take time for America's financial system to catch up. Verifying deaths and settling estates in the traditional manner would be nearly impossible. Electrical issues crashed several city and financial databases, forcing them to rely on paper records long ago archived, or worse, destroyed.

Property rights were the least of her concerns. She cared more about keeping the population safe from the next wave.

So much work to do, Ruth thought.

It will take at least a decade to get back to normal...whatever normal can be.

She worked on her daily speech some more. With fewer new cases of the virus being reported, she wanted to convey hope without encouraging people to get reckless. It was a fine line.

She looked at her legislative calendar. Tom planned to return in two weeks.

That horse's ass! He was getting away with murdering the President, and all those innocent agents, on top of causing the death of millions.

She suspected Defoe was lying when he initially reported the President's death. But it confirmed her instincts when Kiki told the entire story to Walt—describing the extent of Defoe's treasonous actions.

Rage swam through her veins. She slammed her fist on her desk and then drew in a slow, cool breath of air.

I can't deal with him right now.

I need to keep shit together.

But if he thinks I'm letting him be our President, he's sadly mistaken!

Chapter 27

Day 145

A month had gone by since he arrived at the bunker. Tom was keeping tabs on Ruth's daily radio addresses. He used the landline to call her to check in from time to time.

He wasn't pleased with her attitude. She dismissed all his ideas and did whatever the hell she wanted. Yesterday, Ruth told him she was drafting a new Constitution. That was the last straw.

These women were turning our country into a socialist's paradise. The founding fathers must be rolling in their graves.

I'm the goddamned President! Where does she get off?

He wondered if his vacation underground had cost him too much politically. *I need some leverage,* he thought. *I can't run the government from this damned hole in the ground and she knows it.*

The quarantine was ending soon. He would need a small army to take back what was rightfully his.

He looked down at the memento he kept by the phone. The ear was shriveled and black now. Pei had cut it off for him as a gift. "Ha! You still have the ear of the President!" he joked. It was funny at the time. Now it looked sad—like a rotten mushroom.

He called the Pentagon and asked for Secretary Shelton. The corporal who answered said that Shelton was gone.

"What do you mean, gone? Where is he?"

"Sir, he left a note that he retired. Something about spending time with his family. There really aren't many officers left here in the Pentagon. Is there someone else you might want to talk to?"

"Who's the highest-ranking officer left?" Tom asked.

"Admiral Bottomley. Should I transfer you?"

"Yes, Sweet Jesus!"

After a couple rings, a female voice came on the line, "Admiral Bottomley".

I'm screwed. The Pentagon was being run by a woman.

"Admiral," Tom said, "This is President Defoe. I wanted to check on the state of our armed forces. Can you give me a high-level overview?"

"Mr. President. So good to hear from you. We were told you may have been infected. How are you feeling?"

"I'm perfectly fine. In fact, I'll be returning to the White House in a few days. So, if you could, tell me how the Defense Department is doing."

"I'm so pleased to hear you are doing better. Vice President Cochran must be relieved. I have to say, she's been doing a great job these past weeks."

Tom paused. *Vice President Cochran? When and how did that happen?*

Tom took a deep breath. He would deal with that later. He needed military backup first. "That's nice. Again, how are things at the Pentagon?"

"Sir, well, our forces are greatly reduced, as you can imagine. Cochran called back most of our overseas troops."

"What?!"

"Sir, many of our foreign adversaries were also hit hard by the virus. Previous ground wars and hostilities are essentially over. Most Army and Air Force personnel were reassigned to their respective State National Guard units. The defense department is now focused largely on maritime missions. We have a couple of carriers still operating around the world, but most other vessels don't have adequate manpower to continue."

No more wars? Inconceivable! Was he hearing this correctly?

"So, what *are* the missions now?" he growled. He twisted the rotting ear between his fingers.

"Well, our hospital ships, Mercy and Comfort, are providing medical and food aid to our island territories. But domestic issues, like energy and water availability, are taking precedence now. Our electronic warfare technicians are being retrained to work on our national communication systems. In fact, most military contractors are working on infrastructure now."

Tom was dumbstruck. Then heat rose up his collar. "Hold on. Are you telling me Cochran disbanded our military?"

"Well, I wouldn't put it precisely that way. She's trying to make the best of our remaining resources. We all are."

He took a deep breath, resolving to remain calm. The Admiral was only a messenger. Ruth was his real problem.

He responded, "Sure, I see. Well, thank you Admiral for the information. I'll be in touch soon." He ended the call.

Tom pounded the table.

Bitch! She has gone way too far now.

He went to a closet and retrieved all the guns and ammunition he had collected from the agents. He stuffed them into a black nylon gym bag.

Wait. No. Guns are not the answer.

He went down the tunnel toward the former President's room. He retrieved a large black case.

This will get Ruth's attention.

She won't ignore me any longer.

DAY 150

The quarantine was finally over. Ruth sent a driver to retrieve Defoe at daybreak. She would have preferred to make him walk back to DC, but it was better to get this over with.

The Senate building had solar panels for power, but it was still chilly in her office in the mornings. She stoked the logs in the fireplace.

The natural gas pipelines had been secured for safety reasons, after several compressor stations blew up across the country. The stations were all computer-controlled. Based on the suspicious timing and precise sequence of the failures, industry experts concluded the pipelines were hacked. Ruth suspected Russia or China were behind the attacks.

The coming winter would be difficult.

During her radio addresses, she implored people to store firewood. They had little time to prepare.

It was almost like colonial times. She was in the middle of re-

reading the writings of Benjamin Franklin. She needed all the wisdom she could get.

Anticipating Defoe's arrival today, she put out some refreshments, including a plate of her freshly baked homemade ginger snaps and chocolate chip cookies. *Tom did not look happy the last time we talked*, she thought with a smile. *I'm sure he'll welcome some home cooking.*

Between the woody smell from the fireplace, the sugary aroma of the cookies, a carafe of freshly brewed coffee, and the soft morning light filtering through the tall paned windows, her reception area felt a Norman Rockwell painting.

Sally stepped into her office. "Ma'am, he's here."

"Great, I'll be right out."

Ruth took off her glasses and straightened the papers on her desk. She smoothed her hair and walked into the chamber.

You can do this…

She strode out toward Defoe with her hand outstretched. "I'm so pleased to see you, Tom! We've missed you so much! I was awfully worried when you said you were sick. But you appear fully recovered, thank the Lord."

Defoe sneered. "Cut the crap, Ruth."

Ruth looked over at Sally.

"I'll leave you two alone," Sally said, as she closed the doors behind her.

"You have something you want to get off your chest. So, shoot."

Tom had a suitcase in his hand. It was handcuffed to his wrist. He got up and walked over to the sideboard. With his free hand, he poured himself a cup of coffee. Stirring in some cream, he said, "Ruth. Ruth. Ruth. I have to hand it to you. Maybe I underestimated you all these years. You are a formidable woman. I didn't think you had it in you."

"Had what in me, exactly?"

"Disband our military? Pass *new laws* without me? Well, this is all going to change. I'm in charge now. I am your President." He sipped the coffee slowly.

Ruth stared up at him with narrowed eyes, her hand on her hip. "I could have had you arrested for murder." She went over to the sideboard and picked up a cookie. She turned to face him. "But it wouldn't be fair to the country. There are issues that demand real attention."

"No, you knew people wouldn't believe you."

She put the cookie back down and laughed. She locked eyes with Tom. "You were away a long time. In case you hadn't noticed, you are *not* the President. You were never sworn in."

He put down his coffee. "Screw the swearing in. Swear me in now. I don't care. I swear myself in."

"Too late," Ruth smirked. "I was sworn in as President by the new Congress last night. After your impeachment, of course."

"What?" Tom shouted, his face turning red. "That's illegal!"

He then paused, smoothed his tie, and cleared his throat. "You're joking, right? Ok, ha ha. You got me."

"I'm not joking. We have a new Constitution. The President is elected by the Electoral College, which now consists entirely of members of Congress. I won by an overwhelming majority. Do you want to go down the hall and ask some of the other congresswomen?"

"Ruth. I'm not playing around anymore. Do you see this?" Tom motioned to the black case in his hand. "This is the football. I can launch nuclear weapons with this. I've been in touch with NORAD. They will comply with my commands."

"Tom, are you seriously threatening to blow us all up if you don't become President?"

"I've worked my entire life preparing for this job. The Presidency is my destiny! God has ordained it! There is no way under heaven I will let you take this from me. Yes, if I have to blow up all of DC! I will do it. Don't push me."

Tom pulled out a gun from his jacket and pointed it at Ruth.

"Whoa! Tom. Relax. Put the *gun down*," she said loudly.

A female voice came out of a speakerphone in the middle of the coffee table. "Ruth, are you ok?"

Ruth said, "Sally, my guest is a little agitated. Did you get all that?"

"All of it. I can play it back if you'd like."

"You've been recording this?" Defoe said, spraying spittle in Ruth's face.

Ruth stared at the red dots on Tom's white shirt.

Defoe followed her gaze—red beams on his center mass. He looked toward the window. "Oh, I see you brought your own fire power! You think I'm afraid?" Defoe began cackling. "Ha ha ha ha ha. You don't have the guts to kill me."

Director Ortega's voice came through the speaker-phone. "Ruth, I have the shot. Go or no go?"

A bullet shattered the window and nicked the side of Tom's ear.

Tom stepped back, touching the wound with his finger while still holding the gun.

"I didn't have to miss," Ortega said through the speaker. "Hand the gun to Ruth now! If you make any sudden moves, I won't hesitate."

Tom took his finger off the trigger and gently handed the gun to Ruth.

Ruth directed her voice towards the speaker, "Eduardo, Sally—I'm ok." She turned to Defoe. "Tom, let's be candid. You've been through quite an ordeal. Take a deep breath. Come now. Breathe with me." Ruth inhaled loudly and exhaled. "Come on, now. You try." She gestured with the gun.

Tom stared at her. Then he looked down at the dots and took a deep breath and exhaled.

"Feels better, right? Now listen. I was trying to get the country through a rough time. I'm a public servant. That's all I've ever wanted to be. You obviously care about the presidency more. No one else needs to die. A nuclear strike is unnecessary." She waved toward the window and the red beams disappeared. "Fine, you are the President. I'll back away. Given the state of affairs, there is more than enough work to do."

"Really? You would give up the presidency just like that? Why should I trust you now?" He touched his bleeding ear and examined the red liquid on his finger. He looked at the gun in her hand.

Ruth lowered the gun, keeping it by her side. "I was a doctor before I was a senator, remember? My goals have always been the furtherance of human compassion—not political power for its own sake."

Defoe smirked. "Right."

"My God, Tom!" She waved a hand in the air. "The human race was nearly eradicated! Public health needs a new direction. Surely, you can see that." She sat down on the sofa and placed the gun on the coffee table. She picked up a stack of paper and held it in the air. "These are the mortality numbers! You must have read them. We can't afford to lose any more people to preventable diseases. While you were gone, I had the power to initiate important public health reforms. This is my calling.

"So, you're going to step down?"

"I'd like to continue pursuing public health initiatives under your administration."

"What, as part of my cabinet?" He did a short side-step but the red dots came back on. He froze.

"Yes, that would be my preference. Head of Health and Human Services."

"Hmm. I'll think about it," Tom said.

"Thank you, Tom." Ruth got up from the sofa and placed her hand on his shoulder. "I have another small request. In the interest of continuity, would you allow me to act as your Vice President for the next two weeks? Then you can pick someone else. We'll use the transition time to implement whatever changes you see fit."

Tom held up the briefcase. "Fine. But don't cross me again. Arrange a real swearing in for tomorrow. With news coverage and everything," he sneered. "I'm moving into the White House today. I need a new Chief of Staff, a secretary, and Communications Director. Oh, and some Marines and Secret Service. Can you send some of your best folks over? Some *men* if you can find any."

"Sure, Tom. Anything else?" Ruth crossed her arms.

Tom smiled. He walked back over to the sideboard, glancing back at Ruth. He finished the rest of his coffee and picked up a chocolate chip cookie. Tom took a bite. "Mmm, not bad." He took three more cookies. "Do you mind?"

"Please take as many as you want, Mr. President. I made them just for you."

Tom pocketed the cookies and walked to the door. "If I think of anything else, I'll call. But don't let the phone ring more than twice. I hate to be kept waiting."

After Tom left the room, Ruth let out a long breath. She said towards the speakerphone, "We did it! Thanks honey!"

Through the speaker, Ortega said, "Anytime, Madam President. Should I follow him?"

"No need. See you for dinner?" she replied softly.

"Yes, hope you don't mind spaghetti again. See you at seven."

Ruth pressed the button on the top of the speaker-phone to disconnect.

Sally came rushing in. "What happened?"

Ruth picked up the plate of cookies and walked over to the fireplace. She slid them off the plate, into the fire. "What do you think? No one can resist my cookies."

"You didn't!"

"The cyanide should take effect quickly. He won't make it to the White House."

"How did you know which cookie he would choose? Or that he would even eat them?" Sally asked.

"If you were in a bunker for a month, wouldn't you crave some fresh-baked cookies? It's human nature. And, of course, I poisoned all of them, not just one."

"Very smart, Madam President. But aren't you worried he might launch a nuclear attack when he realizes he's been poisoned?"

"He's bluffing. All our nuclear missile sites were taken offline at the same time I had the nuclear power plants shuttered. His suitcase is essentially full of junk electronics. Oh, please call Dr. Braff. Ask him to put down 'heart attack' on Tom's official autopsy."

"Right away. Can I get you anything else?"

"Yes, I was thinking we could repurpose the White House for something more helpful." She put her index finger to her cheek and thought. "Maybe a food bank and community garden. Ask the food committee to consider it."

"Of course. They're meeting tomorrow. Oh, before I forget, what do you think of the new bill? Can I give her a go-ahead?" Sally said.

Ruth took the proof sheet of the new twenty-dollar bill off her desk. It was a sweet gesture from Doris at the Mint. "I'm not sure about having my face immortalized. I've come to believe the role of President has become too elevated. Perhaps Clara Barton or Doctor Elizabeth Blackwell would be appropriate for this honor? Call Doris and ask her to draft some other options."

"Very well. Enjoy the rest of your morning, Madam President."

"Thank you. I shall."

Chapter 28

Day 240

Almost three months after the quarantine was lifted, daily life was returning to normal. Jason met Ortega at the National Portrait Gallery in the late afternoon. He sat on the same bench he'd met Ally at all those months ago. The museum was far less crowded and managed by a couple of elderly female volunteers.

"Hey, Eduardo! Nice to see you," Jason said.

"You as well. How have you been?" Ortega said.

"Busy. Helping Ruth. She's working on the plans for a world summit. So, what is on your mind?"

"A few things." Ortega took a seat next to Jason.

A group of three women were crossing the atrium and stopped to gawk at them. But then they turned and continued talking among themselves and exited on the other side.

Jason still couldn't get used to being treated like a side-show attraction. Everywhere he—or really any man—went, women would stop and stare. He was getting propositions from women, young and old, every day. At first it was comical. Now, not so much. On most days he wore his gay pride t-shirt or a rainbow necktie. The women still asked.

"Ok," Jason said, "I'm listening."

"I know Ruth has lots of domestic issues to deal with right now, but I'm still concerned about Petrov."

"I heard Vlad and his oligarch buddies were shacked up on Cyprus. They took over the entire island for themselves."

"True. We have a carrier in the Mediterranean. They verified those reports. But Vlad is a patient man when it comes to revenge. He might not be a threat now—but in five years? I suspect he will be amassing a new army steadily over time. We need to have agents on the ground to keep an eye on him." Ortega looked him in the eyes.

"Hey, don't look at me. I'm out of the spy business."

"Really? So that's why you are on the long-wave radio for hours every night talking to your contacts overseas?"

"Oh, sure. I like to know what is going on. General gossip. Hey, did you know Zhang is now the acting leader of China, but he is leaving most decisions up to regional officials. And there was an uprising in North Korea—they are slated to have their first female president! Oh, and get this, Tibet is free. Finally free!"

"Yes, I know. All of it. Look, the NSA, like every other federal agency, doesn't have the staff it used to. With the internet compromised in most places, we need to revert to old school tradecraft. Spies on the ground. People to sift through the disinformation that does make it onto the Internet. If you don't want to be a field agent, would you consider helping us as a senior trainer? A new class is forming soon."

"Yes, that I *will* do. Maybe in a couple of months. After Ruth has more systems in place."

"Good. Thanks, Jason. But now I want to talk about something else." Ortega wrung his hands and looked up at the ceiling.

"Oh, now you're worrying me. You look nervous. And you are never nervous! What's wrong? Is there chatter about another terrorist attack?"

"No. Nothing like that," Ortega said. "Did Ruth ever tell you we were once engaged?"

"What?"

"Right before your mother and sister died." Ortega shifted his body away and looked at the slate floor. "But the loss hit her hard. She became withdrawn. I wanted to help her through it, but she pushed me away. The next month I got a promotion and a year-long assignment in Afghanistan. We drifted apart."

Ortega turned and looked at Jason directly. "I never stopped loving her. I tried to reconnect a couple years later, but she was running for the State house. Again, bad timing. As you know, over this last year, we began working together trying to figure out what

Roadfuss was up to. It was great spending time together as old friends. But now, after losing so much, I want more. I told her how I feel. I think she still loves me, too."

"That's amazing! I'm so happy for you both."

"I'm working up the courage to ask her to marry me."

Jason clasped his hand to his mouth and let out an excited squeak. People in the atrium turned to look.

Jason got up and shook Eduardo's hand. "This is fantastic! A Presidential wedding. Wait until I tell Ally!"

"Hold on. So, I take it I have your approval?"

"Eduardo, I haven't been this happy in months. Welcome to the family!" Jason pulled him to a standing position and gave him a hug.

Ortega laughed. "She still has to say yes."

Jason released him and helped him straighten his suit jacket. "Oh, don't worry about that. I've seen how she looks at you when she thinks no one's looking. She tries to act like an ice queen, but deep down, she's a mushy marshmallow. Shit, she would kill me if she heard me say that."

"It will be our secret." Ortega smiled, fixing his tie.

Jason looked around. "Um," he whispered, "you know what happened with Defoe, right?"

"Of course, and?"

"I mean, I love Auntie Ruth. But she can be a little ruthless, if you know what I mean. Sorry, bad pun. I just want you to know what you're getting into."

Ortega whispered back, "Defoe was a mass murderer. We both agreed it was the best way to deal with him."

"Whew! Me too," Jason said. "Ok, well I guess you both have my blessing. Hey, speaking of engagements, did you know that Dr. Braff is getting married too? Did you ever meet Maya Rivera?"

"No, I don't think I met her. Good for Walt."

"They began Skyping with each other, working on the wording of the quarantine order. But they kept in touch. Kind of romantic in a post-apocalyptic way." Jason laughed. "Nothing like the end of civilization to bring about true love. Everyone is pairing up."

Jason pointed at another cluster of women staring at them. "It's almost like we are the last men on earth or something. But obviously, I'm not helping the cause."

"Civilization will go on. I hope you find someone, if that's what you're looking for."

"I'm just glad the funerals are over." Jason said. "Ruth is keeping me too busy to even think about a social life."

"What about your friend Ally? Have you seen her lately?"

"She's back in New Jersey, living with her sister and raising her granddaughter. I went up there for the funerals. I don't know how she keeps going. We talk from time to time, but Ally's really busy. Ruth asked her to run for congress. She said she would think about it, but I don't think Ally will. After everything that's happened, I don't blame her. She said she might go back into medical practice. Makes sense. I'll see her at Christmas, during Walt and Maya's wedding in Bermuda. You and Ruth should come."

"If all goes well, that would be great," Ortega said.

"It will. I'll make sure of it."

Jason and Ortega said their goodbyes.

Jason left the museum and walked toward the Capitol. He crossed the National Mall. He received more curious looks from women. The sun was setting behind the Washington Monument, making it glow a spectacular yellow.

As he walked up the Capitol steps, a tall, handsome man passed him, walking down. He was wearing a brown corduroy blazer over a New York City Gay Men's Chorus t-shirt.

Jason stopped cold. He turned around.

"Sir? Hello?" Jason called.

The man in corduroy stopped and turned to face Jason.

Jason jogged down several steps and extended his hand. "Hi, my name is Jason Burns. I work for President Cochran."

"Nice to meet you. I'm the new congressman from Maine, Joe Williams."

"Mr. Williams, here's my card. Call me if you ever need anything. And I mean, anything." Jason winked.

Joe laughed. "Jason, I'm heading out to meet some friends at the American Grille. If you are free, come join me. I'd love to learn more about President Cochran and her agenda."

Jason smiled. He couldn't remember exactly what was on his schedule the rest of the evening, but it would have to wait. "Absolutely, lead the way!"

Perhaps Ortega was right.

Civilization wasn't dead after all.

* * *

Reclining shirtless on a chaise by the pool, Vlad looked out across the estate toward the crystal blue waters of the Mediterranean. In the distance, the rumble of trucks disturbed the quietude. Members of his small Russian militia were still clearing dead bodies from the purge.

The stench was overwhelming. Trucks filled with dead locals circled the streets before heading to the old Cyprus copper mine—to a zone they termed 'the Carcass Pit'.

His Oligarch friends and their families were sorting out which properties on the island to take as their own. For the most part, the militia selectively killed only the adults and spared the youngest of the local population. The children would be trained for general servitude—manual labor, farming, fishing, or sex trade—but the most promising would be indoctrinated into the new Russian army.

For now, Vlad needed to clear his head and adjust to his new surroundings. He didn't like to make rash decisions. Six months of rest and relaxation were necessary before he would begin strategizing Russia's return to power.

Countries led by women would be easy to topple. Where would the challenge be in that?

Still, he reasoned, at some point, the earth's population would normalize again and the same struggles between governments and differing ideologies would emerge. He needed to ensure his successor would be ready. Already three of his young mistresses were pregnant.

If he lived long enough, he could see his master plan become a reality.

No, women would not rule the world.

Not as long as he had breath in his lungs.

ABOUT THE AUTHOR

DS Whitaker is an environmental engineer, wife, mother, grandmother of two beautiful girls, runner, and now fiction writer. She and her husband live in central NJ with their elderly Maine Coon cat Gretchen.

Antigenesis was her first work of fiction after a lifetime of technical writing.

On a cold, rainy October morning, while trail running at Holmdel Park, she was inspired by the notion of "what if women developed super-immunity after a lifetime of raising children?"

The idea stuck with her as she envisioned a story of a pandemic that spares older women, creating a new world order. Because of her love of humor, the story became a blend of action and satire.

DS joined the Liberty States Fiction Writers group in 2019. Her second novel, *Planet of the Creeps*, is a sweet and funny farce about online dating. Other works include: Shower of Lies and Johnnie Finds a Dead Body.

She is no longer writing about mass extinction events.

Follow her on Twitter at @ds_whitaker and visit her website at dswhitaker.com.

{Fake} RAVES FOR ANTIGENESIS

"A masterpiece. A new classic. Now feed me already." - Gretchen, my cat.

"If you love senseless death and tragedy, you'll love Antigenesis." - Me.

"I'm confused. What genre is this?" - My inner critic.

"[blank stare]" - My husband.

"A funny story about a pandemic? A real winner. Why are all the men in your stories bad?" - My Dad.

"Not funny. Not cool." - Pres. D. Merriwether.

"Feminists unite! Please, take a cookie. I baked them myself."– Sen. Ruth Cochran.

repair 3/21

CPSIA information can be obtained
at www.ICGtesting.com
Printed in the USA
LVHW080334220221
679575LV00001B/97

9 781734 259544